CRITICS' NOVELS

Tibetan Cross

"A thriller that everyone should go out and buy right away. The writing is wonderful throughout, and Bond never loses the reader's attention. This is less a thriller, at times, than essay, with Bond working that fatalistic margin where life and death are one and the existential reality leaves one caring only to survive." (*Sunday Oregonian*)

"A tautly written study of one man's descent into living hell…Strong and forceful, its sharply written prose, combined with a straightforward plot, builds a mood of near claustrophobic intensity." (*Spokane Chronicle*)

"Grips the reader from the very first chapter until the climactic ending." (*United Press International*)

"Bond's deft thriller will reinforce your worst fears about the CIA and the Bomb…A taut, tense tale of pursuit through exotic and unsavory locales." (*Publishers Weekly*)

"One of the most exciting in recent fiction…an astonishing thriller that speaks profoundly about the venality of governments and the nobility of man." (*San Francisco Examiner*)

"It *is* a thril   Thank you!   iciated Press*)

"Murderous intensity…A tense and graphically written story." (*Richmond Times-Dispatch*)

"The most jaundiced adventure fan will be held by **Tibetan Cross**…It's a superb volume with enough action for anyone, a well-told story that deserves the increasing attention it's getting." (*Sacramento Bee*)

"Intense and unforgettable from the opening chapter…thought-provoking and very well written." (*Fort Lauderdale News*)

"Grips the reader from the opening chapter and never lets go." (*Miami Herald*)

A "chilling story of escape and pursuit." (*Tacoma News-Tribune*)

"This novel is touted as a thriller – and that is what it is…The settings are exotic, minutely described, filled with colorful characters." (*Pittsburgh Post-Gazette*)

"Almost impossible to put down…Relentless. As only reality can have a certain ring to it, so does this book. It is naked and brutal and mind boggling in its scope. It is a living example of not being able to hide, ever…The hardest-toned book I've ever read. And the most frightening glimpse of mankind I've seen. This is a 10 if ever there was one." (*I Love a Mystery*)

Holy War

"Mike Bond does it again – A gripping tale of passion, hostage-taking and war, set against a war-ravaged Beirut." (*Evening News*)

"A supercharged thriller set in the hell hole that was Beirut…Evokes the human tragedy behind headlines of killing, maiming, terrorism and political chicanery. A story to chill and haunt you." (*Peterborough Evening Telegraph*)

"A profound tale of war, written with grace and understanding by a novelist who thoroughly knows the subject…Literally impossible to stop reading…" (*British Armed Forces Broadcasting*)

"A pacy and convincing thriller with a deeper than usual understanding about his subject and a sure feel for his characters." (*Daily Examiner*)

"A marvelous book – impossible to put down. A sense of being where few people have survived. The type of book that people really want to read, by a very successful and prolific writer." (*London Broadcasting*)

"A tangled web and an entertaining one. Action-filled thriller." (*Manchester Evening News*)

"Short sharp sentences that grip from the start...A tale of fear, hatred, revenge, and desire, flicking between bloody Beirut and the lesser battles of London and Paris." (*Evening Herald*)

"A novel about the horrors of war...a very authentic look at the situation which was Beirut." (*South Wales Evening Post*)

"A stunning novel of love and loss, good and evil, of real people who live in our hearts after the last page is done...Unusual and profound." (*Greater London Radio*)

Night of the Dead

"A riveting thriller of murder, politics, and lies." (*London Broadcasting*)

"A tough and tense thriller." (*Manchester Evening News*)

"A thoroughly amazing book...Memorable, an extraordinary story that speaks from and to the heart. And a terrifying depiction of one man's battle against the CIA and Latin American death squads." (*BBC*)

"A riveting story where even the good guys are bad guys, set in the politically corrupt and drug infested world of present-day Central America." (*Middlesborough Evening Gazette*)

"The climax is among the most horrifying I have ever read." (*Liverpool Daily Post*)

"*Night of the Dead*, named after the time each year when the dead return to avenge wrongs, is based upon Bond's own experiences in Guatemala. With detailed descriptions of actual jungle battles and manhunts, vanishing rain forests and the ferocity of guerrilla war, *Night of the Dead* also reveals the CIA's role in both death squads and drug running, twin scourges of Central America." (*Newton Chronicle*)

"Not for the literary vegetarian – it's red meat stuff from the off. All action…convincing." (*Oxford Times*)

"Bond grips the reader from the very first page. An ideal thriller for the beach, but be prepared to be there when the sun goes down." (*Herald Express*)

The Last Savanna

"The central figure is not human; it is the barren, terrifying landscape of Northern Kenya and the deadly creatures who inhabit it." (*Daily Telegraph*)

"The imagery was so powerful and built emotions so intense that I had to stop reading a few times to regain my composure." (*African Publishers' Network*)

"An unforgettable odyssey into the wilderness, mysteries, and perils of Africa…A book to be cherished and remembered." (*Greater London Radio*)

"An entrancing, terrifying vision of Africa. A story that not only thrills but informs…Impossible to set aside or forget." (*BBC*)

"Shot through with images of the natural world at its most fearsome and most merciful. With his weapons, man is a conqueror – without them he is a fugitive in an alien land. Bond touches on the vast and eerie depths that lie under the thin crust of civilization and the base instinct within man to survive – instincts that surpass materialism. A thoroughly enjoyable read that comes highly recommended." (*Nottingham Observer*)

ALSO BY MIKE BOND

The Last Savanna

Holy War

Tibetan Cross

Night of the Dead

Assassins

SAVING PARADISE

Mike Bond

MANDEVILLA
PRESS

MANDEVILLA PRESS
Weston, CT 06883

Published in the United States by Mandevilla Press

LIBRARY OF CONGRESS CATALOGING-IN-PUBLICATION DATA

Bond, Mike

SAVING PARADISE: a novel/Mike Bond

p. cm.

ISBN 978-1-62704-001-3

1. Hawaii – Fiction. 2. Political corruption – Fiction. 3. Crime – Fiction.
4. Environment – Fiction. 5. Afghanistan War – Fiction.
6. Surfing – Fiction. 7. Renewable Energy – Fiction.   I. Title

www.MikeBondBooks.com

To the memory of George Helm,
warrior, musician, leader and poet,
who gave his life to defend his beloved Hawaii

and to the memory of my ancestor, Elias Bond,
who tried always to give to Hawaii and never took

HAWAII

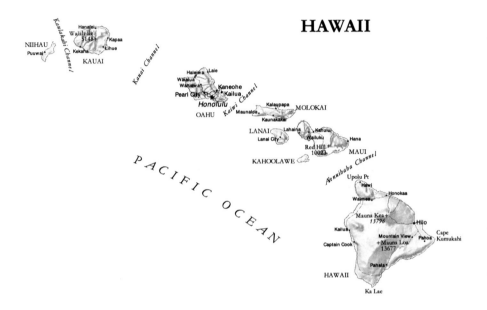

NIIHAU
Puuwai•

KAUAI
Hanalei•
Waialeale 5148+
Kekaha•
Kapaa•
Lihue

Kaulakahi Channel

Kauai Channel

OAHU
Haleiwa• •Laie
Waialua
Wahiawa•
Pearl City• •Kaneohe
Honolulu •Kailua

Kaiwi Channel

Kalaupapa
Maunaloa• **MOLOKAI**
Kaunakakai

LANAI Lahaina• •Kahului
Lanai City• Wailuku• •Hana
Red Hill+ 10023 **MAUI**

KAHOOLAWE

Alenuihaha Channel

Upolu Pt
•Hawi
Honokaa•
Waimea•
Mauna Kea+ 13796 •Hilo
Kailua• Cape Kumukahi
Mountain View• •Pahoa
Captain Cook +Mauna Loa 13677
Pahala•
HAWAII
Ka Lae

P A C I F I C   O C E A N

Ua mau ke ea o ka `aina i ka pono.

The life of the land is preserved in righteous action.

Lovely, Cold and Dead

IT WAS ANOTHER MAGNIFICENT DAWN on Oahu, the sea soft and rumpled and the sun blazing up from the horizon, an offshore breeze scattering plumeria fragrance across the frothy waves. Flying fish darting over the crests, dolphins chasing them, a mother whale and calf spouting as they rolled northwards. A morning when you already know the waves will be good and it will be a day to remember.

I waded out with my surfboard looking for the best entry and she bumped my knee. A woman long and slim in near-transparent red underwear, face down in the surf. Her features sharp and beautiful, her short chestnut hair plastered to her cold skull.

I dropped my board and held her in my arms, stunned by her beauty and death. If I could keep holding her maybe she wouldn't really be dead. I was already caught by her high cheekbones and thin purposeful lips, the subtle arch of her brow, her long slender neck in my hands. And so overwhelmed I would have died to protect her.

When I carried her ashore her long legs dragged in the surf as if the ocean didn't want to let her go, this sylphlike mermaid beauty. Sorrow overwhelmed me – how could I get her back, this lovely person?

Already cars were racing up and down Ala Moana Boulevard. When you're holding a corpse in your arms how bizarre seems the human race – where were all these people hurrying to in this horrible moment with this beautiful young woman dead?

I did the usual. Being known to the Honolulu cops I had to call them. I'd done time and didn't want to do more. Don't believe for a second what anyone tells you – being Inside is a *huge* disincentive. Jail tattoos not just your skin; it nails your soul. No matter what you do, no matter what you want, you don't want to go back there. Not ever.

So Benny Olivera shows up with his flashers flashing. If you want a sorry cop Benny will fill your bill. Damn cruiser the size of a humpback whale with lights going on and off all over the place, could've been a nuclear reaction – by the way, why would anyone want a family that's *nuclear*? Life's dangerous enough.

So I explain Benny what happened. He's hapa pilipino – half Filipino – and doesn't completely trust us hapa haoles, part white and part Hawaiian. To a kanaka maoli, a native Hawaiian, or to someone whose ancestors were indentured here like the Japanese or in Benny's case Filipinos, there's still mistrust. Didn't the haoles steal the whole archipelago for a handful of beads? Didn't they bring diseases that cut the Hawaiian population by ninety percent? And then shipped hundreds of the survivors to leprosy colonies on Molokai? While descendants of the original missionaries took over most of the land and became huge corporations that turned the Hawaiians, Filipinos, Japanese and others into serfs? These corporations that now own most of Hawaii, its mainline media, banks and politicians?

I'm holding this lissome young woman cold as a fish in my arms and Benny says lie her down on the hard sidewalk and the ambulance comes – more flashing lights – and she's gone under a yellow tarp and I never saw her again.

Couldn't surf. Went home and brewed a triple espresso and my heart was down in my feet. Sat on the lanai and tried to figure out life and death and what had happened to this beautiful woman. Mojo the dachshund huffed up on the chair beside me, annoyed I hadn't taken him surfing. Puma the cat curled on my lap but I didn't scratch her so she went and sat in the sun.

I'd seen plenty of death but this one got to me. She'd been young, pretty and athletic. Somehow the strong classic lines of her face denoted brains, determination and hard work. How did she end up drowned in Kewalo Basin?

Benny's bosses at the cop shop would no doubt soon provide the answer.

House of Sharks

A S MENTIONED, I've seen lots of dead people. A tour or two in Afghanistan will do that for you. I sat there with my feet up on the bamboo table and tried to forget all this. Mojo kept whining at the door wanting to hit the beach but I didn't. Once the sun moved past her spot Puma jumped back in my lap and began kneading her claws into my stomach.

By afternoon the surf was looking good, and when you're under that thunderous curl you don't even think about Afghanistan. Or about Sylvia Gordon, age 27, KPOI reported, a journalist for *The Honolulu Post*, dead in the surf this morning near Ala Moana Beach.

But I had a raunchy feeling in my stomach like when you eat bad sushi so I quit surfing and went down to the cop shop on South Beretania to see Benny and his friends. Benny was out cruising in his nuclear Chrysler but Leon Oversdorf (I *swear* that's his name), Second Lieutenant Homicide, wanted to see me.

"Look, Lieutenant," I said, "I been cool. I don't drink or smoke weed or indulge in premarital sex or habituate shady premises –"

"So how the fuck you find her?" Leon says by way of opening.

I explained him. How it happened. All the time he's looking at me under these gargantuan eyebrows and I can tell no matter what I say he won't believe me. Just because I been Inside. I could tell him Calvin Coolidge is President and even then he wouldn't believe me.

"So she drowned," I said after a while, looking to leave.

Leon watched me with his tiny sad eyes. Him that helped put me Inside. "No," he said.

And what he said next changed my life. "She *was* drowned."

"I didn't do it," I said right away.

Leon leaned forward, meaty palms on his desk. "Pono," he chuckled, "you think we don't *know* that?"

"Know what?" I said, covering my bases.

"She was dead six hours before of when you found her."

The thought pained me horribly. This lovely person floating in the cold uncaring sea. When I could've held her, kept her warm.

"She was dead," Leon said matter of factly, "from being held underwater till her lungs filled up with good old H20."

"How do you know she was held?" I risked. "Even if she just normally drowned there'd be water in her lungs –"

Leon scanned me the way the guy with the broadaxe smiles down at you when you lay your head on the block. "This water in her lungs ain't ocean, it's fresh."

"Fresh?"

"Like from a swimming pool or something. You get it?"

WHAT'S BAD ABOUT TIGER SHARKS is they don't kill you right away. They're not fast like a great white, where you get maybe two seconds and then half of you is down his gullet and the rest spread across the ocean. But these damn tigers, they like to play with you.

There's a reef on the south side of the island of Molokai called Hale o Lono, which means *House of Lono*, who was one of the four gods brought to Hawaii by the ancient Tahitians. Tiger sharks breed there by the millions, hammerheads too, with their widespread heads and eyes on the end. I don't mind hammerheads – they bug you when you're down forty, fifty feet you just sock them in the eye. In that wide-faced appendage of theirs.

Tigers however a different deal. How they play with you. Rake you across the ribs with a quick twist of their jaws and then backpedal to watch the blood uncurling from your body like a holy flag – I swear they *like* this – and wait to see what other brothers and sisters show up for the *luau*.

The human *luau*. Tiger sharks, they're never in a hurry. Always have time to watch you bleed.

So when you're sitting far out on your board waiting for the next wave, your legs dangling into the deep, in the back of your mind there's tiger sharks. Occasionally they take somebody, leave a shred of bathing suit or a chewed board. But you can always hope it'll be someone else.

So what I didn't understand when I found Sylvia Gordon is why the tigers didn't get her. She'd been dead six hours, Leon said. Trouble with Leon is he hardly ever lies except professionally.

Not only did she get held under till she choked out the last air and sucked in fresh water that filled her lungs like embalming fluid, after that she got dumped in the ocean and the tigers didn't get her.

Why was that?

Leon didn't seem to care. "We're lookin at this," he said. "From *The Honolulu Post* stuff she was doin. She was some nosy broad, yeah?"

Thing about Hawaiians – and you can tell a true Hawaiian by if she or he does this – they often end a sentence *yeah?* It's reflexive, like scratching your balls when they itch. I've caught myself more than a few times doing that in polite company.

So I asks Leon what's he mean. He says she was doin articles – in the *paper* even, on crystal meth. So the meth dealers wanted to clean her. And they did.

Now crystal meth is a horrible disease and like leprosy and most other diseases in Hawaii it came from the haoles – the white folks. A partial list of the plagues the haoles brought to Hawaii includes malaria (mosquitoes), influenza, tuberculosis, cholera, mumps, diphtheria, smallpox, high blood pressure, high cholesterol, obesity, diabetes, syphilis, gonorrhea, rats and then the mongoose to kill the rats, fleas, head lice, pubic lice, poverty and servitude.

Men who had been free to fish and hunt all day, rejoice in their large families and the pleasures of love and life were now forced to work twelve hours a day six days a week bent over in the pineapple plantations, or swinging the machete in the sugar fields, while the plantation owners relaxed in the shade, sipped mint juleps and discussed how to get richer.

The word haole comes from ha and ole, meaning without breath. The whites were so pale they were assumed to be dead, also they did not exchange breath or hug each other as Hawaiians do.

Tourists who stay on Waikiki (a horrible place – the antithesis of Hawaii) or some sham Maui condo furnished with top-of-the-line formica, Wal-Mart dishes and phony Hawaiian prints, or even in the fake Kona resorts where (I *swear* this is true) they have ersatz Hawaiian celebrations with gas-fired torches and fat ladies dancing hula (more on this later, but as a clue, hula came from the same place as rock'n roll) – almost never get to see the sleazy side of paradise.

To tourists Hawaii is an air-conditioned tanning booth with shopping, booze, bikinis, and lots of smiling low-paid help. The real Hawaii is something else – the greatest mariners the world has ever known, brave warriors and wise healers, a deep-hearted family connection reaching hundreds of people and across whole islands, love of the ancestors, a magical way of life.

So Leon bless his narrow little soul tells me how a bunch of guys on the North Shore were brewing meth big time and Sylvia went out to investigate and they're the ones who drowned her. "We arrested seven these guys already," Leon says under his big black brushy brows. "Get the rest the motherfuckers tomorrow."

What strikes me right then, if these methheads did in this beautiful person how come they're hanging out in their hammocks by the seaside high on meth and getting blow jobs from their cranked-out sweethearts when the cops arrive? If it was me that killed her, by now I'd be deep in the mountains of Molokai.

Leon didn't assist with this theory. Because he hates methheads. With good reason. You can walk in a house full of methheads and the kids haven't been fed in three days nor had their shitty diapers changed. And some skinny little dog is lying dead on the carpet. So I'm not fond of methheads either.

But that doesn't mean they killed Sylvia Gordon. Because methheads are not proactive.

In Afghanistan we had what we called instant response. The ragheads nail one of us, we nail them right away three times harder. But our mission in Afghanistan was entirely humanitarian. And anyways methheads aren't so bad as ragheads.

So I figured Leon was practicing instant response. Going for the usual suspects.

I left feeling Leon was less than half full of honesty. Which is a precious commodity these days. I wandered over to Kahala and talked to some surfing buddies. Including Grunge.

He's one of the best surfers on Oahu and I trust him because he's an ex-Marine. From GW's fabricated Iraq War. "She was here," Grunge said. "God what a pretty lady. One a them that walks softly, you know, not even knowin how pretty she is and we just want to bow down and say can I lay my cloak under your feet?"

Trouble with Grunge is he's prone to overstatement, as he got his head mixed up in Iraq from too many IEDs, and every time a 747 of pudgy pale tourists roars over he just hears incoming and reaches for his guns. So he's always a little furtive, glancing about.

"So they kill her?" I says. "The methheads?"

"*Kill* her?" Grunge sounds offended. "Hell no."

"So who did?" I says, but really to myself.

THAT NIGHT I did the strangest thing. I'd been out on the rocks with my rod trying to get dinner. I get a nice hit and it's an oholehole, lovely delicious fish. About eight inches. He stared into my eyes and I unhooked him and set him free.

Went home and tossed a pound of frozen hamburger on the fire and cut open a papaya. You could argue that the steer wanted to live too, but cattle aren't free, can't survive in the real world, and are stupid as shit, whereas most wild fish are fast, wise and beautiful. Sadly however we are what we eat.

So maybe it was stupid to turn on the TV. I hate the damn thing but tonight felt lonely in the reminder of death and wanted some distraction. And caught KHON just as a photo of Sylvia's smiling bright-eyed face filled the screen, the announcer saying, "The drowning of *Honolulu Post* reporter Sylvia Gordon," his charming TV voice all sad and wistful, "police now say was an accident."

True Aloha

"**S**O WE MADE A MISTAKE," Leon says next morning when I drove down to see him, his eyes like candles far back in a cave.

"Nobody makes that mistake," I answered. "You said she had fresh water in her lungs –"

Leon massaged his lugubrious jowls. "Coroner changed his mind. Musta re-analyzed it."

"What's his name?"

"Joe Krill. Says she musta floated in from Black Point, the way the currents flow. "Anyway," he looks at me, "what's it to you?"

"I want to talk to him."

"Look, Pono, when you have your last piss test?"

"Last week," I lied.

"You keep this up we do one a day."

"Keep what up?"

"Fussin about this girl."

"You said the methheads –"

"They was clean, good alibis. Didn't even know she was writin articles…"

"Leon," I says like we was old friends. "You said her lungs were full of fresh water. How's *that* accidental?"

Leon picked up the phone. "Sergeant, send this man down for a piss test."

I got up quick. "I was just leaving."

"Now you ain't."

"I got an appointment."

"Yeah you do. Downstairs."

I walked out real fast and Leon didn't call me back, but now the cop shop was off limits. And whatever I did for Sylvia I had to do on my own.

ALOHA is an often-misunderstood word. It can mean hello or goodbye, but also affection or sympathy or the warmth that holds people together. Among Hawaiians there's a lot of this subliminal connection – like *sympathy*, whose Greek roots mean *to experience emotion together*. And for Hawaiians that emotion includes being ruled by westerners for the last two hundred years, who stole your land, killed lots of your people, banned your language and wiped out your entire way of life.

But unlike the missionary thieves who pillaged Hawaii in God's name and kept the spoils, my missionary ancestor Elias Hawkins returned the land King Kamehameha had granted him back to the Hawaiian people. While the descendants of all the other missionary hit men morphed their holdings into the super-corporations that run Hawaii today.

But even if you're half haole you can cross over. If the Hawaiians trust you. So I went to see Bruiser, security chief at the *Post*. A boxer, six feet two with a Hawaiian barrel chest, a clan tattoo down his arm and a smile so big a boat could sink in it.

Speaking of security, that's what everyone wants these days. Go anyplace and there's a dude with a sidearm watching you. Couple decades ago no one carried handguns and nobody walked into places killing people. Now thanks to the NRA, the politicians and the Muslim fundamentalists we need security everywhere. Might as well live in Afghanistan.

Bruiser doesn't care from that. It's a job. "Sylvia was nice to everyone," he says. "You know how office people they look down on the rest of us? Sometimes they're friendly just to pretend they ain't ho'o kano. But Sylvia she wasn't like that. When my Auntie Gracie passed last month, Sylvia she come the service…One time she went to Maui she bring me back mangoes right off her friend's tree –"

"She had a friend in Maui?"

TWENTY-FIVE MINUTES will get you to Maui from Oahu on Island Air. A lovely view of the sapphire ocean, past the translucent aqua of Molokai Reef, the longest and most pristine coral reef north of Australia, then over the magnificent National Humpback Whale Sanctuary, then Penguin Banks, the richest feeding ground in the Pacific, and you land in Los Angeles only they call it Kahului. So Maui isn't the green garden it used to be unless green to you means money.

Because lots and lots of money was made building these huge concrete hotels and condominiums casting their dark shadows across the spindly beach. Shopping centers, fancy boutiques, chain restaurants and multi-lane highways going off in all directions and at night there's all the three hundred dollar hookers you could want and any kind of drug you can imagine. Like Reagan used to say when he shilled for General Electric before he became president and shilled for big money, *Progress is our most important product.*

One thing Reagan did say certainly applies to Hawaii: *Politics is supposed to be the second-oldest profession. I have come to realize that it bears a very close resemblance to the first.*

But there's nothing wrong with being a hooker. The wrong politicians commit is pretending that they're not. And while a whore actually gives you something for your money, a politician just takes your money and screws you in a different way.

Sylvia's friend Angie lived in a ramshackle plank house up a dirt road in an area where due to the present recession everything hadn't been torn down yet to make condos. She was slight and pretty and blinked a lot to hide her tears, wiping them onto the short cotton skirt she wore with a skimpy halter top, but clearly at the moment she wasn't any more interested in sex than I was.

"Sylvia grew up on Kauai," Angie said. "She and I were roommates at Bates, but after that I came home to Maui and she stayed on the mainland, was working in Boston, came out here to visit me last May…" Angie paused. "If *only* I hadn't invited her…but she decided to stay here and got a job right away – can you imagine it in *these* times, as Maui correspondent for the *Post* – that's the kind of person Sylvia was – could do anything she set her mind to-"

"Except stay safe," I said, feeling mean for saying it.

She sniffed. "After three months they moved her to Honolulu as an investigative reporter. You know," she looked at me pleadingly, "she almost didn't go?"

"Why?"

"She didn't like Honolulu, said she might as well live in New Jersey…" Angie turned away. "Oh what a horrible accident."

I learned long ago never tell anyone anything till you're sure where they're coming from. "An investigative reporter, that could have made her lots of enemies, yeah?"

"Oh no. Everybody loved Sylvia."

Now I never heard of anyone *every*body loved, but I kept quiet on that. "When you saw her last it was when, two weeks ago, did she talk what she was doing?"

"Oh yes," a brief flash of happy agreement. "She was doing research on a big series the *Post* had scheduled…She was really excited. 'I'm finally really getting my teeth into something –' that's what she said."

"A series on what?"

"This huge project that's being planned, billions of dollars…monster wind turbines all over Maui, Lanai and Molokai, blasting a billion-dollar cable through the Whale Sanctuary. It's supposed to bring power from all the other islands to Oahu."

I'd heard a little about this gargantuan taxpayer-subsidized scam but hadn't paid attention, thinking no one could be so stupid as to actually do it. "So she was *for* it?"

"Oh no. 'The more I learn about it,' Sylvia told me, 'the worse it smells. And when I learn enough I'm going to break it wide open.' It was a perfect example, she said, of why *Money* magazine rated Hawaii the most politically corrupt state in the country, and even worse than Russia. Those were about the last words she ever said to me."

"When was that?"

"On the phone, two nights before she died."

"What else she say?"

"That a lot of the other media had been 'bought' – that was the word she used – by the developers of this project, or they were part of the fat money system that's run Hawaii since the conquest…"

"Who's behind this thing?"

"Behind it? Oh everybody who has lots of money and wants more: the Governor, IEEC, Lanai Land Corporation, an outfit called Ecology Profits, which is a bunch of investment bankers, Sylvia said, masquerading as environmentalists. Plus WindPower and all the other mainland industrial wind companies living on billions of taxpayer ripoffs. That's what she said."

Lanai Land Corporation was one of the colossal corporations founded on the holdings of Protestant missionary families I mentioned earlier, that had stolen most of the Hawaiians' land decades ago and made billions on it since, mostly on sugar, bananas, pineapples and subdivisions. IEEC was Island Electric Energy Company, universally hated for its bullying monopolistic ways, bad management, and the nation's highest electricity bills.

"But the government," I pointed out, "doesn't have any money anymore."

Angie half-smiled. "That doesn't stop the Washington pork, though, does it?"

I scratched my head. I do that when I'm thinking. And as a result get lots of dandruff in my eyes. "What's it called, this thing?"

"You don't know?" She widened her eyes as if I was being unnecessarily stupid. "Big Wind and the Interisland Cable."

How I Got Mojo

SO BACK I GO, talk to Bruiser. Seeing as he's my only contact in the media world.

Know how you can have a hunch and often it's right? Not a few times in Afghanistan they saved my life. And about Sylvia I had three:

One: She didn't drown from accident.

Two: If we'd met we might have fallen in love.

Three: If I'd known her I might have saved her.

"What you coming round here for?" Bruiser said. "Surf's good today."

I looked at the sour staccato street, pale tourists, flashy facades and manic traffic, the inane busyness of Honolulu, and wondered why everybody didn't go surfing instead. Which is why Honolulu's traffic congestion is rated the worst in America. "Whacked my head, my board, yesterday. Givin it a rest."

"You get whacked, your board, every day. What's new from that?"

"So, Sylvia Gordon? I hear she maybe didn't drown from accident."

Bruiser looked at me darkly. "What you say?"

I explained him. He looked even darker. Like I said, when they adopt you in Hawaii, it goes deep. And he and his *ohana*, his extended family, had adopted Sylvia. "Last morning before she died," he said, "some guy, he dropped her off."

"You know who?"

"Nah."

I nodded up at the huge building. "Who should I talk to, in here?"

"Managing editor, Godfrey Slink. She was doin the special piece for him. But last day she say he don't like it, he don't want it no more."

"That was all? That she was doin for him?"

"That was all, Bro. She was choosy. Savin herself."

"For what?"

"For what she was waitin for. You dumb or what?"

"You know a lot for a hired cop."

He grinned a knocked-out tooth. "Big Brother watchin. All the time."

GODFREY SLINK was tall and lank and had a monkish pate with a silver fringe. I wanted to mention that *Godfrey* means *God's Peace* but the moment wasn't auspicious.

"What's this to you?" he says by way of opening.

I explained him how I found her. "One of those tragic accidents," he says wistfully. "Here at the paper we're crushed..."

The AC in his office made it colder than January in Fairbanks. "But what if it wasn't an accident?"

"So you know better than the Coroner who examined her?"

"How come he first said she was drowned?"

He looked for his coffee cup on a desk strewn with papers. "Coroners are human. They make mistakes."

"So how come you tell Sylvia to drop the big story?"

He looked at me exasperatedly. "*What* big story?"

"Big Wind and the Cable."

He slid attenuated fingers across pale lips. "That got killed."

"How come?"

"There wasn't any story to it."

"You're ducking me."

He glanced at me sharply. "I believe we're done here."

SHOULDN'T HAVE left so accommodatingly. Because good old Godfrey, *God's Peace* himself, knew more than he said. About Big Wind and the Cable. But I didn't learn that till later. When it was almost too late.

14

A few years ago we had a Republican governor named Penny Blight who of course had lots of friends with money: General Electric, the U.S. Department of Energy (Enron light), defense contractors, Lanai Land Corporation (like I said, one of the companies that stole all the land from the Hawaiians then made them work it like slaves)…Just normal corporate business, if you see what's happening today when we have the Senator from Exxon and the Congressman from General Electric, and anyone who thinks we still live in a democracy is suffering from terminal naiveté…but as usual I'm getting off the subject.

So Penny Blight the good-looking Republican governor (if they'd picked her rather than whatshername from Alaska we might have ended up with an old fart for president instead of this young guy who's still looking for an ass he hasn't yet kissed in Washington), she figured she'd build a high-speed superferry to make sure all the outer islands would get overdeveloped like Oahu. It would also serve as population control on the whales, dolphins and our other sea animals, because it went so fast it would kill them before they could get out of the way.

Well, the folks on the outer islands said no, but that didn't matter; she tried to push it down their throats without doing an environmental impact statement. Even when the courts told her she needed an EIS she still pushed it, so finally the folks on Kauai went out on their surfboards and canoes and blocked the superferry when it came into port, and it finally went away.

Then Penny figured out with the help of her corporate friends that there were billions of dollars to be made with this taxpayer ripoff called Big Wind (it should be called Break Wind except that ain't polite).

But she ran into term limits so now we have this ex-reefer madness guy named Alvin Fitch, a Democrat – no surprise in this fraudulently single-party state. He campaigned on the promise to kill Big Wind, but if you've ever invested any faith or funds in a Democrat you know how far they can fall. Turns out Alvin has set the record of transgressing on his promises and proliferating all the evils he campaigned against.

He ran as an outsider, but soon as he got in office he started pushing all Penny's nasty agendas that the corporations want like superferries and Big Wind and the Undersea Cable that would cost taxpayers billions and kill the whales the taxpayers are trying to protect, because God bless the American taxpayer, they love whales and the environment and what they *don't* want is more wars and trashing what's left of this lovely earth we live on.

So these days it's the politicians' job, after they get elected, to kill the whales and trash the earth – because thanks to that recent Supreme Court vote (5 Republicans yes, 4 Democrats no), corporations can give all the money they want to politicians. So if you send the Governor fifty bucks and General Electric sends him fifty thousand, guess who he runs with?

He said as much, quote: "If you want me to listen to you then you better contribute to my campaign." Now isn't that rare, a politician who *ever* speaks the truth?

And speaking of General Electric, turns out they made ten billion dollars profit last year but paid no taxes. Actually GE got a two billion dollar *tax credit* for building windmills that don't produce electricity and for all the terrible losses they'd had as a result. BP – who gave us the Gulf of Mexico Oil Spill – owns huge wind projects and uses them to offset billions in taxes. But that doesn't matter – our country sure don't need the money.

As usual I'm getting off my story. Makes me want to tell you about Afghanistan. Kind of like politics in Hawaii. Like Penny Blight, now running for Congress, still pushing the Big Wind Cable and collecting campaign donations from all the billion-dollar companies who want the taxpayer welfare payments from it.

Unlike all these evil people, Sylvia Gordon, God bless her, was eating my heart. She was murdered but that wasn't the official story. As if Jack Kennedy was killed by Oswald's bullets – anybody from Special Forces can tell you no way *that* was true.

But I wasn't getting anywhere to finding who killed Sylvia.

That night with Puma stretched across my stomach and Mojo snoring at my side I tried not to think about how she'd died, this lovely smart caring person held underwater by thick strong hands. Her last scrabbling for life. The moment she knew she wasn't going to make it.

And why all night in the ocean the tiger sharks didn't get her.

To Hawaiians *ohana* means family in the wide sense. My *ohana* is hundreds of people on the Big Island, Molokai and Maui. I've got two hundred cousins if I have one. We're linked all the way back to those magician seafarers who, long before the Europeans, sailed their rickety rafts far into the unknown and linked the Pacific.

So when Bruiser's *ohana* took Sylvia in, that means she was a very special person. One who like a Hawaiian reveres the land and sea because the land and sea are life, who loves and protects others because that is the *pono* way, the only righteous life.

If she floated out there six hours, how come the sharks didn't get her?

I GOT MOJO from an Israeli surfer named Alexa who lived a while on the North Shore. She'd rescued Mojo from death row at the puppy penitentiary and used to bring him to the beach when she went surfing.

She'd just come in from a long ride and we sat on the sand talking about the cross-currents and how to take the big ones. She had on a halter top that revealed some of her lovely small pear-shaped breasts, making me feel as I usually do around pretty women, that if I could only get between her thighs just once I'd be happy to die young.

We talked about the waves while Mojo excavated sand and chased crabs and barked at the other surfers. After a while we swam out beyond the surf and made love. It was getting dark, the ocean deep about a hundred feet, and this fifteen-foot hammerhead comes rising up to watch us. Then he turned away and for a moment I could read his mind. *Wow*, he was saying, *so humans do it too.*

When she flew home to Jerusalem I ended up with Mojo. He must've known I'd taken him in exchange for my time with Alexa but for some reason it seemed to annoy him when he should've felt proud.

Next day surfing I parked Mojo's little puppy ass on the beach. The waves were good, I had a new board I'd just run through the sander, there were some nice pipelines and other guys were getting fine rides. But Mojo kept running up and down the water's edge barking his tiny tail off. So I figured little bastard's gonna drown and I won't have to buy any of that disgusting pet food they show on TV with some golden retriever barking for more. Everybody knows golden retrievers rival sea slugs in IQ, but do they have to stoop to that?

To shut Mojo up I put him on my new board and walked it out a few feet. Being a dachshund he was low-slung with a wide stance that fit the board perfectly. He rode the first wavelets easily, wagging his tail and barking excitedly and watching the waves for more. He wiped out a few times but just paddled back to the board sputtering and trying to climb back on with his little bowed legs. I helped him up a few times then let him learn how to do it himself.

Within hours Mojo was surfing like a pro. Other guys had come up to see this, not believing. I'd walk Mojo out about twenty or thirty feet in the kiddie waves, turn the board around and let him catch the foam into shore. In he'd go, barking and wagging his tail and looking around to make sure everyone was watching. And I realized all the time he'd been on shore he'd been learning how we did it.

It got to be a problem because when I'd go out every dawn he'd want to go too. And he wasn't satisfied with just a few rides – for him it was an all-day thing. I had a short board I'd adapted from a windsurfer that became Mojo's board. So there we'd be, the two of us in my old white Karmann Ghia, him standing up in the passenger seat with his head out the window and his ears flapping, our two boards tied to the roof rack, on our way to the surf at six-thirty every morning.

And true to his name Mojo was a real chick magnet. Girls who never would've stopped to say hello were all over Mojo, and needless to say I got plenty of second-hand action. It was like being a roadie in a band – Mojo was Mick Jagger, but hell, I was carrying his board.

In German *dachs* means badger, and of course *hund* is hound. These little guys were bred with short legs so they could go down badger holes and drag them out. A badger is pound for pound the toughest meanest animal on earth. There's a badger in Africa even lions are terrified of. So anybody goes down a hole after a badger is pretty damn tough.

Perhaps due to some early puppy trauma Mojo hated pit bulls. Whenever he saw one he was after it instantly, me running after him fearing for his life. But it was the pit bulls I should've feared for. He'd get under them and bite them in the belly and no matter which way they turned Mojo was faster. It was an unfair fight.

There was a particular pit bull in the neighborhood who killed cats. I'd talked to the owner – a big nasty Texan with one of those silly pickups on huge wheels – about keeping him tied up, but this guy got his rocks off on how tough his dog was. One afternoon I hear this racket outside and it's the damn pit bull has chased Puma up a mango tree. She's on a branch, all seven pounds of her hissing away at him.

The pit bull heard Mojo coming but it was too late. Mojo got under his belly and went to work, the big dog spinning and snapping his jaws but he couldn't catch Mojo. Then Mojo grabbed him by the privates and really ripped. That pit bull squealed and started running, Mojo hanging between his legs, chewing and biting and trying to slow him down by dragging his rear feet. By the time he finally let go the pit bull was howling three octaves higher, and I never saw him again.

As Mojo's renown grew we started getting requests. Tourists wanting to shoot videos. Then a wedding where Mojo was the star act. By this time he was getting good – I'd paddle him out about a hundred feet, spin him around, wait for a soft curl and give him a shove. By now he was doing tricks and running up and down the board. All the time wagging his little curly tail and barking, a big grin on his long dachshund snout. Fame is a real high, and Mojo was getting his full.

Then Waikiki Hilton Village signed him up. Every Thursday afternoon three to five, come watch the amazing surfing dog! Nobody believed it till they saw him. KITV shot him and he was all over the television, then YouTube and all the rest.

Perhaps due to the stress of fame Mojo started hitting the sauce. Afternoons when I sat on the lanai drinking my Tanqueray martini with Puma in my lap, Mojo would sidle over and whine. "Go get your bowl," I'd say. So he'd go grab his empty dinner bowl and I'd pour in a taste of martini for him. *Lap lap lap*. Then whine for more.

"This dog needs to go on the wagon," Susie Brownmiller, who was living with me at the time, would say.

Even worse he was doing drugs. Sad to say but true. Susie was fond of Maui Wowie and every time she lit up he'd be there beside her, sitting dachshund-style on his little ass and rear legs, vertical as a tree stump, waiting for her to blow some smoke at him. He'd sniff in quickly and wait for more.

"This dog needs to go into rehab," Susie would say.

Those were the good old days. Before Big Wind and the Governor's hideous Cable.

Max AC

HERE'S WHAT I KNEW:

One: Sylvia was doing a newspaper series about Big Wind and the Undersea Cable.

Two: She was going to blow it wide open. That meant there was some scam to it.

Three: *The Post* was going to run the series on this scam, but then killed it.

Four: She was drowned in fresh water then floated six hours in the ocean.

Five: But the tiger sharks didn't get her.

Six: Police first said she was drowned by somebody.

Seven: They changed their minds and said it was an accident.

Eight: Since it was an accident the case is closed.

ONE DAY TWO YEARS AGO my phone rings. "Mr. Hawkins?" a cultured Japanese-American accent.

I glance around to check I was still me. "Yeah?"

"I've seen your articles in *Surfer News*...Do you still give lessons?"

The guy on the other end was named Frank Hamata. He'd spent the last thirty years as an electrical engineer, had just retired as vice president of Island Electric, and all he'd really wanted to do all his life was surf.

"I'd sit in my office," he said one day, "and I could see them out my glass wall, down there riding the waves, and I'd think, them or me, who's doing the right thing?"

"That easy," I said. "*They* were."

He smiled. Slim and small-statured with thin silvered hair, he had that deep mix of intelligence, humility, wisdom and kindness typical of Japanese-American business people in Hawaii. So I felt like the piano teacher with an older student: this one's not going to Carnegie Hall but think of the joy you can bring into his life.

Frank would never ride the big ones, but he was going to have a lot of fun out there on the rolling curling ocean. And as any teacher knows, giving someone the gifts of bliss, awareness, fun and knowledge is about the greatest high you can get.

If I wanted to learn more about Big Wind, who better to ask?

"SO WHAT you been doing with yourself?" Frank asks as we sit in the shade of his royal palms, the ocean fussing and grinding on the rocks below.

I explain him that I was growing tired of racing around the world doing surfing articles. And that I'm doing better at forgiving myself.

He gives me that kind, sad look. "You've got nothing to forgive, Pono."

I downed the fresh orange juice Frank always feeds me. "I was wondering –"

"How unusual…" Frank chuckled

"Somebody was talking story, this new windmill project –"

He laughed. Which for Frank is an excessive show of emotion. "Pono," he says, "you didn't come way out here to ask me a utility question."

I nodded. "True."

His eyebrows knotted. He had such a tough wise face that any emotion could be hidden in it. "You want to know about Big Wind and the Cable?"

"Yeah."

"Why?"

I had no choice but to tell him. About Sylvia and all.

He sat there hands clasped in front of his mouth, cogitating.

"I can't believe Big Wind and the Cable are linked to her death," he said finally. "But they're a total scam. Wind projects don't lower greenhouse emissions or fossil fuel use, they have terrible environmental, human health and social impacts, they destroy property values, they don't produce much power, most of them are owned by Big Oil, and most of the jobs go to the Chinese and other foreign companies…"

"That's not how people see them –"

He smiled, perhaps at human naiveté. "Of course wind projects make billions for the wind developers who pay millions in contributions to politicians including the President *and* Congress, who create outrageous subsidies to make the developers even richer…If I were still at IEEC I'd have killed Big Wind and the Cable long ago."

Big Wind's idea, he said, was to construct – I *swear* this is true – four hundred turbine towers, each forty-seven stories high, making them the tallest structures in Hawaii and nearly half the height of the World Trade Center – across fifty square miles of Molokai and Lanai, the two most beautiful islands in the Pacific.

Each of the four hundred turbine towers, he said, has three blades, each bigger than a Boeing 747 wing and weighing 22 tons. For each tower they dig a huge cavity in the ground, dump all that earth somewhere, and pour a two-million pound concrete and steel base that will be there forever.

Then – I swear this is true too – they want to dynamite a billion-dollar High Voltage cable between five islands, through the National Whale Sanctuary and Molokai Reef, the longest most pristine coral reef north of Australia, to send a piddle of electricity to Honolulu, so Honolulu can keep running Max AC to provide the cold weather the tourists all come here to avoid.

"To do this," he added, "they will also blast deep water ports out of the coral reef, dig hundreds of miles of erosive dirt roads, build miles and miles of transmission lines, and more miles of cables that will be left in the ground in twenty years like all the concrete bases when this monstrosity grinds to a halt." He chuckled. "They deny it, of course, but in the end, all these turbine towers will be left in place like rusting remnants of some War of the Worlds, though the developers always make glib promises to set some money aside – *our* taxpayer money, no less – to take them down. The thousand-ton concrete bases? They aren't going anywhere. Where would they dump them – in the Whale Sanctuary, perhaps?"

Big Wind will cost five to ten billion dollars, Frank said, but the developers don't risk a cent – it's all funded by overcharges on electricity customers who don't need it and us taxpayers who can't afford it.

"And here's the best part," Frank says ironically. "It makes hardly any electricity at all."

"But I thought renewable energy…" I started to say.

"Wind is very erratic," he explained. "So we have to keep fossil fuel plants running full-time as backup. And usually when the wind blows is when we don't need the power, so we have to curtail it…Many studies from around the world have shown that wind power doesn't reduce greenhouse gas emissions or fossil fuel use. It's just Big Oil masquerading as pro-environmental and making billions in the process."

Frank leaned forward. "The easy way," he said, "to make Hawaii energy independent? Put rooftop solar on every house. But IEEC doesn't want it, because if everyone's generating their own electricity then IEEC loses its cash cow, the captive consumer, and the company goes broke…So they're blocking rooftop solar every way they can, putting a false fifteen percent limit on it…In five years IEEC won't exist anymore, solar will win out, but in the meantime, they're going to build Big Wind and the Cable if they possibly can."

Big Wind was like, he added, the old Soviet Union, where the Commissars in Moscow decided on some huge wasteful project, and would flood whole regions chasing thousands of people from their homes to build monstrous dams, but by the time the electricity got to Moscow you couldn't even fry an egg with it.

KNOW YOUR ENEMY is one of the first rules of war. It's the basis of *Six Strategies*, an ancient Chinese text, and of Sun Wu's *Art of War*, and of the writings of Sun Bin, who taught me more about protecting my country than any other person alive or dead.

With these thoughts in mind I reconnoitered the Honolulu offices of WindPower LLC, located near the top of a glossy high rise off King Street.

Feeling awkward and overdressed in a blazer and slacks I took the elevator to the thirty-ninth floor and stepped into a spacious entrée with floor to ceiling windows overlooking the tiny streets and flea-sized cars.

The dizzying height made it seem impossible that Big Wind's turbine towers would be even taller.

WindPower's walls were tastefully hung with posters of pretty landscapes, sparkling streams and happy animals. It was calming and gave one unwarranted hope for humankind. A wall of clocks showing the time in cities around the world added a cosmopolitan touch.

The brightly dressed young receptionist smiled in my direction. "Hi," I said earnestly. "I'm a journalist doing a story on renewable energy –"

"Great!" she burbled. "You'll want to talk to Gavin Hughes, he's our media guy. But," she added sadly, "he's not here right now –"

"Actually, I'm looking for someone more scientific."

"Oh Gavin he's scientific all right. He tells me stuff," she added in her breezy semi-Brit accent, "that I don't *at all* understand."

A bleary tall bald guy with a mustache erupted through a side door. "I'm off to see Napoleon," he announced. "Tell Damon I want a team meeting at four –" He goggled at me through large spectacles. "And you are?"

"A journalist, I…"

"Speak to Gavin." His mouth snapped shut like a turtle's and he scuttled out the door.

"Who's that?" I said, in my role as investigative journalist.

"Oh that's Simon Lafarge. Our CEO."

"I thought Napoleon was dead – you guys brought him back to life?"

With a conspiratorial hand aside her mouth she whispered, "The Governor – Simon calls him that because he's so small, you know? In the Legislature they call him the Gnome…"

Since she was sharing secrets I popped the next question: "You must get a lot of journalists coming around?"

She made a quick moue. "Not many."

"What you're doing is so great – getting rid of fossil fuels, changing us over to renewable energy. It must feel good to be in such a line of work."

"Good to be on the good side, right?" she added, but it seemed rather sarcastic.

"Another journalist I knew said she'd interviewed Simon about this, that he made a good impression."

"Really?"

"She really liked him, maybe you remember her? Sylvia Gordon?"

"You knew Sylvia? You think she *liked* him?"

"That surprises you?"

Again the conspiratorial aside her mouth. "Simon didn't like *her*. He said no one was allowed to talk to her. He stood right there," she nodded at the door, "and told her get lost." She studied me. "How did you know Sylvia?"

I ducked that. "Why didn't Simon like her?"

She shrugged. "He gets a little tetchy sometimes."

"Tetchy?"

"You know." She said the words bravely, as if no one had ever dared say them before: "Pissed off?"

"We all do I suppose. I get like that when the waves aren't good."

"You're a surfer?"

I nodded, a little humbly.

"Gee I've always wanted to do that."

"Actually, I teach surfing. I'd be happy to show you the basics some time."

She studied me, considered this. "That'd be nice."

I glanced at the clocks. Nine p.m. in New York, three a.m. in Paris, daybreak in Moscow. "When you finish here?"

"Five. Unless Simon makes me stay late."

We settled on tomorrow. She'd bring her bathing suit to work and I'd pick her up. She was from New Zealand and her name was Charity. I didn't like fooling her, but as Sun Bin says, it's essential strategy to have an agent in the enemy camp. Now, despite myself, I had one.

Though I thought she didn't know.

Scorpions and Centipedes

WHEN I CAN'T FIGURE what to do I get down on myself. For being lazy, not solving things. Mojo senses what's amiss and plumps his butt on my lap and licks my mouth before I can turn away wondering where his tongue has been recently – and somehow in his furry, ocean-salty rufous presence I remember I'm *not* guilty and that it's okay to listen to lessons from the heart.

I spend so much time up on big waves where your decision time is a hundredth of a second, and the wrong decision can be painful or even fatal, that I'm not very good at regular cogitation. And I'm not the investigative type, don't know how to find information or scan the internet. I'm not talkative, and bad at asking questions. And since I'm on parole I have to be very careful who I annoy. If they put me back Inside I'll never find out who killed this beautiful woman.

Plus I'll go crazy.

TEACHING FOSTER KIDS how to surf took my mind off Sylvia. Twice a week I bring seven of them down to the beach to work on getting out on the water, staying on their board, reading the waves, all the usual.

These kids are a reason to hate crystal meth. Their parents were so zoned out that Social Services placed the kids in foster homes. You can't just root a kid up from his family any more than you can tear a tree from the earth and plant it elsewhere. But in this case you needed to. The parents barely knew the kids were there, didn't feed or clothe them, didn't do anything. That's the wonders of modern chemistry: a little Sudafed or Contac and anhydrous ammonia is all you need.

One kid, Anthony, still has burn scars on his arm from when his Mom poured hot water on him instead of in her instant coffee. Nine years old and skinny, he got knocked around so much his smile's a little bent, but he's got guts and he wants to learn how to live. And there's no better way to learn how to live than surfing.

First I teach them how to swim. Nobody goes out on a board till they can swim well. Crystal meth kids tend to be afraid of everything, particularly the water. Week after week we work on it, and now it's great to watch them cut through the waves doing the crawl just like an Aussie.

"What's with you, Pono?" Anthony punches me in the gut. "Didn't get no lovin today?"

I hand-punched him back. "Just getting old, man."

"How old *are* you anyway," Cynthia asks, a brown urchin with a big-toothed grin, tugging at my finger.

"Seven hundred and seventy-nine."

She scowls. "You said you wouldn't lie to us anymore."

"But I didn't say I'd do it any less –"

But they don't want to talk, they want to surf. It does your heart good to see them out there leaning into the waves, scooting their boards back and forth over the crests as if they were born to it.

Which we all were. It's just that we've forgot.

ANGIE HAS A FEY SEXY look she doesn't know about. As natural to her as laughing at complicated thoughts or scratching between her toes.

The more I got to know her the more I realized she was absolutely no one but herself, and didn't care to be anyone else. A complete package, a compact well-balanced whole with nonetheless half the mysteries of the universe locked up inside her.

Not that I was back on Maui because of Angie. I needed to understand Sylvia, learn her last activities and what the moment was that doomed her. The moment when someone decided she knew too much. Because if I had *that moment* I'd have her killers. With no chance that any of them was going to jail. That's one of the things you learn in Special Forces – how *not* to send people to jail.

I suppose with all this talk about SF I should explain you. When the Islamic madmen destroyed our beautiful towers I was seventeen. A senior at Punahou headed for UCSD in marine biology. I'd surfed all my life, taken ocean-related courses at U of H, dived with the best and swum with the whales – if there's anything purely religious it's swimming with a mother whale and calf – so ocean life was what I loved.

When the crazy Muslims hit us I felt bereaved. Sat in the Punahou dining room crying. Finished the year then decided *Screw marine biology I'm joining the Marines.*

"Nah, don't do that," Pa said. As a former Seal he hates the Marines. "Mindless cannon fodder. Bullet sponges."

"I want to get Al Qaida."

"So go in Special Forces. Those guys have all the fun. And they don't have to spend their lives like Seals, in the damn ocean."

THE HAWAIIAN TOURISM Office will tell you how multicultural we are – all the types and colors of different humans in these little islands. That's because when the U.S. military invaded Hawaii and overthrew the Hawaiian Monarchy, and President McKinley appointed Sanford Dole to become Hawaii's first territorial governor, Dole tried to turn the Hawaiians into serfs on the plantations he'd stolen from them, but the Hawaiians didn't buy it. So Dole and the ex-missionary thugs banned the Hawaiian language and imported impoverished folks from other places – the Philippines, Japan, Korea, even Mexico, and a mixing of the races ensued.

In fact the Tourism Office, and all the other multi-million-dollar tourism campaigns make a big show of our smiling friendly people but don't mention the low wages, health issues and all the other problems they face. Nor does the Tourism Office tell you about our exciting multicultural arthropod community, one that can give you the bite of your life.

Arthropod, from the ancient Greek, of course means *jointed feet*. Arthropods are eighty percent of all living things – all insects and crustaceans, including two that are quite poisonous and widespread in Hawaii: scorpions and centipedes. If you have to get bit by one, take the scorpion. Like our Governor, the centipede is far worse.

It's interesting how these evil creatures showed up in Hawaii: our islands rose from the sea when the Pacific plate slid slowly northwest over a hot spot in the earth's mantle, at a speed of 30 miles every million years. That led to spurts of volcanic activity which created the islands, Kauai 5 million years ago, Oahu 2.5 million years ago, and the Big Island only 400,000 years ago.

Everything that now lives on these islands either floated or flew to them – including us. So how did centipedes and scorpions get here? Probably on flotsam from Malaysia – or did the ancient Polynesians unknowingly bring them in their sailing ships so long ago?

Either creature will give you a bite to remember – the centipede can put you in the hospital. An Afghani trick is to put scorpions in your bed, which can make you never want to sleep again.

Like the people who killed Sylvia, centipedes hide under the detritus of everyday life, seemingly innocuous yet deadly. So if you want to find a centipede or scorpion you look where you normally wouldn't go – in dead leaves, under rocks or old lumber.

I'd been to WindPower LLC, a place I'd normally never go. Where else was I not looking for whoever killed Sylvia?

LIKE MOJO, PUMA arrived without invitation. It was a rainy night, windy and cold for Hawaii. I lay in bed listening to the patter and spatter of rain, reflecting on Afghanistan, prison life and the vagaries of humankind. I was happy to be alive in the loveliness of the rain, which to the ancient Hawaiians was a gift of the gods.

A slight mewling tugged at my awareness. Bamboo leaves rubbing against the house, a trickle in a gutter. The rain came back in gusts, thundering on the tin roof, and I forgot the sound, but soon it was back again.

Mojo was sleeping in his usual position beside me and grumbled when I moved him. Flicking on a headlamp to check the floor for scorpions and centipedes I went to the kitchen window but could hear mostly the *drip, drip, drip* off the eaves. Distant tires howled on the highway; water gurgled in the gutters, the surf rumbled, and the rain swept over the roof and hissed through the mango leaves.

I opened the back door and glanced out. It was a beautiful night; everything shone with the glossiness of rain. Something cold and wet brushed against my foot – a little ball of soaked fur.

What could I do? I wrapped her in a towel and held her against my chest till she stopped shivering. She snuggled closer and started purring. Is there a person on this earth who would have put her back outside?

She was all black but for a patch of white on her chest. I rubbed her down with the towel and gave her some of Mojo's hamburger and rice which she ate instantly and looked for more. At the sound of his food being eaten Mojo trotted into the kitchen and growled. The kitten clawed his nose and Mojo backed away. He who would take on a pit bull any day was not going to mess with this little cat.

She slept that night on one side of me with Mojo on the other. When she wanted to change sides she went to his side and made him move. It was clear from the beginning that this two-pound kitten was going to rule the house.

Over the next few months she grew to full size, all seven pounds. My vet Paula calls her a Burmese, due to her relatively flat face. "What's her name?" Paula said.

"Cat."

"C'mon Pono, you have to do better than that."

"Okay, what do you suggest?" I always defer to Paula as she is a star skydiver and I'm afraid of heights.

She cradled the cat between her lovely breasts. "When I worked at the San Diego Zoo we had a black puma with a white spot on her chest. You should call her Puma –"

So "Puma" it was. An absolutely fearless, affectionate and wise friend. A dog is a loyal, loving companion and protector, but a house without a cat is like a body without a heart.

She knows when I'm feeling down and leaps into my lap and does everything she can to boost me up – rubs herself against me, purring, licks my fingers with her scratchy little tongue, kneads her claws in my stomach – trying to make me feel loved and wanted. Usually it works.

Supposedly there are cat people and dog people, but us lucky folks have both. Our window into the minds and lives of creatures halfway between us dumb domestic humans and the wild world we lost so long ago.

Only thing I held against Puma is she wouldn't learn to surf.

Thieves and Liars

A FGHANISTAN WAS HOW I ended up Inside the first time. Second time was right here in Honolulu. But that's another story.

You'd think there's little connection between Afghanistan and Hawaii, but in reality they're very close. Honolulu politics is like Kabul: a few good honest politicians but enough thieves and liars to ruin everything. Perhaps this is why Hawaii gets continually rated the most politically corrupt of the fifty states – not an easy accomplishment these days.

Like Pa said, the trick was get into Special Forces, don't be a bullet sponge in the Marines. First requirement was Ranger training at Fort Benning – day after day of the most exhilarating exhaustion you could ever wish for, running, rucksack marching, climbing wicked hills and jumping off tall walls into muddy rivers and nasty bush and all the time the drill sergeant abusing you in every legal and illegal way while your companions sweat and moan and collapse around you as if it were a real war.

Like most kids growing up half-wild in Hawaii I was running around barefoot before I was two, surfing by five and windsurfing monster waves at ten, swimming long distances and running up the fourteen-thousand foot slopes of Mauna Loa and Mauna Kea as if they were stairs – to me they *were,* to a level of physical excitement beyond any drug. I was *crazy* about running – about *any* form of physical exertion that made my blood hot and the sweat pour off me like a Molokai waterfall.

So in the Rangers all that physical exertion was a turn-on. Young American guys today are nowhere near as tough as they used to be – too many carbs, TV and video idiocy, and the misconception that watching football games makes them men. So while my companions were dropping like flies I was having the time of my life.

And after all that fun and games came the Special Forces Selection course at Fort Bragg – another twenty-four days of exhausting physical rigors, after which I was admitted as a Weapons Sergeant candidate to Special Forces Qualification Course, which made everything before it seem like kid's play.

Next thing I knew I was in Afghanistan.

And if you aren't crazy by the time you leave Afghanistan then you were crazy to begin with. Because you'd have to be crazy not to go crazy there.

SYLVIA HAD GONE TO MOLOKAI to see where they planned to put all these huge wind turbine towers. So Angie and I flew out of Kahului across the National Whale Sanctuary and around the north side of Molokai.

Molokai may be the world's loveliest island. It's just been rated one of the world's ten best by Yahoo Travel and MSNBC, and *National Geographic* rates it the sixth most beautiful island in the world, but it's better than that. With the world's second-longest coral reef on one side and the world's tallest sea cliffs on the other – incandescent green peaks with two-thousand foot waterfalls tumbling down their black volcanic faces to the frothing sea. Peak after peak topped by impenetrable rain jungles, valley after vertical valley of sparkling rainbowed cascades, and far below great muscular waves pummeling the black sand.

They unroll forever, these gorgeous cliffs, then you pass over the emerald peninsula of Kalaupapa where the haoles banished the lepers, shoving them off their boats into the huge waves crashing through the volcanic rubble. And where Father Damien was one of a few who dared to care.

Then more cliffs and magical waterfalls till you swing over green grazing lands then the rich farms of the Hawaiian homesteads, where anyone with Hawaiian ancestry gets forty acres of fertile volcanic soil, enough for a huge garden and chickens, pigs, and a cow or two, as well as papayas (my favorite), bananas, mangoes, coconuts, oranges, lemons, limes, passion fruit and all the other delicious stuff that just leaps out of the soil.

Oh my god if you've ever eaten passion fruit right off the vine...

Then you're into cattle country, steep ridges red and raw with erosion, everything sliding toward the sea. Then Hoolehua Airport, a wide spot in the road where all there was to rent was a huge blue Chrysler like Benny Olivera's nuclear cruiser, and with Angie reading the map upside down I drove our Armageddon vehicle west toward the setting sun that gilded the jutting hills and set the sea afire.

They say you have no idea of beauty till you've come to Molokai. Some people call it the friendly island, but for most Hawaiians it is *the Sacred Island*, the only one that's kept its Hawaiian character despite the tidal wave of haoles. Even in the past, they say, enemies attacking Molokai died in their canoes before they ever reached the shore.

We stood on a lovely ridge with green forested valleys and grassy savannas on all sides sweeping down to the agate white-capped Pacific where whales spouted and slapped their huge tails. It was ecstasy – the perfumed warm air, the salty tang, the brilliant green bushes and grass, the explosions of yellow, purple, white and red flowers, the distant thunder and crash of the sea. The sun sank warmly into my shoulders, the air tasted fresh and cool. The endless sky covered us like a beneficent cloak. If the industrial wind developers had searched the world for the most beautiful place to destroy, they'd found it.

"Everywhere here," Angie said, "is our precious a'ina – and ancient graves and sacred sites that will be destroyed, and the kupuna, the ancestors, will be lost forever."

"Fucking paradise," I added in my usual cogent way.

And not a breath of wind.

THAT NIGHT ANGIE and I stayed with her friends Mitch and Noelani high up on the edge of the Molokai rain forest where the mists unfurled like Afghani veils and spattered off the towering trees and luminesced the long grass, and when you ate mangoes off the branch they were slippery with it.

"You can kill some kinds of trees up here," Mitch said, "just by walking under them. Before people came to Hawaii there were no mammals, no four-footed predators or herbivores, so these trees evolved with a network of surface roots you can easily crush."

Mitch has an earnest fast way of talking, using his long-fingered hands. For twenty years he'd been a studio guitarist in LA, one of those impeccable musicians who back all kinds of famous singers but are never named on the album notes. That was fine with Mitch; he loved music, not fame. And he made plenty of money, enough to buy this place and live with Noelani and work on saving the rain forest and the world-famous Molokai Reef and all Molokai's other unique mysteries.

Angie said Noelani, whose name means *beautiful one from heaven*, had been dancing the hula since she was two and is now one of Hawaii's best at this infinitely complex art. The hula is a way of telling a story without words, expressing an emotion too complex to relate, a time in history, usually done to a chant or instrumental music.

"It started right here on Molokai," Noelani said. "Did you know that?"

I shook my head. The haole side of my family came to Hawaii in 1837 and I've lived here most of my life, but every day I learn something new about this marvelous place.

"When the missionaries came in – like your ancestor," she smiled at me sweetly, "they tried to stamp out the hula, called it evil, the work of the devil."

I thought about my ancestor Elias Hawkins. He hadn't believed any of that. And he had nine kids and spent his life earnestly trying to help people, gave far more than he took.

"And now," she added, "High Stakes Ranch, the Governor and IEEC want to put these wind turbine towers on the sacred spot where the hula was born –"

I still wanted to defend old Elias but kept silent on that.

"Before the Europeans came," Noelani went on, "all Polynesians had very relaxed attitudes about sex. Kids started having sex when they hit puberty, most adult relationships were polyamorous and couples raised kids that were often not from both partners –"

"Polyamorous?" I said, not wanting to miss any interesting tidbit.

"*Poly* in Greek means *many*. Like Polynesia means *many islands*? I think you know what amorous means."

"So what's that got to do with hula?"

"The missionaries of course were horrified at all this fun and happiness. So they made people stop dancing, wear clothes, and go to church, and told them that having fun was a sin, and if they didn't stop having sex they'd burn in Hell forever. Just to practice Hawaiian religion got you a year in prison . . .

"So all this sex got buried," Noelani added earnestly, "and came out in the hula. It can also be a poetic rendition of the sex act, and of a woman's ability to entice a man to sex."

"Most guys don't need any enticing," I said, thinking of myself.

"In Polynesian times the women often initiated sex. Any time, and as often as they wanted."

Paradise, I thought. And now we have Paradise Lost.

Mitch and Noelani's house looks out over cloud-wispy valleys and across Molokai Reef to Lanai, another magical island now owned by Lanai Land Corporation and run by an ancient harridan named Miranda Steale, and where Mitch said the developers want to build another forty square miles of turbine towers.

Watching the moonlight turn Lanai's western slopes ivory and silver it didn't seem possible anyone would want to do a thing like that, but you know how some people are – the only thing beautiful to them is money. Like that Spanish conquistador so in love with gold the Incas tied him to a stake and poured it molten down his throat.

Dinner was venison – I hate to keep talking superlatives but Molokai and Lanai have the world's best venison – deer originally given to King Kamehameha by an Indian rajah. The grass here is so sweet the deer have no gamey taste, just rich deep mouth-watering protein. And with it came Molokai purple sweet potatoes and string beans out of Mitch's garden, a salad of wild tomatoes and lettuce so delicious you want to keep chewing and chewing it.

"Building wind turbines on Molokai or Lanai," Mitch said, "is like a hunting season on rare and endangered birds. Some turbine towers kill two hundred birds a day or more, and Hawaii is already the bird extinction capital of the world…"

"What they do to bats," Noelani said, "is the wind implodes their lungs. Our bats are already dying out. This will finish them off."

"And the towers with their thousands of blinking lights will kill the few pueos we have left," Mitch added. Pueos are short-eared owls, already endangered, attracted to lights.

"We keep killing off these species," Angie said, "that have been here for millions of years…As if it didn't matter –"

"Our few remaining monk seals are on the edge," Mitch added. "Any cables across their breeding grounds and they'll go extinct. When was it, two years ago, Caribbean monk seals went extinct?"

Noelani turned to me. "Our problem is that we're fighting huge and powerful enemies. This project makes no sense – it will cost billions, destroy a large part of Hawaii, is totally opposed by everyone who understands it. But none of that matters."

"None of it *matters*?" I said.

She shook her head. "The governor and the legislature don't care that in terms of science, engineering and economics this will be a disaster. President Obama doesn't care – he doesn't understand that industrial wind projects don't lower greenhouse gases or fossil fuel use."

"No matter what we say or do," Mitch added, "they run right over us. They use our tax money to hire consultants to prove what they want, hire PR firms to sell the project to us – they lie and we don't have the millions of dollars to fight back." He said nothing, then added sadly, "People don't realize we don't live in a democracy anymore."

As they talked, I began to see Big Wind and the Cable for what they were – a monstrous War of the Worlds metallic evil stalking these beautiful islands – one more corporate thing to crush the beauty of the world.

Like the Iraq War – a vast costly disaster built on lies.

But some folks made billions on that too.

ANGIE SLEPT in the spare bedroom, and me on the lanai listening to the symphony of a million insects, the sad screech of pueo owls and the *plunk plunk plunk* of dew off the eaves. It was so beautiful I couldn't sleep, went out on the deck to follow the stars' slow slide across the ebony sky. There's so few lights on Molokai you can see the stars and planets just as God made them, thick as a sparkling mist – you can reach right up and pull them down by handfuls – an endless universe that puts everything in perspective.

But the question I asked the stars that night was an old one: *In this world of thieves and liars how do we find truth?*

Sylvia, wherever you are – can you tell me?

TRUTH WASN'T HIGH on anybody's list next morning when Angie and I visited the folks who run High Stakes Ranch, which owns most of western Molokai – a place so beautiful your eyes can't stop feasting on it – and where these miles and miles of wind turbine towers would go. Though High Stakes Ranch sounds American as cherry pie, Mitch said it's really owned by a Hong Kong gambling company that bought it in hopes of bringing casinos to Hawaii.

Three years ago they tried to install a mega-development of vacation mansions on sacred Hawaiian lands along the southwest Molokai coast, miles of untouched gold-sand beaches and forested volcanic cliffs and headlands. When the people of Molokai rose up like a tsunami and killed the project, the Ranch punitively shut down most of its other Molokai operations, fired two hundred employees, poisoned all the palm trees in their resorts, emptied the swimming pools, abandoned the golf courses and stopped fixing the roads, tried to cut off the water and other services they are required to provide.

I guess that's called big business, but Mitch said it didn't have the desired result. The folks on Molokai are tough and don't like being stepped on. Though the job cuts hurt, what it did was harden the hatred most Molokai people feel for High Stakes Ranch.

"WIND TOWERS are not in our interest at this time," said Ian Christian, the jovial slick-palmed CEO of High Stakes Ranch. Tall, avuncular and fat, Ian was sweating although the AC in his office would've killed a polar bear. Everything about him said *emoluments*, though I had to wait till I got home to look up what that meant.

"What do you mean," Angie said, "not at this time?"

He smiled down at her, palms open on the table. "Corporations aren't like people. We have to constantly reevaluate what's best for our stockholders."

"Corporations are considered persons under American law," Angie snapped. "Unfortunately."

"When Sylvia came out here," I interjected, "did she talk to anyone at the Ranch?"

Fingers steepled, Ian thought. "No," he shook his head slowly. "No, not that I know."

"Not that you know? *Who* might know?" I was beginning to feel that cheery Ian was being less than open.

He smiled like I'd just answered a difficult question. "Now that she's dead no one would know."

THAT NIGHT SYLVIA came into my dreams as if I'd sent her an email, her lovely soft voice with a rough catch in the back of her throat, the lovely Hawaiian accent, the feminine immanence of her. "You're going about this the wrong way," she said.

"Of course. I can't figure it out."

"*Think*! You know I was killed. *Who* would want to kill me? And *why*? Who has the most to lose?"

"Jesus, Sylvia. You tell me."

"I know," her voice slipped away. "I know, but I still don't know."

What did that mean? And how can you find someone's killer when even *they* don't know who killed them?

PEOPLE SEEM to think me happy though I'm not. Probably Afghanistan is too much with me – ambushes, firefights, bomb blasts, the endless dying. The filth and despair, the horrible men and benumbed women, the insanity of religion.

But even before Afghanistan I wasn't happy. In a way our beautiful earth is going through the same thing as Afghanistan – slow dismemberment by human hands – and this preoccupied me in a way I couldn't alleviate. All around me my beloved Hawaii was dying – ruined by crooked politicians and ruthless companies building concrete towers and concrete freeways, pouring sewage into the sea and pollution into the once-fragrant air.

Often as a kid I hitched from Hilo to the Kona coast of the Big Island. There were times I waited for two hours or more on the little country road at Waimea and not a car passed. Today it's a car-clogged four-lane highway hemmed by shopping centers, condos and chain restaurants, the air thick with greasy emanations and windblown trash. People who live there have no idea what it once was. This is what sorrows my soul: we have lost the earth and don't even know it.

And Big Wind and the Cable, I was learning, would destroy it even more. Giving Hawaii the *coup de grace*, the bullet in the back of the head.

Anyone might think, I imagine, that I have an easy life. Get up early to surf, a job that pays enough to keep me surfing and canoe racing and chasing women, a car that often runs, pets I love and a roof that rarely leaks. What more is there in life?

But since Afghanistan, I was realizing, I'd lost purpose, given up marine biology, commitment to a cause, a caring. And when Sylvia bumped into me, lovely, cold and dead, I began to remember there'd been a spirit life back in my past, and deep joy in many moments.

So like the people who live in Waimea and don't know what they've lost, what it once was, I had imagined I was happy because I didn't remember what happiness was.

Love and Death

MOJO WAS FURIOUS when Angie and I got back from Molokai. She had decided to stay with me on Oahu as there was no late flight to Maui. My neighbor Zeke had fed and walked Mojo but that didn't count. For two days he hadn't been surfing and wasn't going to let me forget it.

Puma took out her annoyance by devoting herself to Angie and ignoring me. "Mojo has to pull himself together," I said, annoyed. "He's got a gig this afternoon."

"The one at the Hilton?"

"Seagrams is doing a marketing shoot, using him to promote some new energy drink – I get twelve hundred bucks for letting him do it."

"How much of that does *he* get?"

"Enough to keep us both in Tanqueray."

I should've known things were going to turn bad when he wouldn't get in the car, didn't want to sit in the back because Angie was in the passenger seat. When we got to the beach I noticed there was a bit of cross swell out there. Kind of like a rip tide, it can make riding tricky. The camera crew was ready, lights and expensive gear all over the place, a Zodiak inflatable pulled up on the sand. Ted, the Seagrams project director, was walking up and down watching the sun, looking nervous and harassed.

"You're going to have to watch the cross current," I tell Mojo, who's eyeing the cameras. The sun comes out from behind a cloud and I call him over, he hops on his board and we push out.

All's looking good, he catches the first wave just right, the camera crew tracking alongside in the Zodiak. Mojo turns to watch them not paying attention to the curl and it surges over the board and knocks him off, the board spins around and whacks him on the head.

I'm there in no time, put him back on the board but he's having none of it. We go into shore and he sits on the sand shaking water out of his flappy ears but won't get back on his board. For a good half hour I plead and coax, even promise filet mignon, but nothing works. Ted's very ticked off, and I would be too.

"He's never done this before," I explain.

"He got banged on the head," Angie adds.

"I've just blown four grand on this camera crew," Ted seethes.

"You're going back to the pound," I tell Mojo when we get home, but he just smirks and jumps in Angie's lap.

I'M STANDING THERE after dinner on my lanai looking up at the stars – we dumb humans have been doing that since we climbed out of the muck and we *still* don't know what's really up there – and the door slides open behind me and Angie comes up beside me with her arm against mine making my heart thunder and I said very diplomatically *what a fuckin beautiful night.*

"Yeah," she slid her fingers up my arm. "Let's do something about it."

It was ardent and lovely, each inside the other's skin, and afterwards we lay there bonded, having finally said with our bodies what we had long felt. We made love all night and again in the morning on the breakfast table knocking aside dishes and papaya and banana skins, a coffee cup clattering, Mojo barking, Angie giggling and the sting of perfect pleasure neverending.

That afternoon we tried surfing but the waves weren't good so we went back and made love in the shower and sat on the lanai drinking Tanqueray martinis and talking about Sylvia like she was a dear friend who might show up any moment. And like a jealous lover I wanted to know about the men in Sylvia's life. "Was she seeing anyone lately," I asked Angie.

"Not really. There was one guy, Manny, the last few weeks he was really after her but she didn't like him much. A leech, she called him...

Manny St. Clair – that was his name…When we last talked, a week before she died she'd met a guy she really liked, somebody named Lou…"

"Any guys before that?"

"Not many, a few college boyfriends, then she got engaged to a guy in grad school but he died in the second Bush invasion of Iraq…I used to ask Sylvia," Angie said, "Don't you miss sex?" And she'd say every once in a while she'd meet some guy, even did a couple of one-nighters but it didn't click…I remember how she said it, kind of looking down at her long hands draped over her knees, and I knew she was thinking of Brian, the guy who died in Iraq."

I looked out the window saying nothing, seeing the faces of dead friends.

"So who died?" Angie said, that way she had of seeing inside my head.

Startled, I pulled back from my friends, the IEDs, RPGs, bullets, grenades, falling buildings, bombs and screams of human beings. "What?"

"In Afghanistan?" She ran her palm up my thigh. "You don't have to tell me…"

"It'd only make us both feel bad."

She tickled her fingers over my ribs. "You feel pretty good, actually." She leaned back pulling me with her. "I like the feel of *all* of you."

It made me laugh, she was so funny and so good. Her kindness just overflowed into me, made me feel safe and protected. I had this sudden feeling of letting go. "We were on patrol. Up north, the mountains. This starving puppy had followed us, begging, and I turned to pull some MRE from my pocket and one of my guys stepped on a mine and two guys died because I glanced at that dog and didn't see the wire."

"Oh Pono –"

How do you put in words, I wondered, what you've lost? "Next day the squad – we're down to seven guys now – we're doing a weapons check in this Godforsaken village of about thirty stone huts on a rocky mountainside. It's sleeting, the thermometer on my wristwatch says eighteen degrees – and I'm watching every detail for the danger I'd missed yesterday. Ahead of us I could smell a fire, rancid smoke. They were searing a sheep skin, I thought, to get the last wool off the pelt. Horrible stench and then screams, almost-human, then this awful moan, a woman, '*Allah please kill me –*'"

"Oh my God," Angie whispered.

"I ran for the sound, into a courtyard, a bunch of guys with AKs standing around a writhing woman, her body charred, half her face coals, an empty gasoline tin. I screamed *What happened?* They turned at me, all angry, the woman gasping and shrieking –"

"Pono this is horrible."

"This old guy with a long beard grabs my shoulder, says *She looked at a man not her husband.*

"She what? I yelled at him.

"In the market. Raised her eyes to him. A woman's eyes trap men in Hell, the Koran says –

"Her eyes were gone but maybe she heard my voice, this foreign soldier's voice. *Please kill me*, she's screaming, *Oh God please kill me!* and one of my guys grabs my shoulder, 'C'mon, man, let's go, this shit happens all the time here –'

"It is a just punishment, a young Afghani in a dirty headscarf says. *God's will –*

"Who did it? I'm screaming at the old man, shaking him. *That is her husband*, he nods at the young man. *It was his duty.*

"She was dying. In the most horrible pain. There was no way to save her. I shot her in the head."

Angie said nothing, clenching my hand, her jaw trembling.

"Criminal! the young guy's yelling at me. *She was to suffer!* So I swung my rifle up and shot him."

"Oh Pono."

"I shouldn't have maybe. But what he'd done to the woman was so awful, I just reacted…She wasn't even a woman…just a girl, fifteen… These honor killings, they call them, so common in Muslim countries, a girl can be beaten to death by her father and brothers just for showing her face in public.

"Anyway, three days later I'm on a plane back to the States, and after two months and seven days of lockup at Fort Carson in Colorado I get a two-hour trial and twenty years in Leavenworth army prison. A civilian massacre, they said. Bad for our image."

"When?" Angie said.

"December 2005. Four years after Bush let Bin Laden walk from Tora Bora, when we'd won the war and then lost it again."

"But you didn't do twenty years –"

"Another lawyer took my case, a West Pointer just out of law school. She got it reviewed, was going to make a big public fuss, so the Army commuted my sentence."

Angie leaned back in her chair stroking my arm and looking out to sea. I sensed she was seeing the long unrolling of human history, all the wrongs and rights, the horrors imposed on each other, the sacraments of love. "Oh, Pono," she said again, each time meaning something different. And I sensed I'd opened a secret chamber in my heart, a poisoned locket, had emptied it and now it might heal.

She squeezed my hand. "But you were in twice, you said."

"Yeah." Out to sea the waves were breaking better, steep and tall and steady. "I'll tell you some time."

Military prison's horrible but it's better than civilian prison. In military prison you get three squares and the guards are tough but they're Army too and aren't trying to sell you drugs or shorting your rations or wanting blow jobs, and they don't get you in a corner and work you over like civilian guards do, not unless you provoke them. And the other prisoners are Army too, trying to live out their time, and they don't try to cornhole you in the shower or break your ribs in the exercise yard.

"I learned a lot in Leavenworth," I said.

She had pulled her chair closer, her head against my shoulder, stroking my arm.

"You're treated like who you are," I went on. "You can withdraw, focus on yourself. Or you can give yourself to others, listen to their stories, love them for the good in them, try to *help* the good in them. If you do, I learned, your time goes faster. And at night when you lie down on that concrete slab you sleep easier."

She nuzzled against me. "I love sleeping with you. We've only spent one night together but I want more."

Another of the things I was learning about her was she lets you know right now what she feels. None of this coy stuff. I kissed the fragrant top of her head where the hair parted. "We didn't do much sleeping."

She snuggled closer. "I'm not planning on sleeping tonight, either."

SO FALLING FOR ANGIE just brought me closer to Sylvia. That's the thing about loving, it brings you closer to everybody. Except those who do evil. Like people who build wind "farms". Like whoever killed Sylvia.

Next morning after breakfast we went over our list of everyone who might have wanted to kill Sylvia. We started with her recent exposés and those we knew were behind the Big Wind and Cable scam:

1. *The methheads*? Probably not. But we'd keep the idea open.

2. *Lanai Land Corporation*? "The most crooked company in the most crooked state in the nation," a news magazine once called them. Not only did they "own" Lanai, they were rumored to own part of the Legislature and the present Governor. Lanai they stole in 1928 by a devious maneuver: filing "quiet title" to lands owned by the native Hawaiians. The notices mailed to the Hawaiian landowners were in English which most didn't understand, nor could they afford to travel to Oahu to defend their ownership of lands that had belonged to their ancestors for centuries. Nor did they realize that the haole legal system could literally take their land. It did, and they were homeless, serfs to work their own lands. It is this stolen land Lanai Land Corporation now wanted to cover with windmills.

As Vonnegut said in *Cat's Cradle* about a similar outfit, "*Castle's operations...never showed a profit. But, by paying laborers nothing for their labor, the company managed to break even year after year, making just enough money pay the salaries of the workers' tormentors.*

The form of government was anarchy, save in limited situations where Castle Sugar wanted to own something or to get something done. In such situations the form of government was feudalism. The nobility was composed of Castle Sugar's plantation bosses, who were heavily armed white men from the outside world. The knighthood was composed of big natives who, for small gifts and silly privileges, would kill or wound or torture on command. The spiritual needs of the people caught in this demoniacal squirrel cage were taken care of by a handful of butterball priests."

As I said earlier, Lanai Land Corporation was now owned and operated by Miranda Steale, the "Horrible Harridan" as folks on Lanai call her, a maleficent virago with multiple jets, fourteen homes, children who despise her, a stable of muscular studs, and seventy years of creating misery and dirty deals. And just as junkies always want more junk, she always wants more money, ready to resell the soul she's already lost to the next bidder. Would she have killed Sylvia? Of course not. Could she have had her minions do it? Of course – it was practically her business model.

3. *The unions?* Old lady Steale had already set union thugs to terrorizing Lanai residents who opposed Big Wind and the Cable. Though the unions would get far more jobs if Big Wind's funds were used for rooftop solar across Hawaii, the unions seemed to neither care nor understand. Could they be behind Sylvia's death? If Lanai Land Corporation told them to?

4. *The Oahu subdivision developer* Sylvia exposed? Unlikely. He went broke and moved back to the mainland leaving twenty million in unpaid bank loans.

5. *The state senator on the take?* Most of them are, so why should he worry? In Hawaiian politics taking bribes is almost a status symbol.

6. *The church burned down for insurance money?* If they believe God's on their side, no need to take out their vengeance personally.

7. *The hit & run driver, a famous local athlete?* He'd already promised to do a hundred hours of community service (signing autographs), so nothing there.

8. *The Governor's team?* Quite possible. A little man, the Governor appears a vindictive soul, taking any disagreement as a personal affront. And rumor had it he is fully owned by Lanai Land Corporation and the mainland industrial wind companies.

9. *IEEC?* Possibly, but they're all engineers or accountants. They may be nasty but they have no balls.

10. *The Big Wind contractors?* Very likely. They've been spreading the virus of wind power all over the globe. Their Mafia partners in Italy

are now in jail, but ex-Enron miscreants and the British Petroleum guys who caused the Gulf of Mexico oil spill are still running the wind power show.

11. *High Stakes Ranch* or their Hong Kong owners? Few things are more ruthless than a tong, which is basically what these guys are. Very possible.

12. *A Filipino gang* trafficking cocaine? Doubtful. The last thing they would want is to attract further attention to their highly profitable operations.

So the ones who made the most sense were Lanai Land Corporation, the Governor, the Big Wind contractors, and High Stakes ranch and its Hong Kong gambling company.

But I didn't have the faintest idea where to go next. I was so far out of my league it was laughable. I, who had always more or less tried to do good, had no idea what drove evil people to do what they did.

Okay, Sylvia, I said. What next?

Her answer came back instantly: *Why do you keep thinking it's only one?*

I SWAM OUT before sunset about a quarter mile and lay there on my board thinking about all this, waiting for a good one. The swells were long and easy, the ocean green and lovely, the fragrance of the universe and the feeling of being *there* in the existential flow, was with me. If you'd asked I could not have imagined why humans fight and hate and steal when there is so much beauty in each moment.

Beyond the reef the crests were climbing, more muscle in them. You could feel the ocean tighten, and in the tautened water I felt something beneath my board, a reef shark maybe, and as I slid back it grabbed my ankle, yanked me off the board and pulled me deep under.

Two guys in black wetsuits, masks and rebreathers, spinning me down into cold darkness.

Bait

I HAD NO CHANCE. They could breathe and I was choking, they had fins and my ankle was leashed to my surfboard , they had goggles and knives. One had me by each wrist, pulling me down, powered by their diving fins. Tethered to my board I couldn't reach them. My lungs were screaming, my body writhing for air. They were going to drown me and let me float up again, just another incautious surfer.

Thrashing and twisting with my last bit of air I yanked one guy close enough and head-butted him. He let go my wrist to push me back; I jabbed my fingers under his mask into both eyes and he jerked away. Leveraged against the buoyancy of my board I pulled the other close, tore out his mouthpiece, poked him in both eyes, digging at them till he dove away and I spurted to the surface choking in glorious air, rolled onto my board and caught a fast wave to the beach.

I sat on the sand shaking and coughing. A couple of guys came up asking what happened. "Caught a bad one," I gasped. "Axed."

I didn't want to tell Angie but had to. Had to get out of her life. If they were going to come for me I didn't want them hitting her. Or using her for bait.

"WE'RE GOING TO THE COPS," she said.

"No we're not. The moment Leon sees me he gives me the obligatory piss test and I'm in for ten years."

"We can solve this, Pono!"

"We're not a *we* any more, Angie. It's too dangerous."

"They'll kill you!"

Standing there so slim and pretty with her blondish hair stringy down her cheek and her eyes bright with tears, she sundered my heart. Why couldn't we just have met without all this tragedy? No Sylvia, no death. Just Angie and me, the beach, surfing, doing what we love?

"I can watch myself," I said.

"Yeah, like you just did."

"I wasn't expecting it. Now I am."

"These people are powerful, Pono. They can get you a hundred ways. Anyone who sends two divers to drown you isn't fooling."

"Maybe it was just a warning."

"Yeah, like they were about to let you go –"

"Don't make fun of me, Angie. I'm scared."

She held my wrist. "Whatever happens, we do this together. Sylvia was my friend, remember? In fact, she wasn't yours at all. You didn't even know her."

"Whatever happens, you're out of this. I do it alone."

She gripped my arms hard, holding me with her eyes. "We can find them."

I took a breath. Being able to breathe still seemed an amazing gift. "Yeah?"

"You hurt their eyes, you said?"

"Not enough to blind them, they pulled away too fast. But they're hurting."

"Where do people go when they're hurting?"

I nodded. "Why didn't I think of that?"

Angie took my Karmann Ghia to Queen's Hospital while I started calling every ophthalmologist's office on Oahu. I said I was a diver and two of my friends had injured their eyes and I was trying to find where they'd gone. Most answered that they hadn't seen anyone like that, and a few said, "We can't give out personal health information," that kind of thing.

I was half way through the list of over a hundred eye docs when Angie returned. "Nada," she sighed and flopped down in the chair beside me.

"Anybody with the money to pay for killing me," I reasoned, "would have access to a private doc, someone who won't talk."

"The police might know."

I snickered. "You trying to put me back Inside?"

We split up the rest of the list of ophthalmologists and by five o'clock had finished. No one on Oahu seemed to have injured their eyes. "You're right," Angie said. "It's a private doc."

Seeing her sitting there all frustrated and angry, her lovely hair in tangles, sweat glistening in the hollow of her throat, made me want her again. I've noticed that about near-death: it makes you horny as hell. One last time, I decided, before I say goodbye.

Afterwards lying naked and achingly fulfilled on my rumpled sheets I had the kind of epiphany lovemaking is famous for: I thought of another lover. She's a slender sexy Filipino named Kim who was a great lay till she turned out to be an undercover Honolulu cop who helped put me away the second time. She was now a homicide lieutenant and owed me big time because after I was Inside she learned I'd taken the fall for a Special Forces buddy who couldn't do the time himself.

With that in mind I sat on the edge of the bed watching Angie all lovely and disarrayed and called Kim. I was in the middle of leaving a message when she cut in. "Hey you," she said.

"Hey you," I answered, our standard greeting, but trying to sound dispassionate for Angie's sake.

I explained Kim what happened. "They try to kill you?" she said incredulously, as if who would *bother*. She thought a moment. "That's attempted homicide."

"I figured it might be," I answered, jauntily as I could.

"You call anybody?"

I told her about the million ophthalmologists and Queen's hospital, and about not wanting to call Leon Oversdorf because he'd put me back Inside.

"Yeah," she said. "He's like that."

"By the way, Kim, you remember that woman got drowned, few days ago?"

"The reporter? Accident, yeah?"

"No way. I'm the one who found her."

"So what you know from how she died? What, you do it?"

"I want to *find out* who did." Watching Angie out of the corner of my eye, seeing the grim line of her mouth.

"You're making trouble for yourself again, Pono," Kim said. "You go in this time you'll never get out."

"Can you do me a favor?"

"I don't owe you no favors."

"Ask around, the other cops, is there a doc, an eye doc maybe, who might take care of people who don't want to go through the system?"

"If somebody try to kill you, Pono, I want you downtown, make a statement."

"Not till Leon's on vacation."

"Wherever you go, Pono, trouble follows you around like a hungry puppy."

That reminded me of Afghanistan, of how my two guys died. "Don't say that."

"Listen, why not check the dive shops? See if they have any customers who got trouble seeing lately?" She paused. "Anyway what you care, this dead woman?"

Then I made my big mistake: "She was a friend. I cared about her. I still do."

In the background I could hear a police radio squawking. "Got to go," Kim said.

Angie slid out of bed and shrugged into her clothes. "She's got the hots for you, that woman," she said, with the perspicacity females have about each other.

"Nah," I lied. "She helped put me Inside. The second time."

"The time you don't want to talk about."

THERE'S 42 DIVE SHOPS on Oahu. Some of them you don't *ever* want to rent from, 'cause they don't clean the regulators or make sure the air's fresh. But some of them are great, and you can stake your life on them. Those guys I knew; it only took a couple hours on the phone to work my way through them.

About number seven was Clyde Fineman. A tough barrel-torsoed guy, trim beard, hands like vise-grips and twinkly eyes. Ex-Seal like my

Dad, and like my Dad had learned that defending freedom ain't always what it seems.

Clyde has done over five thousand dives – can you imagine? – and there's few things about being underwater he doesn't know. "How's your damn dog?" Clyde asks.

"We were doing this Seagram's thing last week, and he wipes out, board hits his head and now he won't ride any more. We could have made twelve hundred bucks."

"Maybe he's riding the wrong board."

I explained him my problem. "Day before yesterday," Clyde says, "I rented two rebreathers, all the gear. Mainland guys. Then this afternoon this redhead chick in blue sunglasses and a black Subaru drops off the gear. No sign of the guys. She paid cash, didn't want me runnin the credit card. Strange, yeah?"

"You keep the original copy, the deposit?"

"Nah, she wanted it."

"You remember their names, anything?"

"I noted it down, somewhere, when they called to reserve the stuff…" Clyde rustling around in papers, in the background Robert Plant is screaming about he's got a little woman in that weird falsetto of his. "Got one guy," Clyde comes back on. "From Pittsburgh – what the fuck they know about the ocean, yeah?"

"What's the name, Clyde?"

"Rico Morales." Clyde snorted. "*Rich morals* – now there's a conundrum for you. From what I see, the rich don't have no morals. If they did they wouldn't be rich, now would they?"

SPEAKING OF THE RICH, it's funny how some folks still believe in due process. That this country is run by the good for the good. It's a well-perpetrated myth that works to the benefit of the myth-makers. If you believe the system works, how can you complain when it screws you?

So when it screws you maybe you think there was a mistake this time, that usually it works for the good. When in reality the system is set up by the powerful for the powerful, and when you run afoul of it that's just your tough. But that don't mean you should go down without a fight.

And the rest of the time you try to stay away from the system and love who you love and take care of everyone you can. That way you can still be a human being even though the system preys on you. Preyed on by the rich and powerful, who try to convince you that you're in the freest, best country in the world, and if you're not making it very well it's your fault.

So it irks me when I see good people worn to the bone working ten, twelve hours a day for nine bucks an hour. They have a lousy place to live and their kids don't have good clothes and their car if they have one doesn't run well, and you can see from the beaten, exhausted look in their eyes they think the reason they aren't doing better is their fault. When in reality everything is stacked against them, and the system wants them to be broke and work hard because that way it squeezes the maximum out of them for the minimum investment. They think they're failures in life when in reality they're trapped, serfs in our modern feudal world.

Worth Killing For

R ICO MORALES DIDN'T EXIST. Nobody in the Pittsburgh white pages by that name. Over a hundred people in Google and Facebook named that, but none of them seemed likely to be my perp.

"You shoulda known that," Kim said when I called her. "If you was killing people, you'd use your real name?"

So I called Clyde back for Rico's description. "He was about six feet, ripped, dark hair, that kinda unshaven look dumb guys think makes them look sexy. The usual dark glasses and greased-back hair. Kinda guy pisses you off by being there, on his toes, you know, thinks he's tough. Kind you wanta smack upside the head, just on principle."

"Thanks, Clyde. That helps a lot."

"Any time, Bro."

"No tattoos, nothing?"

"Not that I saw."

"The other guy?"

"He never come in. This Rico guy rented for both a them."

"The chick, what was she like?"

"She was hot, man. Slender, nice tits, long curly red hair, the blue shades. Hey, I remember, when she went out, she had a cobra tattoo on her ankle."

"Which one?"

"What kinda cobra? Christ I don't know –"

"What ankle, you dumbfuck Seal?"

"Oh yeah. The right one. Nice ankle, too. Nice long legs."

Nothing makes you feel stupider than when somebody tries to kill you and you can't get them back. Like in Waziristan – not that we were *there*, mind you – when some asshole opens fire on you from a ridge, and by the time you get there there's no asshole, no spent cartridges or tracks, just the nasty frigid wind howling at you and the sound of a chopper coming in to pick up your dead buddy.

WHEN PEOPLE TRY TO KILL YOU, no matter how tough you think you are, it's scary. And you get pissed off. A mix of terror and anger that becomes fury.

My first thought was to call a few buddies. But what was I going to tell them?

Maybe later, I decided. Tell them *if I get wasted or disappear, even if I drown and it looks like an accident, it isn't. And here's the possible perps*...Listing the usual suspects – Lanai Land Corporation, High Stakes Ranch, the Governor, WindPower LLC and the other windmill contractors who'd lose five billion bucks if this deal went south. How much money, I wondered, is it worth killing somebody for?

Sylvia was in the ocean but had fresh water in her lungs. From a swimming pool? Or had her head been held under in a bathtub or some other horrible place?

Drowning worries me because I've nearly died that way several times, most recently due to the two dudes who now had eye injuries. Even got waterboarded once, by some Seals doing practice interrogations and trying to prove us SF guys couldn't take it. Despite all the fuss, waterboarding isn't as awful as some folks make out. More like choking on your own vomit, which any eighteen-year old may end up doing at a high school party, and no worse for wear thereafter. Unless of course he's Jimi Hendrix.

IN WAR you see lots of bereaved people. The GW Bush Iraq thing created millions of them, either from our direct bombing and shelling or from the internal violence that broke out because we'd torn the country apart. And people who lose someone they love, they act in predictable ways.

One way is they hate you. You see it in a mother's eyes as she stands over her bloody child – a black pool of hatred. Or a little boy holding his dead brother's mangled body close, and you know he's just decided to get his hands on a gun, soon as he can, and come after you.

Another way is they're just stunned. Broken by weeping. By sorrow and loss. They come to hate you too. But for now they're just crushed. Numb.

So when I found Manny St. Clair, the guy who'd been seeing Sylvia, in the phone listings and went to see him, I was surprised he wasn't full of sorrow. He wasn't full of anything. He was like, impartial. I decided he didn't care about Sylvia. I was wrong.

It was a cluttered building in a three-story development huddled around a windy parking lot. The stairs were dingy and the walls soiled. It smelled of Vietnamese food and barbecue sauce. His apartment had a NASCAR flag on the wall, basketball players running around on the TV and about twenty empty Bud Light cans on the table.

"So you still believe it was an accident?" I said.

He was a tall tough-looking guy with a two-day blond shadow, a gold incisor and big knuckly hands. "What's it to you, Dude?"

"Because I found her."

"She was," he hesitated, "a magnificent person. She was kind and thoughtful and direct and I loved her."

"So how was she in bed?" I risked, to shake him up.

He glanced at me angrily. "Divine."

He looked away and I felt bad for the question. "She have other guys? Anyone who could have done her harm?" I wondered why it bothered me to ask this.

"No." He looked up at me with blue surprised eyes. "Just me. That's why I had hope. When we were together it released her. *Friends With Benefits* – you see that movie?"

I shook my head. The *ny* at the end of *Manny* seemed pejorative, diminutive, at cross purposes with his rugged demeanor and hard face.

"When she was with me, she said, she stopped worrying."

"About what?"

"About what's wrong with the world."

That's a bottomless pit, I wanted to say. "So what are you going to do now?"

A passive shrug. "Go to the Big Island, get away. I have a house there I've been wanting to fix up…"

"You're the one decided Sylvia should be cremated?"

He shrugged again. "Since her Mom and Pop were dead, no relatives – her friend Angie on Maui was too stunned to think about it…You meet Angie?"

I ignored this. "So it was your decision?"

"Where was I going to bury her?" He realized what he'd said and backed off. "She loved the ocean…I thought maybe she'd want to be in it." He raised his hands imploringly. "I couldn't just have her buried at sea, could I?"

"Sharks would have got her."

He winced. If ever one wanted him to talk, I decided, some time in a pool with an eighteen-foot tiger would do it. "How'd she get fresh water in her lungs?"

He shivered. This guy was no good at acting. Or too good. "I didn't know that." Palms out, supplicating. "How could that be?"

"If you hadn't cremated her," I stood. "We might have found out."

"I GOT A NAME FOR YOU." It was Bruiser on my cell phone. "The guy dropped Sylvia off, last morning before she died?"

"Yeah?"

"I rolled back our videos, found him. Seven-fifty nine a.m., Thursday April 19. Red BMW, plate FAQ 505. Guy name of Lou Toledo."

"Not Manny St. Clair?"

"No."

"You run his stats?"

"He's a professional diver. Works salvage, does tours, the usual."

"Think he's had an eye injury lately?"

"How the hell would I know?"

I called Clyde Fineman. "Ever hear of a diver named Lou Toledo?" Clyde turned down Led Zep. "What?" he yelled.

I asked him again. "Lou Toledo?" Clyde said. Behind him Robert Plant was singing *the piper will lead us to reason.* "Never heard of him," Clyde said.

LOU TOLEDO lived in a white bungalow near the Punchbowl Crater, where many of our nation's finest fighting men are buried. There was a red BMW parked out front with a red diver decal on the back bumper.

I knocked three times before he answered the door. It was 07:40 and I'd woken him up.

"What you want?" He was about six feet, slim, muscular and tanned, in a T-shirt and jeans, bare feet, a beautiful clan tattoo down his right bicep.

"It's about Sylvia Gordon."

He stared at me, angry. "What the fuck?"

"I'm the one who found her body. I'm trying to learn what happened, thought maybe you could help."

He gripped the door like he was going to smash it into my face. "She drowned. It's a goddamn tragedy. I don't want to talk about it."

He started to close the door but I held it. "She *was* drowned."

We sat on his small back deck made of Trex with a nice view of the waterfront. "I only knew her a week," he said. "We had this sudden very hot thing. She was amazing." He shook his head. "I'm thirty, never been married. But I would've married her any day."

I felt sorrow for him. And a moment's pang for Manny St. Clair, who didn't even know he'd been displaced. "How'd you meet?"

"The Outrigger Club. She'd come in from paddling practice and I'd just done a dive and we got talking." He looked far off. "That was a Wednesday night…She'd been on Molokai researching some story. We had some drinks, some food, came here…"

For some reason this annoyed me. "When was the last time you saw her?"

"We went out every night after that…the next Wednesday night…" he swallowed, "the night before the night she died…we went to see that movie, *The Descendants*? Silly damn thing. What do people think Hawaii *is*?"

"They don't know for shit," I answered.

"The next night, the one she died," he looked out at the hustle of downtown Honolulu, "I had to work all night…or maybe she wouldn't have died…"

"So you never saw her again?"

He shook his head.

"IT'S THAT WOMAN." Angie handed me the phone. Outside my window dawn was breaking. I tried to shake myself awake.

"Hey you," Kim, all bright and cheery. "I did you the favor I don't owe."

"Hell you don't."

"There's an MD out on Pali Highway," she says. "Lost his license for doing too many barbiturates, yeah?"

"You bust him?"

"Never could. But paid him a visit last night. After we talk story, go over old times, he admits treating two guys yesterday had hurt eyes. A bar fight, they said. One had a torn retina, even."

"He mention a redhead with blue sunglasses and a black Subaru?"

"He didn't say nothing about that. Anyway they pay him cash and they're probably already back on the mainland somewhere. That's all he knows."

"Thank you," I told her. "You still owe me one."

"You're tilting at windmills, Pono."

"I'm not tilting at them, I'm taking them down."

"Yeah," Kim said. "Good luck."

"That woman's a bitch," Angie mumbled, still half asleep. "Don't trust her."

CHARITY HAD A COBRA on her right ankle.

I'd picked her up in front of WindPower LLC and we drove to Kuhio Beach, small waves, an easy entry. She got out of the KG and peeled off her tight jeans and there it was – a lithe cobra tattoo snaking up her ankle. I almost said, "I like your tattoo, where'd you get it?" but instead pretended not to notice.

She had a blue bikini under her jeans and blouse, and it was hard to keep my eyes off her. I'd brought Mojo's board for her as he was not into surfing lately and I was still ticked at him for blowing our twelve hundred bucks.

It's hard to teach surfing to someone without bumping into them but I was trying to keep my distance. She seemed as naïve and cheery as before, couldn't seem to master the trick of getting up on her knees at the right moment in the wave and then standing. So we switched to boogie boards and she got that right away, swerving in and out of the crests.

Afterwards we sat on the beach and I pointed out moves other surfers were making, how they judged the waves, the usual. The sun was low and the little hairs on her forearms turned golden. I felt bad about my motives but after a while just liked her for who she was, and felt better.

I took a picture with my phone of her standing at the water's edge holding Mojo's board, and without her noticing a close-up of her ankle. On purpose I didn't talk of WindPower LLC, waiting for her to bring it up. Which she did after our second gin and tonic at Pipeline, a surfer's bar by the Aquarium. "I was afraid Simon'd make me stay late tonight," she said. "So I told him I had a dentist appointment."

"How long've you worked there?"

She thought back. "Year and a half. I'm actually thinking of quitting."

"I don't really even know what it does, WindPower."

"It builds wind towers. Wind farms. Though I'm from a farm in New Zealand and these towers aren't exactly farming. How do you call that, a euphemism?"

"From the Greek, to use good words for something evil."

"Whatever." She shook her bracelets. "The way they put these deals together, it *is* evil."

"Explain me."

"They go all over the country trying to find places to put those huge towers, then they work on the local politicians, offer them money, find out who in the area is really broke and try to buy them, promise them all kinds of things that they have no intention of doing. They say there'll be a big tax income for the county but then they cook the books to show no income and therefore don't have to pay taxes. They promise that after twenty years when the turbines wear out that they'll take them down and take out the concrete bases…But there's two million pounds of concrete in every base – how are they going to get that out of the ground and where are they going to put it?"

"You tell me."

"They promise to contribute to a fund to remove them, but they're gone long before that. That's why they're an LLC."

"What's that?"

"It means Limited Liability Corporation, so that you can screw up any way you want and your parent company can't get touched. Like WindPower, it's just a front for an investment group. And the lead investor is the former president of BP, the guy they blame for the Gulf of Mexico oil spill."

I tried to take this in. It was monstrous, malicious. "You know that Sylvia was killed, don't you?"

Her mouth dropped. "Killed?"

"Somebody drowned her."

She shook her head, more to clear her thoughts than deny it. "Oh my God."

"What?"

"Something Simon said. That afternoon after he threw her out."

"Yeah?" I waited.

"Simon was joking with Damon. He's our construction manager…and he flies the company plane."

"Yeah?"

"Well, Simon said, like he was laughing, *that woman should take a long swim somewhere.*"

I nodded, unable to speak. Did this Simon guy order her death? Or was he just talking, like when you say *I'd like to kill the bastard*, you really don't intend to? Wishing someone ill isn't the same as killing them.

Yet Simon could have been telling this Damon guy to have Sylvia killed. That way there'd be no comeback to him. If Damon did it and got caught, Simon could say *I was only joking.* Damon, what a name. From the ancient Greek: *daimon.* Devil.

The best way to learn about Simon *et al*, I realized, was to get close to Charity. But she was thinking of quitting WindPower. So I had to move fast.

I could have asked her home except Angie was there and I didn't want to anyway. I was beginning to like her more and more and feeling guilty as if two-timing her, because my interest in her wasn't romantic. And I was feeling bad for two-timing Angie. Not that I was, but it felt like that.

I dropped Charity off at the WindPower parking garage with a kiss from me and a tight hug from her, and when I got home Angie was gone.

Breaking and Entering

I FEARED A MOMENT for Angie's safety then saw her note on the table under Mojo's collar:

I went to Pipeline tonight to get the scarf I forgot when we were there... That girl you were with is real cute – I wish you good luck with her. And with all those girls who keep calling for you...

> *Thanks for everything,*
> *Angelica*

"Shit!" I stomped around, furious with myself – why hadn't I called Angie this afternoon? Because I'd thought it didn't matter, and I wasn't interested in Charity, didn't have my cell phone with me – all stupid excuses.

What was this about girls calling me? Since when?

I called Angie but her cell went straight to message. I checked my watch: *20:27.* She was on the last Island Air to Maui and I couldn't reach her for another half hour. I left her two messages, the same: *Please call as soon as you get this.*

For something to do I emailed Charity's photo and the close-up of her tattoo to Clyde Fineman asking *Is she the one?* but got no answer, called and left him a message.

Mojo was in a surly mood when I warmed up his hamburger, rice and veggies. "Why didn't you tell her not to leave?" I snapped, but he walked out of the kitchen without touching his food. Puma was nowhere to be seen.

I called Angie three more times but she wouldn't answer, so I left three more messages. It didn't seem like her to be so irrational and it made me mad.

With Mojo sulking on the lanai and Puma absent from my lap I felt even worse. I made a martini but didn't feel like drinking it and Mojo wouldn't touch it. "Even *you're* pissed off at me," I grumbled. "When I didn't *do* anything."

I tried Angie one more time then sat trying to figure things out. According to Charity, Simon at WindPower had told Sylvia to get out. If I told Kim about that, would she feel it worth investigating?

What had Sylvia asked Simon that freaked him out? As a journalist she would have had solid proof of any charges she made. Where was it?

That's when I got the bad idea of breaking into Sylvia's place.

SHE'D BEEN DEAD a week, so it was possible all her stuff was still there. Who was going to claim it anyway? Not Manny St. Clair. Probably not Lou Toledo. Angie hadn't mentioned it. Today was the 26th; most leases run to the end of the month.

It was a rainy night. I left the KG four blocks from her place, a white two-story apartment building off Punahou Street, a deck on the rear facing the sea. With a pencil light I checked the addresses; luckily hers was top rear.

It was so dark and wet you couldn't see. I went down the alley at the rear and climbed a tippy fence behind her building and sat a half hour under the bougainvillea with the rain running down the back of my neck, to make sure no one had seen me. Then I climbed the redwood post of her deck and went to the sliding doors.

They were locked and I could see nothing inside. I waited another fifteen minutes then quick-popped the slider lock and stepped inside.

It smelled stale and cold. Everything was a mess. Papers and clothes on the floor, dresser drawers hanging open.

I was too late: somebody had already been through the place.

With my pinlight I checked the whole place but found nothing. A small file cabinet under her desk was empty. No computer, printer, modem or

WiFi. The papers scattered on the floor were all part of somebody's thesis on the pueo, the endangered Hawaiian owl.

There was a *Newsweek* beside the toilet, female stuff in the mirror cabinet, and shelves of interesting books in the living room. Clothes were piled on the closet floor, running shoes, flipflops, underpants and bras.

No credit card bills or bank statements. They'd taken everything. I picked up her land line phone and wrote down all the recent numbers on the CID.

Her silk underpants exuded a faint sweaty sexy smell. I wondered if she'd worn them on one of her hot nights with Lou Toledo.

Headlights flashed along the windows: a car cruising the alley. I killed the penlight and looked out: cop.

I stuffed the underpants in my pocket, waited till the cop turned the corner, crossed the deck and slid down the redwood post as another cop car swung into the alley.

His headlights bounded up and down as he bounced across the gutter. I sprinted around the corner down a steep street with his engine howling behind me. "Stop!" he yelled through the speaker. "Stop! Hands up!"

I dashed across the avenue, his tires and siren screeching closer, dove over a fence into thorn bushes, down a slippery hill, tumbled over a concrete wall and slammed down into trash cans, bottles and cans clattering, stink of garbage everywhere.

Another cop was roaring down a side road, searchlight dancing, blue lights flashing. I scrambled back up the hill through the thorn bushes and ran the four blocks to the KG. It started instantly; I drove off shaking and shivering, sweating and gasping for air, my scrapes and scratches burning and my bruises thudding with pain.

"This sucks!" I yelled furiously at myself, wiping at the windshield mist with the back of my hand. "Idiot!"

Back home Puma still wasn't there. I called her a few times but feared waking the neighbors. She was old enough for her first heat; maybe that was it. I took Sylvia's underpants from my pocket and put them in a bedroom drawer. They had an intoxicating female odor, alive and feral.

Sylvia I begged her silently, *I want you back.*

I mixed a double martini and sat out on the lanai and tried to catch my breath.

If I'd got caught the charge would've been breaking and entering. That was bad enough. But if they could prove I'd intended to commit a crime, that's burglary – serious hard time.

But if I wasn't intending to commit a crime it was just illegal trespass, a misdemeanor. Though Leon would try to prove I was intending to commit a crime, because he wanted me back Inside.

What crime was I committing by seeking clues to who killed Sylvia? But Leon would say *only reason you didn't take nothing is that it was already took.*

Why didn't Leon care who *had* taken it?

Interestingly enough, why was he so hot to get me?

I was a mouse locked in a cage with a cat, and I didn't like it.

CLYDE CALLED AT NINE. "Why you send me this picture?"

"She the one paid for the two rebreathers? The famous Rico Morales and friend? Girl with the cobra on her ankle?"

"You know I can't tell, man. Coulda been, coulda not been. With those big sunglasses she had on. And she was in here real quick, and gone."

"I'll bring her by to see you."

"Yeah? And if she was the one?"

He was right. It wouldn't work, to let her know I knew.

But what *did* I know?

CHARITY AND I had our second surfing lesson and she was beginning to get it. She could stand for ten or twenty seconds on a small curl and even one time went crosswave till she slid off the back.

She'd got off at five and it was five forty when we hit the beach. I'd brought Mojo but told him he couldn't surf – I was going to show him who was boss. She was out in the water on Mojo's board, got up on the first wave. The sun setting gloriously over the Waianae mountains turned her skin almost ruby and her hair red-golden. I was beginning to like her – her enthusiasm, honesty – no interest in being a brilliant sophisticate.

Sure, she was indirect, but seemingly more from shyness than deceit. She was truly from New Zealand, where one imagines people live wisely, with concern for each other, surrounded by endless ocean and the huge sky.

But her cobra tattoo still bothered me. Though from what Clyde said she maybe wasn't the girl whose friends had tried to drown me.

"How'd you get all scraped up?" She pointed at my bruises from escaping the cops at Sylvia's.

"Came in too close and hit the rocks."

"Ouch." She jabbed her board into the sand, as if hitting back at the ocean for hurting me. "I gave Simon my two-week notice today."

Oh shit. "What'd he say?"

"Bastard said he couldn't find someone in two weeks and would I stay a month?"

I relaxed. There'd be time to learn about WindPower. "That gives you more time to find a new job –"

"So I said no."

"No? But you need time, to get a new job –"

We grabbed a table at Pipeline. "So why you quitting?"

"Simon's a groper."

"A what?" With her Kiwi accent I thought she'd said *grouper*, a fish.

"He likes to put his hands on you." She cupped hands under her breasts, patted her sides and thighs.

"That's gross. He ever make a pass at you?"

"All the time."

I thought of his sour wincing face, goggle eyes and freckly pate. "Somebody should beat him up."

Her eyes widened. "He's married, too –"

"Kill the guy," I said rhetorically, the way one does.

She crossed her long lean thighs way up under her blue beach dress. *Oh Jesus*, I prayed. *Oh Jesus.*

"You would?" she said.

With you? I wanted to say. *Absolutely.* "Would what?"

"Kill Simon?"

"For being a gross prick?" I thought of Kim. "The cops can arrest him."

She grinned, amazed at my naiveté. "I don't want them after me."

"The cops?"

"WindPower. They're quite nasty with people they don't like."

I waited a breath. "Explain me."

"People who fight the windmills, their houses get burned. They lose their jobs, get arrested for stuff they didn't do – one poor guy even got arrested for child porn – I heard Simon and Damon laughing about how they'd had the stuff put on his hard drive…"

"How'd you ever get tied in with these idiots?"

"I was flying from Christchurch to New York and stopped a few days here. Saw WindPower's ad in the *Post* and figured *why not?* Being from New Zealand I'm pretty environmental and I thought that's what they were."

"Lots of people think that."

"It's all in a name, isn't it? The oil companies are totally co-opting the environmental movement with this garbage about wind. That's what I've learned."

I'm trying to find Sylvia's killer, I wanted to say, *and to learn about WindPower. Can you help me?* But I didn't want to chase Charity away. Or get embroiled with her. I was beginning to like her too much.

She glanced at her watch, snatched her bag. "Bye!"

"Hey, I was gonna ask you –"

"I'm late," she gave me a peck, "for a very important date."

I felt chastened. "See you Friday?"

She wiggled fingers turning away. "See you then." Tall, slim and stately she vanished into the Pipeline crowd, her blue beach dress dancing over the cobra on her calf.

19:14, time to go home and feed Mojo and Puma. And even myself, if I wanted to.

That was part of solitude. You ate whenever. Before Angie, that had been the deal. And seemed it was going to be again.

Two days with no return call from her. I'd only known her a few days, how could I have known how jealous she'd get? And how silly was that?

Or was it? Charity was erotic and seductive as a dream. One who promises you everything then gives you so much more you're stunned, in ecstasy. Then gives you even more. Maybe the reason Angie was pissed.

Was I being distracted from Angie just as she'd distracted me from Sylvia? Only difference was Sylvia was dead.

When I got home the place had been turned upside down and Mojo's headless body lay in spattered blood on the kitchen floor.

Retribution

MOJO'S HEAD WAS SPIKED to the bedroom wall like a trophy, his blood and brains down the headboard.

I found a flat wooden wine crate and laid his body in it, tugged his head off the spike and set it on his neck so that diagonally he fit the crate.

I will not pull you out, I told the spike in the wall, *till I kill them all.*

All night I sat at the kitchen table deciding what to do, and wondering what had happened to Puma. Before dawn I filled Mojo's crate with stones and nailed down the cover. We drove in the KG to Kahala Beach, Mojo in the passenger seat as always, but not standing with his head out the window.

I swam way out with Mojo on the front of my board, out past the big ones, way out where I'd made love with the lovely Israeli girl who gave me Mojo, where the hammerhead had come up and watched us.

"Okay, little brother," I said, saltwater in my throat. Mojo sank through dawn's pearly seadrift, the box glistening smaller and smaller then just a spot that glinted and died out far below.

He'd stood for everything good in life: courage, loyalty, tenacity, kindness, humor, fairness, and great joy.

And all I wanted to do was say *I'm sorry*.

MY GUT WAS UPSIDE DOWN. I kept seeing Mojo's head on the wall, his bloody body on the floor.

Why did they do this? *Who* did it?

Did they think it would scare me?

What had Sylvia found that they killed her for, and now made them come after me?

How was I going to find them?

To find them I had to get close to Charity, learn about the thugs behind Big Wind. Had to visit Sylvia's boyfriends Manny St. Clair and Lou Toledo again – for different reasons. Had to track down Rico Morales, the non-existent diver from Pittsburgh who with a friend had tried to drown me.

Crazy ideas avalanched through my head: grab Simon and make him talk? Ask Kim to have my house checked in case Mojo's killers had left prints? Talk Leon into opening an investigation?

All idiotically untenable.

I thought of a man named Jim Corbett who hunted man-eating tigers and leopards in India in the 1930's. These animals were very smart and dangerous – some had killed hundreds of people. When he was tracking a particularly tricky tiger, Corbett would sometimes stake himself out as bait.

And let the tiger come to him.

YOU WANT ACTION, call Kim. She can have cuffs on somebody quicker than they can scratch their ass. That's been my experience.

So I says, "Can you get me any background on Manny and Lou?"

"What you want that for?" Her usual suspicious tone.

"Sylvia was going out with both of them."

You could hear Kim's lip curl in derision. "Pono, this lady died from drowning."

"I'll make you a deal," I says.

"I don't do no more deals."

"You help me with this and I'll never ask you again."

"That's not a deal. That's blackmail."

"Whoever killed her killed my dog."

"*Nobody* killed her, Pono. And like you said, maybe the guy with the pit bull – getting retribution? Or just some burglar, he kill Mojo to shut him up."

"Like the guys who tried to drown me?"

She thought about this. "Maybe you really *should* talk to Leon, his guys."

"And he puts me back Inside?"

It was time to call Kapu. He was the toughest guy in Halawa prison, which is how he got his name, the Hawaiian version of the Polynesian word *Tabu*. Because no matter how tough they were nobody dared to mess with him.

HE ANSWERED on the first ring. "Pono you dumbfuck, you finally call me?"

"I called you, what, couple months ago. We had dinner. You don't remember?"

"No I mean since you got in this shit."

"Got in *what* shit?"

"You putting the heat on brothers –"

"*What* brothers?"

"Hippolito Urbano, the whole ohana. They say you fingered them."

"Fuck you, Kapu. I don't finger people."

"They saying you did. That you blew smoke up that cop-whore's skirt and she dropped a rock on them."

Now I was getting mad. "You think I'd turn somebody?"

"I didn't say that, dumbfuck. I said everybody *thinks* you did."

"I don't even know those guys. I don't even *want* to know them."

"That don't have nothing to do with it."

He was right. Being blamed for shit is far worse than actually doing it. I explained him again that I didn't do it. Told him about Mojo, that I had to find his killers.

"Hippolito and those guys, they wouldn'a done that. They want you, they hit *you*, not some dumb little animal…Trouble is, now they got this retribution going against you."

"So I need to straighten them out."

"I can call Hippolito," Kapu paused, "Tell him meet with you? You up to that?"

That made me even madder. "Why wouldn't I be?"

"When you see him ask him who's fucking with you. He might know something."

"They have to cut this retribution shit."

"Incredible," Kapu added. "How anybody do a thing like that –"

"What, blame me for something *they* did? It's normal, these days."

"No, dumbfuck. How anybody do that to a poor little animal."

THAT NIGHT CHARITY told me more.

We'd done the usual lesson. She was getting good enough she could learn the rest on her own, didn't need me anymore. But I needed her, her access to WindPower LLC.

After surfing as usual we stopped at Pipeline. All I could think of was Mojo. My heart wasn't into talking or drinking. Strangely though I didn't want to be alone, liking Charity's bright cheery garble and long sinuous legs.

I couldn't decide if I should tell her about Mojo. It might scare her off, the idea that knowing me was dangerous.

"I can't believe," I said, "that WindPower actually goes after people who don't want windmills –"

She shrugged. "Wouldn't tell you otherwise."

"Why?"

She leaned forward, eyes into mine. "Because you *want* to know. Because you think *they* killed Sylvia Gordon and you're using *me* as a way into them."

The thrill of recognition flashed up my spine, the joy of honesty. "I started out that way. And now I just like you."

"Thank you." She took my hands in hers. "You know they're watching you? I'm supposed to learn all I can about you. Where you go and when, who your friends are…" Her eyes danced over mine. "I'm even supposed to sleep with you, if I *have* to –"

A shiver ran through me. How lovely that would be, for a moment not to be lonely and hunted. I shook the idea from my head. "I never asked you, what car you drive?"

"Me?" She seemed startled. "Honda. An Accord. So?"

"Can you prove it, that Simon and Damon go after the people who oppose windmills?"

"Pono my dear –" she clasped my hands. "Stop being naïve. What do you think these companies really are? One of our competitors is run by guys from Enron, another is part-owned by the ex-CEO of BP who is blamed for the Gulf of Mexico spill, another's partner is now in prison in the largest Mafia bust in Italian history – the Italian government took over the windmills and everyone but the Americans got a million years in jail – Pono my dear these are *not* nice people."

I thought of the guys who'd tried to drown me. They'd been serious and tough; if I hadn't grown up fighting Seals I wouldn't have had a chance.

She shook her bracelets, irritated by my credulity. "They even go after the scientists and engineers who testify against them…But," she shrugged, "there's nothing in the files. Nothing on the computers."

"So how do *you* know all this?"

"I hear them talk about it. And they call Hong Kong, discuss it with them. Hong Kong does the rest."

"The *rest*?"

"They have people who can put things in your computer, get you arrested. People who set things on fire. They're a gambling company, they want to bring casinos to Hawaii."

"They ever talk about killing Sylvia?"

She thought a moment. "No. Not except that time I told you, when Simon said she should drown."

"That's not what you said."

For an instant she looked scared. "What?"

"You said Simon said, *that woman should take a long swim somewhere.*"

"Yeah," she nodded. "That's what he said."

"So *how* do we prove that they go after people?"

She gave me a sarcastic look. "*We?*"

"Can you get the phone logs? We can see how many calls, and to where?"

"So? They're trying to do a deal with these Hong Kong guys, to build all these windmills on Molokai. Why *wouldn't* they talk to each other?"

"So what do you tell them about me?"

She posed her chin on her hands. "Nearly nothing. That you're a good surfer and don't talk much and don't seem very interested in me –"

"*Interested* in you?"

She dimpled. "Oh, you *know*, physically."

I waited. "Did you tell them where I was going to be, last Wednesday?"

"Last Wednesday? When we came here? Of course not."

"You didn't tell them we were going surfing? And then we came here then I went home and Mojo was dead?"

"Mojo?" She looked at me, lips parted, eyes wide. There was horror in her eyes, but I couldn't tell if it was plain shock or a realization of something she'd done.

WHEN THE FEDEX TRUCK pulled up next morning I couldn't have cared, expecting it was the ten author copies from my latest article in *Surfer News*. It now seemed so pointless to write about surfing: you should think about surfing when you're doing it. And when you're doing something else you think about that.

I had to sign for it though usually I don't have to. The box felt light – no doubt a thin issue of the magazine this month. I cut it open on the kitchen table and Puma's headless body tumbled out.

Fear Kills

"I KNOW THIS PLACE!" Charity exclaimed as we parked the KG at Deep Blue. I'd picked her up as usual at WindPower, said I needed to make a stop to buy a regulator for going diving tomorrow.

"How come you know it?" I said.

"I was here last week. Dropped off some diving gear, I –"

"Who for?"

"Remember the guy at WindPower I told you about, Damon? Some friends of his were using it."

I started the KG. "Hey," Charity said, "don't you want to pick up your regulator?"

I dropped into neutral, idling. "Can you get me inside WindPower?"

"You mean, like the office?"

"You have a key?"

"No. Only the bosses have keys."

"That patio you told me about, off Simon's office – does it have sliding doors?"

"Sure, but –"

"You can get into the main building, up to the thirty-ninth floor?"

"Yeah but there's cameras running twenty-four seven. They'd see me."

"Wait." I shut off the car and went into Clyde's. "She's the one," I said.

"What dropped off my gear?"

"Yeah."

"Tell her she owes me. That stuff weren't rinsed."

"I'll tell her. You got a rope, about a hundred feet?"

"What kinda rope?"

"Something you'd trust your life with?"

"I got some nylon mooring, you want that?" He went in the back and brought it out. "It's salt-weathered, pretty frayed," he said. "You wouldn't want to rappel on it –"

I tossed it in the KG's back seat, started the engine and pulled from the curb. "Where we going?" Charity asked a little anxiously.

"We're going to make love, have Chinese food, and break into WindPower."

"Wow," she said. "At least it's in the right order."

WE MADE LOVE in her apartment which coincidentally was in the same complex as Manny's. The way she was acting had made me want to do it, to test her honesty maybe. Though bed's the most dishonest place on earth – no doubt why politicians like to get in it with each other.

She *was* honest, and lovely and sexy. The horror of recent days was briefly gone. Then as I lay alongside her, both of us sweaty and sticky and panting, it all came back, Mojo and Puma, Sylvia's death. Whatever else these people had done.

We ate at Little Village on Smith Street, a great place for real Chinese food, started by a couple who arrived from China in 1974 with nothing but a hundred bucks to their name. From there we drove to WindPower and parked two blocks away. "So what's your story?" I said.

"I came back for my purse, hoping someone's working late and could let me in. If my purse isn't in the office I have to call the credit card companies tonight."

I held her close. She smelled of sex and Chinese food, two of my favorites. Making me want to start all over again. "Check your watch."

"Nine forty-two."

Her lower lip was trembling; it made me feel sorry and upset. "Nothing bad's gonna happen."

She squeezed my hand. "I know."

I felt a surge of warm affection for this frightened girl who'd been happily making love with me barely an hour ago. "But if I don't open the door in forty-five minutes, go home."

She walked down the sidewalk toward WindPower. I took off my shirt, coiled Clyde's rope round my torso and put the shirt back on. Feeling unnaturally portly and hot, the rough salty fibers itching my skin, I walked to the garage exit behind the WindPower tower and waited till a car came out. Swinging my keys conspicuously I ducked inside the closing door, crossed to the stairwell, unwrapped the rope and looped it over my shoulder, and started climbing.

It took eleven minutes to jog up the thirty-nine floors to the roof access door. Then another seven minutes and forty seconds to pick the door lock. I crossed the flat gravel to the edge and looked down a sheer concrete cliff to the tiny streets so far below, antlike buses and taxis scuttling back and forth between my toes.

As mentioned earlier I lost my liking of heights in Afghanistan, and being on this roof edge made my guts congeal and my muscles weak. I checked the building's other sides till I found the one with patios. Simon's was the closest, three floors down.

The roof was flat with no place to tie off the rope except around the bar handle of the access door. But from there it was not a direct drop to Simon's deck, but rather off to one side. There was no other place to tie off.

I tugged on the rope. It felt safe. I didn't.

I looped it in a simple climber's harness around my torso, folded my shirt on the roof edge where the rope would hang over the side, and stood there trying to get up my courage. Ignoring the vertiginous drop to the tiny city below, I backed off the edge and dropped over the side, banging against the rough concrete, caught a toe on a window rim and slid down the glass to the concrete wall beneath, spun out from it and banged back. Shaking with fear and dizzied by the kaleidoscope of streetlights so far down, I took three long breaths and rappelled further down the wall to the level of Simon's deck.

It was a good twenty yards to the left. I hung there, terror numbing my arms and hollowing my guts. Fear made me want to let go and fall the forty stories, get it over with. I couldn't imagine having the strength to climb back up.

It's fear that kills you, a voice said, *not the enemy.*

Thinking that thought I began the climber's pendulum: using my feet to push my body away from the wall I ran sideways against it, away from Simon's deck then swung back toward it. The scuffle of my shoes on the vertical concrete was loud; I had a moment's insane fear someone on the sidewalk forty stories below might hear. With each swing I got closer to the deck but then couldn't run any further away from it because I'd reached the corner of the building. I hung there for a moment. The sight of moonlight on the sea was terrifying. I dove back down across the abyss and jerkily upward slapping along the concrete, touched the rail of his deck with one toe and fell into the abyss again.

Something flitted past like a large bird. My shirt. It had worked loose from under the rope, and now the rope was fraying on the concrete edge.

I reached the corner, spun round and sprinted back. The deck swung near, I was upside down, feet in the air reaching for the rail and I hooked one leg over it and lost the rope as I pulled myself up and over the rail and lay there shaking.

After five minutes I stood carefully, hurting all over, went to the patio door and popped it open, walked down the half-lit corridor across the nice entrée with the pretty pictures and clocks and opened the front door.

"Where've you been!" Charity hissed, rushing inside.

"Scaring myself." I shut the door behind me.

"Where's your shirt?"

"Where's the files?"

She led me to a narrow interior room with two walls of filing cabinets, closed the door and turned on the light. I gave her two USB flash drives I'd borrowed from a former SF buddy named Mitchell Paige. "Get everything off Simon's and Damon's computers. Then come back." As she turned away I grabbed her arm. "And listen for anyone coming."

There was an entire file drawer for Big Wind. I started the first file, shooting pictures as fast as I could, arms still shaking, nausea in my guts. "You're bleeding on the floor," she said when she came back.

"You get all their files?"

She gave me the two flash drives and began opening folders and handing documents to me and putting them back when I finished. "Simon watches kiddie porn. He doesn't know I know. Is there a way that shows up in his files?"

"If he did it we can find it."

She was quiet awhile, then said, "I could get in real trouble."

"How?"

"The cameras. What are they going to think if they see I was in here a whole hour?"

"You came in to get your purse then decided to work on something."

"What if the hall cameras see you when you leave, going to the stairwell? And they remember I was here too? What if –"

"When were you born?"

"Me? March twenty-five. Why?"

"You're an Aries? Oh Jesus."

"You believe in that stuff?"

I kept taking pictures. "Sometimes."

"How long will it take?"

"After I finish Big Wind you need to show me the other projects where they screwed people over."

"There's plenty of them." She brought me a new folder called *Vermont Public Relations*. "Where were you, anyway?"

"Up on the roof."

"That's a song."

I finished the folder entitled *Merrill Lynch JV*, put it away and took out *Montana Legislators*. "You have a good memory."

"For songs I do."

She kept opening folders and putting them away when I was done. "It's really brave of you, you know. To do this."

I flipped through *New Jersey Power Authority* and turned to *National Renewable Energy Laboratory*. "Brave of you, too." I was remembering the voice I'd heard on the tower wall as I hung there: *It's fear that kills you. Not the enemy.* Ike Gleason, a Rangers sergeant, years ago. Said in the hope that it might one day save our lives.

"You go," I said. "I will when I can. No one'll think we were together."

"You coming by my place, afterwards?"

I should have said yes. But with a thousand photos to download, a dead dog and cat and people trying to kill me, people who *had* killed Sylvia, I just couldn't.

The only reaction Charity showed was a slight crimp in her smile. When she left I picked up speed and by 02:40 had used up my phone's 1,245 pix capacity. In the company kitchenette I found a large cloth napkin, cut eye holes and wrapped it around my head so no one could identify me if the hallway cameras caught me. I took the stairwell to the roof, untied Clyde's rope and coiled it. Where it had rubbed on the edge it was half-cut. The memory of hanging on that forty-story concrete cliff made my body shiver.

I turned on my phone. *You have 7 messages.* There wasn't time now. I ran down the forty flights, tossed the rope in the KG and drove home.

When I put the flash drives in my computer they were empty.

Nothing. *Damn you!* I swore at Charity.

I went into the bedroom for a shirt and Puma's head was hanging on the spike.

Why'd You Do It?

MY PHONE was ringing. No, that was my head. I was going crazy.
No, the phone was ringing.

"Where've you been?" Charity, sounding upset.

"These damn sticks have nothing on them." I *was* going crazy.

"Somebody broke in. My computer's gone, my camera!"

I sat on the bed looking at Puma's head. "How'd they get in?"

"The patio door. The lock's bent."

I sighed. "Probably junkies."

"You know it's not! They *know* about me! I'm *scared*, Pono –"

My watch said *04:47*. "Get in your car and come over here."

IT RANG AGAIN. "Damn it, Charity!" I said.

Silence. "I've been trying to find you all night," Angie said. "Who's Charity?"

"Where the hell have you been?" I yelled. "For days I've been leaving you messages –" I was so angry I couldn't talk. "Why didn't you call back?"

"I was upset, what *you'd* done."

"I didn't *do* anything!"

"That money you stole? From that old woman?"

"*What* money? *What* old woman?" I almost hung up. "I don't even *know* any old women!"

"And that other bitch – Claire's her name, isn't it? – and if you don't send this month's payment she'll tell the cops about you screwing her thirteen-year old daughter? You expect me *not* to care about that?"

I started to throw the phone at the wall, stopped and hung up. Angie'd gone nuts.

I pulled Puma's head off the spike, got her body out of the reefer and put her in a New Balance box. The phone rang again. "But then the Maui cops came," Angie said, "and I thought I'd better tell you."

I felt the last hope go out of me. "What did they want?"

"That you should come in on your own, it'd make things better." She sighed. "Damn it, Pono! Why'd you do it? Couldn't you just go straight? We were doing so well! Couldn't you have just…cared more about *me*?"

"Angie," I sighed. "I haven't committed any crimes." *Oh but I had: two counts of Breaking and Entering.* I thought of WindPower, how they messed with people's lives.

"I came to see you but you haven't been home all night. And already you've got some other woman. They *are* true, Pono, all those things –"

"They're nuts. Let's talk, tomorrow."

"Tomorrow Hell! We'll talk right now."

"Now?"

"I just turned onto Pali Highway. See you in five minutes."

Charity's headlights swung into the drive. I put Puma back in the reefer. Charity got out of a black car and ran to me. "*Thank you*," she said, "*Oh thank you thank you.*"

"For what?"

"For letting me come…I'm so scared –"

A big Chrysler like Benny Olivera's cruiser pulled up out front. "Oh damn," I said.

"Where are you going?"

"Out the back. Tell them I'm not here."

"Tell who? Wait, come back!"

I climbed the mango tree, hopped over Zeke's wall, ducked along his cabbages and lettuce to the front and looked out. Angie got out of the Chrysler and banged on my door.

I whistled. "Angie!"

She turned. "What are you doing out *here*?"

I hugged her. She pulled back. "I came to tell you about the Maui cops. But that's all. I don't want to know you anymore."

"Angie don't be crazy."

My door opened. "You came back!" Charity said to me, saw Angie. "Who's this?"

Angie smiled. "You must be Charity."

"Charity just had her place robbed," I explained.

"And Pono here," Angie said to Charity, "screws thirteen-year-old girls."

"Let's go," I said to Charity, walking her toward her car. It was a black Subaru.

"Go? I want to be *here*." She hugged me. "With you."

I got in. "Drive."

Angrily she shoved it into gear and roared up the street. "I thought you had a Honda," I said.

"This is Manny's car."

"Manny?"

"Manny St. Clair. He was my neighbor."

It didn't make sense she could know him. "Was?"

"He's moving back to Kohala. I'm keeping the car till he can ship it over."

"Why didn't you bring *your* car?"

"It wouldn't start."

I leaned back, too weary to think. "Those computer sticks were empty."

"Can't be. I checked before I ejected them. All the files were there."

This made no sense. "You had their passwords?"

"Simon's is *Slit1955*, Damon's is *Greenmoney*."

"Turn the corner," I said, "pull over."

"Why can't I stay with you?"

"Because I need to find those files on those sticks and download those photos, and think about what's happening." I was lying and hated it. "And I need to be alone."

"Yeah, alone with that woman. You bastard, Pono. I bet your really do screw thirteen-year-old girls –"

I got out and leaned through the open window. "And *you* need to go straight to the cops and tell them you want a detective there right now."

"You used me to get into WindPower and now you don't care about me." She shoved it into gear. "I'm going to tell Simon all about you." She squealed away.

Dawn was breaking in lovely blues and purples over the Pacific; the soft breeze smelled of plumerias and diesel. When I opened my front door Angie came at me with hatred on her face. "Why'd you do it?" she screamed. "Why'd you kill that poor little cat?"

"Angie, somebody did that." Tears of sorrow and fatigue slid down my cheeks. "They killed Mojo too."

Hands over her mouth she stared at me. "I went to the refrigerator," she mumbled, "see if you had orange juice…saw the box…poor Puma…" She sat heavily on my couch. "Mojo too?"

I sat beside her, hand on hers. "This all started because of Sylvia."

"Maybe she did die by accident –"

"Yeah, maybe the world's flat."

"Why is all this happening?"

I shook my head. "Those calls you got –"

"First I see you with this Charity woman at Pipeline, then I come back, hear the phone messages being left – I got so angry I just erased them."

"So who were they, the people who called, who's behind them?"

"Check your CID."

"They're too smart." I felt the incredible weariness of battling an infinitely powerful, ruthless foe. "They don't make mistakes." I wondered if I should tell her about breaking into WindPower, but that would make her an accessory.

Waves of exhaustion washed over me. For an instant I was back on the WindPower tower's concrete wall about to fall into the abyss. My head dropped on Angie's shoulder. She dragged me to bed and I drifted into a dazed sleep, woke after sunup remembering the seven messages on my cell phone, found the phone and checked it.

Six of the messages were from Angie when she was trying to find me. The seventh was Kapu: "Hippolito will meet you at the Outrigger Club, nine a.m. Be there."

I had seventeen minutes to make a six-mile drive in America's most congested traffic. "I have to run," I said to Angie.

"Going to see Charity, are we? I won't be here when you come back."

"I'm meeting somebody who wants to kill me."

She gave me an amused look. "You can't think of a better lie than that?"

"Please," I kissed her forehead, "don't go." I ran to the KG but it wouldn't start, perhaps fearing for my life.

I ran back to Angie. "Where's your keys?"

"To my rental car? Get lost."

They were on the table beside her purse. I grabbed them and ran out with Angie chasing me. "I'll call the cops!" she yelled as I pulled away.

THE OUTRIGGER CLUB sits on palm-shaded lawns by the edge of the sea. Morning sun sparkled the water and snaked cool shadows over the velvet lawns. Mynahs squabbled in the monkeypod trees and doves cooed and strutted on the mossy grass. White-shirted waiters scurried to and fro with trays of fresh bread, fruit plates and silver coffee pots. Though set in the roaring center of Waikiki, its wide tranquil acres breathed wealth, luxury and peace – the antithesis of my life.

I tried to catch my breath as the hostess led me across the terrace to a table by itself. Hippolito was a small thin man with short-cropped white hair and a week's gray beard. He motioned with his eyes for me to sit across from him. "So why'd you do it?"

My eyes stung with pollution from Honolulu's traffic jams and from the glittering water; I felt ready for a fight. "I don't finger people. And I know absolutely nothing about you."

"You got this name Pono in the pen?" He grimaced. "You know what it means?"

"*I* didn't give it to me. And I know what it means."

"A righteous person? In your case, a misnomer." He gave me an amused glance. "So now we have to kill you."

"If I had a problem with you I'd have come to you with it."

"Why not make it easy on me – just kill yourself?"

I waited while the waitress poured my coffee. "What is it you think I did?"

"You tell that cop cunt of yours that the fifty bales you dumped in the Bay is mine. You even swim one night onto my sailboat, my big beautiful Beneteau, and stash weed on it. Then you tell *her*, and when the cops come check my boat they find it. They know right where to look –"

I laughed at the absurdity of it, shook my head.

"So the cops impound my big beautiful sailboat that cost me four hundred grand. My beautiful boat I never put a molecule of weed on." He leaned forward, lizard eyes on mine. "I could kill you right at this table, with this little gut gun. It's got one of those new Israeli silencers... nobody'd hear...I just tell a couple waiters throw you in the Bay."

"What gives you the crazy idea *I* did this?"

"...and now I'm looking at five to ten hard time. What, you had to dump that weed, some Navy boat on your ass so you finger me?"

"I don't run weed, Mr. Urbano. If I did and had to dump it I'd be crazy to finger you."

"You said it: you're crazy. And now you gotta pay."

"I got so many people trying to kill me you'll have to wait your turn–"

He smiled, thumb and forefinger pursing his lips. "So you're a popular guy."

"I'm gonna explain you my situation. I want you to listen real hard, because *I* didn't finger you. Maybe you can figure it out who did, from what I tell you."

He chuckled.

I told him the whole story. Finding Sylvia's body, how WindPower, IEEC and Governor were planning to destroy Molokai and Lanai, about the guys who tried to drown me, Mojo and Puma. Didn't mention Angie or Charity, didn't want to put them at risk. Didn't mention the B&E of Sylvia's place or WindPower, something he could use against me. Didn't mention that the Maui cops were looking for me either.

He watched me, steepling long brown fingers. "So why," I repeated, "you think it was me?"

"You think we don't *know* when somebody talks to the cops? Who it is and what they say?"

"Sure I've talked to the cops but it was about Sylvia. Or to talk with this cop, like you say, I've been seeing."

"You're not *seeing* her you're fucking her. And we hear that one night you call her, talk the whole story, where the weed is you stashed on my big beautiful boat."

"She tell you this?"

He laughed. "You're a dumb fuck."

I was going crazy trying to make him understand. "Look, Hippolito…"

"Don't call me, my first name."

"I use your first name, Hippolito, because I'm your ohana." I pulled my knife.

He watched me, the amused smile. "You're half an inch from dead."

I cut a slash across my palm, held it up, blood down my wrist. "I'm offering to be your brother. Blood. I would never have done anything to hurt you and I never will." I slid the knife handle-first across the table. "Cut your palm."

He gave me a big wide white smile, shoved the knife back. "Okay I give you three days."

"Three days for what?"

"Three days to find the prick fingered me. Or *we* find you."

I shook my head. "I don't have the faintest idea."

"You better. Fast." He stood and walked away.

I ordered another espresso and watched a Navy frigate round the point heading for Pearl Harbor. Waves lapped the shore; a warm breeze caressed the palms. I felt safe here.

My cell phone rang *Highway to Heaven*. Kim.

"Why'd you do it?" she said.

"Do what?" thinking of Hippolito.

"Break into Sylvia Gordon's place? We get a 911 from neighbors, somebody's in there. He gets away though. So we run prints – guess whose left index shows up?"

I wasn't sure what to tell her. "Kim, I'm trying to find who killed Sylvia."

"She was dead from an *accident*. Can't you get that through your head?"

"You know it's not true."

"You attract trouble like a magnet, Pono. Nothing more I can do to help you."

"I need to know, Kim, you spending private time with anybody else?"

"That ain't your business –"

"Anybody who's been telling you to hit Hippolito Urbano?"

She said nothing, then, "Who tell you that?"

No Pattern

M Y PHONE CLICKED, an incoming call: Angie. I put Kim on hold. "When you coming home?" Angie said.

"Soon." I switched back to Kim. "So who's been feeding you trash on Hippolito Urbano? Who set him up?"

"Where you at?"

I told her, feeling I shouldn't. "Meet me out front," she said. "Ten minutes."

Every time I get in a police car it's bad news. That it's unmarked makes no difference. This was a low-slung black Mustang with a 315 V8 that rumbled like a P-51, tinted windows, black leather, a chrome steering wheel and 6-speed stick, and purple dash lights.

"So why'd you do this?" I yelled at her. "You know who *he* thinks did it? *Me!*"

"No way." She slid into first and took off down Ala Moana.

"Goddamn it, Kim, *who* told you? Who got you to hit Hippolito?"

She left rubber in second. "Don't try to impress me," I snapped.

"We get calls, most of them just somebody trying to screw over somebody." She hit third jerking my head back. "But sometimes they're real. Folks acting in the public good."

"So *who was it?*"

"I'm asking my head that, just now." She crossed the double yellow and accelerated to pass two trucks and weaved back.

"Will you fucking *slow down!*"

92

At the War Memorial she pulled over and stood watching the sea while I explained her the whole deal. "Crazy," she said. Her phone rang and she sent it to message. "I was gonna get a promotion for this."

"What, for getting me killed?"

"Don't you wish," she snickered. "No, for finally putting away Hippolito Urbano. Whole thing's gonna fall apart now." The phone rang again and she thumbed it off. "I got five minutes, don't know what to tell you. This tip came in hot. A person of interest wanting to buy our love by screwing somebody else." She shrugged. "We're whores – we'll try anything, see if it pays."

"Who's this person of interest?"

She shook her head. "I tell you, you'll kill him."

"Give me the name, Kim."

She looked into my eyes. "How many times we made love?"

The question surprised me. "I don't know…why? A hundred?"

"Ever figure why it's called *making* love?" She gripped my arm in steel fingers. "You love me, Pono? I don't mean any romantic shit. I mean, *Do you love me*?"

I eased back a little. "Course I do."

"Okay then. If you promise *by our love* not to hurt this guy –"

I could always shoot him in the head and he'd feel no pain. "I promise."

"His name's Lou Toledo. He lives out on –"

"1811 East Pierce."

She stared at me darkly. "How you know this?"

"He had a hot relationship with Sylvia. The last week before she died. I mean before she *got killed*."

"He's a diver, this Lou Toledo. He wouldn't kill nobody."

"It was a diver and his buddy tried to drown me –"

She cocked her head. "Explain me again that one."

Highway to Hell rang again: Angie. "If you're not home in fifteen minutes with my goddamn rental car," she breathed, "I'll tell the cops everything I know about your sordid little life."

"Angie I love you. I'm close to finding who killed Sylvia. And Mojo and Puma. And who tried to kill me."

93

Silence on the other end. "So what are you telling me?"

"That I love you and I'll be home soon as I can."

Kim gave me a vicious look. "You tell this chick you love her too?"

"Yeah," I nodded. "I love her too."

"I should shoot you. And save everybody else the trouble."

"That's what Hippolito said. That I should shoot myself."

She put her hand on her piece. "Want to borrow a gun?"

I smiled, kissed the side of her head, the short dark curls. "God you smell good."

"Shut up."

"All of you smells good. Jesus I do love you."

"Yeah and you love this other chick."

Strangely I wondered where Charity was. "You've got a husband, Kim –"

"Yeah? You can have him." She gave me a long loving look. "I'll give you a day, sweetheart. Then I bring you in."

"For *what*, for Chrissake?"

"For B&E on Sylvia's place. Why didn't you at least wear gloves if you were going through her shit?"

"I did. They tore. I didn't notice till after."

"Yeah, when you were bein chased."

I was thinking hard. "What if, like I told you, I say I was there before? Knew her?"

Her eyebrows rose. "But if she *was* murdered, wouldn't that make you a suspect?"

LOU TOLEDO WOULD DIE once I told Hippolito about him. So before I told Hippolito, Lou and I would have a talk. Of all the people who could've fingered Hippolito, that it was Lou was almost too easy. But I couldn't understand why he had. Or why he'd framed me.

Supposedly Lou was bringing fifty bales of weed from the Big Island and got chased by a Navy boat so dumped them and then planted evidence on Hippolito's boat. But why set up Hippolito, one of the most dangerous people in Hawaii? Was it some old feud? To deflect attention from himself? Or was Lou doing it for somebody who wanted to nail Hippolito?

And what about the connection between Sylvia and Lou. Coincidence?

And why spread the story that it had been me? One answer was that I'd just been to see Lou so I was fresh in his mind. But that didn't make sense.

More likely was that whoever killed Sylvia wanted me dead too. Only because I was trying to find her killers. There seemed no other reason for anyone to kill me. Not since Afghanistan, anyway.

Lou had a hot affair with her the week before she was killed. On the films my friend Bruiser the security guard at *The Post* had seen, Lou's license plate showed clearly when he dropped her off that last morning. And they'd met at the Outrigger Club – nothing unusual about that. Except that's where I'd just now met Hippolito.

Lou was a diver, like the ones who tried to kill me. But half the guys in Hawaii are divers. No matter, Lou Toledo had tried to bring about my death by framing me. And he'd been with Sylvia all the week before she died. No, was *killed*.

When drowning me didn't work they set up Hippolito and framed me so Hippolito would kill me. In that case, Lou was working for whoever wanted to kill me.

In normal situations when people want to kill you, you kill them first. That's what Afghanistan's all about. Or Iraq. But now I was in a nice peaceful place like the United States where you sometimes get in trouble for killing people. Particularly if you're a guy like me with a history.

It went around in circles; I didn't have enough pieces to see a pattern. When you walk into a valley in Afghanistan that can kill you, you try very hard to see it all, take it apart with your senses and instincts. You look for inconsistencies in the pattern. But this was *all* inconsistencies. There was no pattern.

I tried to remember what had gone down since yesterday. Yesterday morning, I decided, was when the FedEx truck delivered the package with Puma's body. Later I took Charity to Clyde Fineman's to see if he could ID her, but she recognized the place anyway and said Damon from WindPower had sent her there to return the rebreathers.

We made love, ate at Little Village, went to WindPower and I rappelled down the wall at forty stories to avoid the security cameras (*Breaking and*

Entering + Burglary Two), took pix of all the files while Charity dumped Simon's and Damon's computers on the sticks that turned out vacant anyway, and when I got home Puma's head was hanging on the spike.

Then Charity called to say she'd been broken into as well and I said come to my place but Angie was coming too so I met Charity outside and made her go to the cops but Angie shows up and thinks I killed Puma. Then I get the message to meet Hippolito – who wants to have me killed too. I snatch Angie's car (*Grand Auto Theft?*), talk to Hippolito who gives me three days to find the scumbag that fingered him.

Then Kim calls to say my prints have shown up at Sylvia's (*Breaking and Entering all over again*). She finally tells me it was Lou Toledo who fingered Hippolito, and everything begins to fall together. Or fall apart, depending how you look at it.

All this in twenty-four hours. I was sick with exhaustion, dizzy and numb. Wiser to go home, I decided, and catch some sleep before I took on Lou Toledo.

When I got there Angie was sitting on the lanai in a philosophical mood. "I've always been attracted to bastards," she said, "but you take the cake."

I explained her my last twenty-four hours. Didn't mention making love with Charity or about Kim and me. Then I lay down with my head on her lap and fell asleep, and had a dream of Mojo riding a beautiful wave, barking and wagging his tail at the joy of it. I woke and looked around for him. Then remembered.

THE WINDPOWER FILES had nothing on Lou Toledo. At least not in the pix I'd taken. That was a shame because I wanted something on him that he didn't know I had. In addition to knowing he'd framed me for fingering Hippolito.

One thousand two hundred forty-five pages were a lot to go through. Just to get my head around them seemed impossible. Pages of hotel receipts (how can a room cost a thousand bucks a night?), airplane tickets (always first class), limousine services, chartered jets, all the usual that our soldiers in Afghanistan are dying to protect.

The biggest files were what you'd expect: *Governor*, *High Stakes*, *IEEC*, *PUC* and *DOE* – all the acronyms made it sound like some Pentagon operation. Which in a way it was, I later found out.

Governor was full of printed emails – as if Simon didn't trust the digital world, needed a paper trail. Or maybe these files weren't on the computers any longer – no way to know unless I could get the flash drives to reveal their secrets. But there was page after page of stuff like this:

FROM: Tim Friendly (t_friendly@HI.gov.gov:)

TO: Simon Lafarge (S1@W_Powerllc.com)

Good to talk this morning. As agreed, we will not admit that the Big Wind and Cable costs will exceed revenues. Or that it will raise rates not lower them. To do so would kill the project.

Our mantra is once IEEC pays const. costs + gov funds then BW will levelize rates – this in a spidery scrawl signed "Simon". What kind of personality, I wondered, had handwriting so stultified and small? It seemed introverted, non-empathetic.

Stapled to this email a blue half-sheet torn from something, in another handwriting: *Calhoun @ PUC will oppose charging elec customers for Cable. Keeps fussing re billion dollars. Deal with him.*

Another email, this one from David Pruehoff, Deputy Director, U.S. Department of Energy:

I agree with you Simon but Joel Nashimoto at IEEC is still fighting us. We have to find a way to deal with his arguments. I have listed the major ones below and await your suggestions:

- *Wind power requires more oil-fueled generation than a fossil fuel plant due to spinning reserve.*
- *Wind power won't lower CO2 emissions.*
- *The winds on Lanai and Molokai are too intermittent.*
- *Wind power is very expensive compared to all other generation.*
- *IEEC could build a combined cycle plant fired by American LNG at one-twentieth the cost of wind power.*
- *Rooftop solar in Honolulu is far cheaper and more effective.*
- *The billions of dollars spent on the cables will make the project even less cost-effective.*

We have to find a way to discredit these points or they will kill us.

In the next file: *Solar Risks*, *Danneham says residential PV very dangerous for IEEC.* I tossed it aside, then wondered how rooftop solar could be dangerous for a utility, and flipped back to it:

Asked us if we could come up with arguments against rooftop solar. Fears it will become widespread and cut their revenues. Says it could kill IEEC. Therefore they will not allow over 15% of generation from rooftop solar. Who was Danneham?

I called IEEC and asked for Mr. Danneham, got routed to the Chairman's office and hung up. That was easy.

In the next file, *NPR*, in Simon's spidery scrawl: *Les Nelson (Hawaii Tonight) very pro our viewpoint. CW to send another $10k for NPR annual drive.*

In the *Molokai* file was a seventy-two-page report from Dansen & Fieler, a Honolulu PR and advertising firm. From its one-page Executive Summary:

Opposition to Big Wind is nearly 100% across the entire population of Molokai. Attempts to promote it only seem to increase resistance…To impose an industrial wind project on Molokai would likely result in revolution…

Following this, a short letter from Annheuser, Diglitz, Mannehan and Bush, Attorneys at Law, Honolulu and Los Angeles: *Given the intensity of Molokai opposition, a potential tactic would be Department of Defense participation in Big Wind and the Cable to avoid the EIS requirement and sidestep any possible legal challenge. Any physical challenge to the project would then be covered under Anti-Terrorism statutes and would result in long jail terms. If the Cable and its landings can be made a military project they cannot be stopped by public outcry or legal measures.*

Next in line was *Lanai*, most of it dedicated to Miranda Steale and her worldwide empire. The Honolulu PR firm had done a report on Lanai also, though it was only thirty-one pages. From its Executive Summary:

Although opposition on Lanai is nearly as strong as on Molokai, Lanai Land Corporation is threatening evictions and job loss to anyone who opposes the wind project. Most Lanai residents are originally from the Philippines and fear losing their green cards. Lanai Land also working with a local union to intimidate these people into realizing where their best interests lie.

Behind this was a brief memo from Damon McNight to Simon: *Governor would like a trip to London – I suggest we fund it (first class, best hotels, beautiful escorts, fine restaurants etc, plenty of spending money) – in return for the inside track if PUC requires an open bidding process.*

Then in a file called *Other* that I almost hadn't copied were several xeroxed news articles, one about sewer line extensions on Maui, one on Waikiki hotel occupancy, another on a new exhibit on Hawaiian art at the Bishop Museum – seemingly irrelevant till I noticed they were all written by Sylvia Gordon.

The Governor is Adamant

NOWHERE IN THE FILES was there another reference to Sylvia. None of the articles in *Other* related to Big Wind or the Interisland Cable – but that was because Sylvia was still researching the story when she got killed, hadn't written it yet.

One email from the Governor's office had been mis-filed in *Other*:

FROM: Tim Friendly (t_friendly@HI.gov.gov:)

TO: Simon Lafarge (S1@W_Powerllc.com)

The Governor doesn't care about the intensity of public opposition to Big Wind. People can fuss all they want, but in the end what they want doesn't matter. Per our earlier agreements the Governor is adamant this project will go through even if every person in Hawaii is against it.

I took Angie's Chrysler to Lou Toledo's, wondering was the Governor so "adamant" he'd have someone killed? Had Sylvia been trying to find information on him? Was he, or some minion in his office, a suspect?

And why did he want Big Wind and the Cable so badly? How much of the five billion dollars would he get?

I parked two blocks away and walked to Lou's house. It was a bright sunny morning with a fresh wind rattling palm fronds and making the birds twitter. His red BMW was parked in the same place; I climbed the front steps still not sure how to begin this.

When I rang the bell nothing happened. I whacked hard on the door and it eased open. Lou Toledo was lying in the living room in a little lake of blood.

The smell of blood was nauseating. I felt a terrible sorrow for him. I was stunned, speechless, didn't know what to do. Had Hippolito's guys found him already? Or else who? Now I'd never learn who he'd been working for, who'd wanted me killed.

I stepped around Lou and went into the bedroom. There was a computer case in the corner with nothing in it. The desk was clean and empty. The modem socket on the wall hung empty where the cord had been yanked out. Once again I was too late.

I thought of calling Kim to tell her Lou Toledo was dead, but then I'd be a suspect. Otherwise how could they prove I'd ever been here?

I tiptoed out, pulled the door shut and wiped the handle with my shirttail. The door of the next bungalow swung open suddenly with a blast of TV and a burly woman with a laundry basket in one arm and a little girl in the other stepped out. She gave me a red-faced glance as she crossed to the clothesline and I walked slowly away, heart thundering, short of breath.

I WAS STILL SHAKING when I got home. Angie wasn't there. I sat on the lanai with a martini but couldn't drink it. Looked down at my shoe and saw the edge of the sole was red.

Blood covered the edge and between the sole waffles – I'd apparently stepped on an edge of it at Lou's. I wrapped the shoes in a plastic bag, went to the morning trash pickup and dumped them in. Then I went home and washed the floor where I'd walked, went back to the trash bins and tossed the rag in too.

I called Kapu and told him I needed to see Hippolito. Five minutes later he called back. "He's too busy."

"Tell him his problem's solved. That he should watch the papers. And get off my ass."

Kapu chuckled. "You want me tell *him* that?"

"Yeah. Tell him that. For me."

I went back to the lanai and tried to watch the ocean. My gut was churning and my muscles felt weak. I had the crazy desire to call Leon Oversdorf and tell him the whole story but that would be like swimming with a tiger shark.

Now there were two people dead, plus my dog and cat. And people had tried to kill me. I'd gotten into something far bigger than I could comprehend. I was a fly stuck in a spider's web and the spider was wrapping me in its web before it drank my blood.

Angie came home but I could barely talk. The fear and disgust were so bad they were eating my heart. I was facing a ruthless and determined enemy and still had no idea who they were. And no one to turn to for help.

Angie was barefoot in the kitchen cooking peppers and pork loin. "It's not safe for you here," I said. "And I need to get away."

"You think whoever's after you won't follow you?"

We'd been trained in SF on how to disappear. It's much harder in a place like Afghanistan where you don't look like the locals. But no matter where you are it's best to have a safe house with plenty of supplies so you can stay a month or more if you need to.

But I also needed to move about, talk to people. And do it alone.

"You have to go home," I said to her.

"Why, so you can hang out with Charity?"

"Don't be silly," I said, feeling evasive. "Charity has nothing to do with this."

She gripped my jaw in her hard little hand. "You balled her yet, Pono?"

This was no time to lie. "Of course not."

She pushed my chin away, disgusted, not believing. This relationship I'd cared for so deeply was exploding and I couldn't stop it. Like being on a rabid Ferris wheel, high overhead and out of control.

"I have to track down who it is," I said. "Though I think I know –"

"Who?"

"WindPower. Maybe the Governor too."

"IEEC?"

"They'd have loved to see her killed but don't have the balls to do it."

"What about Lanai Land Corporation? High Stakes Ranch? They're the worst of all."

"I haven't gotten to them in the files yet."

"So let *me* do the files, take notes –"

I shook my head. "It's not safe any longer, Angie."

She didn't say another word. In five minutes she was gone. I put the two computer sticks in my pocket, got the KG going after a few minutes' negotiations, and drove across town up into the hills to see Mitchell Paige.

With every dead or injured buddy I've always felt I had to live for them. A debt. With Mitchell it's different. He lost his legs on a mission I was leading, and I did time to keep him out of prison. So our history makes us sort of equal. Though he'd give everything to be like me and I'd give everything not to be like him.

I rang the bell and waited for the sound of his wheels down the corridor. "Yeah?" he yelled through the door.

"It's me, asshole. Open up."

"Go away!" he called as he slid the bolt, swung the door open and reached up in his wheelchair to give me a hug. "How you, brother?"

He wheeled into the kitchen and rolled back with a tray on the front of his chair with two glasses of ice and a bottle of Stolichnaya. "What you been up to?" I said.

He scanned me. What does a guy do, I wondered, who has no legs, no balls and no dick? How does he fill up his life? "I been busy as hell," he said.

"The job?" By this I meant Naval Intelligence, where he spent his days patrolling the network looking for infiltrations. Just like we'd done in a different way in Afghanistan.

"Not just that. When I took the job I demanded the right to work nights and weekends on my own – you know that. So now I'm getting all this free-lance work, companies, agencies, wanting to securitize their systems." He shook his head as if amazed by this need for security, and poured two glasses full of vodka.

"Everybody's suddenly afraid?"

He drank, thinking. "Yeah, it's getting worse and worse."

"Why?"

He shrugged. "Anarchy. The four horsemen. Everyone fears the world's descending into chaos. America's going to hell – the politicians and corporations have ruined us." He shrugged again, as if to hide how much he cared about this. "We ruined ourselves, I guess, by tolerating it."

Seeing Mitchell's lean pain-worn face brought back so many others. Guys in Arlington now. Or in family cemeteries all over America. "You still counseling?"

"The VA? Yeah. These poor young guys, nineteen, twenty maybe. They're paraplegics now, no more girlfriend, no more car, nothing but emptiness..." He coughed. "I try to help them find a way..."

"Find a way?"

"To stay sane."

"I got a letter from the VA yesterday," I said. "Asking did I have any symptoms."

"PTSD?" Mitchell smiled. "What you tell them?"

"No."

"The VA's really trying but they're so understaffed, and there's an avalanche of shit coming at them." Mitchell paused, thinking of it. "Not just PTSD but the whole psychological thing, the brain damage from IEDs, the lung destruction from explosives dust, the denatured uranium...That one's like Agent Orange, it's gonna be the iceberg under the whole deal, and just like Agent Orange, the guys at the top won't admit it." He gave me a hard glance. "You look like shit. What's up?"

I showed him the flash drives from Simon's office, explained what had happened. He took them into his cave, a wide tall-ceilinged room with about ten computers humming away on benches and a thick carpet where Mitchell could wheel silently back and forth between them.

He popped them in and out of one computer, then another. "These guys are amateurs," he said. "They thought they had it securitized. But I can get into it backwards. Just takes time."

"How long?"

"A night, maybe."

I thanked him and went back where I'd hung a hammock in the thick trees of a vacant lot two blocks from my house. Like Jim Corbett, waiting for the maneater.

False Face

A T 03:17 A WHITE VAN circled my street for the second time. Cold and stiff, I swung out of my hammock, slid down the tree and crouched at the edge of some ferns. It came around the third time, eased down the alley and halted with a blink of brake lights.

I slipped back through the ferns along the ratty edge of the vacant lot, watching for broken bottles and beer cans, crossed the street farther up, went half a block then down the alley.

At this point I was about two hundred feet from them. If they turned on their headlights they'd see me, but their lights were off and they were moving toward the house, three guys dressed in black, black face masks, metal bars in their hands, another guy in black by the van.

The alley was slippery with leaf rot, garbage, rat shit and mud. Papaya trees hissed, a palm tree so frilly and loud I feared they'd come up behind me and I wouldn't know it. Far away the surf was breaking, steady and loud. Through the smog and city lights you could see Orion's sword.

I moved fast along the alley till I was fifty feet from the guy standing with his back to me watching the van. The other three had vanished. Again I had the fear of someone behind me, glanced back but the alley seemed dark and empty.

Twenty feet behind him I hid behind a clump of bamboo in Zeke's garden fragrant with basil, mint and tomatoes. The wind in the bamboo leaves was so loud I could hear little else.

The guy turned and started pacing, ten feet away, ten feet back, chin tucked into his palm. I could take him now but so what? This jerk wouldn't have the faintest idea who had hired him.

I trotted across the garden and around the house, came out on the next street, ran to the corner and around the block and came up through the shadows toward the white van. In the windy darkness it stood out like a white ghost. I could see the guy moving behind it, still pacing.

I leaped Zeke's garden fence and crouched along it till I came to my property line. The other three guys were moving around inside my house, their headlamps flashing.

It was a GMC van, JKL 509. A plastic panel on its side said *Courtesy Electric* in bold Italic, and underneath in smaller letters the phone, fax and email and an address, 449 Ahua Street.

The best thing was to take this guy, learn real fast what he could tell me. Then? Knock him out, or just hurt him bad enough he drops out of the game. Still trying to decide I edged nearer and somebody smashed into me from behind knocking me into Zeke's fence, my hand splintering the pickets. I started to fight back, realized it was Zeke's damn goat. I slapped him hard across the face and the pain in my hand nearly knocked me out – I'd done something to it, held it up to the foggy night and saw black stuff dripping out.

"Hey!" the guy yelled. "Yo, Clancy! Dick! Code Three!"

I took off across Zeke's garden with the goat butting me, dove over the next fence through a chicken run, hens screeching and a dog yowling as I cleared the front gate and sprinted down the street, up another alley, then back across my own. The van was gone.

I ran a half mile through the streets with no one after me, back through back yards and alleys where no one could follow, to my vacant lot and climbed one-armed up the palm to my hammock. My hand was pounding and the blood kept pulsing out. The blood on my clothes felt sticky and cold.

In the light of my headlamp it was a long ragged slash across my right palm. It hurt to open or close the hand or move the fingers. The hypothenar and transverse muscles had been sliced part way through. I bit the fingers to check the nerves were okay.

I went back to my house. It was empty. I went in and got my bottle of Tanqueray. It was a waste of good gin but I poured a good shot into the wound, held my breath till the pain subsided then sewed it shut awkwardly. Something they should teach you in SF, I thought stupidly. How to stitch your wounds left-handed.

I took a long hit of Tanqueray and left the house, walked a few streets to ensure I wasn't followed, climbed back up my tree and snuggled into my bag ignoring my throbbing hand and beaten muscles and the hissing and scrabbling of rats in the branches. It felt good to fall into sleep. I'd have almost two hours till dawn.

There were so many things to do, so many dangers. The fear and dread came crashing back and I forced them aside. If I didn't surmount them I'd never win. Never survive.

AT DAWN I slid down the tree and drove the KG into the hills above Palolo Valley till the shabby housing developments petered out. Off a side drive stood a corroded sheet metal barn from the days when this area was a thriving Japanese family farm, before the developers changed the zoning and raised the taxes to drive the farmers out. The slidebolt on the door was rusty but opened after a good kick, inside was straw-floored, a pile of greasy tractor parts in one corner, the air thick and dusty. I parked the KG inside, hid the key up under the eaves, patted the fender and promised to be back.

After a two-mile hike downhill I took the bus to Marguerite Place.

The neighborhood was poor even by Honolulu standards: three-room shacks with peeling paint, hanging clapboards, missing shingles, rusting roofs, punctured screens and cracked windows, abandoned pickups and broken bottles in the tall grass, children staring thumb-in-mouth from shadowed doorways.

Many times I'd tried to get Ken to leave but he liked it here. It was cheap; with his disability payments he made ends meet. I visited him regularly but it broke my heart: this guy who'd once rappelled the toughest cliffs, had logged hundreds of HALO and HAHO insertions, spoke four languages including Farsi and did calculus in his head, now reduced by an instant's random violence to a mild benumbed confusion.

"It's like he has an IQ of seventy," the VA docs told his family. But he wouldn't live with his family or me or any of his old buddies, hung out alone in this Honolulu ghetto.

"Who are you?" Ken said when I knocked, as he peered through the screen, gripping the latch.

"It's me, Ken. Can I come in?"

"He hasn't lived here for a long time –"

I glanced around. "Ken, let me in."

"I'll let him know," he gripped the door tighter, "when he comes back."

I backed down a stair so he could see me better. "C'mon Ken –"

"Okay you win," he opened the door. "You knew all along it was me."

I checked the view from his windows but nothing looked out of place. "I can make you some tea," Ken said. "I only drink green tea. Do you like green tea?"

"Don't have time now," I said pacing to the next window.

"You're not really here to see me are you?"

"Not this time. I got the badguys after me, Ken."

"Al-Farouk?" he said sharply, one of those amazing links with the past that sometimes pop up in his head. Al-Farouk had led a band of guys from the Waziristan hills, would harass NATO forces in Afghanistan then slip back across the border. Finally under Obama we were allowed to go after them.

"Like Al-Farouk," I said.

"We dealt with him."

"It's some other badguys, so I needed to ask can I borrow your truck?"

He scratched at the long pink dent in his skull. "Two nice policemen came yesterday."

"Really?"

"They said if I see you I have to call them. They said it was national security. That's very important you know."

"You gonna call them?"

"Only if you want me to."

"I don't want you to."

"Okay I won't then."

"What number they give you?"

"I've got it somewhere." He fumbled among toast crusts and jam jars on the kitchen counter, gave me a blank card with a handwritten number. "That's what I'm supposed to call."

"Who they say to ask for?"

"Oh they didn't say." He thought a bit. "No, just to call that number."

I pocketed the card. "That's all right," Ken said. "I remember it."

I glanced out his windows again. "I just need your truck a few days. Till I deal with these badguys."

"What if it doesn't have gas?"

"I can get some." I cleaned up his kitchen, changed his sheets and towels, put his frozen dinner in the microwave and took the truck keys off the nail by the back door.

"I wish you could stay more," he said.

"Me too."

"Where you going?"

"On an op."

"An op?" It took him a moment to remember. "Oh," he said.

It was a white Ranger pickup that hadn't been driven in months. I wiped the dust and pollution off the windshield, drove to the Best Buy on Pearl Ridge and bought a Toshiba laptop, and then to Sand Island Road and the old marina where Attila the Hulk floated calmly among the mangroves, a white egret standing one-footed on her bow.

She'd been a good boat once, fast and low, with a fishing deck over the cabin and a sharp prow. Now she needed a good cleaning, her paint had powdered in the ocean sun, her engine wheezed a little and her tappets clanked. But she was wide below decks, with a nice galley and plenty of storage and extra fuel tanks for a long cruise. She was safe as a safe house could be: if trouble comes you just move it away.

Chained under a tarp on her rear deck were a Suzuki dirt bike and a Spectrum sea kayak. I don't like dirt bikes – too many idiots ruin the back country with them – but they're a great escape tool because they're fast and can go practically anywhere. And at 160 pounds it was light enough I could get it in and out of the Hulk when I needed to.

For a few moments I sat below deck enjoying her old-boat odor and the slight nod of the hull on the Bay ripples, wanting to fall down on the big double bunk with the orange bedcover and sleep for a week. Instead I hitched up the new computer, created a Gmail account and checked *Whitepages.com* for Courtesy Electric. They were right there, 449 Ahua Street. I drove Ken's Ranger downtown, bought a throwaway cell phone with a thousand minutes and drove to Ahua Street.

Courtesy Electric was in a long low off-white concrete block building, two garage doors and an office beside them. A short-haired pretty woman about forty-five sat at a computer behind the counter. The nameplate on the counter said Mrs. Aquino.

"I was wondering," I said, "how many trucks you have."

She looked at me strangely. "How many *trucks* we have?"

"Yes, Ma'am, I –"

"We have two trucks. Why?"

I explained her about one of them being at my house at 3:15 a.m. "That can't be," she said sharply.

"Ma'am, I –"

"They're locked in here all night. We have master locks and a burglar alarm. No one can get in here but my husband and me and our son Reno. He drives one truck, my husband the other."

One of the garage doors began to rumble open, making me jump. She watched me, nimble-eyed. A white van pulled up on the sidewalk and into the garage. It was a Ford not a GMC, and the lettering on the side was different and was painted on the metal, not on a plastic panel. A big guy with clan tattoos on his arms and neck got out, tossed the keys on the seat, looked at me and nodded his chin: what can I do for you?

I explained him the same thing. He shook his head. "These trucks don't go out. They're locked in here."

"Is the other one a Ford? You got any more?"

He grinned. "The way things are now, man, we can hardly run two."

I stood on the bright windy sidewalk, pissed off and exhausted. Every path I took went nowhere.

I NEEDED A FALSE FACE. Even with the Hulk I couldn't hide all the time. To keep hunting my enemies I had to be constantly on the move. I had my backup life with the Hulk and Ken's truck, but with the new security cameras everywhere I'd soon be caught.

For a false face I went to Smyrna. She has a beauty salon on the rich end of Waikiki, all glossy granite, chrome and potted palms, women in rows with stinky metal turbans on their heads.

As usual she was in her office with the interior Japanese garden and the marble fountain of the Greek girl with the water sliding down her tits. She has a mahogany desk so big you could land a plane on it. "Hi Sweetheart," she said. "Where you been?"

I explained her some of it. "I wondered," she said, "why I haven't seen you." What I need to add is that her long-time girlfriend is my cousin Sally. They even talked about getting married under these new gay marriage laws but decided why do what the crowd does when they've done the opposite all their lives?

What I also didn't add about Smyrna is that she was a disguise technician for the Agency in the nineties, can make you a false face you can wear all day. It's thin, it breathes, you can't even see the match around the eyes, mouth and nose. I've been told that the CEO of Enron who supposedly died before they could sentence him, the body in his casket had a false face that looked just like him.

She looked worried. "I can do that."

"How soon?"

"I take an impression now, you have it Friday."

"What about the hair?"

"Hair?" She scanned my tangled sunburned locks. "You're going to be an older man. Maybe bald?"

I let out a weary half-chuckle. "It won't work."

"Horn-rim glasses, maybe a cane." She scowled at me. "How much do I tell Sal?"

I shook my head. "Nothing."

Gala Investments

HOW MANY TIMES I wished I'd never gone surfing the morning I bumped into Sylvia. I'd be free now, living my happy uncomplicated life. Surfing every day, girls and music at night, my lovely dog and cat, working just enough to get by.

But I *had* bumped into Sylvia. So what could I have done? Pretend she drowned by accident? Pretend no one tried to drown me a week later, killed my dog and cat?

So this was my new normal. With no way to resurrect the past. And sometimes I wasn't even sure I wanted to.

Either way, I first had to survive. I called Hippolito Urbano. "I don't need to see you," he said.

"But I need to see you. I need you to save my life."

"I don't give a fuck your life."

"I'm your ohana Goddammit. I gave you my pledge. You owe me."

He thought this over. For a Hawaiian these were powerful words. And I meant them. He let out an exasperated sigh. "I told the guys you were okay."

"You knew I was okay all along. Now I want payback."

"You little shit –"

"I've ducked more bullets than you've ever fired." I realized I was gaining and pressed it. "I'm coming over, to tell you everything, then I want you to help me."

"Oh Christ," an old man's pissed-off sigh.

He had a rambling oceanfront estate off Kahala Avenue near the Waialae Country Club. At the gate a little muscular guy frisked me and another took me inside. It was simply furnished, maybe Japanese but more the style of someone who did what he wanted and didn't care what other people thought he should do.

He met me at the door and shook my hand and smiled his old man's smile at me, avuncular and protective. Somehow everything had changed between us and I didn't know why. This worried me.

The living room was spacious with a northeast ocean view. I tried to imagine the beautiful islands of Molokai and Lania out there – with thousands of wind tower red strobe lights flashing all night, got my mind back where it belonged. "I didn't do Lou Toledo," I said.

A flash of sharp regret passed over Hippolito's face. "Do *you* know," he said softly, "who did?"

"Don't have the faintest." I started to tell him about going to Lou's place and finding him dead, but decided against it. "You did know it was Lou," I said, "was talkin story on you?"

"We were told this. Same time you were." He shook his head, the same grim face. "It made no sense."

This surprised me. I tried to remember when I'd been told it was Lou. It was when Kim drove me in the undercover Mustang out to the War Memorial and told me. So did Hippolito have her car wired? How else would *he* know?

He looked at me clearly. "You hear something, you tell me. Agreed?"

I nodded, looked into his eyes. "Agreed."

He smiled, paternally. For a moment I understood this man's immense charm, that he could make you feel safe when you were far from it. "What are you drinking?" he said.

That made me laugh. "Tanqueray."

"Martini?"

I nodded and he called to the guy by the door, "Two, Vincent." He turned to me. "We want to know."

"Someone didn't like him."

In a couple of minutes Victor came in with two martini glasses and a big aluminum shaker. "We're fine here," Hippolito told him. "So you can keep you-know-who company, yeah?"

Victor vanished and Hippolito poured us full glasses. "Five to one, I assumed."

"More gin the better –"

He raised his glass. "She did it."

"She?"

"Your hot little cop cunt."

Anger snaked through me. "Don't call her that."

He nodded. "Agreed." He watched me speculatively. "She's not who you think."

I wanted to defend her. "None of us are. Not even you," I added coldly.

He took this, no problem. "So," he said. "You wanted to see me."

I explained him again, repeated what I'd said at the Outrigger Club, about what I'd found at WindPower, their link to the Governor, to Lanai Land Corporation and High Stakes Ranch. Told him everything had happened since, the guys in the GMC van that turned out not to be Courtesy Electric.

He sat with his martini, thinking. I watched the flicker from the Diamond Head lighthouse dart round the walls, the bougainvillea nodding in the seashore wind, waiting for him to speak. All the time I'm wondering was he right, that Kim had killed Lou. No, I shook my head. She was tough but she wasn't a killer. She was a good cop. Or was she?

"This Governor," he said after a while, choosing his words, "is the worst we've ever had. The most crooked. When he got elected I thought *Wow* maybe he can do some good, get our schools going, our urban systems, work on prison reform, stop lobbyists from buying all our politicians, bear down on illegal developers, crooked bankers, lying lawyers and all the other scammers who've been destroying Hawaii for years –"

He said nothing more, looking out to sea, that pensive lower lip between thumb and forefinger. "Humans never change."

I shrugged. What could I say?

"What happened, your hand?" he said.

I explained him about Zeke's fence and the billy goat. He chuckled. "Now you got two hands don't work. Being from cutting your other one showing off to me."

"I meant what I said."

"The Governor's a crook," he went on. "But Lanai Land Corporation's far worse. They will do anything to get what they want. And what Miranda Steale wants right now is lots of money."

"Christ, she's got three jet planes, companies all over the world –"

"She's got a bank loan she can't pay. Almost a billion bucks. The lender pool, they're about to pull the plug. Then her whole house of cards comes down."

"What's this have to do with Big Wind and the Cable?"

"If she can get this sham project built she gets thirty percent of the cost up front. Nearly a billion bucks. *Pocket money*, they call it. From our very own Barack Obama." He shook his head. "Christ, I worked my ass off for that guy. Look what he does to us."

He collected himself. "And High Stakes Ranch? What do you imagine a Hong Kong whoring and gambling company would do? To get what they want?"

I'd thought about this and it wasn't pleasant. "So how you going to help me?"

He paused. "The Governor's security detail, they often visit Gala Investments…You know it?"

I shook my head.

"It's a place with beautiful women. Governor goes there too, when he can get away from the Dragon –"

"The Dragon?"

"What he calls his wife. When she isn't listenin." He sat back. "How you suppose the Governor, on an annual salary of a hundred twenty grand, pays for Gala once a week?"

"Must be his good looks."

"You should find out," he said, "who's paying for the Governor's fun. The girls at Gala, maybe they can help. They know who comes with him, who pays the bills. And his security detail knows everything he does. So we get the girls to learn."

"Learn what?"

"What the security detail knows."

"Why would they tell some hooker?"

"You're being a moralistic fool. And you haven't met Severina."

WHEN I GOT TO THE DOOR it didn't say Gala Investments. It said **Blue Ocean Planning Group**.

So what the fuck is this, I said under my breath in my usual succinct way. I banged on it, thinking of *Knockin on Heaven's Door* whatever that means. It was huge and made of some thick dark Indonesian hardwood. Tiny TV eyes were set in high up on both sides. The handle, anchor knocker, lock and hinges were polished brass.

I knocked three times and as I turned away an old guy opened it, a Filipino with a straggly chin beard, dressed in a yellowed wife-beater. Hovering there like I just woke up Paul Bunyan or whoever it was who slept so long.

"What?" he says.

"I'm here for Simon Lafarge. He wants to reserve a table, tonight, eight people? Who do I talk to?" Clearly *he* wasn't it.

"Come back later."

I looked at my watch. *14:11*. "When later?"

"Tonight seven clock. People be here then."

I went back to Ken's truck wondering what kind of business was this that only opened when everything else was closed?

Simon and the Governor were beginning to take shape, oozy and evil. And how many others? I didn't understand the pattern but felt it was there.

IT WAS THE U.N. made Hawaii a state. In the late 1950s it began working on a resolution against colonialism. At the time Hawaii was a U.S. territory and would be covered by the resolution. This forced the U.S. to either let Hawaii go back to being its own nation – as most Hawaiians wished – or to make it a state, which most Hawaiians did not wish.

The foremost military base in the Pacific, Hawaii was central to U.S. domination of the hemisphere and the oil fields of Indonesia and the Middle East. Too many mainland companies had investments here. The appropriate politicians were told what to do, a lot of fuss took place in public, and the coonskin was nailed to the wall, as a later President, Lyndon Johnson, once said of Vietnam.

Such tidbits occurred to me now as I drove in Ken's white Ranger to Gala Investments. If Hawaii had become its own nation, Sylvia would not have died, because Big Wind and the idiotic Cable would never have been considered. The people who live here love this place and would never tolerate such a disgrace to the land and culture.

But in the U.S. it's easy to own politicians. All you have to do is give them lots of money. So the big corporations own most of our politicians. And when these huge companies are looking to make money off our citizens, our government is always there to help them out.

Also if Hawaii had become its own nation, I wouldn't have fought in Afghanistan and Iraq, wouldn't have done time. And if anyone *had* killed Sylvia, there would be no delay in finding them, no pretending it hadn't happened.

I parked the Ranger. It was nearly 19:00; the rigging lights of cruise ships looked like little bridges to nowhere out on the sparkling sea.

I rang the bell. High heels came to the door; I glanced up at the TV eyes and the door opened.

"You're early," she said. She was pretty, about five-six, Hawaiian, long-limbed and slender.

"I'm here for Severina," I said.

She looked me over. "She doesn't take clients."

"I'm not a client."

"Who sent you?"

"I'll tell that to Severina."

She hesitated, beckoned me in. It was a wide classy foyer with Oriental carpets on the marble floor and Kama Sutra paintings on the polished hardwood walls, a Rodin-like koa statue of a standing man and woman making love. "Wait here."

Severina wore a little blue shadow under her eyes but she didn't need it. Her eyes were pure cornflower blue, wide and unflinching, so entrancing you didn't care how beautiful the rest of her was.

She had on a powder-blue dress with a nine-inch semi-transparent hem half way up her thighs. It sheathed her thin waist like serpent skin then tapered lovely over breasts I tried not to look at. Her thighs under that amazing see-through hem were lithe and golden, legs of a woman who runs five miles a day. Her face was incisive, that carved marble look some Russian women have.

"Wow," I said, "you're even lovelier than I thought."

"Than you *thought?*" She had a throaty Russian accent. "How vould you *know?*" Her lovely exhalation at the end *you* and *know* made me dizzy.

She led me to a cramped office with two chairs and an oak roll-top desk. She took a chair and nodded for me to take the other. "I don't have so much time. It's a busy night –"

"Hippolito said come see you."

"He told me about your problem." She smiled, eyes sparkling, as if this were a game. "Many powerful and wealthy men come here. Tell me who they are, these people making trouble for you."

I told her quickly, worried about her time. Her face revealed nothing, a carved porcelain mask so beautiful that any man would hunger for her, would do almost anything to have her, if only for a night.

She looked straight into my eyes. "You are lucky, having him for a friend."

"Hippolito? But why's he care about me?"

"He takes care of good people. So they take care of other good people. Don't look a gift in the mouth."

"What's the gift?" I said recklessly.

"Apparently, your life." She looked at me humorously. "That's not enough?"

No Way

DID KIM KILL LOU? No way. But Hippolito said she did. How did he *know*? I thought back over the two years I'd known her and it didn't make sense.

I should explain you about Kim. She was the cop who put me away the second time. As I learned later, she was undercover in a combined operation with the DEA to stamp out the plague of weed smoking among Iraq and Afghanistan vets.

In Iraq you spend a lot of time patrolling the desert, the bedraggled villages and barren hills. Or you walk the deadly streets of Baghdad or Fallujah. Doesn't matter how much Kevlar you wear, the snipers find the seams.

Or you get blown up. Working a street with your buddies and suddenly a crushing roar throws you across the street, smashes you into a building, your body screaming with pain and fear, and you scramble for defense positions wiping your friends' guts off your face.

Or you kill people by accident. Pregnant women, school children, white-whiskered grandfathers. You see their rumpled bodies on the side streets, or under slabs of concrete after an attack. Nearly a million Iraqi civilians dead. That haunts me. Everywhere the smell of spent explosives and rotting flesh. Afghanistan is the same but worse. Because there you also have to deal with the mountains.

When you come home you realize most people barely know there's a war, let alone two. They're busy trying to get a job and get laid and have fun. So you're an outsider. You wake up ten times a night with horrible memories you can't talk about.

Weed is peaceful. It heals wounds, diminishes the pain, allows you to slide part way back into how you once were while keeping the awareness of what you've been through. So lots of vets use it. And so the DEA wants to stamp it out.

And like Mitchell Paige and everybody says, weed is a great therapeutic. If GW and Cheney had smoked it in the White House maybe a million Iraqis and four thousand Americans would still be alive. If weed was legal Sylvia would never have died, for such an evil calamity as Big Wind and the Cable could never have been imagined.

Mitchell buys it by the kilo then divides it into half-ounce baggies he provides to other vets at cost. He makes nothing; spreading weed's therapeutic benefits is all the payback he wants. Lots of vets don't dare get medical marijuana cards for fear the VA tracks them, so he gets them weed without their risking jobs or benefits.

Funny thing is Mitchell has a Top Secret clearance with Naval Intelligence, spends his days online patrolling the Navy's networks and his nights and weekends teaching others how to secure their systems.

So I met Kim at Wipe Out, a downtown bar, a great place for new bands, surfing tales, half-pound local burgers and double martinis. We danced a few times and I liked how lithe she was, how fast she moved. I went back a week later with Grunge and she was there with a tall red-haired guy I instantly disliked. I asked her to dance and then we went out on the deck and I kissed her and she damn near killed me kissing me back.

We went down the back stairs out on the beach and made love on the cold wet sand. You know how with some people you make love with, you like and care about them but it isn't an instant connect? With her there was an immediate deep carnal link making me trust her. But like I said I didn't know she was a cop.

We're sitting afterwards side by side on my shirt, she with her knees drawn up and her chin on folded arms. "You a vet?" she says.

"What makes you say?"

"How many tours?"

"Don't matter."

"I can see it in your eyes."

I told her. "Wow," she says, "three tours –"

We talked about what she said was her job in real estate, condos and homes, how slow the market was, then she says, "Got anything to smoke?"

"In my car."

"Want to?"

We sat in the KG sharing a smoke then she had to go. "Who's the red-headed guy?" I said.

"He's from my office. Ran into him inside. No bother."

"Can I see you again?"

She gave a side-shrug of her head: *if you want to hope for it, go ahead.* An almost rueful smile. "Once was enough, no?"

"There's no such thing as enough."

"Yeah," she laughed. "How true." In one lithe move she was out of the seat and the car door clicked and she walked away slender and fast toward the parking lot.

"Fuck you," I said, hurt but not knowing why.

Three days later I drive to Nanakuli to pick up Mitchell's weed (with no legs, how's he going to drive to get it?). A full kilo, two point two pounds. On the way back I get pulled over by one of Hawaii's finest who wants to see my license and insurance and tells me I got no brake light.

While he and I are inspecting this supposedly dead brake light his partner comes around the other side of the KG with a German shepherd who puts his nose in the rear seat and in five minutes I'm on my way downtown with hands cuffed behind my back and Mitchell's kilo in a yellow evidence bag in the cop's trunk.

Of course the newspapers and TV made a big fuss, the DEA saying they'd uncovered a major marijuana ring led by an ex-SF guy once jailed for killing Iraqi civilians (they didn't even have the right country), and I'm arraigned on a Class B felony so fast it makes my head spin and I end up in Halawa Prison doing ten to fifteen.

Now Halawa's the worst prison in Hawaii, which is why many guys try to get sent instead to the CCA (Corruption Corporation of America – sorry, my mistake, I meant *Corrections* Corporation) prisons in Arizona. Though the CCA slammers are noted for their violence and dreadful guards, just like Halawa. And any Hawaiian there is far from his or her ohana, from the fabric of loving and togetherness that binds Hawaiians together.

But Halawa's worse than third world. The ACO's (Adult Corrections Officers) are vicious, the food's atrocious, the whole place is filthy, and you can get a shiv in your liver just for looking at someone. Although native Hawaiians are a relatively kind and peaceful people, the courts and prison systems are biased against them – they're a quarter of the state's population yet over half the prisoners, and the chances of early parole are nonexistent if you're Hawaiian.

So Halawa's where I got the nickname Pono. Like I explained you it means righteous – the correct and good way to live. When I hit Halawa I realized my outside life was over – I'd be forty-two when I got out, providing the system didn't give me more time for some dreadful pointless reason. So it was how I was going to live for a long time.

At first I was crushed, hopeless. But I began to realize it was my fate and I had to make the best of it. And making the best means taking care of others, our *kuleana* – responsibility to the greater good. So though I was heartbroken I tried to work with others, make *their* lives better, and that's why other prisoners named me that.

Anyway, what could I have done, ratted on Mitchell? Then he would have been jailed too and lost his career with Naval Intelligence, and I'd still be doing time. And you don't ever, *ever* rat on people. That's another Hawaiian principle: *ho'oponopono* – the spiritual process of making things right, between yourself, others and the spiritual world.

After Mitchell learned what happened he came every day to see me – can you imagine how easy that was, in his wheelchair? He wanted to reveal his role in this but I told him even if he did I'd still be Inside, they'd just jail him too…And in a perverse way we both knew I was taking the hit for him like he'd once taken the RPG for me in Afghanistan.

Over the next months he kept trying to get me out. Through a NavInt buddy he got copies of my arrest files, eventually learned about Kim, tracked her down and told her the real story. Then what was she going to do, arrest him? No way, she's a good cop.

At the time I'd never realized she was the one who put me Inside. In my memory she was just this really hot chick I'd met at Wipe Out, who worked in real estate or something, and we'd had a fantastic time and then she didn't want to see me again.

And for her I'd been a routine takedown – we'd smoked weed so she passed my name and license plate to the DEA, and to the road squad for random checks, and that's who pulled me in. The kind of mess your private parts can get you into.

When Kim learns the real deal from Mitchell she vanishes the stored evidence, gets the cop who arrested me to reevaluate, and asks her brother who's a leading Honolulu ambulance chaser to file an appeal in my case. Two weeks, two days and seven hours later I'm out.

That evening I'm sitting on the lanai with a martini watching the waves and not believing where I am when the doorbell rings, and it's Kim in a short black skirt and a black silk blouse and nothing underneath. I'd been without sex for a hundred and thirty-two days, and what she did was overwhelming. So pretty soon I fell in love with the woman who'd put me away.

Trouble was she had a husband, a state legislator and big-time pol, Randall Akawa, former bagman for an illustrious ex-US Senator, and a nasty get-even kind of guy who had run an earlier Governor's campaign. She'd agreed not to divorce him till his next campaign was over, but he was still making her miserable. Sadly, given my recent history I couldn't even offer to kill him or anything helpful like that.

SO NOW I had to call her, prove to myself it wasn't true what Hippolito had said, that she'd killed Lou.

"Hey you," I says when she answers, what we always say to each other.

Silence, then, "Where you at?" All warm and sexy.

"Downtown."

"I got a little time. Want to meet up?"

This was code for making love, something she'd normally never do on duty. "I want to talk to you about who killed Lou," I said.

More silence, then, "You want to tell me about it?"

"*About* it?"

"About how you fucked up again, Pono? You left a shoe print in Lou's blood, after you killed him."

I *had* stepped in Lou's blood. My mind raced. "Everybody wears shoes, Kim –"

"But not soles that match the print you left in the mud outside Sylvia's house."

"Lou was dead when I found him. I hear *you* did it."

"No way." A sarcastic laugh, then softer, almost teary, "What you kill him for, Pono? After you promised not to?"

21ST Century Serfs

"I READ THOSE FLASH DRIVES," Mitchell said. "Lots of good stuff."

By habit I scanned the room as if someone might hear. "Like what?"

"Their emails. I pulled up the last three months. Plus Simon's files. Creepy."

"See anything about Sylvia?"

"Not yet. But these WindPower people are evil, man. The bribes, the back-room deals, just like Kabul. This Governor's worse than an Afghani drug lord. Just wants to ride over everybody. And collect his millions on the side."

"Maybe that's how the world is. And we just didn't know."

"World isn't like that, man. Most people's good people. It's the politicians who work for the corporations that ruin our lives. We're Twenty-first Century serfs." Mitchell watched code dance across his screen, turned his wheelchair toward me. "What's an old guy like the Governor going to do, anyway, with all that money?"

I thought about what Mitchell had said. When you looked at what had happened to him, losing his legs and balls in a war that two draft-dodging pretzels in the White House had created out of lies and propaganda for the sake of the oil and defense industries, you had to agree.

Or when you thought of the trillions of dollars – how to imagine a *trillion*? – that Americans were paying for the Iraq War out of their paychecks and income, like they pay for food and mortgages and taxes while their jobs are destroyed by the stock market, much as you didn't want to, you had to agree.

"How about this one?" Mitchell read off the screen. "Email from S. Lafarge to WP BD: *Damon and I spent two successful days walking the corridors in Washington. We've given the politicians so much money they leap to attention when we enter a room.*"

This made me sick so I tried not to think about it. "Can you make yourself copies of those sticks and keep them for me?"

"Already done. They're there if you need them."

I stood. "Just like you are."

"Yeah," he took my hand, not wanting me to leave. "You too."

"Any way to hack into their network? See what they're up to?"

"Already done." Mitchell smiled up at me. "You told me how Simon's into kiddie porn? I checked his emails and saw what sites he visits, then sent him an email with an attachment almost identical to one of them. The moment he opened the attachment I had remote control of his computer, could read or download anything we want. By the way, what's Gala Investments?"

"Expensive whores. The Governor's work stimulus program."

"Man, the taxpayers are making those girls rich –"

Feeling worn out, my injuries pulsing pain, I headed for the door. "Maybe it's always been this bad, the world."

Mitchell shook his head. "Even if it is, man, that don't mean we don't have to fight it," and I felt both shamed and heartened by his words.

MAYBE LOU'S DEATH had nothing to do with me. Maybe Kim had been wrong and Lou hadn't fingered me. Maybe Lou hadn't set Hippolito up. Maybe all that mess had nothing to do with me, was some dance the cops and bad guys had going among themselves.

Yeah and maybe our forefathers lived with the dinosaurs.

Somebody had told Hippolito it was me. Who?

I sat in the Ranger on Beretania watching for cops and called Hippolito. "What, you again?" he said, but his voice was kind.

"Back when this started, who said I fingered you?"

"You don't remember nothing? Like I told you, we keep tabs on the cop store. Everybody knows that, everybody but you apparently."

"*Who* was it?"

"Shit, that I don't know. I'm not Einstein."

"You could have killed me for nothing –"

"Guy like you so many people want to kill, has to be a reason."

SO THE DILEMMA still was:

Somebody killed Sylvia.

Why?

Somebody got the cops to say it was an accident.

Somebody tried to kill me when I started asking questions, killed my dog and cat.

Somebody told Angie stupid stories about me, tried to turn her.

Somebody told Lou Toledo to finger Hippolito then told him it was me.

People broke into my house, most recently four guys in a white GMC van.

Somebody cleaned out the computers, files and papers from Sylvia's.

Somebody killed Lou and cleaned out his stuff.

Kim and the other cops thought I killed Lou and were going to nail me with it.

They had my prints from Sylvia's place (why had I been stupid enough to think I might find some clues there?) – *that* was B&E.

If Charity told Simon about my visit inside WindPower, *that* was B&E too.

They had my shoe print in Lou's blood – *that* was Murder One.

Once the cops got me I'd never get out, never be able to prove it all wrong. And this time Kim wouldn't save me.

Kim knew me well and now was determined to find me. How could I escape her?

How much longer was the Hulk going to be safe?

Where else could I hide?

How was I going to find the answers? Because if I didn't I was going to spend the rest of my life *Inside*.

And all I wanted to do was go surfing.

SPEAKING OF WHICH, it was Tuesday so I was supposed to do a surfing lesson with my foster kids. It bothered me that they'd go down to the beach and I wouldn't be there. The way so many adults hadn't been there for them, all their lives.

I hadn't seen Angie in two days but didn't dare call. The cops can triangulate you on a cell phone in thirty seconds. They wouldn't expect me to call Hippolito, but Angie they would.

Charity worried me. It was almost three days since she'd been burglarized and had driven off angry after I didn't want her to stay at my place because Angie was there. And she'd promised to tell Simon all about me.

Charity had been driving Manny St. Clair's black Subaru. Manny who'd been in love with Sylvia. And who she'd ditched for Lou? None of it made sense.

15:42. I drove the streets near Charity's but saw no sign of cops or tails, and parked the Ranger in a cul-de-sac four blocks from her place. Manny's black Subaru was in the same place it had been at the back of the parking lot. I ran my knuckle over the dust on its fender and took the stairs to her apartment.

It was on the fourth floor of a four-floor walkup. The stairs continued past her door landing to the roof, which was locked. From a seat at the top of the stairs, under the locked door to the roof, I could watch her door and not be seen. The metal step had corrugations in it, surprisingly comfortable. I settled back and took a light sleep.

Light-sleeping is a useful thing you in learn in SF. You drop into a zone where you can watch and listen to everything yet be at peace, resting, in your body and your mind. Very lovely sensation when you're not in danger, a Buddhist mindfulness. You learn to wake up if you slip too deeply toward real sleep – a mental rumble strip alerting you if you start to drift off the road.

So I was deep into it, relaxed yet ready, when a click of heels comes up the stairs.

"Hey," I said when she got to the top. "I've missed you."

"Where have you..." she said as she let me in. "What are..."

I glanced round her apartment. "Don't look like much got stolen."

"I was scared." She tossed her head. "You didn't help me."

"What'd the cops say?"

"It was probably junkies."

"Like I said."

She stepped into the kitchen. "So what did you get off the files?"

"Like I told you, nothing."

She reached for a glass on the counter. "Not possible."

"How's Simon these days?"

She tried a bored look. "Same old."

"What do you hear from Manny?"

She filled the glass with water and drank it. "Still in Kohala. Fixing up an old house. Whatever."

"Tell me again how you knew him?"

"He lived in this apartment development. I told you that."

"Has anyone mentioned Sylvia – Simon or anyone?"

She shook her head again. "No one. I think you're grabbing at phantoms, Pono. I really do."

"Ever hear of Gala Investments?"

She gave me a crooked smile. "Too many times."

I held the lovely curve of her jaw in my palm. "I can't tell whose side you're on."

She smiled again, a real one. "Sometimes neither can I."

"You tell Simon about me?"

"I should have."

"That a threat?"

"Play it as it lays." She slid against me. "Can't we just be friends?"

I paused in the doorway. "How's your surfing?"

"Haven't done it since the last time with you."

As I went down the stairs I couldn't understand why I'd come, what if anything I'd learned. Something tugged at me but I couldn't tell what it was.

One Sure Thing

O N THE FLASH DRIVES that Mitchell recovered from Simon's computer were twenty-two Big Wind and Cable folders plus all the icky personal stuff.

The first folder was *Project Financing*. There were twenty-seven projects listed, each in a sub-folder of its own. Each held multiple financial contracts between huge banks, many of them Chinese, and WindPower, full of terms like debentures, accelerated paydowns, failure to perform, and defeasance. And each project, apparently, was paid for largely by American taxpayers. One letter, from Shimogura International Bank of Tokyo, stated it succinctly on page 472 of the Initial Offer of Project Financing for an Oregon 200 MW Wind Farm: *It is the understanding of this Offer that all sums lent by Shimogura Bank are fully and adequately guaranteed in U.S. dollars by the United States Department of Energy. It is also the understanding of this Offer that 30% of full project cost will be wired to Shimogura Bank by the U.S. Department of Energy at the moment of contract signature.*

In other words, the Japanese bank was going to lend money to WindPower only after the U.S. Department of Energy had given the money to the Japanese Bank. It seemed worse than crooked, but then I'm not an international banker.

The next folder was *Turbine Mfg*. Most of its files seemed anodyne – 400-page contracts with turbine manufacturers in China and India (why is

our government going further into debt to buy things from foreigners?),
buybacks and financing plans offered by the turbine manufacturers, specs
and performance data, lots of detailed drawings of funny machines.

Site Work was filled with plans and working drawings for inverter
stations, transmission systems, road networks on Lanai and Molokai – and
as I glanced hurriedly through the site and location maps I realized that
each was separated into Phases One through Three, and covered nearly all
of both islands. This meant, I reflected sleepily, that Big Wind was only
the first step to completely covering Molokai and Lanai with industrial
windmills.

Many files dealt with the planning of Big Wind and the Cable, all
immensely complicated and deviously written, and in my fatigued state
hard to understand. But in essence the process was, to quote from A_
Haggard@WindEnergyEnterprises.com:

How we do it:

1. *Pick a site with some wind potential (doesn't have to be much, just
    indications).*
2. *Ensure that the landowner(s) are amenable, or become so.*
3. *Bring in local politicos as partners. Some politicians don't even need to be
    paid – a little flattery, a few dinners and a girl or two will do it.*
4. *Arrange zoning changes as needed. Run over anyone in the way.*
5. *Get the media involved on your side (tell them it's "green" and
    "renewable", and how good it will be for town, county, whatever).*
6. *Get the enviro organizations behind you. This is easy – a few donations
    and some nice words about how wind power lowers CO2 emissions
    and fossil fuel use. Most of them have swallowed the whole story
    already.*
7. *Be generous with funds. You're going to make billions, remember?
    Whatever bribes you give, call them "community benefits".*
8. *Crush all opposition early and hard. Make fools of them, question
    their knowledge, accuse them of NIMBYism, putting private gain over
    public good. Ignore all environmental impact arguments (this project
    is "green", remember?).*

9. *Get PR, lots of lawyers and polling involved. Polls can be structured to guarantee any result you want.*

10. *Push hard and fast before the public realizes what the project will do to them.*

11. *Once the contract is signed grab the 30% up front pocket money, pay off everyone, then run the project on the remaining 70%, and you have a 1000% ROI! Not bad for a no-risk deal! Given that you hardly put a penny in it in the first place!*

12. *And since the government guarantees the loan, even if the project falls apart (good old LLC) you never owe a penny back.*

Such tactics, we have found, practically guarantee success. As long as Obama keeps pushing the loans and guarantees (does he really think these damn things work?), we are in gravy. So let's go like Hell.

Your buddy Edwin –

I HUNGERED FOR PEACE, badly wanted just to disappear, take my backup life to some island in New Guinea, the Kenya coast or Patagonia. There were still plenty of places to get lost. The Hawaii cops would frame me with everything and Interpol would put me on the hot list but after a while maybe they'd assume I was dead and stop looking.

It seemed better than what I had.

Sleeping at my desk I dreamt I swam through warm waves to a mangrove shore and climbed a grassy slope. Standing in warm sunlight I felt elated to be free, glorying in the beauty of green hills, golden savanna and blue sea. I climbed higher, soft grass underfoot. Nearing the crest I heard a thumping at the earth and voices. Four Hawaiians, golden-skinned, muscular and nearly naked, were digging a hole in the earth with pointed sticks and lava shards, piling the dirt to one side. One saw me and beckoned me over. He had a sunny square smile and big white teeth.

"So here you are!" he said.

"Where's this?"

"We're ready for you," another said, a cheery tattooed face.

"Who is?"

"Didn't you know?" the first grinned, pointing at the hole.

"Jump in!" the other said, turned to hide a laugh and I woke, hunched and cold over the computer, back aching, cold coffee spilled in my hand.

03:21. In the galley I washed the coffee off my hand, took a rag and wiped it off the table. I washed my face and went topside. The sky was bright with Honolulu nightlight, the day that never dies, the stars invisible behind the glare. *There is no answer*, a voice said in my brain. My voice. *No answer to all this.*

I shut down the computer and killed the WiFi. Could the cops somehow track you by your internet connection?

I was like one of Jim Corbett's goats. Staked out on the man-eater's ground.

Every backup life, I realized, needs a backup life of its own to retreat to when times get tough. A second cover unknown to the first. Infinite mirrors, cover inside cover throughout time.

05:40. I went topside and sat cross-legged on the bow. The east was afire, boiling across the water and arching into the sky. If I lost this cover, this backup life, where could I go?

I had to stay cool and think things out. *How many times had I told myself that?*

The sun rose out of the sea huge and yellow, blazing. "Thank you, sun," I said, "for this new day." I went below and set the alarm for ten, woke with a buzzing head to the ten a.m. news, the end of a story about *the former Special Forces soldier Sam aka Pono Hawkins, winner of several medals for bravery in combat, served time in Leavenworth military prison for the murder of Afghani civilians and in Halawa Prison for drug trafficking, now charged with the murder of local diving coach Lou Toledo.*

An all-Islands alert has been posted on Hawkins. He is armed and considered extremely dangerous. If you have any possible information please immediately contact the Police hotline. All information will be kept totally confidential.

THE ONE SURE THING was the link between the guys who tried to drown me and Damon at WindPower – he had been the one who got Charity to bring the gear they had rented back to Clyde Fineman at Deep Blue.

This meant WindPower had killed Sylvia. Or why try to kill me?

Or Damon's friends were just out for a dive, had nothing to do with the two guys who tried to drown me.

Damon would know. How to make him explain?

My false face felt awkward and sticky. It itched and felt heavy on my skin. I parked the Ranger across from WindPower, scanned the area but saw nothing dangerous.

16:45, people leaving the building in hordes, ants out of a kicked nest, staring up at a sky they hadn't seen all day.

17:32, Charity comes out with Simon, waves him goodbye, walks past the Ranger's tinted windows, dressed in a hot miniskirt and a satiny blouse.

18:30, I give up waiting for Damon and drive to Charity's, climb to the fourth floor and tucked my false face in my pocket.

"You again," she says.

"Can I come in?"

"If I say no you'll just climb through a window –"

When she said *that* is when I *really* began to love her.

"DAMON," she answered when I asked who'd told her to return the rebreathers to Clyde's.

"Does he dive?"

"Damon?" she laughed. "He's got a two-inch dick."

"What's that got to do with diving?"

"Pono!" she slapped both hands on the couch. "Don't you under*stand*?"

"If Damon didn't rent the rebreathers, who did?" I was thinking of Clyde's description of Rico Morales, the guy with curly black hair from Pittsburgh.

"Damon," she said after a moment, "plays for both teams. He brings in these diver dudes," she went on. "Pays them two thousand bucks a weekend. I saw one of his emails, telling some guy after a weekend on the Big Island, some nude men's yoga place, that for the first time in his life he really felt like a man."

"Two thousand bucks a weekend?"

She laughed as if it were obvious. "Don't worry, they're expecting the up-front money. The billion dollars they get from Big Wind and the Cable, before they do a thing."

My mind stumbled. "The what?"

"The pocket money. Obama made a law that wind developers get thirty percent of the total project cost as a federal grant – your and my money – up front, the instant the contract's signed." She hitched her head. "That's why I hate my job."

An enormous weight descended on my shoulders. "You care?"

"I don't know." She glanced at the sea. "Don't know any more."

"Sure you do," I baited her. But even I wasn't sure.

"I CAN SAY whatever I want and it's safe with you," I said later. "I'm done with scamming. I'm going with the heart."

She pulled closer. "That's dangerous."

I raised my eyes to hers. "Know why?"

She actually laughed. "I give great head?"

"Because you couldn't lie to me without torturing yourself forever."

"You don't *really* think so –"

"*You* do."

She considered this. "Fuck you," she said finally.

"Afterwards let's go somewhere? I'll show you places in the Alps, in Sumatra or Tanzania or Argentina even God doesn't know about."

She gripped my ribs, her eyes bright. "That's a proposal?"

I laced my arms through hers, my hands across her slender back. "Of all the stupid things I do, one of them isn't bullshit."

"I'll hold you to it," she kissed me. "Now go."

If WindPower had killed Sylvia, I thought as I scanned Charity's sidewalks before stepping outside, some indication would have to be in Simon's computer files. I just had to find it.

THE TOSHIBA SCREEN wouldn't stop dancing. *04:17.* I took another sip of cold coffee, rubbed my eyes and kept going.

From Simon's report to BD 10/15/11:

We flew Senator Gable to Molokai today. Ian Christian drove us around what we're calling the "Project Site" (High Stakes is angry at the people of Maunaloa so they plan to put some turbine towers right around the town).

Fed His Excellency a libationed lunch of Molokai prime rib and sent him on his libidinous way with some filet mignons and a promise of $10k if he pushes the bill through the Senate to make ratepayers pay the billion bucks for the cable.

He fussed a bit about birds. Must be getting little-old-lady emails. We said we've got a radar system that stops the turbines if birds are near. He actually bought it.

He's amazingly cheap. Hawaii is a pushover. Now we'll have even more bucks for the big guys.

BOUNCEBACK was the next folder. When I double-clicked it hundreds of items toppled out, all emails.

There were different senders and receivers but all seemed in the same large group. Sometimes an email was from one to just one other, or two, others were "Reply All". Hundreds of people who all seemed to know each other. Maybe a subcontractor of WindPower, I decided, though none of the emails ever went to WindPower, the Governor or any of that crowd. Yet all seemed focused on Big Wind and the Cable.

"Aloha All," said one, *"At our weekly meeting tonight over a hundred new people showed up. Mahalo to all who sent letters to the Legislature. We are certainly growing in strength as more and more people learn about the windmills. Over half the island has signed up, and we're getting a hundred new members from the other islands daily.*

WindPower was on Molokai two days last week, offering people five hundred bucks to sign a petition in favor of Big Wind. No takers so far, so they're apparently thinking of raising it to a thousand. "When poor people turn down money," Aunty Marie said, *"then you know God's with them."*

Another by the same group, to a list of names "and 427 others", seemed a more general advisory: *IEEC had a hearing at the Mitchell Pauole Center on Tuesday to explain the latest rate hike, even though we already have the most expensive electricity in the U.S. This month's hike is 6.7%, with another 30% rate hike if Big Wind and the Cable are approved. However, the IEEC spokesman said no more rooftop solar will be allowed anywhere on Molokai unless people pay a fee of $20,000 per residence for a "study" (all the $20,000 goes in IEEC's pocket), in addition to the $17,000 to install the system.*

IEEC is fighting rooftop solar because if people produce their own power they don't need IEEC except at night. So IEEC's income drops 80% and they can't pay the inflated salaries of their top brass, nor pay the interest on their $1.6 billion debt. Their credit rating, already one point above junk bonds, will get even worse, and all the stock options of the top executives will be worthless.

So even though rooftop solar is the best solution for Hawaii (with 320 sunny days a year), the Governor and IEEC have created this enormous shell game called Big Wind and the Interisland Cable, intending to build it principally for federal government handouts to keep this dysfunctional utility alive...

We will continue to defend our island from this insane scheme.

This didn't sound like any subcontractor. Bit by bit it dawned on me that these emails were from the groups trying to *protect* Molokai, the 97% of Molokai residents who opposed Big Wind.

So how did Simon get them?

And if WindPower had the emails of people trying to protect Molokai, what else did they have?

More and more I was sure that WindPower was behind Sylvia's death and the attempts to kill me.

Then I hit pay dirt.

IT WAS 06:49. My eyes wouldn't focus, the Toshiba screen a white-blue blur. I was shivering with caffeine and damp cold, stomach burning with strong coffee, drifting to sleep on the chair and dreaming, lurching awake and dreaming again.

It was another email from someone named Tank Alani to the rest of the group. *Aloha All*, it began, *A reporter from The Post is doing a series on Big Wind. She is coming to Molokai tomorrow. We will meet with her, show her the project area, introduce her to some of our people. She is also meeting with Ian Christian of High Stakes Ranch and a few local folks who work for the Ranch and have been told to say they want Big Wind.*

She seems very interested in the project's financing, which is what the developers refuse to discuss.

Her name is Sylvia Gordon.

I read it again and went to the galley sink to wash my eyes with ice water and then read it again. Not only had Sylvia gone to Molokai to uncover financial information that Big Wind's developers didn't want revealed, but Simon knew she was going before she even got there.

After this was a string of emails explaining that Sylvia had spent an extra day, had talked to many people including Ian Christian, and had told several people afterwards that Big Wind *"seems like a crazy scheme."* She kept asking, *"Why are they really doing this?"*

These emails seemed the first time Simon had heard of Sylvia.

The last email from the group about Sylvia was tough to read. *"Aloha All, very sad news that the young Post reporter Sylvia Gordon has died... She was a lovely person, truly caring for our island and we ask all Molokai people to pray for her...*

I went topside to wait for the sun. The dawn was yellow-gray, full of high tumbled clouds. A little chop wrinkled the bay. Every time I scanned it the harbor looked safe.

I went below, checked the engine, started her up and putted out of the harbor around Diamond Head and straight east into heavy seas toward Molokai and the rising sun.

Follow the Money

NAVIGATING THE 32-MILE Kaiwi Channel between Oahu and Molokai I kept watching for planes, fearing the cops had broken my cover and were hunting the Hulk.

One of the most dangerous ocean crossings on earth, the Channel is known for its huge swells, crazy currents, endless depths and 30-foot waves that can swamp your boat in an instant and toss you into the crashing seas. Site of the world's most challenging paddleboard, outrigger, and canoe races, the ocean's ultimate long-distance measure of mental and physical toughness, it has killed many fine paddlers and surfers.

Among these was Molokai's champion surfer Eddie Aikau, who vanished in 1978 after leaving on a surfboard in the middle of a huge storm to seek help for crewmates of a capsized canoe. You can still see tributes to him on bumper stickers all over the world: *Eddie Would Go* – meaning no matter how bad the situation was, Eddie would be there to help you.

But this morning was calm with a soft rolling swell, a few flecks of foam, no vog or fog, an early sparkling sun. The engine kicked out a steady cadence, no rattling valves or howling shaft, and I kept hoping she wouldn't die and leave me crosswise in the waves.

Molokai rose out of the ocean like a goddess, the sacred way Hawaiians see her, lovely low green slopes up to the tall treelined crests of the great central rain forest. Beyond her Lanai gleamed ochre and green, black cliffs and steep landscapes, and beyond it, hazy with distance, towered the huge blunt shoulders of Maui. Seeing the beauty of these islands it seemed impossible that any human would seek to destroy them, but then some humans aren't so human.

The western half of Molokai's 40-mile south coast is empty – nothing but rocky forested headlands and golden beaches. The small town of Kaunakakai and its harbor lie in the middle of the south side, between the island's tropical east and dry west. There is an abandoned pier at Hale o Lono fifteen miles west of Kaunakakai where I tied up, pulled the dirt bike ashore and took an oceanside trail till it crossed the east-west road and climbed into the hills past rows of coffee bushes and open fields, the asphalt wet with midmorning dew, an occasional car puttering past.

Passing by the turnoff to Mitch and Noelani's made me realize how happy I'd been back then, wandering Molokai's back roads with Angie. Thinking of her I almost rode right by Tank Alani's place.

It was a dirt road that led to three houses. Tank's was the middle one. I parked the Suzuki by a rusty jeep, climbed the stairs, crossed the porch and knocked on the screen door.

The woman who came to the door was young and pretty and held a baby in her arms. "Yes?" she said through the screen.

"Tank around?"

"Out back," she nodded her head toward the coffee fields behind the house. "Up the middle, you'll find him."

It was a quarter mile gentle slope, the grassy earth soft between the old trees. He was cutting new shoots off the trees with a saw. "Tank?" I said.

He put down the saw. "Yeah?"

"I'm a friend of Sylvia Gordon's –"

"I know who you are," he said. "They say you killed her. And also some other guy."

"I didn't. And I want to find the ones who did."

He chuckled. "That *all* you got for alibi?"

I sat on the crinkly dry grass. "So when Sylvia came, you showed her around, introduced her?"

"Not much. She rented a car, drove herself." He sat across from me, arms round his knees. "We met with her, showed her the project site."

"When did she see Ian Christian at High Stakes?"

"The second day. Afterwards she told me, 'I'm following the money and it keeps leading nowhere.'"

"This is the problem."

"IEEC now insists Big Wind and Cable financial agreements are too confidential to release. Of course the Governor's backing them. As are the Public Utilities Commission and Consumer Advocate…or as most people call them, the *Protect the Utilities Commission* and the *Corporate Advocate –*"

"Question is, who killed Sylvia?"

"High Stakes."

"You think so?"

"I'm sure. But not these assholes on the hill," Tank nodded west, indicating Ian Christian's office at the Ranch headquarters. "The guys back in Hong Kong."

"The Tong? Had to be because of something she'd learned. About the money."

"If we could get our hands on it, it'd bring the whole project down."

"And get the people who killed Sylvia."

"Hong Kong? How you ever gonna get back to them?"

I was stunned. Since the start, my lizard brain had been on the same path – *find the bastards*. But maybe no matter how lucky I was I wasn't ever going to find them. Maybe, though, it might help to explain Tank the whole story, let him see it with fresh eyes.

So I talked while he chewed a coffee bean, his dark eyes watching the sea and beyond it Lanai's golden hills where more miles of turbines would go. "This financial stuff she was after," he said, "had to be some big payoff."

"To who?"

"That old Roman saying – *A Qui Bono? Who's this good for?* Or like we say here on Molokai: *When tracking evil, follow the money.*"

"So who would make the most money out of Big Wind and the Cable?"

"Is what I'm saying. High Stakes."

His conclusion, simple enough, was that High Stakes Ranch was a painful failure for the Hong Kong tong. They'd hoped to convert its fifty thousand acres of sacred Hawaiian lands into casinos, resorts, golf courses, multi-million dollar housing lots, all the usual that big companies have always done in Hawaii. But like I explained, the Molokai people shot down the Ranch's vast development scheme, so the Ranch fired all its employees, threw people out of their homes and shut down everything (*We'll teach them not to oppose us!*).

Trouble is, the Ranch makes no money grazing Molokai beef. It needs to show its investors some return. If not a real return at least a paper one. Thus the useless industrial wind factory, paid for by the good old American taxpayer and the hapless IEEC electricity customers, with all its billions in profit going to Hong Kong.

"Of course the Tong wants to make money," I said. "But that's no reason to kill Sylvia –"

"I hear the Tong is a gambling and whoring company backed by Chinese money. So if Sylvia was asking why should Obama's Recovery Act funds go to a foreign whoring and gambling company, you think that wouldn't threaten them?"

"Couldn't that bring down the Governor, if he's tied to it?" Tank was right, I realized, when you consider that half the five-billion-dollar taxpayer subsidy for a useless windmill "farm" would go to the Ranch and the developers, including a half of the nearly two-billion up front pocket money they'd get the moment the contract was signed. Given that the Tong paid only fifty million for the Ranch, they'd have a thousand percent return and still own the land, however disfigured it was by windmills.

"But even better," Tank said, "When the Tong bought the Ranch they paid only eight percent down…Eight percent of the fifty million purchase price is four million bucks. So if they get a billion and a half Obama pocket money up front, that's actually *thirteen thousand times* their investment."

"I still don't understand why they'd need to kill to prevent this getting out."

"Because if it gets out, everybody sees what a scam it is, how crooked they all are, and it gets stopped. If enough people in Hawaii learn about Big Wind and the Cable, that will kill the whole project."

"And how much," I realized aloud, "of that one point five billion goes to pay off all the politicians who've lined up behind the Cable and Big Wind…" The number of Sylvia's potential killers had just gone up astronomically. If ten or twenty politicians from the Governor on down were getting a cut, any one of them could have arranged her death.

"You should go see Marcus Wild," Tank said. "On the Big Island. He and his wife Rebecca are big-time lawyers. She got thrown off the state ethics board by the Governor for trying to reveal all this. So she might have something to say…"

I shook my head. "It can't happen –"

"It *is* happening. WindPower has already put wind measuring towers on the ridge west of the airport, where they want to build the first hundred turbines."

"That's on the flight path from Oahu –"

"They're getting the FAA to change the landing approach." He gave me a quick glance. "You're a brave guy, to take this on. You and Sylvia, how long you was together?"

"Only time I met her, she was dead."

His eyes widened. "So why you caring about this?"

Again I was stumped. Except at the beginning, my lizard brain hadn't asked why. And once I got involved there was no stopping. "Not sure," I said. "Maybe because she got killed…and then the police lied…She seemed such a fine person, so bright and caring – how could you not –"

"Too bad," he said, "you don't know computers."

I thought of Mitchell. "I do a bit."

"Ian Christian at the Ranch, he's the nexus of all this. Even though he's dumb as a mule's ass, everything in and out of Hawaii goes through him. If you can download his computers, we can get you in there."

"In there?"

"His office. Tonight."

Mitchell had been unable to get through their firewall. Maybe this would do it. "Explain me."

"You know Maunaloa Town? The cemetery by the rodeo grounds? Be there midnight, someone'll get you inside, you can copy what you want."

I scanned him, thinking of traps. "Why tonight?"

"WindPower's bringing more Senators on binge trips to Molokai. And the Governor's energy director says Big Wind and the Cable are essential for our future. The crooks are lining up against us. They own or control most of the legislators and media, got the TV stations pushing the Big Wind Cable."

He cleared his throat, looked at me directly. "Molokai and Lanai are in a battle for our lives. Our enemies include President Obama, the Department of Energy, the State of Hawaii, the governor of Hawaii, most of the Hawaiian legislature, a bunch of international investment banks, a bunch of foreign and U.S. wind developers and cable companies, and most of the Hawaii media, which are either owned by, beholden to, or overly influenced by those in power."

He shook his head. "Now someone's killing our monk seals, they're shooting our owls…We can't catch them, can't prove it, but we think it's the people behind Big Wind – when we have no more endangered birds and seals it will be harder for us to fight the project –"

He sat there a while, thinking. "But our biggest enemies are all the knee-jerk politically correct folks who still don't understand that wind power doesn't lower greenhouse gases or fossil fuel use, but it destroys environments, property values, human health, millions of birds and bats and many other things. And that it only exists because of huge taxpayer subsidies, billions and billions that can never be repaid, money that goes straight into the pockets of the oil companies and investment banks behind these schemes…They make billions but never risk a cent."

Same old same old, I thought. "What else?"

"If we can't solve Sylvia's murder very soon, Brother, you're gonna spend the rest of your *life* Inside."

That thought, as you might imagine, chilled my soul.

He stood. "The politicians have to understand that what remains of the real Hawaii is sacred. If they try to destroy Molokai and Lanai, it will be over many dead bodies. Including mine."

No It's IEEC

THE COP CAME OUT OF nowhere with lights blazing as I turned the Suzuki onto the mountain road. *Oh Shit what can I do* flashing through my head as I raced down the steep twisting pavement slick with rotten leaves, the speedometer bouncing on seventy, the bike skidding near horizontal on the curves, the cop's blinding lights, siren and thundering engine at my back as I saw a road to the right and grabbed it, the bike slamming high into the air and whammed down and up again, fast down a long pasture path barbed wire on both sides, the cop car whanging and banging behind me but losing ground, and when the track split I took the worse one then shot off through the trees, my headlight darting among the trunks, the tires spitting dirt and roots, branches whacking my face.

The cop gave it up, far behind. But there'd be others on the main road now – how to get across it? I stopped on a knoll and cut the engine to listen. A few distant cars, the far rumble of the sea. My thundering heart and tick-tick of the cooling engine. My legs shivering in the aftermath of fear. Burnt grass stench on the muffler.

Why had the cop chased me? Had Tank betrayed me?

Was my cover blown?

Did they know about the Hulk? Could I even go back to it?

The main road was a narrow black two-lane snaking down from the western hills but flat as an arrow across the plains, with nowhere to cross that the cops wouldn't see me half a mile away. I would have to go north along the windy bluffs above the sea cliffs, in open country, hoping the cops couldn't follow.

I tied my shirt over the headlight to dim it and puttered through the coffee groves circling the town of Hoolehua and north of the airport, working west toward Maunaloa Town and the Ranch HQ.

There was a thrum in the distance I recognized instantly and knew I was finished: Chopper.

He flitted up and down the main road flashing searchlights to both sides then swung back toward where I'd lost the cop. He danced around there for a while making me think he'd lost me, then he roared toward me right along the little trail I'd taken, fifty feet off the deck with searchlights blazing. I shoved the bike under a fallen kiawe tree as he snarled over shaking the ground, and pinioned there in his afterblast I sensed what it had been like to be Vietnamese.

When he pulled away I ran the bike along the trail, no lights. The throb of his rotors grew fainter, his lights twinkling as he headed back toward Hoolehua.

The bike was heavy to push but I didn't dare start it, even with no sign of cop lights now on the main road. *23:18* – I stopped and listened for five minutes, heard nothing but a pueo hunting and the ever-present distant growl of surf. I started the bike and drove without lights west toward Maunaloa Town. If all went well I could still be at the cemetery by midnight.

A MAN IN A CAMO MASK and a black sweatsuit led me on foot from the cemetery through star-shadowy forest over a stony hill to the back of Maunaloa Town and down a dirt road to the Ranch HQ. Another masked man, slimmer and smaller, and also in black, took me through a back door down dark corridors to Ian Christian's corner office, closed the drapes and turned on a headlamp, pointed to the fat desktop computer beside Ian's desk and said, "Everything goes through this one," and I realized it was a woman.

I pulled out the flash drives and went to work. Somehow Mitchell's calm diligence filled me, as if I were he and could do this.

The flash drives ate through those files in minutes. I didn't bother to think how insane that so much information could be transferred so fast and easily, remembered Pa trying to explain me what life was before computers. "We had peace," Pa had said. "We had downtime."

It felt strange to be in Ian's office where Angie and I had sat only days ago. This made me miss her even more and wonder who this masked young woman was.

She led me back across the hill to the cemetery and stopped a few feet from my bike. "Mahalo," she whispered and was gone.

"Mahalo!" I answered. In the distance a rooster was crowing. *00:43* as I rode out of Maunaloa Town. The trail was bright under the stars.

A half mile before Hale o Lono I hid the bike and checked the trail down to the pier. The Hulk sat out there quietly in the star-spangled bay. But who was in the trees waiting, between here and the beach?

If my cover hadn't been blown the Hulk should be safe. But how had the cop found me? Why had he chased me?

The woods were thick with long-thorn kiawe; you have to move slow and careful or they rip you to pieces. I worked my way through them behind the beach, saw no one in the woods or out on the pier. The beach in the starlight was pearl-white and looked empty. There were no tracks in the sand newer than mine.

I ran back through the forest, grabbed the bike and pushed it downhill and across the beach onto the pier hearing nothing but my own hoarse gasping, the rustling tires and *click-click* of rear axle. With the bike aboard I reversed the Hulk out very quietly and headed across Molokai Reef toward open ocean.

The stars were mirrored in the sea like thousands of diamonds, as though I floated through deep space. For an instant it seemed absurd to be caught up in some human drama and not aware of the universe. Then I was back to worrying and watching for planes and trying to figure things out.

I turned east toward Maui, tied the wheel, went below, plugged in the first flash drive, found Ian's emails under Firefox and scrolled back through them to April 9, the day Sylvia first called him. Right away it leaped out at me:

TO: N.Dangerfield@drvmsolutions.com
FROM: I.Christian@HSRanch.com
Please advise IEEC that Post reporter Sylvia Gordon is seeking info on BW and Cable financing. They may wish to deal with her directly. Or through our friends?

The chop grew deep, waves towering over the thwarts and crashing across the deck. I started to fear we'd get plowed under, thought of the great Hawaiian musician and warrior George Helm who helped free the island of Kahoolawe then drowned swimming the thunderous seas back to Maui. I sensed George's strong warm hand on my shoulder, heard his deep sure voice and for an instant felt safe.

The chop worsened, poor Hulk rocking despite her solid keel, the running lights knocked off the deck by fierce waves, a window smashed out of the cabin. I went down to put on a life vest and tied myself to the wheel, thinking of all the solitary sailors washed overboard and watching their boats float away, aware how soon they would die.

The waves were up to twenty feet now, short and nasty, white and windblown at their crests and shuddering the Hulk each time they crashed across her. The ocean was black, the sky was black, even the white crests were black with anger, the anger of a disputed sea, a disrespected sea, one that would get you back, teach this antlike stupid human for attempting to traverse it.

Then I could see stars. Holes in the black clouds, the seas calmer, the Hulk's prop digging in, pushing us forward. For half an hour I didn't dare believe it till the lights of Lahaina hove into view. I tied the wheel and went below to change into warm dry clothes, brewed a tall whisky and coffee, and went topside to watch the fading stars.

The seas grew soft and lustrous as I pulled into the harbor, as if the ocean had gone on good behavior now that lots of people were around.

06:57. I maneuvered the bike onto the kayak and paddled ashore, leaped on the bike and headed for Honolua Bay in the hope of finding Cal Levine.

Cal is a well-known surfer, a guy most everyone respects. After years in the Navy he worked for IEEC overseeing electrical distribution on

Oahu, and now works free-lance as a power lineman, high-voltage stuff, and surfs when the surf's good and he doesn't have to work.

The surf at Honolua's best in early morning before the wind comes up and before it gets too crowded. He was way out there, riding a long right-hand barrel. He finally dropped off and coming up saw me wave, came ashore shaking water from his long graying hair.

He's a short powerful guy with a surfer's sinewy arms and a trimmed gray beard. He's efficient in everything he does, how he moves, a lithe instinctive certainty. And when he speaks it's the same way: short, precise.

"Big Wind and the Cable are nuts," he said. "Wind projects lose money even when they're sited where the power's needed, but to site it on three or four *different* islands, with billions of dollars in undersea cable costs added to it, is…" He held out his hands, reaching for a word. "Totally nuts."

"So why are they doing it?"

"IEEC's a dinosaur kept alive by screwing its customers and the American taxpayer. The product of years of bad management, political collusion, gouging customers, kickbacks and lies. *And* they're going under. They *need* the billions of taxpayer bucks they get from Big Wind."

"The Obama pocket money –"

"Their credit rating's so low they can't borrow money to keep their financial house of cards going. But with Big Wind they'll have a new asset to borrow against…Plus the up-front depreciation. Plus subsidized power, also paid for by us –"

"Subsidized power?"

"The taxpayers pay IEEC to take the power. The power the taxpayer's already paid for."

I almost laughed at the insanity of it. "But why?"

"The wind companies have bought enough politicians and environmental groups, convinced the public to create this enormous boondoggle, a direct transfer of billions of taxpayer dollars to investment banks and oil and electricity companies, with no environmental gains and huge environmental losses." He stared at me. "You know why?"

"Why?"

"Because utilities have to keep creating large capital investments in order to make a profit. And the only way their top executives gets a bonus is to keep building crap they don't need and then charge their customers for it to show a profit...It's called rate of return regulation." He began to thud the bottom of his board into the sand. "It's really the past versus the future."

"Explain me."

"The difference between distributed versus centralized generation. Every home should have enough solar panels on its roof to produce its own power. Solar is cheap now, and getting much cheaper. But utilities are based on the idea of producing lots of power in a central place then transmitting and distributing it, at a great loss in power, to some other place where it's used. So the moment folks are making their own power on their own rooftops – or most of it – the utility ceases to have value, all the money it owes on its obsolete equipment can't be paid, all the execs lose their bonuses...You get the picture."

"But would they kill someone?"

He looked at me, surprised. "Why?"

I explained him about Sylvia. He stood there for a long time watching the waves. "They could," he said finally. "Not IEEC officially, but someone, maybe two-three guys at the top. Ones with the big bonuses and the most to lose, they could do it."

"I hear somebody named Dangerfield warned IEEC about Sylvia. So IEEC could *deal with her directly*. Or *through their friends*. What do you think that means?"

"Whatever you want it to."

The waves were perfect and I sensed he wanted to be out there. "What about this CIA guy?"

"In the Navy we called him Admiral Dingy because that's about as big a boat as he could safely operate, but also because he never seemed to have a straight idea in his head. That he got to run the CIA is hilarious. And now he's fronting the group wants to buy IEEC – in a democratic country for the former spy chief to take over a state utility would be absolutely *verboten*...Even funnier, the director of the Hawaii department that's pushing Big Wind and the Cable, he has a million in IEEC stock, and if the company sells he makes another million. Who was it said, *We jail the small thieves and vote the big ones into office?*"

"This CIA guy and his other investors, would they have worried about Sylvia's investigations?"

"Probably not. Why fear bad news about IEEC? It would only drive the stock down further, make it even easier to buy."

"Would they have killed her?"

"The CIA? You have to ask me that?"

"I still don't understand what they'd get from it."

"Nor do I. Doesn't mean they didn't do it."

The Cable to Nowhere

I FUELED UP IN MAUI then took a fast cruise across to the Big Island's Kohala coast and tied up at the wharf just north of the Puukohola heiau, an enormous stone pyramidal base built by the ancient Hawaiians. In those days the Hawaiians used the heiau for worship and for sacrificing people; now tourists gape at its rugged immensity and try to shelter themselves from the blazing sun. But the wharf just north of the heiau is a nice place to tie up where nobody pays attention to you.

From there I took the 270 coast road north, trying to figure what to ask Manny. Since he might be the only one who knew what Sylvia did her last night, except for the people who killed her. And maybe Lou Toledo, who'd said he didn't know, but he wasn't answering questions anymore.

Had Manny known about Lou Toledo? Did he wonder where she was those last nights? Had he tried to find her?

If I gave him a chance maybe he'd say.

Maybe he could explain me why she left her apartment that night… Who had called her? No one, according to the CID on her land line. And her cell phone had never been found.

Manny might know.

THE OLD WHITE HOUSE stood on a knoll with a battered chicken coop behind it and a big mango tree in front. Some of the windows were boarded, mango leaves lay deep on the front porch, and a gutter hung diagonally across it.

The stairs looked mossy and soft. Stepping on the joists I climbed them and crossed the porch. Through a dusty pane I could see an empty living room, clothes scattered on the floor, an upended plastic bucket, a Raggedy Ann missing a leg and arm.

I popped a window and stepped inside. A scorpion ran off tail-high. The floor was thick with dust. Behind this living room was a small kitchen. The sink had been smashed and the reefer tipped over. Alongside it was a small bathroom with marks on the floor where a clawfoot tub once stood.

There were two small bedrooms, one on each side of the living room. Nothing but a plastic clothes hanger in an open closet, a child's upended sneaker on the floor.

I wiped out my tracks in the dust, stepped outside, shut the window and checked the chicken coop. Just the dry ammoniac odor of manure, feathers and mites. From many years ago.

I sat in the woods trying to understand. Two weeks ago Manny told me he was going back to Kohala to fix this place up. A week later, Charity said he was already here working on it. But nobody had touched this place in years. Nobody'd even been inside it for months.

So where was Manny?

And why did he lie?

Now all the questions I'd had for him still had no answer.

Maybe I was crazy. Maybe none of this was real.

"IT'S ALL REAL," Marcus Wild said. "And a vicious scam." Since I was already on the Big Island, I had gone to see him and his wife Rebecca as Tank on Molokai had recommended. Marcus and Rebecca were big-time lawyers, Tank had said. The Governor had thrown her off the State Ethics Committee for criticizing the Big Wind Cable.

Marcus paced the room in a blue pin-stripe rolled up at the sleeves, worn jeans and sandals, his brush-cut hair silvery against his earnest, tanned face and shocking blue eyes. "You won't believe what happened today –"

"I haven't been really keeping up with the news," I said sarcastically.

He ignored this. "Today IEEC released a request for Big Wind planning studies that doesn't even *allow* alternatives like rooftop solar…It requires an undersea cable, so you can't even site your production on Oahu where it *should* be…It allows *four days* for response, so insiders are the only ones who can respond. It's so crooked it's…" He paced out on the lanai, returned. "It's corporate *chicanery.*"

Chicanery made me think of Manny's chicken coop. "Would they kill someone?"

He halted. "They're not above anything."

His wife Rebecca came in brushing her palms. "You have to make the salad," she said to him. "So we can eat."

He rinsed the lettuce from their garden in water and vinegar and spun it, sliced a handful of wild tomatoes. "And get this," he said, "IEEC is now requiring every bidder to work with Lanai Land Corporation, that paragon of bribery, kickbacks and dirty deals. So in essence the most corrupt private company in Hawaii gets to select bidders for a *public* utility contract…"

We ate on the lanai watching the voggy sun set through the macadamia trees on the slope below. Dinner was Big Island prime rib with the salad, purple sweet potatoes and a bottle of amazing French wine. "Sometimes the vog's so bad you can't see the horizon," Rebecca said.

"You move here because it's beautiful," Marcus said, "and the mountain decides to erupt and for the next two hundred years we get vog."

"You should live so long," she said.

"As a corporate lawyer," he went on, "I've seen every type of graft and corruption the human mind can invent, but what IEEC and the Governor are doing is worse…"

"Enough already," Rebecca said.

"Now the Governor's pushing a bill to exempt Big Wind and the Cable from environmental and public review –"

"And to think," I said, "I never used to care about graft and corruption."

"Look at all these trees," he gestured out at the slope silvery in after-sunset, the broad-leafed old trees in soldierly ranks down the slopes. "When we bought this place the income from these trees was forty thousand a year. So we could swing the mortgage, with that income." He raised an admonitory finger. "Two years later our politicians in Washington decide to cut a deal with Australia to let cheap Australian macadamias into the U.S. without a tariff, even though they're far lower in quality and everything else-"

"Trouble is," Rebecca said, "now nobody knows the difference."

"The politicians got campaign funds from lobbyists working for the Australians. And every macadamia producer in Hawaii went broke."

"Happens all the time," she said. "Get over it."

"Hell I'll get over it," Marcus snapped. "Anything you buy these days – a toaster, a pet toy, a gas grill, a cordless saw – it's all from bloody *China*!"

"Marcus," she snapped back, "Pono and I are *not* the enemy!"

"Of *course* the Chinese can undersell American manufacturing – they pay their workers a dollar a day, let them go home only two weeks a year, dump all their pollutants in the nearest river and all their emissions into the atmosphere, they get their raw materials cheap because they poison *every*thing with toxic chemicals –"

"All chemicals are toxic," she said patiently, "in quantity."

"It was my ancestor," I said conciliatorily, "brought the macadamia nut to Hawaii. So maybe it's his fault."

"I forgot that," Marcus said. "Father Hawkins."

"All of this would've really pissed him off," I said. "He loved God."

"Yeah," Rebecca sighed. "Don't we all."

"But all this politics is beyond me," I added. "All I want to do is sit out on the waves on my board and wait for a big one."

"Not happening. Not anytime soon." Marcus raised the bottle. "More wine?"

I wanted more but feared losing my edge. "Has IEEC ever threatened anyone, could have hurt or killed them?"

He cocked his head, thinking. "You should tell him," Rebecca said.

He glanced at her. "No privilege?"

She shook her head. "Not in this case."

"Three years ago," he said, "several people died in car crashes, difficult to prove, but they were making trouble about a transmission line, then there was the guy in IEEC who tried to blow the whistle on some fuel purchase deal..." He turned to her. "He drowned, yeah?"

"Out on the reef, in four feet of water."

He raised eyebrows at me. "There've been others. If IEEC did what it did today with this proposal request, how it's tailored to steal billions of taxpayer money for itself, Lanai Land Corporation and the Governor's other friends – what *won't* they do?"

"I used to wonder, how little money would one kill for? A million, five million?"

"Or with Big Wind and the Cable, five billion?"

"It could cost ten billion," Rebecca said.

"The Governor, his people, would *they* have someone killed?"

Marcus made a face. "He's a ruthless guy. The teachers helped to get him elected, then he turns on them. Thousands of elderly and poor people voted for him and what's he do? Cuts their benefits, which are already minimal. Denying them the medications, the funds to stay alive…There's more than one way to kill people."

"I mean would he have Sylvia Gordon drowned?"

"Why not? And then there's Lanai Land Corporation. The Horrible Harridan's close to bankruptcy – the banks are close to calling her loans. She needs the half billion up front pocket money she'd get from Big Wind to keep from losing it all – the three jets, the husbands on alimony and all the young studs, the trophy horses, the rafts of politicians she's bought over the years who are still on her payroll…"

"Would *she* do it?"

Marcus laughed. "She's the nastiest, meanest, most vengeful person I've ever dealt with. Like you said earlier, there's probably nothing she wouldn't do. Or have done." He grimaced. "But there would never be a trail back to her."

My brain was swimming with it all. "Every time I try to exclude somebody, I realize *they* could be the killers."

"Go back to your computer files. Got to be something in there."

"I've been through every file from WindPower and High Stakes. Both have emails about getting rid of Sylvia, but nothing I can prove. And in the meantime I'm being charged with it all."

"That's the best proof," Rebecca said, "that you're on the right track. If you weren't a risk they wouldn't bother with you."

"Who is *they*? That's my problem."

"Think of this: now they want to build an underwater cable from Oahu to here, the Big Island, to tap geothermal, and they're trying to build the cable before they even know if there's enough geothermal – all because IEEC can borrow money against the cable once it's built –"

"The Cable to Nowhere," I said.

"The Two-Billion Dollar Cable to Nowhere." Marcus half-smiled, perhaps at the idiocy of humans. "Shine the light on darkness, and you will see."

"You sound like Father Hawkins."

"He did a lot to help the Hawaiian people. The first girl's school in Hawaii – he did that, no?"

"And the second boy's school," I added, feeling proud of him that he'd never taken from the Hawaiian people like all the other missionaries, the ones who became the rich thieves who now own Hawaii.

"We used to have so-called Sunshine legislation," Rebecca interposed. "To keep government dealings in the open."

Marcus chuckled. "Until the Governor killed it."

I thought of what Tank had said yesterday. "A wind industry newsletter just had an article that the more people learn about wind factories the more they hate them."

"That's why the wind Nazis try to buy up all the politicians, to override public opposition. They make it legally impossible to defeat…Like Obama arranging fast-track legislation for wind projects so there's no public hearings…" He turned to his wife. "Rebecca's from Maine originally."

"What's happening there's even worse than Hawaii," she said. "The previous two governors and a big environmental group wrote legislation exempting industrial wind projects from most environmental and public review, and now the magnificent mountains of this beautiful state are getting filled up with turbine towers, even where there's no wind, the environmental group got a half million from the wind Nazis and the two governors are going to become billionaires on taxpayer subsidies…"

"But why," I said, "would an environmental group do this?"

"They don't understand that wind projects don't lower CO2 and fossil fuel use," Marcus said. "They just don't get it. Some environmental groups are like people who don't believe in evolution – no matter how much proof you give them they won't listen."

"They used to call Maine Vacationland," she said. "Now they call it Wind Turbine Land. Maine can't even use the electricity – so it will get sold at a loss to New Jersey or Pennsylvania, a lot of it lost down the transmission lines."

"The wind Nazis prey on the backward states," Marcus added. "The poor states with easily purchased politicians."

"Protests are going on all over the world," Rebecca said. "Against Wall Street, these huge banks and corporations that own our politicians, steal everything, companies like Lanai Land Corporation, High Stakes and IEEC...It's time to bring this into the open."

"In Hawaii?" Marcus smiled. "Who cares?"

"Even in Hawaii," she said, "even in Maine. Let the truth be told."

AT SOUTH POINT on the Big Island, as Marcus said, a huge wind project follows the coast in long rows of rusting, broken turbines. Unlike on Molokai and Lanai there is wind here; it howls through the dangling blades and warped towers, the turbine housings and other detritus scattered over the eroded roads and monolithic concrete foundations.

An old Hawaiian who'd been fishing on a seaside boulder pointed at them. "Just look, you can see they are evil. They send signals to another world. An alien world. Telling them to come here and destroy us."

FRUSTRATED, I headed from the Big Island over to Maui then across the strait towards Lanai's great sea cliffs. I couldn't risk going into Manele harbor so dropped round the north shore and pulled in beyond Polihua beach. There was no way to get the bike ashore so I kayaked in, hid the kayak in some kiawe brush and jogged up the steep red eroded slopes of the Garden of the Gods, where Miranda Steale wanted to build two hundred wind turbines on the most sacred and beautiful land in the Pacific.

From there I crossed the forest reserve, dry leaves and bark crackling underfoot, the ancient trees gaunt and haunted, and up into the cool pine-clad slopes east of Lanai City along a snaky ridge road to a small gray house peering over the great cascade of hills down to Maunalei Gulch and the rolling peaks and ocean beyond.

"You come at the right time," Tom Shapiro said. "Gin's under the sink. Ain't no vermouth."

"I'll live."

Tom chuckled. "That's in doubt."

I made us each a tall glass of gin with some ice. We clicked them. "Here's to you," we said. "Where's Sue?" I said.

"Mainland."

"Why?"

"I sent her." He nodded at the lanai fronting the house. "Know why we ain't sittin out there?"

"You're suddenly afraid of heights?"

"Somebody nearly got me last week. Bullet made that crack when it went by my ear, you remember that sound –"

I scanned the lanai, the hillside beyond. "They can hit you just as easy inside –"

"Not from that shooter's angle. He was out on that crest there, in the trees. When he fired I dove inside and grabbed my Sig, ducked round the back into the forest and went for him, but he'd gone when I got there."

"Tracks?"

"Size eleven Nikes with the herringbone sole."

"No cartridge?"

"Of course not." He said nothing, then, "I think they were just warning me."

"You should vanish."

He shook his head. "Lanai Land Corporation and the union are trying to terrify us all. They threaten everybody who shows up at a windmill meeting –"

"The lord and his serfs."

"Last week the Miranda Steale staged a touching airport departure, about fifteen people were paid to cheer while she talked about how wonderful the windmills would be and threatened anyone who doesn't line up behind them. She's so out of touch with this project she boasted it could 'power the whole state'. A lie, of course, it will only produce about four percent of Oahu's power, half what they could get by efficiency programs, a tenth of what they could get with rooftop solar. But most everything she says is nonsense anyway. "

"You know what we *fought* for in Afghanistan and Iraq. Why we protect our country. So shit like this *won't* happen. So Americans can be free, not thrown out of their homes, lose their jobs, get beaten up just because they don't want what the king wants. This ain't Afghanistan."

"You so sure?"

"Remember Minny? How'd he ever get that name?"

"Was named Minton. Don't know why."

"Minton from Montana. God bless him. What a wiseass. But such a good guy. Always looking out for all of us."

"Like we all were."

"When he got wasted, man…" Tom looked away, out over the Gulch. "Think what he died for. We gonna allow *that* to be destroyed?"

My eyes stung. "Our country."

He nodded grimly. "That's why I'm staying."

"You're no good dead."

He grinned, tossed back his gin. "You neither."

Almost Forever

IT WAS DARK AND DANGEROUS hiking down the crumbly washouts of north Lanai on my way back to Polihua beach and the Hulk, too easy to misstep and slam fifty feet down the near-vertical slopes of razor-sharp lava. And rocks kept clattering down, making me fear searchlights and guns.

All the time I was trying to figure out that even though both the Governor and IEEC could've killed Sylvia, what if they didn't?

In SF training we learned to both analyze and challenge everything you thought you knew – that the Afghani you most trusted was the one who'd walk in one day wrapped in C-4. So I had to keep thinking that IEEC or the Gov was behind her death, but not forgetting the others –

Lanai Land Corporation because Sylvia was blocking an immediate half billion dollars of Obama pocket money they desperately needed to keep from going bankrupt?

High Stakes Ranch because they were stuck with a property they couldn't develop into the casinos, whorehouses, golf courses and million-dollar lots they wanted? And then Big Wind and the Cable had come along, promising them billions in taxpayer bucks, but Sylvia was going to ruin it all?

Or WindPower? What would they do to preserve a five billion contract? Of which they'd share nearly two billion up front, before the project even started?

We were down to the same five perps: Lanai Land Corporation, the Gov, IEEC, WindPower and High Stakes. All intertwined in a circle with the killer in the middle, and lines going inward from each of them to the killer.

Sylvia was always the key: who did she threaten most?

All five.

Being any of them, what would *you* do?

Tank on Molokai said High Stakes killed her. True, they'd warned IEEC about her, but was that proof?

Cal the former IEEC distribution manager said IEEC could have killed her to protect their piece of Big Wind's five billion, the only thing that could save them from junk bond status...And they were cooking the books, too, to look sexy for potential purchasers like the CIA guy and his team.

So why did the CIA want to own IEEC? Were they a perp too?

The eroded slopes leveled out into jumbled boulders and thorned kiawe then dropped down a bluff to the beach. Keeping in the trees I worked back to the Hulk. She bobbed quietly at anchor a hundred yards out; there was no one in the trees behind the beach or up on the point, no new tracks in the sand.

I'd been thinking of trading the Hulk for a sailboat and heading south, to the Marquesas, anywhere a guy could vanish into the succulent landscape, the little seaside towns where nobody ever went anywhere and the only cop was five islands away. Or your own atoll, living on coconuts and fish – I'd done it before and could again. But right now seeing the Hulk made me feel at home.

To be sure she was safe I swam to her, the last fifty yards underwater, and came up under her keel, listened for fifteen minutes to the soft waves slap at her hull, heard no human sound, slid aboard and checked her out: *No one.*

I swam back for the kayak and pulled her aboard the Hulk, started her up and headed west for Oahu. With luck I'd be there before dawn.

MY ALL POINTS BULLETIN on the radio as I pulled into Honolulu harbor was scary. The cops had reversed their story on Sylvia dying from accident and now were saying it was Murder First-Degree – and I did it. According to the list of charges:

One: I'd had a relationship with her before she died (*untrue*, but unfortunately I'd told Kim that, to shut her up).

Two: I broke into Sylvia's apartment after she died to erase clues but left my prints and tracks (*true*, but I was looking for clues, not erasing them).

Three: Underwear carrying her DNA were found at my house, supporting the claim that we had had a relationship (*untrue* – I'd taken the underwear for her DNA, in case it was needed later).

Four: My whereabouts could not be established for the night of her death (true, but how many of us remember all our nights?)

Five: My description matched the guy the cops chased from her back yard (*true*).

Six: I had repeatedly attempted to sabotage the investigation by challenging police officers and intimidating potential witnesses (*this sounded like my good buddy Lieutenant Leon Oversdorf talking*).

Seven: I had been detected by security cameras in the downtown office building where the offices of WindPower LLC, a company trying out of the goodness of their hearts to lower greenhouse gases and bring jobs and money to Hawaii, had been burglarized at the same time (*true*, but my face had been covered so how did they identify me? Had Charity told them?).

Eight: I'd been identified as a person of interest in the murder of Lou Toledo, an Oahu diving instructor. A neighbor had identified me as leaving the scene shortly after his death (*the burly woman with the laundry basket*).

Nine: As a two-time jailbird I was a habitual criminal. Therefore there was nothing I wouldn't do.

The announcer continued with all the flapdoodle about me being armed and dangerous. It made me realize how big business and politics are just like crime – what they tell us via the media they own is nowhere near the truth. And usually they're trying to talk us into something bad for us but extremely profitable for them.

I tied up at my slip, killed the engines and fell down on the bunk for an hour. You can live almost forever without sleep, I told myself. *Almost forever*.

SINCE I COULDN'T RISK going to Mitchell's and didn't dare use my cellphone I stopped in the Waikiki Village Hilton basement to call him on the one payphone that still took quarters.

"How long before they get you?" he said.

"God knows."

"Too bad. There's so much good stuff in WindPower's new emails. A real cornucopia…" His voice got that distant tone it had when he was scanning a computer screen. "Here it is, thirteen days ago – From Simon at WindPower to Hen Lu of the Hong Kong tong…*That company you used before*," he quoted, "*we need them again for a similar issue…*"

I thought of Simon's spindly fingers and innocuous eyes. A man who'd dare nothing. "This could be for cleaning apartments," I said, "fixing a sidewalk."

"The cc is to ION Security, out of Jakarta, a private security and investigations firm tied to the Indonesian government."

"That paragon of justice and democracy –"

"No website, no telephone, no nothing."

"So?"

"*So*, you doofus, they're big time! *They're* the ones who tried to kill you."

"You're jumping to conclusions, Mitchell."

"No, baby, you're the one who won't jump. Even when the alternative's the abyss."

"Keep looking," I said. "Let me know."

"They arrest you," he said, "I'm coming down in my wheelchair to sit in front of the Justice building and starve till they let you out."

"Won't matter. They'll say you're PTSD. Put you away somewhere."

"Yeah," he chuckled. "Let them try."

WHEN I CALLED HIPPOLITO on my cellphone a weird voice said, "This's Manny." I glanced at my phone. I'd misdialed, hit Manny's number in *Contacts*, not Hippolito's. "Manny," I invented quickly, "this's Chris Roberts. I was a friend of Lou Toledo's."

He actually gasped. "Who is that?" he said meekly.

"You *know* who Lou was. So you and I need to talk. I know where you are," I invented again, "but let's meet somewhere neutral, a Starbucks or something."

"What do you want?" he said weakly.

"You *know* what I want," I hazarded.

"Okay, I could meet you sometime –"

"We'll meet in one hour. You pick it."

"Okay okay," he swallowed. I remembered thinking, couple weeks ago, that if I needed answers, hooking him up with a tiger shark would do it. "Yeah okay," he said. "The Starbucks in Pearlridge shopping center?"

Now I knew what part of Honolulu he lived in. *09:47* my watch said. "Let's make it half an hour."

"I can't get there that soon."

"How long you want?"

"Gee, forty-five minutes anyway…"

Now I knew even better where he was. "And don't bring any friends. Because I have so many that if you do they'll make a real mess out of you."

"I don't deserve this," he pleaded. "I really don't."

"You know the old song, Manny. Can't always get what you want –"

I hung up. A double-wide tourist in an aloha shirt staggered out of the john, a urinal hissing behind him. I got in the Ranger and drove to the mall with twenty minutes to scope out the place before Manny got there.

Conspiracy Theories

PEARLRIDGE SHOPPING CENTER hops and skips down the hills above Pearl Harbor, a loose agglomeration of shops, restaurants, parking lots, side roads, beauty parlors and other tricks and trades. Starbucks has come to rest near the bottom, outdoor tables with a view of a potholed parking lot, scraggly brush, rooftops, roads and concrete highways, Pearl Harbor and the choppy sea.

I parked the Ranger outside Bed Bath & Beyond, popped in their front door and out the employee back exit, did a quick recon around Starbucks seeing nothing out of the ordinary. But that's the sign of a good team – you never see them till they take you down.

Pearl Harbor was a reminder of how easy it is to ignore your instincts and other people's warnings, but all my instincts were telling me it was safe and how would the cops know I was going to be there unless they were covering Manny's phone?

And there was no reason they should.

Or unless Manny had really been only five minutes away not forty-five, and had set me up? Or rather, set up Chris Roberts, this friend of Lou Toledo's?

Manny had sounded afraid – would he have called the cops? Only if he felt safe with them, had nothing to hide.

Maybe not even then.

I sat in a front window of a nearby restaurant watching Starbucks and every parked car – the soccer mom's blue Windstar that could be hiding five SWAT guys in their little black suits, or the FedEx panel truck parked under the monkeypod that wasn't really FedEx.

In which case I was looking at several consecutive life sentences.

11:47. A tan Accord pulls up in a Handicap space and Manny gets out. He locks the door then heads to Starbucks, turns around, goes back and locks the car door again. Pocketing the key he hitches up his shoulders valiantly and marches into Starbucks. Through the window I catch glimpses of him glancing around, worried and unsure. He gets in line, pays cash, waits at the counter for a large thing with foamy yellow stuff on top, and sits in the corner by the restrooms.

For twenty minutes he fidgets, crosses and re-crosses his legs, holds his cup upside down over his skinny mouth tapping the bottom to get the dregs. He picks his nose assiduously and wipes it under his chair. He goes to the window and peers at the parking lot, sits down again, gets up, pulls a *Star-Advertiser* out of the old newspapers but doesn't read it.

I cross the street below the parking lot and wait behind the soccer mom's Windstar twenty feet from the tan Accord. About ten minutes later Manny comes out wiping his palms on his pants and looking almost pleased with himself. He doesn't see me till he pops the Accord's doors and quick as Bob's Your Uncle I jump in beside him.

"You're..." he stumbles at words. "You're the guy who asked me all those questions –"

"And I'm a friend of Lou Toledo's."

He's silent a moment. "Lou's dead now." As if that would end all further inquiries.

"Did you do it?" I hazard, out of the blue.

"Me?" Mock shock: do you really *imagine* I'd be enough of a man to do *that?* "Why would *I* care about Lou Toledo?"

"Because he was banging Sylvia."

"I knew she was seeing him." Manny looks down at his folded fingers. "I knew that. I, I tried to deal with it." He looks at me searchingly. "I knew I wasn't good enough for Sylvia, not for a lifetime –"

I have this surge of pity for him, like you do for a run-over mongoose – that this guy should be so poorly equipped to survive, to succeed. "But you always hope, you know," he adds primly, "that she'd tire of him, come back to me." Again he stares at me. "You have to hope, don't you?"

"I don't believe in hope," I say.

He shakes this off.

"Drive."

He drives up Kaonohi Street and I make him pull over at the turnaround. "You're not going to hurt me are you?" he says.

"Not unless you lie to me."

"Why would I lie to you?"

"I know almost everything, just want to fill in some details. So what was the real deal between you and Lou?"

Fingering the door handle he glances at the empty turnaround. "I didn't do it."

"I have this little gut gun." I slid my hand under my shirt, thinking of Hippolito's offer to shoot me with his little gut gun at the Outrigger Club. "It will rip you apart before you open that door."

"I *told* you, you don't have to *threaten* me –"

"You know how many unsolved murders there are in Honolulu every year? Bodies found in places like this?"

He turns on me, fear in his eyes. "What *possible* benefit to me was Lou's death, when Sylvia was already dead?"

"But you know who did it."

"Anybody could know. Nothing's ever *sure*, you know."

I sigh heavily. "You're pissing me off."

"I'm *trying* to be helpful. Lou was a heartless self-centered prick who'd do *anything* for money."

"You're saying he deserved to die?"

"Lots of people didn't like him. He was in trouble with the cops so he was trading them information about some dope deal that was going to happen…" Manny tries to shrug, show some self-confidence. "Two weeks later he was dead." He smirks: *Lou had it coming.*

"How you know about this?"

"He told me. *Boasted* to me. After she died and he called me and I went to see him."

"*You* went to see him?"

"I sure did," Manny adds bravely. "Wanted him to know if he hadn't messed with her, she'd be alive today."

"How would you know that?"

"Why would this smart, committed beautiful journalist hang out with a two-timer, the bottom of the dive barrel – *you know what I mean?*"

"Like you said, Manny, for the sex?"

"Who likes sex *that* much?" he scoffs, reminding me why he's never going to make it in the real world.

I don't know where to go next. It was Lou, though, who falsely fingered me to Hippolito. "So how'd Lou find out about *me*? Why, out of nearly a million people on Oahu, did he choose me to lay the blame on? I know ninety percent of this," I added, "and want you to fill in the other ten."

"If this gets back," he says dramatically, "I'll be dead." He looks manfully through the dirty windshield. "The cops. They got Lou to finger that guy." He looks at me softly, "So maybe they told him to use you?"

"There's over two thousand cops in Honolulu. Give me names."

Manny wipes his nose with the back of his hand. "How would I know?"

How much of this story is true, I wonder, and how much just Manny's jealousy and hatred of Lou? "So why did Lou," I say, "tell you this? Or did you just make it up?"

He near-smiles, links fingers. "Me and Lou became like sort of friends, after she died. We were both missing her."

I try to imagine muscular tattooed Lou and random ineffectual Manny ever sitting down together. "You ever go diving, Manny?"

"Diving?" he shivers no.

"Ever hear of WindPower LLC?"

He shivers again. "I have a friend, she works there I think."

"What's your friend's name?"

"*Oh* I couldn't tell you *that* –"

"I already know it. You tell me the first name and I'll provide the last. And if you're lying I'll shoot you."

He muses on this a while. "Charity," he admits weakly.

"Danver."

His eyes widen. "How did – how come you know?"

"I know almost everything, Manny. And I know you've been lying to me so I have to shoot you."

He raises his hands. "I'll *tell* you. Whatever you *want*, stop *frightening* me!"

"Tell me everything you've left out."

His Adam's apple dances. "The cop, Lou told me was some woman. She was DEA too, always leaning on him for information, because he was such a small-town sleaze."

"I bet you know her name too."

"I swear I don't."

"Do the cops know you went to see Lou, before he died?"

"It would just confuse them."

"Confuse them?"

"Well," he turns his hands palm-up, eager to explain, "they might think *I* killed him. When I didn't? What good is that?"

"You told me, that time we met, that you were headed to the Big Island to work on some house. How's that going?"

"Yeah, it's hard work…Man, I can't afford much right now."

"You did some work, on the house?"

"Well yeah," he glances at me, "I mean no, not physical work, you know –"

"What kind of work then?"

"Talking to the bank about a construction loan, the County about permits, you know –"

"When was the last time you were there?"

"There?"

"The house."

"Oh *when* was it," he sighs. "Oh it's been a while –"

"I'm going to kill you, Manny."

"Oh no you're not. You don't know *half* you say you do."

"What don't I know?"

"You don't know which cop told Lou to finger you, you don't know," he raises a splayed hand, counting fingers, "you don't know who killed Lou – it wasn't me, you *do* know that – I couldn't kill *any*body, why would

170

I *want* to? – and *you*," he smiles mischievously, "you don't *know* how close the cops are to getting you, and how *fucked* you'll be when they do."

I smile at this sudden onset of bravery. "I think you killed Lou."

"You're never going to make it to prison alive, you know that –"

"And if you go to the cops on me, I'm going to bring it down on you."

"They'll never believe you. A two-time jailbird who killed civilians in Afghanistan? You think everybody doesn't *know* that? It's all *over* the news."

I got out. "Beat it," I said. When he turned uphill I ran through speeding cars across the four-lane and grabbed a bus downhill, jumped in the Ranger and was back on the Hulk in twenty minutes, wanting to pull out for the Marquesas, anywhere they might not find me.

Manny was a lying whore but what if it was true what he'd said, that Kim had named me to take the hit for Lou's fingering Hippolito with those fifty bales of weed? Kim my lover for over a year. Who'd put me in the pen then got me out.

I loved her. She said she loved me.

Guts empty I listened to the howl of tires on the distant freeway, the hiss of jets coming in, a seabird's lament and the oily slap of riffles on the hull.

Kim.

Had she done this whole thing?

Why?

Small Change

A COARSE WHISPERY VOICE on the phone, "Go see my friend." By the time I realized it was Hippolito he was gone. I stared at the phone – no CID number, just the quick memory of his words scratchy as palm fronds in the wind.

Go see *which* friend?

It'd been Kapu who introduced me to Hippolito but he wasn't his friend.

00:47. I rolled out of the bunk, feet on the cold hull, down the dark dank galley to the head, washed my face in the galley sink, found jeans, running shoes and a semi-clean shirt, downed the dregs of yesterday's coffee and drove cross-town to Gala Investments.

The streets were deserted, streetlights throwing yellow stains across the littered pavements, lurid graffiti and sea-grimed walls. A cop going the other way gave me a glance and I watched him in the mirror as I'm looking for a place to ditch the Ranger and run, but he shrank into the distance, going his own way.

You're running out of time, I reminded myself.

SEVERINA WORE another stunning gown, this one a simple russet sheath cut low in the front and high up her thighs and clinging to her body. "You must stay in more touch," she said as she took my arm and led me to her office and sat me again in the oak chair beside the roll-top desk.

"I have good news." She laid slim cool fingers on my wrist. "The night before last night I send three of my best girls to a big penthouse in Waikiki. Is a party for something with the Governor and this guy you know of, Simon from this company they call WindPower, no? And two guys we know of from IEEC, this horrible little man from Ecology Profits, a couple others. One a Chinese guy, they were talking to him about Hong Kong."

"A sex party?"

"With the Governor?" she laughed. "No, my girls are there to serve drinks and they're dressed very nice and they're smart, some even have advanced degrees, and if any of the men wants to go somewhere with one of them afterwards, it's paid for."

"By who?"

"Who do you think? Not that engineers and accountants have a sex life."

"Hey, I knew a woman engineer once. She was amazing."

"A *woman* engineer? *That's* different. I have one here, she's got a Masters in Electrical Engineering and she's the most magnificent lay in Honolulu, I swear you –"

This made me feel very religious. "Maybe when this's all over…"

She chuckled, a big sister again. "We see. If this gets all over."

Yeah, I thought. *We'll see.*

She opened the desk's middle drawer and pulled out a flash drive. "It's on this."

Excitement ran through me. "You recorded it?"

"Your friend asked me to."

"And they didn't know –"

"It's a Tampax tube in a girl's purse. Who's ever going to check a Tampax tube?" She held it out in two hands like a chalice, rose and kissed me gently. "Stay safe."

"If I ever get through this –"

She hushed me. "If he is your friend, so am I."

"WE'RE IN TROUBLE." A high screechy voice on the recording I recognized as Simon's. "Hostility to Big Wind keeps growing, and despite all the money we've thrown at the Legislature they may kill our Cable bill." There was a brief silence. "You all know what that means – if IEEC's ratepayers don't pay for the Cable the whole deal falls apart."

"We won't allow it to fall apart," said another. "We offer the legislature more money. The Governor. They'll come around."

I backed it up to listen again. Yes, the first voice was Simon. But I didn't know the other voice.

"Big Wind has two enemies," Simon went on. "The first is *time*, because sooner or later the federal cash cow's going to dry up –"

"I can't believe," somebody else laughed, "that we've kept it going this long –"

"The other enemy," Simon continued, "is *disclosure*. We get some journalist on our back and the project goes south. Because as we all know, the more that people learn about wind power the more they oppose it. So we move fast. And take no prisoners."

An appreciative chuckle echoed through the room. "So what do you suggest," the other voice said, "if we *do* get a prisoner?"

"We resolve it quickly as possible."

"We thought we *did* that," someone else said, a Chinese accent.

"We *did*," Simon answered. "But it's come back to haunt us."

"Because you didn't do it right," the Chinese voice said.

"Because *you* didn't do it right," Simon answered.

"You're accusing *me* of screw up?"

"Doesn't matter who's to blame," Simon said patiently. "We just have to do better."

You could feel the tension in the room. I wondered why they'd let the girls stay, then realized it'd just been a girl's purse on a sideboard somewhere – who would've noticed?

I went up on the Hulk's deck. Impossible to believe some people would order another person's death just to make money. Or for any reason at all.

Simon and the Chinese guy had basically admitted they'd had Sylvia killed, but in a way that would never prove anything. But why had it come back to haunt them? Because I'd found her? It was haunting them, the Chinese guy said, because Simon hadn't done it "right". But Simon said it was because the Chinese guy hadn't done it right. What had they done wrong? The fresh water in her lungs? Letting her float to shore instead of sinking her? Something else I hadn't thought of?

Where did I go with this?

Who would believe me?

And what did Lou Toledo and Kim have to do with all this?

Amazing to think that more Americans want to live in Hawaii than in any other state. Sure, the big companies, Lanai Land Corporation and IEEC and those crooks, of course they want more folks to buy their split-level termite-infested new developments, buy more Chinese crap from Bed Bath and Beyond.

But what's in it for us? The folks who live here?

And who has the right to decide? Who gave the money people the right to destroy things for the rest of us?

I went below and listened to the rest of the recording. Lots of foolishness and dirty jokes, the sour humor of powerful old men who can barely remember what sex was like, the drooling comments about the girls when they were out of the room.

"I could plank her all night," a voice said, IEEC maybe.

"Which one?" someone drawled. "I could plank them *all*."

"The redhead. Christ she must be six feet tall."

"You're going to have to climb up there, Oscar," another voice chuckled.

"When she comes back in we need another round –"

"I'm a married man, believe it or not."

"Question is, do *you* believe it?"

"Hard to with these girls…"

"The redhead, let's get her to strip down to her underwear –"

"Christ I'll go crazy."

"Hey," a new voice said, "We have the solution for your endangered bird problem on Molokai and Lanai."

"What's that?" Simon said.

"We get guys out there with shotguns and kill them all. That way you don't have any endangered bird problem…"

"Let's do the same with those damn endangered seals," someone adds.

Quiet chuckles, another voice, "You're a genius, Gerry. A true genius."

"Species go ex-stinct all the time," Gerry adds expansively. "So who gives a shit?"

A clatter of glasses, men's voices, a girl's high tilting laugh. "When you come back in, Honey," someone called, "we have a job for you."

The recorder hissed with no voices for a while and I almost turned it off. "While the three of us are alone," Simon said, closer to it, "let's go over things."

"If you want," the Chinese voice said.

"Works for me," Gerry said.

"This guy making trouble, the cops want him for multiple crimes. He doesn't stand a chance. Prison for life. But if he makes it to trial, gets in the witness stand..."

"In this country you have too many laws," the Chinese voice said.

"That's what I think."

"People who cause public problem must be resolved. For benefit of all."

"But your guys didn't 'resolve' him last time –"

"You didn't tell us," Gerry said, "that he'd been in Special Forces for Chrissake –"

"We didn't know either," Simon said. "Now we do."

"Nobody finds this guy. Cops can't find him. How you want my guys find him?"

"Our connections are close to locating him. As we speak. And if the cops locate him first, they tell us before they pull him in. So *we* can go get him. Simple as that."

"You always think complicated thing simple."

"As I said, we're close. Your people should be ready."

"Five people now I have here. Waiting. Many thousand dollars already it costs me, these guys. We must add that cost to my share of the deal."

"We've always agreed it's fifty-fifty for Molokai and Lania," Gerry said. "One point six billion pocket money up front, divided down the middle. Then the other three and a half billion also. So don't hassle us about your damn travel expenses."

"You got us into this trouble. You costing us this money."

"And I'm paying twenty-seven elected officials from Obama on down," Gerry hissed back. "His damn reelection committee keeps calling me, plus Senators, Congressmen, all the way down to some dogcatching legislator from Oahu...The Governor, look at him over there, that oblivious ass –"

"True –" Hen Lu said.

"Last year I blew ten grand on him in London," Simon said. "And had to promise him two million a year in consulting fees for the next five years. Plus after he leaves office, Gerry here has to give him a seat on the Lanai Land Corporation board, at half a mill a year."

"That's right," Gerry put in.

"Politicians are always deductible expenses. *Before* we divide pocket money. That has always been agreed. But my expenses for my five guys to be here – is different."

"And now this DOE guy, Landsford, wants a seat on *our* Board."

"Like you we have two boards: a public one and a real one."

"We got all these community payoffs to make, Christ there's a guy on Molokai, former community activist, he wants a grant of two million...And I've got these IEEC guys looking for post-retirement consulting fees..."

"That is, how you say, small money."

"Small change. But it adds up. That's what I'm trying to tell you, Hen Lu: all of this adds up."

A silence, then, "You the guys fuck here up. And now this Governor you buying, he in bad shape. Big Wind scandal breaking his bones. He has worst poll rating any governor America –"

"I know," Simon said patiently. "We have the money to fix that."

"So I ask my friends, they study American politics. They say he not get elected next time. Everybody hate him."

"If that happens we buy the new Governor," Gerry said. "Not to worry."

"Him that not worry not succeed."

"It's all bought and paid for," Simon said, "so get off our backs –" then he was drowned out by men's voices, the sound of high heels, laughter and clapping. More laughter, a click and the recording ended.

Hard Evidence

I HAD TO MOVE FAST. But like being hunted in darkness, I couldn't see my enemies or which way to move. Simon's "connections" were close to finding me – it was two days ago he'd said that. So they could be even closer now. And the Hong Kong killers were waiting to finish me off. Even the cops, Simon said, would hand me to them.

Situations like this don't make me feel brave. Usually going into combat I was scared – there were too many unknowns, potential accidents, "goatfucks" we called them, to ever feel safe. And then the incidents out of nowhere – IEDs, hostages and ambushes, the trusted Afghani who blows himself up to kill your friends.

But at least in combat there's other guys looking out for you just like you're looking out for them. You're not facing the enemy alone.

Here I was totally alone in a wasteland of sorrow and fear. Anyone I turned to for help could be Simon's "connection". Anyone who knew me was an accessory just for not turning me in. Any person coming up behind me could have a Glock with a silencer, and there's little you can do about a bullet in your brain.

As it had a way of doing, however, the sun came up, warm and bright. "Thank you, sun," I said, trying to feel grateful, "thank you for this new day."

How miniscule, it said, *are human worries in our infinity of universes.*

Yeah, I answered, *but the only universe I've got is mine.*

Then I made the decision that nearly cost me my life.

SHE ANSWERED ON THE SECOND RING. "Hey you," I said.

Silence as she fiddled with her phone, trying to key in my number to locate me.

"Don't waste time, Kim," I lied, "you're not going to find me." A downtown corner McDonald's, cars, sandy windblown trash.

"I can find you anytime!"

"I didn't do it, Kim. Not *any* of it. But I'll give you the names."

"Yeah, right."

"The two people who arranged Sylvia's death are Simon Lafarge, the CEO of WindPower, some guy named Gerry from Lanai Land Corporation and a guy named Hen Lu from the Hong Kong tong that owns High Stakes Ranch. You taking this down?"

"In my head."

"She was killed by members of a Jakarta private security company called ION – all capital letters."

"That's crap. They're well-known, work for their government *and* DEA. You're going to have to do better than this, Pono."

"Can you get me feedback on them? Has anyone opposing WindPower died or disappeared?" I listed the suspicious deaths linked to IEEC that Marcus and Rebecca Wild had given me.

"This's all *crap*, Pono!"

"Please do it," I said. "I'll call you back, you can tell me…" The silence, the vast canyon of pain and love. "Remember, when you put me away?"

Silence. "How many times," I went on, "did you wish you hadn't?"

"Don't fuck with my head."

"You've *got* to help me, Kim. I've got no one else." *That was a mistake*, I realized, *to tell her how isolated I am.*

"Let's get together. Talk."

"Not a chance. I need you but I can't trust you."

"Why not?"

"Because you killed Lou Toledo. And I don't know why."

"You're full of shit."

"What would your husband do, in my situation?"

"Him? I don't think about him."

"Think about him."

"He would've lied his way out of this, long ago."

"What am I doing?"

Her voice caught. "Don't you hustle me."

"What am I doing?"

"Yeah, okay. Maybe."

"What am I doing?"

"Like always trying to find the truth, you damn fool!"

"You'd do the same."

"Not so sure."

"Can you think of a time you *ever* lied, Kim, except for work?"

"Pono you have to get away," she said softly. "No way you can solve this. No way I can help you anymore. It's over, my love. God bless you."

The phone clicked. I went out, jumped in the Ranger and took off down Nimitz, watching in my mirror for the cops who never showed.

"I BEEN TRYING TO CALL YOU," Clyde Fineman said. "Your phone don't answer."

"I haven't been around." I scanned the Kmart parking lot. "Don't tell anybody I –"

"Them two guys you asked about, remember, rented the rebreathers? Can you believe it, they just come in for more gear. With a new guy, ugly as the other two."

"When?"

"Hour ago maybe."

"What'd they get?"

"Same stuff: rebreathers, suits, fins, whole deal."

"For how long?"

"They said a week but that probably they wouldn't need all that time. I said they bring it back early I can't give them the weekly rate, has to be the daily multiplied by –"

"Clyde for fuck's sake what'd he *look like?*"

"What'd *who* look like?"

"The third guy."

"The third guy? Oh yeah, he was big. Big blond guy, looks Russian, you know what I mean? Easy to recognize, though."

"How's that?"

"One ear's shorter than the other. Like the earlobe, you know, got bit off –"

WHILE WAITING FOR CHARITY to come home I tried to figure if she was Simon's "connection". She worked for WindPower, Sylvia's probable killers. She had dropped off the rebreathers at Clyde's for the two guys who tried to drown me, but said it was Damon at WindPower who told her to. Said she'd never met the guys, didn't know anything about them.

But she'd let me into WindPower and helped copy the files and download Simon's computer. But the cops found out I was there – had *she* revealed me to them or did they pick me off the security cameras? But I'd covered my face – how could they?

But even though she'd gone with me to Clyde's and knew I knew about the rebreathers, she must not have told anyone, or they never would have returned to rent them again. Unless they *did* know, and it was a trap.

When she dropped off the rebreathers she'd been driving the black Subaru owned by her neighbor Manny St. Clair, who'd had a dubious love affair with Sylvia till a week before she died, when she supposedly took up with Lou Toledo.

Manny St. Clair found out about Sylvia and Lou, and after she died he went to see Lou to condemn him, but they became "almost friends", united in sorrow. That made little sense: from the one time I'd met Lou I couldn't imagine him having anything to do with Manny.

Manny says my lover Kim killed Lou because he was a small-time sleaze. But that wasn't true: he'd seemed a cool guy, cared about the ocean, had that combination of strength, power and gentleness you see a lot in your SF buddies.

But someone got Lou to set up Hippolito then finger me. So the man who had the last ardent week with Sylvia had then been hired to get me killed.

And if Kim did kill Lou could it have been to protect me?

Since Lou was trying to get me killed, and I had been trying to solve Sylvia's death, then he was working for the same people who killed Sylvia. Or he'd killed her himself. A big muscular diver, he'd pulled her down in a swimming pool somewhere. Or held her down in a tub. The images in my mind were awful.

With her usual clunk clunk of high heels Charity came puffing up the stairs. "Oh hi!" she said when I met her at her door, as if we'd crossed a few times at the mailbox.

"Can we go in?"

Only an instant's hesitation. "Sure."

As she went ahead of me inside I felt an instant of lust at the mix of her perfume and sweat from the hot Honolulu afternoon. "Make yourself a drink," she called. "I've got to pee."

"You want one?"

"Same as yours."

I made the martinis and the shower started running. I went into the bathroom and took off my clothes and got in with her, water splashing in our martinis, and then I put the empty glasses high up on the ledge so they wouldn't break while we made love.

We made more martinis and she cooked bonita in passion fruit butter. "I'll testify for you," she said. "Any time you want."

"Simon's emails and what you've overheard just show feelings of hostility, they don't prove these guys did anything. It's not hard evidence."

Standing at the stove she slid a spatula under the bonita and eased it over. "There's a new tension at WP. Something different going on." She turned toward me. "Like desperation, maybe?"

"What about?"

"That Big Wind and the Cable are falling through. I hear them talking, about the huge public opposition. They didn't expect it. Normally they just blow through, bribe who they need, get it signed and pull in the money. But they've been trying to buy people all over Molokai and not one will take anything. Apparently all seven thousand people on the island are totally against Big Wind."

"Yeah but it doesn't matter, any more, what people want –"

"And Simon's terrified about the Governor being so far down in the polls because of Big Wind, the Cable and other idiotic stuff he's done. He's afraid he won't get reelected and that will kill the project."

If the Governor's defeated, Gerry from Lanai Land had told Hen Lu, *we buy the new one*. But I couldn't tell her I knew that.

Simon had told Hen Lu *not to worry*. But Simon was scared.

"Simon told the Governor to hire a PR firm," she said. "Hundred fifty grand of taxpayer money for an advertising campaign on Lanai and Molokai, to convince them to take Big Wind."

"Taking money from us to force us to do what we hate." I looked out at Honolulu at night blazing like an artificial sun, all that electricity going to waste. "Where's Manny these days? Still in Kohala?"

"He's back."

"Oh? Where's he been?"

"Don't know. I've just seen him once. He didn't say."

"He living here?"

"He quit his apartment here. Said he's staying with a friend."

"If he comes round, let me know."

She sighed. "I wish I'd never introduced them."

"Who?"

"Manny and Sylvia. You *knew* that –"

"Knew *what*?"

"It was me brought them together."

Recipe for Death

"**Y**OU KNEW SYLVIA?"

"Of course. I *told* you."

"No you didn't."

She looked at me exasperatedly. "I *know* I told you."

"Christ I'd forgotten." I exhaled, feeling trapped and stupid. "Tell me again."

"I met her when she came to interview Simon. The second time she came he escaped by the back elevator. So she and I talked a while."

"She interview you?"

"Not really."

"You tell her how you feel about WindPower?"

"Some."

I looked at her. "A month later she was dead."

"I really liked her. We…"

"Is it your fault?"

"Fault?"

"That she got killed."

"Sometimes I think that, and I don't know what to do."

"Go to the cops."

"You want *me* killed?"

"Why'd you put her together with Manny?"

"I could tell she was lonely. She'd been engaged once and it didn't work out."

"He died in Iraq. That's why it didn't work out."

"I didn't know." She looked even unhappier. "And Manny seemed a nice guy...She came for dinner one night and I invited him too..." She looked down at our plates. "We had bonita that night too."

"So why do you think you shouldn't have introduced them?"

She watched me, waiting. "What if Manny killed her?"

I shook my head. "Why would he?"

"He was in love but she wasn't? He *did* know about Lou Toledo and was jealous?" She raised her hands. "There's lots of crazy reasons why men kill women."

I couldn't get my head around it. If Manny killed Sylvia then it was he who was trying to kill me, ludicrous as that sounded. So who was the other diver?

No, there was a larger scale to their efforts – the four men in the "Courtesy Electric" van who broke into my house, the two divers who tried to drown me, whoever it was that got Lou Toledo to frame Hippolito and finger me...It wasn't Manny all by himself.

But what if Manny *had* killed Sylvia, and for a totally different reason someone was trying to kill me? But again, WindPower and High Stakes had as much as said they were behind it.

But why would Manny have killed Sylvia? I'd asked Charity and she'd said didn't know, just had a feeling. Clyde had said the three divers rented the gear for a week but didn't think they'd need it that long. If they were coming after me in the water that meant they knew I had a boat. And maybe where it was moored.

If I didn't return to the Hulk I'd lose everything – the computer with Simon's files and the pix of the WindPower files, my clothes, money, gear, my false face, five hundred bucks stashed in the ceiling over the head. I'd be down to living out of Ken's Ranger with fifty-two bucks in my pocket and no way, any longer, to prove a damn thing.

I didn't dare spend the night with Charity so drove back toward the harbor. If the Hulk seemed safe I'd head out of the harbor and tie up somewhere on the north side.

THE HULK SEEMED SAFE. I'd parked a half mile away, stripped down and swum up through the moorings, staying in the shadows.

Three boats ahead of me the Hulk had swung stern into the faint current, nodding in the ripples. I swam under two hulls, bumping my head on a keel in the oily darkness, came up one hull away, under the slip.

She did seem safe. I was cold and needed to sleep. I could climb aboard, leave the Ranger where it was and get it before dawn. *23:24*: five hours' sleep.

I slid from the dock, ducked under the last keel and came up on the Hulk's starboard side. Palms against her rusty flank I listened but heard nothing.

But there was *some*thing.

Once in a scrubby juniper forest at ten thousand feet in Afghanistan I'd smelled something. Waved the guys down and waited. Yes, a smell, and then I knew what it was. The camel grease the Taliban sometimes used to waterproof their shoes. We turned back and came up behind them. We had no casualties.

Now the *some*thing was a smell too. Deodorant. Somebody on the Hulk was wearing one of those musky deodorants that are supposed to make women melt in your arms. From toxic fumes maybe.

"Midnight," a man's voice, in the cabin.

"Fucker ain't coming," another said, by the stern.

"Oh yes he is," said a third one right over my head. "I can smell him."

I sank under and swam away, got dressed, checked the Ranger, went down the dock a few hundred feet, crawled under a stored boat's canvas, set my phone alarm for 03:30 and crashed into sleep.

By 03:50 I was alongside the Hulk again, naked but for my shorts, my K-Bar in my teeth. I couldn't smell the deodorant but figured the three guys were still there. Till 04:15 I watched the other boats and the tree line and listened for motion inside the Hulk, for footfalls on the docks or a swimmer coming up behind me, hearing only the mechanical wail of mosquitoes and the hiss of tires on the highway. In a shadowed corner of the bow I reached up and hung there, slowly increasing my weight so as not to rock the hull, pulled myself up and crept barefoot across the deck to the front of the cabin.

For a long time I heard nothing. Staying on the dark side of the cabin I slid inside. Both sleeping benches were empty. I listened at the hatch then slowly opened it so the city lights reflected off the sky shone in. For fifteen minutes there was no sound of breathing, not even a pulse, just the lap-lap of ripples under the hull.

I hated this. To move into a dark place where you are highlighted by an open door is a recipe for death.

There was no one inside, just a trace of *Musk for Men*.

I went out. The deck was clear, no movement on nearby boats.

At the far end of the ramp something crossed a band of shadow.

A man, almost to the parking lot. I leapt off the deck and barefooted down the dock but he was already in a pickup and drove off with parking lights on but they also lit his plate: 095 TSR.

But where were the other two guys?

NOW I'D LOST my boat. Before the three guys left they'd surely wired it, and no matter how hard I looked I'd never find the transmitter. So wherever I went in the Hulk they'd know. And could come get me whenever they wanted.

I went aboard for my computer but it wasn't there.

I lifted the rectangle of greenboard over the toilet and my five hundred bucks was gone.

I'd cut my foot chasing after the guy in the pickup and was leaving sticky blood smears everywhere but there was no way to go back and erase them. I got dressed, climbed into the Ranger and drove up Likelike Highway into the hills.

The sun rose in gorgeous raiment over the Waianae range. Nauseous with exhaustion I climbed several hundred feet through the forest, lay down under a tree, set my alarm for 08:00 and fell asleep.

At 08:35 I parked five blocks from Mitchell's, checked the neighborhood then knocked on his door. "You again," he said.

I explained him the latest. "You are totally fucked," he added encouragingly.

"Find me that license plate."

He rolled his wheelchair back to his bank of computers. "Belongs to a Virgilio Mendes. 3224 Bougainvillea Terrace – can you believe a name like that?"

"Mendes?"

"Bougainvillea Terrace? What kind of sad marketing scheme was that?"

"Mitchell," I said, "you got too many things going on in your head."

"Here's it is. Mostly single family ranch style or two-story apartments," he muttered as Google's street view slid past on the screen. "Looks kind of raunchy. Nearest cop shop 2.4 miles, he's in this bungalow here –" It was a small white four-room house with a nice lanai and a palm tree in front, bananas and other stuff behind. "You should follow him," Mitchell said.

"Follow him? I'm going to *interview* the fucker."

"He won't know shit. Find out who he works for. Then you'll know."

"Know what?"

"Everything you need to." Mitchell peered at a new screen. "Wait, I've got his pay stubs. Paid every two weeks, Waimano Foundation."

Waimano Foundation. Why was that familiar? "Hippolito."

"Hippolito?"

"That's who owns Waimano Foundation: Hippolito Urbano."

Up to God

PARKING THE USUAL few blocks away I surveyed Hippolito's estate. The eight-foot stone walls along the lane and down both sides to the sea cliffs shone with midmorning sun and a warm breeze nodded the glossy leaves of the naupaka. I took out my phone and punched him in.

He answered on the second ring. "You promised me protection," I said. "I shouldn't have to ask again."

"I gave you it."

"And now you're trying to have me killed again –"

He coughed, spit. "Where you get that dumb idea?"

"Virgilio Mendes."

"What, you *found* him?"

"Where's the other two?"

"What, you really *found* him? You're good, kid. You're good."

"Who are the other two?"

He sounded surprised. "*What* other two?"

"Three guys were in my boat. Him and two others. Where are they?" I grew angrier thinking of the man waiting in my boat calling me a *Fucker*. I wanted to grip Hippolito's tendony neck and choke the truth out of him.

"Never my man was in your boat. We were watching you to protect you, you dumb fuck."

This stunned me; I instantly believed him. "Where you at?" he said.

"Out front."

"Get your ass in here."

He met me at the front door in his bare feet and led me back through the cavernous kitchen to the vast living room peering over the ocean. He sat in a corner of the long white leather couch looking toward the sea. "What?" he rubbed his face in exasperation, "you think my word's no good?"

"What was he doing on my boat?"

He padded across the wide bamboo floor, opened a door at one end of the great room. "Virgilio!"

I glanced round; there was no quick exit, no available weapon. Hippolito sat back down. "Want coffee?"

"No."

I stood quickly to face the guy who came in, slender about five-ten, muscular, lithe and lantern-jawed, skull shaved. "Aloha!" he said to me, surprised.

I circled, watching him and Hippolito, the room. "You the guy down at my dock last night?"

Virgilio glanced at Hippolito. "I've had somebody with you," Hippolito said, "ever since you come back Oahu."

Virgilio grinned at me, perfect white teeth. "I waited for you last night, yeah? To tell you there's three guys hiding in your boat. But you never showed up."

I was in the water, I started to say but didn't.

"Finally they leave yeah? So I go home, get some sleep, new guy take over."

"New guy?"

Hippolito smiled at my credulity. "The one doubling you now."

I felt disgusted I'd been so focused on hunting my pursuers I hadn't watched my back. "I can't use my damned boat."

"They wire it?"

"I assume so."

"So one of my guys takes it somewhere and they follow it."

I hated the idea of losing the Hulk. "Like where?"

"Meantime I got a safe house for you. And another car. You leave that truck." He turned to Virgilio, "Where you think he should leave that truck?"

"In that parking lot, yeah.? That way they think *he* take the boat –"

For a while I said nothing, then, "Why are you doing this for me?"

He shot me that amused smile that made me feel stupid. "You don't know?"

"If I knew I wouldn't ask."

"Remember Jimmy Diamond?"

I thought a moment. "I remember him."

"In the pen when those Hilo boys wanted to make him somebody's girlfriend, you said you'd kill them first –"

I tried to remember. "I told them leave the kid alone."

"You saved him."

"So what?"

"He's my nephew for Chrissake. Don't you know shit?"

I felt a wash of joy and relief, an instant's sense of protection, of how powerful this ancient rule of the clan. Hippolito smiled. "You're a damn smart kid – how you found my guy Virgilio, him that's so good at keeping invisible?"

I explained them. "Why do you think they left my boat?" I said to Virgilio.

"Decided you wasn't coming."

"If they come back…" *If they came back I'd follow them –*

"We're doing that," Hippolito said. "We'll get answers."

"From these guys?" I explained him more about the Hong Kong tong, the ION guys with their legacy of death.

"My first rule is *Don't hurt nobody*, like Hippocrates said, that Greek doctor –" Hippolito scanned me, waiting for it to sink in. "Don't even hurt your enemies. That way pretty soon you don't have any enemies. Do business with honor, the ancient Hawaiian way. The rest is up to God."

"So you guys didn't kill Lou Toledo?"

He sighed. "You remind me of somebody don't believe in evolution. No matter how much wisdom you give them they just won't listen."

HIPPOLITO'S SAFE HOUSE was at the top of Hahaione Valley, a two-level place glued to the cliffs with one hard approach and several easy exits up into the mountainous forest even choppers can't see through. The living room balcony had a rope drop down the cliff; both bedrooms had trapdoors down a tunnel to a hidden exit deep in the scrub. Inside the house were more motion detectors than the Pentagon; outside it had an old bathtub full of fresh water that herds of deer drank from. They were the world's best motion detectors, uttering their sharp barks and thudding off whenever anybody came near.

Virgilio drove me up there and came back two hours later with new used clothes, a backpack, tube tent and sleeping sack and other emergency gear. "I ask Hippolito if I should bring you a gun," he said, "Hippolito says *Hell no.*"

"Guns don't kill people. People kill people."

"You are a brave guy, no? To be in all this trouble and still making jokes?"

The new car was a blue Dodge caravan with a *Soccer Mom* sticker on the bumper and a row of little human decals on the rear window denoting a dad, mom, two girls and a boy in the middle, a curly-tailed dog and a cat. All in a descending line like reverse evolution. And a brass fish clamped on the trunk and inside it the word *Jesus.*

AFTER DARK I took the road down the mountain to the harbor, parked the Caravan in a busy corner of the lot and took up a position on the brushy bank above the Hulk.

Sitting there I tried to figure why Charity thought Manny killed Sylvia. Even if he was jealous or suffering from unrequited love he didn't seem the violent type. And he'd seemed to love her in a rather unselfish way.

Why might Charity finger him, set him up? She *was* working for WindPower and if they *had* killed Sylvia and wanted to deflect suspicion, Manny was their best bet. A guy who was involved with Sylvia but couldn't remember what he was doing the night she was killed.

He and I should talk some more. Maybe Charity would know how to find him.

Cars were coming and going in the parking lot, their headlights snipping through the trees. Twice people came down the ramp, both times a man and woman who turned the other way and boarded boats further up the line. It was hard not to envy what I imagined as their quiet evening repose in warm companionship and love.

If Manny was being set up by WindPower, then they were hoping I'd take him down. Another murder they'd be free of; another murder pinned on me.

Hurt no one Hippolito said.

Should I tell Manny he's being fingered? Who else might want him?

All night I watched but no one ever neared the Hulk. She sat placidly haltered at the bow, stern following the tide.

How could I find Manny except through Charity? Or did she even know?

I caught an hour's sleep in the Caravan parked outside Deep Blue, and when Clyde opened at seven I got the copy of the credit card receipt and took it to Mitchell.

"You look worse than shit," he said. "Go lie on the couch, get a few hours' sleep. I'll track this down."

When I woke it was late afternoon. I took a cold shower but still couldn't wake up. When I wandered into his computer cave he was staring at one of his many screens. "This guy don't live in Pittsburgh Pennsylvania," he said. "Lives in California. Pittsburg without the *h*."

I yawned, still trying to wake up. "He doesn't exist."

"Yeah he does. Look, I got all this dope on him…Give me a minute, credit card statements can be slow – no, yes – *here* it is: Visa ending in 0092 most recent charge this morning at the Chevron station on Dillingham, *here* it is – rental of dive gear from Deep Blue…Yesterday – get this – he flew Mokulele Air from Lanai to Honolulu, paid for three tickets…Yesterday – wait a minute – yeah, yesterday he charged four hundred eighty-eight dollars and forty-seven cents for breakfast at the Manele Bay Four Seasons in Lanai…No, Pono, this is a real credit card. This is a real guy."

Rich Morals

RICO MORALES had come back into my life. But he didn't know I knew.

He was out there hunting me. But he didn't know I was hunting him too.

The thumbnail photo on his California driver's license showed a narrow-faced big-nosed guy with swept-back curly chestnut hair, flat ears and a wide thin mouth. Age twenty-eight, at six-two and 195 he was probably in very good shape. I remembered the strong hands gripping my ankles when they'd tried to drown me. That kind of guy.

The second guy, Clyde said, was the one with Rico two weeks ago, a red-headed burly guy about twenty-five with a jutting jaw and green eyes. The new guy was the tall tough Russian-looking blond guy with the lobe of his left ear gone. Maybe twenty-five, Clyde said.

So where were the other two guys that Hen Lu from Hong Kong had complained about paying for? And why was he hiring guys from California instead of Hong Kong, who are faster, deadlier and totally immoral? Next to those guys anybody like Rico would be an amateur.

Didn't make sense.

And why had Rico and his two buddies been on Lanai?

Had he met with Miranda Steale, who needed Big Wind's billions of taxpayer grants to keep her empire from collapsing?

NATURALLY I CALLED HIPPOLITO. "Your guy, he can take my boat somewhere?"

"To fuckin Patagonia, you want."

"The north shore. Kalaupapa?"

A moment's silence. Kalaupapa's a haunted place for many Hawaiians. As mentioned earlier, it is the roundish peninsula jutting north from Molokai's cliffs, a separate small caldera of a few square miles where thousands of unfortunate souls, mostly Hawaiians, who had or were suspected of having the white man's gift of leprosy, were banished. Because of the immense sorrow, bereavement, atrocity and misery suffered by these people and their families, to many Hawaiians Kalaupapa remains a kapu place. A place you don't even speak of, let alone visit.

"Okay," Hippolito said. "He drives your boat there."

"He drops anchor on the west shore, up by the airport, takes the plane out, same day?" Other than this tiny airport the only other way out of Kalaupapa was the two-mile zigzag trail cut into the cliffs.

"You know what you're doing?" Hippolito said.

"Tomorrow," I said. "Tell him wait till tomorrow."

Intense, I told myself. *You have to be more intense.* I was missing something extremely important but couldn't figure what it was.

I WAS SO HUNGRY I gorged myself at an IHOP on high fructose corn syrup and LDL cholesterol masquerading as blueberry pancakes and bacon. Like eating poison to stay alive, but it gave me a glycemic high while I crossed town and climbed the stairs to see Charity. Who as the saying goes begins at home.

But she wasn't. At home, that is.

That was unfortunate because how else could I find Manny's new location, so he and I could chat?

Finally about 20:17 I jumped over the side, popped her patio door and went looking for anything that might show Manny's new location, hoping she'd written it down. I was only there a few minutes, having a little snooze, when she, having tiptoed barefoot into the room, flipped on the lights and faced me with a funny little gun I figured was a Colt.

"It's you!" she said, disappointed.

"Who'd you think?"

"I was hoping someone from another planet, whisk me away from all this."

"Would you put that damn thing down –"

She glanced at the gun as if it were an unfortunate excrescence having just grown out of her hand. "Sorry. I got it after I was robbed. You remember–"

"That silly thing won't do you any good. Where's Manny?"

She looked shocked then relaxed. "How would I know?"

"Take me there."

"I misled you." She swung a shawl off her shoulders. "Maybe he didn't kill her."

"So who did?"

She threw her hands in the air, a theatrical gesture.

"*Please* tell me," I said, "*where* is Manny?"

"He called me, what is today, Saturday? Must've been last Tuesday." She pointed to the phone. "Check the call history."

"What time?"

She tried to remember. "Maybe seven p.m."

I pushed through the buttons. She'd had seventeen calls on Tuesday, eleven after five p.m. I handed her the phone. "Which one?"

She glanced them over, pushed one. I could hear it ring, far away like under the sea. "Manny!" she said, low and succulent. "How've you been?"

I could hear his voice, high and squeaky, either nervous or happy I couldn't tell.

"I'm feeling real lonely," she said. "I know it's a little late but can I come over?"

I could hear the silence. His calculating silence. What was in it for him versus what he was risking. "You're a sweetheart," she said. "How do I get there?"

HE WAS LIVING in one of those expensive digs that litter the upslopes of suburban Honolulu. You know the kind, three architecty levels surrounded by tropical landscapes down to a swimming pool with a view over roof-crowded ridges and car-thick valleys to the sea. Where you can almost imagine what Oahu used to be.

We drove there in Charity's Accord, a muddy white thing with a stick shift that she handled expertly. The car felt as if I'd seen it before, but then how many Hondas do you see every day in Honolulu?

When he opened we both walked in. "You!" he jumped back seeing me. "I didn't expect *you*."

"I keep not expecting you either."

He turned on Charity. "You *cheated* on me –"

"Why'd you kill Sylvia?" I said.

"– Sylvia cheated on me too," he said to her.

I grabbed him round the neck and pushed him into a chair. *Hurt no one.* "Sorry, Manny. Just tell us all about it."

He sat up like an aggrieved chicken rubbing his neck and gulping. I glanced at Charity and she nodded: her recorder was on.

"I told you be*fore*," Manny mumbled. "First time you came to see me. Who the fuck you think you *are* any*way* mister?" His rage flared then died out. "I *told* you I loved her. I love her still. She was sweet and angelic and kind and *I don't want to think about this anymore!*"

"But she cheated on you," Charity said.

"*Never!*"

"She was banging Lou Toledo," I said to goad him.

"You just told us," Charity said, "that I was cheating on you and Sylvia did too and look what happened to her."

"She wasn't 'banging' Lou," Manny sneered at me. "I watched them. It never happened."

"You *watched* them –"

"At his place. They'd go in and they'd get undressed but they never did it...I swear it," he almost wept, "I was looking at it."

"So *why*?" Charity pursued, "did she get punished?"

"God knows so much we can't know." He glared at us. "Who do you think I am, God?"

"How'd she die, Manny?" I said. "How do *you* think she died?"

The out-flung hands: *how could I know?* The eager self-abasing smile. "You're the one told *me*…"

I wanted to smack him. "I told you she had fresh water in her lungs… How'd she get it?"

"In a lake? How should *I* know?"

Hurt no one. "Tell us again all the things you did the night she died. The whole story. Make it good."

He gave me a white-eyed look, the *side eye*, Hawaiians call it. "I phoned her that afternoon, left a message could we have dinner that night. That I really *needed* to see her. Was afraid she was sliding toward the dark side…"

"Lou Toledo –"

"Yeah, that and…"

"And?"

"She was trying to blackmail this company downtown, had information on them that would cause lots of damage." He looked up at me. "Yeah?"

"*What* downtown company, Manny? You're not leveling with us."

"I am. I *am*. She said they would give her a half million dollars. Just to shut her up." He drew his hands to his chest. "I told her that was *wrong*. That was *evil*." He turned to Charity. "*We* don't have to punish evil. *God* does."

"What downtown company, Manny?"

"Follow the money –"

"Lanai Land?"

"My *my*," he minced. "What a smart boy."

"Watch it, Manny," Charity said. "Pono can break every bone in your face in ten seconds."

"What a *man*!"

"Sylvia was blackmailing Lanai Land Corporation?" I said. "So *they* killed her?"

He twitched shoulders. "Why else?"

"How you know it was them?"

"Who else?"

"Charity works for WindPower. What about them?"

He splayed fingers across his face, an actor's gesture. "Know nothing."

"You knew I didn't like them," she said.

He smiled. "Did you say that?"

"If it *was* Lanai Land Corporation," I said, "how'd they do it?"

He looked at me blandly. "How hard is it for two strong men to hold a hundred twenty pound woman five minutes underwater?"

"Why two?"

"That's all you need. One holds her arms behind her, another grabs her legs."

"That doesn't make sense, Manny. How do *they* breathe?"

"Oh they have aqualungs or something. What do they call them these days – rebreathers?"

"You know lots about it."

"You think I haven't *suffered* it, this vision, since she died?"

"What vision, Manny?"

"Just like I said, two guys pulling her down…" He buried his face in his hands. "I *can't* get it out of my head."

"But it was punishment, you said," Charity persevered.

"Because she was blackmailing Lanai Land. God punished her."

"You said *I* cheated on you, Manny," Charity said. "How?"

He pulled back. "You women, all the same –"

"We are? How comforting."

"The moment I trust you, you cut my throat. Just like Sylvia."

"*I* cut your throat?"

He pointed his index fingers like two pistols at her. "You let *him*," he pointed them at me. "You let *him* come here. You *betrayed* my trust."

"And how'd Sylvia cut your throat?"

"Going to tear it out of me, aren't you? Going to make me go through it, all over again." He sighed. "God help me."

We waited, a clock ticking in the next room, the far wail of the sea. "How'd you get this place?" I said softly.

"My auntie on the mainland owns it. I'm supposed to help her sell it but, you know, the market's so bad –"

"She know you're living here?"

He looked at me hopefully. "I have the key don't I?"

"How'd Sylvia cut your throat?"

"I knew you'd get back to it. Tearing it out of me…"

"You should get it off your chest."

"Even though she wasn't doing *sex* with Lou, how could she be *naked* with him? How could she *do* that to me?"

"You had every right to punish her," Charity said. "For that."

He smiled at her sweetly. "But I didn't *have* to. God did."

"So the night she died," I said, "you sent her the email that afternoon wanting to see her. Did she reply?"

He stared down at his hands. "She was working on the Big Wind and Cable story. But next week she'd have more time." He grinned up at us. "Next week never came, did it?"

"So what'd *you* do, that night?"

"Got Korean takeout – you know Kun Chu? Really good and *not* expensive…"

"Then what?" Charity said.

"Honey, I came back here and watched American Idol. I never told you, did I, how I love that show?"

"If you're playing with our heads," I said, "I'll kill you."

"Oh I don't need to do *that*. You'll do that to yourself."

"HE'S EVIL," Charity said accelerating downhill. "Maybe he did kill her."

"You believe she was blackmailing Lanai Land Corporation?"

"Not for a second." She turned to me, hands off the wheel in disbelief.

"Don't do that."

"I'm not going to kill us."

I watched the passing cavalcade of houses, mothy streetlights, salt-stained cars and stooping palms, the flitting yellow line. "When I get done with this let's go somewhere."

She put her hand on my thigh. "Can you come back, tonight?"

"See that dirt road –"

"There?"

"Take it."

She swung down tire tracks between old pineapple fields and killed the headlights. I reached for her. "I love the smell of your hair."

"I love lots of things about you –"

"I'd love to go back to your place, spend the whole night…"

She pulled down her shorts and kicked them off. "It's safer this way."

We made love fast not even bothering to go in the back seat, then she dropped me a half mile from the harbor. I came in on the dark side and fed mosquitoes for an hour while I watched the Hulk then went up a couple hundred yards, took off my clothes and swam down, climbed aboard and checked her but no one was there. I got my clothes, started her up and chugged quietly out of port around Diamond Head toward the north shore of Molokai.

Somewhere on the Hulk was the transmitter the three guys had hidden. Not that I'd ever find it. I didn't want to. All I cared is that it was there.

Money Whores

THE NAKED EYE can see ten thousand stars in a true night sky. Not in a city or suburban sky, but in the sky the way God made it – vast and black and afire with stars and planets, asteroids and galaxies – the way you can see it as you round the cliffs of Ilio Point on Molokai and turn east along the island's north shore, now hidden from Oahu's glowing melanoma.

Even in my present predicament I was thankful for this star-spangled night, its vision of eternal life and space in which we'll probably be the tiniest of unremembered extinctions. And considering the likelihood of my own approaching extinction I took a last glance at the heavens and turned back to the wheel.

Huge rollers that had come all the way from Japan were thundering into the Ilio cliffs, surging in great white billows far up the rocks and cascading down again. It seemed the wrath of the ocean against this flake of land that had had the temerity to push itself up from below, to challenge the ruthless sea. *How soon*, the sea was telling it, *you will be gone.*

In the years before Afghanistan, Ilio was my favorite Molokai haunt, jutting like a prow from the island's northwest shoulder, where the Shark God went ashore and became a Dog God and has forever tried to protect humankind – *why* I can't imagine. But I love this place, you walk its splintery basaltic crust laid down atop the island's uprisen volcanic cliffs, the clean salty air from thousands of miles across the Pacific, and the gorsey scrub and sun-warm soil, it puts you in a deeper place, happier and in touch.

Heading east around Ilio the cliffs grew higher and more vertical, glistening blackly with starlight, great white waves booming up their feet. Ahead in the first crimson of sunrise stretched Kalaupapa peninsula and the stark, enormous and unscalable cliffs blocking it off from the rest of Molokai.

The sky grew rosy bright as I neared Kalaupapa. I steered north of the town with its low empty buildings where once hundreds of people awaited slow gruesome deaths, swung east past the airport and dropped anchor in a little bay. I stuffed binoculars, my K-Bar Marine Corps knife, my false face, paracord and a few other things in a small backpack, paddled ashore and hid the kayak in the thornscrub.

05:48. Dawn was bursting in great yellow streaks across the cliffs. My enemies needed a few hours to locate the Hulk and fly in the troops. Now I had to figure where to lead them.

As mentioned earlier, the Kalaupapa peninsula is about eighteen square miles in a half-oval jutting north from the three-thousand foot cliffs of north Molokai. Formed by a now-extinct volcano, it is flat, thorn trees and tall grass, here and there a dirt road, a barren caldera in the middle and the half-empty town haunted by sorrow and love.

On the lonely east end, where the cliffs are highest, stands the classic hand-hewn church Father Damien built, with the graveyard beside it. From there the land slopes down through dense trees to a stream channel and a strip of boulders under the black cliffs, windy and desolate in the unending crash of the waves. From here the only exit is straight up the cliffs or a low-tide scramble eastward over the boulders to the next vertical valley.

Beyond town on the west end a footpath in the cliffs zigzags twenty-eight times to reach the top. It's wide enough for a mule or a person but very easy to fall from. Especially at night.

I ran the five miles across the middle of the peninsula and climbed a couple hundred feet up the cliffs to where the jungle creepers gave way to bare rock, found a niche a good six inches wide and made myself comfortable.

I had a perfect view of the tiny airfield in my binocs, a good half of town and the roads in and out from Damien's church on the east end to the wharf on the west.

13:54 when the plane came in, a single-engine high-wing straight from HNL. It dropped into the runway wind and pulled up at the hut which serves as a terminal. Five guys got out, all in camo, with camo backpacks over their shoulders. I scanned them carefully: this wasn't Rico Morales and his friends: all five looked Asian.

The pilot opened the luggage area behind the wing and two of the guys lifted down three big crates. They popped open the doors and three large brown dogs bolted out. The big thick-chested square-jawed fearless beast known as the Molokai boar dog. It can hunt down anything, anywhere, and kill it faster than a human can.

This made me mad at myself that I hadn't thought of dogs. I slithered down the creepers to the steep bouldered jungle floor. Already I could hear the dogs baying as they led my pursuers west toward where I'd hid the kayak, and soon swung south toward my niche in the cliffs. When I took a last glance in their direction I was even more annoyed to see the Hulk heading back toward Honolulu with my kayak on the deck. That's okay, I told myself. Now my pursuers were down to a maximum of four.

I ran back along my trail a half mile then cut left toward the sea, through the dilapidated silent streets of town to the beach. From there I ran a quarter mile toward the airport then back ankle-deep in the water past where I'd come in and along the beach, sloshing and exhausted in the heavy waves and wet sand, till the beach thinned to cliffs. There I climbed from the waves up the cliff a few hundred feet, fingertips and toes hunting holds in the slippery rock, then lateraled through vertical creepers to the trail.

Above my head, coming down the trail, was the sound of more running dogs and human voices.

Now I was cornered, really scared because I had nowhere to go.

I ran down the trail ahead of the dogs and east across the peninsula to Father Damien's church, where the land narrowed and the dogs couldn't follow me up into the cliffs. Now both sets of dogs were on my trail, the ones from the plane coming in from the north, five different bays and howls. I was truly exhausted when I reached Damien's cemetery and the church all white in sunset, the wind whistling around it.

Over the surf thunder in my ears I heard the dogs nearing. I ran past picnic tables across the stream along the narrow low-tide strand of boulders under the cliffs to the next vertical valley where long ago a few people grew taro and lived cut off from the world.

Running toward the back of the valley I heard the dogs cross the strand and come after me into the valley. In the growing darkness I climbed a wedge of stone to a lava cliff that I could move across with finger holds, the dogs yipping and whining below.

Steadily in the darkness I moved across the lava cliff back toward the strand. Far behind me the dogs were baying and barking as if they had me treed. I was about a hundred feet up the cliff moving down to the strand when a man splashed his way through the boulders and into the valley. *20:17* – in another hour the tide would be coming in so high that no one could make it back across the strand.

I descended the cliff fast as I could and worked carefully back toward Damien's church, ducking between the boulders when a second man splashed by grunting and swearing. In the darkness he looked big and burly, not like the Asian guys from the plane.

The surf was knocking me into the boulders by the time I reached the creek bed. *21:12*. With how the tide was rising no one could cross the strand behind me now. The dogs and the two guys were stuck in the valley till dawn. But where were the four Asians?

I climbed uphill toward the church, staying in darkness and watching for the third guy. I reconnoitered the back side of the church and the cemetery above it, was working down to the lower cemetery when someone whispered, "Yeah?" soft and low to the left, from the cemetery. "I'm at the church for Chrissake. Where you at?"

He was silent a few moments, then, "You can't get back?"

More silence. "Yeah, okay. They're gonna be pissed...I know it's not your fault, I didn't say it was."

More silence, then, "So can I go back to town? You know, no point in my sleeping out here, I'll be back here six a.m. –" He said nothing, then, "All right! *Jesus!* I just asked...Yeah, okay, I'll call him. I said I would..."

He rang off and walked back and forth muttering, I could get only the occasional word, "advantage...too smart, mother fucker...thinks he's God..."

He turned back, sat on a fallen tombstone, huffed and quieted. I was readying to go in on him when he pulled out the phone and punched in a number. "Yeah," he said. "No, hey listen, it's not bad...No, he isn't taken care of yet. But we'll get him!"

He let the phone squawk a while then said, "The dogs have him pinned on the side of a cliff up some fucking valley where there's nobody and I can't get in there till tomorrow because of the high tide."

The phone squawked more and then he said, "Yeah I know I won't get the money if it isn't done right. It's *gonna* be done right...Yeah I'll call you right away..."

He walked up and down again a while then pulled out the phone. "Yeah, of course it's me. He says we don't get this done tomorrow he's gonna pull us and leave it to the Koreans. He so pissed he was jumping up and down – I could hear it over the phone."

He listened a moment. "So, you can see this guy, up on the cliff? I don't care he's hiding, you got to locate the fucker. Yeah," he went on, "yeah. From what I been told isn't anybody living up that valley, so soon as you locate him shoot the motherfucker. Don't worry the sound. Just nail him good and drag his ass out on the beach so the waves can take him. Shark food, that's what he's good for. Fucking shark food."

As I came up behind him I recognized his smell, the musk deodorant one of the guys on my boat had worn, remembered the voice. I gave him a nice tap on the back of the head, removed his weaponry (typical PPK under the arm, a little Russian thing on his ankle, a high-impact super-plastic razor knife on the other forearm, the kind you can wear through airport security), trussed him tighter than a Thanksgiving turkey, dragged him to the cliff edge and poked him with his knife to wake him up.

He moaned making me fear I'd hit him too hard. He'd just ordered the guys in the valley to kill me so I had no particular concern for his life, but if he died he wasn't going to tell me a thing.

Shark Food

"WHO YOU GONNA KILL?" I asked him. When he didn't answer I slid him a little further off the cliff. "Go ahead," he gasped. "You're going to kill me anyways."

So I slid him a tad more. Starting to hurt my arms now just holding his weight. "Okay Rico," I said, taking a guess. He stiffened.

"I know all about you," I added. My mind was racing, couldn't think what to say next. "Who you just talk to?"

"You heard me, the guys in the valley. How the fuck you get out?"

"The other call?" I let go a little and he slid a couple inches. "The guy who was jumping up and down?"

"Get it over with," he said, but we both knew that was bullshit. In Rico's place we'll all do almost anything to live a little longer.

"Did you go to Catholic high school, Rico?" I said, guessing again. This stunned him. "Yeah. So?"

"Ever read about chivalry? The knights when they fought, the one who lost could either choose to die or swear to always obey the other one, forever after? Remember that?"

"Sure," Rico said, feeling a little safer. "Sister Marie, she taught us that. Sometimes the loser didn't have to die –"

"Explain me that other call, Rico."

"What, I'm lyin here half off the edge, your rope's killing my hands, and you want me to talk?"

I slid him up a little. Easier on my arms too. "So talk."

He said nothing and I realized he was stalling, waiting for someone to come in on me. I dropped him off and let him dangle, big and heavy as he was. "No," he begged, "No please no I'll tell you – Please pull me back up –"

Now don't think Rico a coward for breaking like this. The sudden drop into the void, the instant realization of smashing death in a couple seconds, makes your body scream to live. It's mostly in the movies you get wordless tough heroes, actors who in the real world wear pink underwear and go to boy-boy parties.

"'D'you know, Rico, I got a bullet through this shoulder, back in Afghanistan? So I can't hold you but a few seconds longer."

"His name's Gerry Cruwell. Lives on Lanai. I can take you there you want. *Please* pull me up now."

I pulled him up a ways. "I think I know him. Explain me more."

"Okay okay this guy Gerry Cruwell works for the old bitch. But everything gets recorded, the old bitch listens to it all, anything to do with Big Wind and the Cable, the old bitch is listening in…"

"Miranda Steale?"

"That one. She's so old everybody's thinks she's dead and has been, what you call it, resurrected."

I had flash of liking for Rico even though he'd wanted me dead. "What'd they want you to do?"

"You know it: take you out. Vanish the body, though. That was the problem last time."

"*What* last time?"

"You know that reporter got killed. The one sticking her nose into everything."

"I never heard about that."

"The one worked for the paper. She was causing trouble, some big project the old bitch was working on. But she got killed, yeah?"

"How'd she get killed, Rico?"

"I never heard. She showed up dead, in the ocean no less. Maybe was an accident."

208

I slid him right off the edge, dangling again. "No!" he screamed.

I pulled him up. "Who killed her?"

"God I don't know. We had *nothin* to do with that – Oh please please pull me up –"

"What were you hired for then?"

"Just to deal with you, make you vanish…I'm sorry, it's not my fault, I wouldn't hurt you now, please let me up…"

"You and who else tried to drown me, that day surfing?"

He thought about this. "I didn't know it was you. I wouldn't hurt you now."

I reminded myself someone was coming in on me, there was no time. I pulled him up. "You have to swear to me, Rico, you will quit this now. You won't hunt me anymore or try to help anyone hunting me –"

"My God I swear it."

"Never hurt me again in any way –"

"I promise on my mother's grave. On Jesus' name. I will *never* harm or threaten you again."

I untied him and backed away. "I want you to walk back to town and fly out tomorrow."

He reached down and pulled out the little Russian gut gun. "I sure will, motherfucker, after I kill you."

I should've explained you that when poor Rico was knocked out I dumped the bullets out of his Russian gun and put it back in his ankle holster. The Walther I'd kept for myself, along with his deadly plastic knife.

He pulled the trigger and it snapped on an empty chamber. There was an instant of shocked stillness, he pulled the trigger again and with a roar leaped at me.

I didn't want to but had no choice. After I'd shot him I tossed his sorry ass off the cliff. Shark food.

One down, two to go. Plus the four Asians out there somewhere. And now they knew where I was because they'd just heard the gun.

What Would Genghis Do?

R ETREAT IS OFTEN the best attack. It provides temporary safety and time to prepare, and induces in the pursuer the illusion that you're afraid, exhausted and running for your life.

Genghis Khan won many victories by retreating, luring pursuers into killing grounds with no exit. He seemed to work from a level of deep intuition, to be inside his enemies' heads.

Rico's two buddies and the dogs were stuck in the blind valley beyond Damien's church, but I had no idea where the four Koreans were. But after the shot they had a pretty good idea where I was.

As I made my way in darkness along the dirt roads across the peninsula I began to question whether I should have led my enemies here. Without my boat how was I now going to get off Molokai, get back to Oahu to confront them all?

As usual, part of me wondered about naively telling *The Post* the whole story and asking them to broker my surrender in exchange for a total revelation of what I'd learned and who the villains were, a chance to bring out the truth.

But I'd be killed before they ever brought me in, and if I ever did make it to jail I'd never get out.

To beat them I needed pure evidence. There were the emails and files I'd copied at WindPower, and now the recording Severina had given me, and though all of them had disappeared with The Hulk, Mitchell had copies.

But none of them proved anything stronger than a dislike for Sylvia and thereafter for me. Hippolito had said I hadn't killed Lou Toledo, that Kim had done it, but that wouldn't save me, nor would he say it to anyone else. Charity might testify to some of the things she'd told me, but she could also take me down. I could've tried to bring Rico Morales to the police so he could explain about what Miranda Steale had hired him to do. But that was too idiotic to even consider: why would Rico have told the truth once he was safe from me?

I needed proof on who ordered Sylvia's death and who killed her. Problem was, once it was clear who they were, why didn't I go deal with them myself? It was an appealing prospect but meant I'd be on the run the rest of my life or, more likely, Inside.

My boat was gone, I couldn't take a plane, the Koreans were surely watching the trail up the cliff. In about four more hours the tide would recede enough for Rico's two buddies, the curly-red-haired guy and the big Russian, and their Molokai boar dogs, to get out of the valley and come after me.

I had no boat, no money and no way to get off Molokai. Yet I had to get to Oahu, literally to save my life.

There wasn't time to think about this as I crossed the thornscrub savanna toward the cliff trail, watching the dirt road through the trees but never daring to take it. Everything was dark and shadowy, the lava boulders were huge black blocks, the trees and knee-high grass blackly visible, the breeze clacking the dry branches and making it hard to hear.

The stench of mule manure and urine grew thick on the air: it was the meadow where the mules the tourists ride are penned, so the trail up the cliffs was just ahead.

The problem with going up the trail was that the Koreans would be waiting, no doubt with night vision glasses, probably GEN III or some other good technology. I had to get out of the valley but there was no other way except the cliff trail. Somehow I'd have to see them before they saw me.

Patchy clouds were crossing the stars. For ten million years we've lived like this, I thought as I climbed the cliff above the first two switchbacks, fingers and bare toes seeking holds on wet rock.

My fingers ached and my arms and legs quivered. No way I could climb the rest of this cliff. I was so tired I couldn't remember when I'd slept but maybe it was two days ago. I moved back to the trail telling myself if I was going to take it I had to go slow because the Koreans were waiting. And the slower I climbed it sooner the tide would go out and Rico's two buddies and their dogs could cross the strand and come up behind me.

So I kept climbing the switchbacks fast as I dared, had passed seven out of twenty-eight, then worried I'd missed one or counted one too many, had that creepy feeling one gets when we know we've screwed up but don't know how to fix it.

Kept on climbing, gave up worrying, maybe they weren't there, amazing how you can time your breath to your steps and climb fast forever even if you don't know who's watching, wants to kill you.

Afghanistan taught me that killing people never solves anything, just makes things worse. So I didn't want to kill these guys, but *they* were here to kill me. Two of them already nearly *had* killed me. So to Hell with what Hippolito had said. I had no reason to pity or preserve them.

Then I smelled them.

Amazing how your sense of smell improves under the threat of dying. And when people wear synthetic fabrics their smell is stronger because the fabric doesn't absorb it. It was a raunchy, sweaty smell: they too had been running all day, trying to cover my exit, hunting me down. You could even smell the spicy food they'd last eaten.

It wasn't that hard to climb around them. All I had to do was move laterally along the cliff slippery with sea dew then find handholds up it, wondering as I groped in darkness if anyone from Kalaupapa had ever escaped up this cliff and how many had fallen off trying.

After maybe two hours I'd passed around and above them, fingers bloody with rock burns, ankles and forearms shivering with fatigue. I rejoined the trail above the Koreans, ran the thousand remaining feet to the top and down through the rain forest where Mitch and Noelani were no doubt sleeping quietly in their lovely home, and my heart was begging me to stop and ask for help, but wouldn't that be first place the cops would look? I ran on, down through the cattle pastures then the coffee farms, past Tank's farm wishing again to ask for help – but if he didn't turn me in wouldn't he face five to ten?

The hills widened into the brushy lowlands toward Kaunakakai and the shorefront huts where the Molokai Paddle Club keeps its Polynesian canoes. Like everywhere on Molokai the huts weren't locked – no one on Molokai steals anything so why lock it?

This made me feel bad as I slid a canoe from the rack, picked an old but sturdy one – there was no reason to take a newer one when chances were slim I was going to make it.

And when I set out through the tall threatening waves toward Oahu I tried not to think about that I'd never canoed forty miles at one time in my life. But we can do amazing things when death's the alternative.

The waves rose huge above the reef and came roaring across it to crash over the canoe. I jabbed the paddle into the swell, driving the canoe out fast, smashing into the next huge crest as it broke over me. But I drove through it, half-knocked out by the force of the wave, paddling intensely, digging into the waves, pushing the power down my chest and up from my torso and legs into the arm and out the paddle that clawed me forward.

Out a half mile the waves grew more regular, just a seven foot swell like a rocking chair, easy to paddle, sliding down the trough and biting deep on the way up and thrusting across the top. Hour after hour the wide dark hulk of Oahu never seemed to grow nearer, but behind me the starlit silhouette of Molokai grew steadily smaller.

And it's true that we can go on almost forever if we have to. Paddling had become a rhythm, leaning forward to bury the blade deep into the wave where the power is strongest, arms, shoulders, neck, chest, stomach and legs right down to your toes, all together driving back, forcing the wave behind you, the prow forward. Your breathing paces the paddle's drive, or your paddle your breathing, and if you need to you can stop a few seconds to rest your aching shoulders, knowing that you are suddenly drifting away, out into the vast and empty southern ocean, so you bite the paddle in again, check for Oahu's mass against the stars as you hit the crest, and push your way across the waves.

It is impossible to describe how joyous were the first touches of dawn. Nearly imperceptible this vague lightening of the ocean's supple crests, the eternally flexing black musculature of the late-night sea. Oahu grew larger, the stars over Diamond Head dimming as the mountain loomed closer, then the great volcanic ridges of the Koolau Mountains growing clearer, even the waves calmer, less dangerous.

It was a lovely sunrise. The mountains gleamed like onyx. I could make out cars on the Kalanianaole Highway, an early glint of house windows. My every muscle was torn and dead but I was beginning to think I might make it.

When I was two miles from shore a little gray Cessna dropped from about five thousand feet right down to the deck and began circling me.

I expected someone to lean out the window and shoot at me as I paddled in a frenzy for the shore, so close now I could see individual trees and rooftops. The swell was deep and curling white on the crests, shoving me closer, faster.

Then the chopper came.

Properly Done

I ROLLED THE CANOE, dove ten feet down and swam underwater for shore, stroking hard, lungs aching, a panicked hunger for air in my throat. When I'd gone as far as I could endure then another thirty seconds after that I spurted up, shoved my face through a frothing crest, sucked in air and dove again.

Trying to stay deep I swam onward, lungs screaming, came up to suck in air and saw I'd swum the wrong way, out to sea, the chopper hovering shoreward. I dove again and swam out further, glancing down for sharks, came up and couldn't see the chopper, swam out further and let the current take me north toward Kailua, and a couple hours later floated into shore to a little empty beach gleaming like a pearl in midmorning sun.

I staggered up the sand and fell down, tried to get up but my legs wouldn't work. My arms belonged to someone else. With a last spurt of strength I crawled under the wide-leaved boughs of a sea grape and passed out.

The sun was low when I woke. My tongue and lips were swollen. I fumbled half-blindly for my backpack with the K-Bar knife, then remembered I'd lost it when I dove out of the canoe after the chopper came. My false face, everything. Gone.

I got up on my hands and knees a while, head hanging. My throat was burning with thirst and salt. I crawled from under the sea grape, grabbed a thick bough and pulled myself up. When I felt steady I let go of the bough and took a few steps and waited for the dizziness to pass.

"What happened to *you*?" a voice said.

It hurt to turn round so fast. She was just a kid, slender and tanned in a red and white bikini, two long chestnut braids, a blue boogie board under one arm and a little red backpack over the other shoulder.

"Lost my board," I mumbled, couldn't control my lips.

"You *what*?"

"I lost my board." I tried to say it more distinctly, pointed out to sea. "I guess the leash broke then I got hit on the head by my board. Anyway I got pulled out a ways and washed all the way down here from Lanikai Beach."

"Wow, you came from *there*? You must be amazing good."

"You surf?"

She nodded gravely, cocked her head. "Are you that man they're chasing?"

I tried to look wide-eyed. "I've been out surfing. Nobody's chasing me."

She inspected me closer. "What kind of board?"

"That I lost? A Bushman Pancho."

"Wow. That's a shame."

I glanced at her backpack. "You have a cell phone?"

"*Every*body has a cell phone."

"Can I use it to call my girlfriend? So she can come get me?"

She put down the pack and pulled out a pink Nokia. "Mahalo," I mumbled and punched in what I thought was Charity's number.

"Builders' Remote," a man said. "This is Charlie –"

"Sorry," I said, "wrong number." But my fingers were so numb I hit Charlie's number again.

She snatched the phone. "Tell me the number."

It took three tries to remember it right. Despite the warm breeze I couldn't stop shivering. Charity's voice sounded so lovely when she answered, just the thought that there was someone out there who maybe understood me. "Where you at?" I said.

"Where you think?"

"I got hit by my board and washed all the way down to Kailua. I'm all beat up and can you come here and get me?" *Please*, I wanted to add. *Please*, Charity, *please*.

There was a moment's hesitation as if someone had nodded to her, given her the okay. "Where is *here?*"

I looked at the girl. "Where are we?"

"63 Mokapu Court." She shrugged as if it were obvious – "in Lanikai."

I repeated it into the phone. "I heard it," Charity said. "Who is she, your latest one-nighter?"

"Hey," I said to the girl, "how old are you?"

She pulled herself up taller. "Eleven. In November."

"You hear that?" I said to Charity.

"I'll mapquest it, take the Pali Highway and be there forty-five minutes."

"What're you driving?"

"Manny's car."

"Come alone."

"Don't be a jerk!" she snapped and hung up.

I tried to wipe the phone clean on my ragged salt-caked shorts, gave it back to the girl. "How do I get to the road?"

"Take the path up past the garage and out the drive."

I nodded at her boogie board, the ocean. "You're not going out there alone?"

"Nuh-uh. My mom's coming. She goes out with me."

I turned and headed uphill. "Don't worry," she called, "I won't tell."

"Dorothy?" A woman's voice came from the house. "Who are you talking to?"

"Nobody, Mom. Are you coming or not?"

The house was dignified and gray with white trim and gave off a sense of quiet wealth. Beyond the four-car garage the drive snaked up through forest and meadow then more forest to the gate, two simple stone pillars, a thick hedge of bougainvillea on each side.

I pushed the button on the inside and the gates slid open almost silently. I walked down the road in the direction Charity would come. It curved through towering forests with tall stone walls hiding each estate, a spiritual peaceful world I would have loved to stay in.

THE BLACK SUBARU tore around the curve below and pulled up beside me. She had changed her hair, it hung down in ringlets and made her seem an enticing stranger. She wore a yellow dress and looked more tanned and pissed off than the last time I'd seen her.

"Thank you," I said, testing the water.

"You didn't need to say that about coming alone."

"Also known as masturbation."

"Don't be vulgar."

"And self-pleasuring."

"You look a total wreck."

I explained her what had happened, not mentioning Rico's fate but implying I'd marooned him with his buddies in the blind valley, telling her about the canoe trip across the strait and the Cessna and the chopper. "Where were you," I said, "when I called?"

"Checking a memo from Simon. Bastard can't even spell."

Simon who ordered Sylvia's death, I thought, but no point to say it. It wasn't just Simon or his henchman Damon, now it was the Hong Kong mob with their Korean killers, and Lanai Land Corporation who'd hired Rico and his friends to kill me.

She handed me a bottle of water which I sucked down and almost threw up. "You need some rest," she said. "Some food and rest and love."

Much as I cared about her I couldn't imagine having energy for the *love* part. "How's Manny?"

"Still house-sitting his auntie's place."

I patted the dashboard. "He doesn't need his car?"

"He's driving his aunt's 500 SL. And my car's in the shop."

"Manny's station in life has certainly improved."

She downshifted for a hill and floored it. "Careful!" I yelled over the gear yowl.

"He must've come into money," she yelled back. "The way he's throwing it around."

I tried to peer through the accumulated eucalyptus leaves, salt spray, road spatter and other detritus on her windshield. "You should clean the windshield," I said.

"It bothers you," she snapped her gum at me, "*you* clean it."

It made me smile just being with her, to be cared for, like Dorothy's kindness when I washed up on her shore after I'd been hunted on Molokai, paddled the strait and swum underwater to flee the chopper. Were the ones in the Cessna and chopper Rico's people or the Koreans? Did I know anything for sure?

I fell into a weary doze in evening traffic while wondering how to prove Miranda Steale had hired Rico and his two chums, including the so-called Big Russian, to kill me. That in itself seemed a serious offence, and though I was taking it perhaps too personally, it was generally against the law.

If as Rico said they hadn't killed Sylvia then who did?

If Lanai Land Corporation hadn't killed her, it had to be WindPower or their accomplices Ecology Profits, the Governor's people, IEEC or High Stakes Ranch. But which? I was beat up, had lost everything I had, and was no further down the road than before.

But seeing Charity next to me driving so intently with those lovely coils of hair windblown down the side of her face and that pert nose I realized all this fussing about money and killing people is so unnecessary, *all we need is love.*

What if, it came to me in a flash, instead of attacking Iraq and since then killing nearly a million people, what if Bush had said to the Iraqis, *Look, it's going to cost America about two trillion dollars to do this war, so why don't we divide the money instead, and each get a trillion? I'll give you a trillion for marvelous new schools and fantastic hospitals, solar panels on every roof so everyone has good power, good roads, lots of environmental restoration, all those good things? And I'll keep our trillion from going further into debt? And no one dies.*

How could everyone not have agreed?

But politicians don't work that way. Big money loves wars. Like this guy Gerry Cruwell from Lanai Land Corporation who on Severina's recording had said, *Am I on board?* about killing me. *Should have been done weeks ago. The moment he found her. Not that anyone should have ever found her. She should have been properly done. Not by some amateurs.*

Okay, but who were the "amateurs" who did kill her?

Then there was Damon's recent memo to Simon:

Been talking to your friend the Gov. He wants a "legally enforceable" guarantee re his Board seat after he leaves Governorship incl amt remuneration. At least $2 million a year for 5 years because that's what his predecessor was offered by the Superferry corp.

The Gov is such a squirrely little prick but we have no choice. I'd like to write the guarantee in vanishing ink or something that explodes when he touches it. But we have to give him the money or he won't back Big Wind and the Cable.

He actually said to me, "You guys are clearing a billion profit on Big Wind and you won't even give me ten million? Me, who brought this to you, when you're handing out lots more millions to everybody else?"

Can you believe, little prick thinks Big Wind was his idea?

No Crime

T HE SWEET RELEASE of love heals many wounds both spiritual
and physical. I was fed Big Island prime rib and mashed potatoes
and spent the night in Charity's lithe arms. In the morning she bought me
new clothes and shoes at Target and gave me the keys to Manny's black
Subaru, two hundred bucks and the kind of hot lingering kiss that makes
you never want to leave.

Wearing my new running shoes, blue shorts, and Punahou T-shirt I
drove Manny's Subaru cross-town to Mitchell's.

"Can you do it?" I asked after I'd explained him what I wanted.

"Of course," he scowled. "But I won't."

I feared a sudden accession of narrow-minded virtue in him. "Why not?"

"You'll get killed."

"What would you suggest that *won't* get me killed?"

"You have two alternatives: *First* is this stupid idea of yours, trying to
trick one of them into a meeting and make him talk. But there's no reason
he would. And if you kill him you're in even worse trouble."

"That's impossible."

"*Second*, we insert something in their email history that proves
their guilt –"

"No lies. I want it done right –"

"It's just to freak them out, you idiot, see what they say to each other."

"They won't reveal anything in an email."

"No problem. Because now I can listen to Simon's phone too, and Gerry Cruwell's from Lanai Land Corporation, download their messages, copy their files, locate them by GPS any time I want. And I'm working on getting Hen Lu and the Gov. *And*, get *this*, we can even take pictures with their phones and they never know."

It hurt to sit so I walked around. "So how do we make this all stick?"

He held aloft a little flash drive like the ones I'd brought him from WindPower. "A stick will make it stick."

"Recorded conversations?"

"Admissions of guilt." He grinned at me. "But sadly, before this all happens the perpetrator will be shot trying to escape."

"Me?"

"Who else? Do you see another perp waiting in the shadows? No, once they get you they're free for good. All that five billion bucks is theirs."

I explained him about the five Koreans. Didn't explain him about Rico, just Rico's two buddies and the boar dogs.

"So even if you kill all seven that'll only piss off their friends, who will send more guys, *etcetera ad nauseam*..." He shrugged his wide shoulders. "So either you totally vanish, become an entire new you with no contact with *this* you's life..." He shrugged again, "or do you *really* think you can keep taking them down, one at a time?"

"I don't want to do either."

He smiled at me as one does at a somewhat intelligent dog. "Okay, there's a third way. We send an email to one of the perps, saying something like *We have the GPS of the person you want. We will transfer it to you for its fair market value.*"

"You want to tell him where I *am*?"

"No, you idiot. We wait and see what he tells the others."

"Remember that recording from Gala Investments..." I tailed off, not wanting to remind Mitchell of hookers and the beauty of fucking.

"The chat in the corner between our three main perps," he says, heading me off.

"WindPower, High Stakes, and Lanai Land Corporation."

"That leaves the Governor and IEEC out. But the Governor's behind it all."

"Let's send it to WindPower." Maybe, I thought, I could get some feedback from Charity on Simon's response. "You sure they can't find you, in all this?"

"Our location's untraceable. They won't know what hit them."

"How much would be usable in court?"

"I'm not your lawyer." Mitchell shrugged. "Maybe fifteen, twenty percent?"

My phone rang, *Private*. "Yeah?" I answered, trying not to sound like me.

"Hey you."

Oh Jesus. I didn't know what to say. Mitchell's words ran through my head: *we can GPS you by your phone.* "Hey," Kim said again, "I can hear you breathing."

"Yeah?" Already I was looking for exits.

"I got good news –"

My good news lately has been Rachel the credit card lady calling to congratulate me on being eligible for a new loan if I buy a dirigible or Hummer or a new war or something. "Yeah?" I cleared my throat.

"I've been sleeping with Joe Krill –"

"Whoever he is he's a lucky man –"

"You *know* who he is. The coroner."

That took me aback. "Him who found fresh water in Sylvia's lungs then didn't."

"That one."

"How was he?"

"Like a terrier. He's got a little one but won't give up."

"I hate it when you sleep with other guys."

"You know why I did it."

"Yeah. I know."

"So shut up." She let that sink in. "That water in her lungs?"

"Yeah?"

"Was fresh."

I felt dizzy, wanted to sit. "How come?"

"How come *what*?"

"How come he changed his story?"

"His brother runs the pharmacy on Lanai."

"So?"

"*So?* Lanai Land Corporation owns his business and his house. So either Joe Krill changed his report or his brother lost a home and a lifetime of hard work."

"Will he talk about it?"

"Would you?"

"So what's this prove?"

"What you already knew."

"Then Manny had her cremated."

"Good old Manny."

"Are you tracking me on this phone?"

"I'm using a throwaway. Just for you."

"I can't stop loving you. I hate it but I can't."

"I can't either. But I don't hate it."

I wanted to say I don't either really, but she'd rung off.

"YOU'RE GOING DOWN, MANNY," I told him. "I've got a good alibi, witnesses, the whole deal. You don't have shit."

I'd driven into the misty hills to his auntie's place and dropped in unexpected via the lanai roof. He'd been watching soaps in his bathrobe, sat there prim as a princess on the edge of the Victorian silk loveseat in the voluminous great room overlooking the terraces and pool, his hairy legs wrapped round each other, fingers clasped over one knee, a pensive smile on his thin lips, seeing Sylvia in his memory. "She was in a prissy mood that last night," he said. "Wanted to go see Lou Moreno…"

"Last time I asked you, you said she was working late on Big Wind."

"Yeah well she was. Lou was helping her."

Now I was really confused. "How?"

His watery pale eyes shifted. "I'll give you a clue –"

"You've been holding out on me?" I wanted to crack his ugly neck.

"She got scared. I told her, *You silly, stop working on this story.* To give it up would've been so much safer…But Lou, he said he'd protect her, that's why she liked him. She really liked *me* better, as a *man*. He was just a lunkhead who could protect her."

"Protect her from what?"

"Like that night, before she died."

Now I really wanted to strangle him. "Explain me."

"I never told anyone, it wasn't their business…"

I waited, clenching my fists. "There was a benefit, the Lanai Land Corporation Foundation?" He said it like I wouldn't know about them. How they and others like them invest a hundredth of one percent of their ill-gotten gains in some public thingy like operas and hospitals and libraries and schools. One hundredth of one percent, and everyone says how wonderful they are and how much they've given back to Hawaii.

"Well they'd invited her," he went on, "but she felt strange about it. *Into the hyena's den*, she said. So I said *don't* go." He held up his palms in surrender. "But she called Lou, wanted *him* to take her. Believe me, I didn't want *that*."

"He *did* take her?"

"He couldn't. Some night dive he had to do. But even *he* told her don't go. That's what he told *me*, anyway…"

Logical next step, of course, was ask Lou. Trouble was, of course, Lou was totally and completely dead. As was Sylvia. By maybe the same killers. No witness plus no evidence equals no crime.

"But she *did* go?"

"Her car was in the shop, she'd have taken a taxi…"

"Or somebody came for her?"

"I never talked to her again. None of us did."

"Why'd you hold out on me, Manny? Not tell me this?"

"Who did you think you were, anyway, asking questions? I didn't know you, why should I tell you *every*thing?"

"What are you holding out now?"

He clasped his hands. "Absolutely nothing."

"The Lanai Land Corporation Foundation…You ever ask them was she there?"

He shook his head. "What difference would it have made? She was dead. I thought she'd gone for a swim on her way home and drowned... How was *I* to know?"

I wanted to tell him another SF maxim: *Always assume the worst till you know better*...But Manny wasn't up for that, wasn't up for much but freeloading off his auntie and watching the days go by. No wonder Sylvia'd had no use for him. *A leech*, she'd told Angie. *He reminds me of a leech.*

As I walked down the stone path from his auntie's house to the street I was thinking if Sylvia said Lanai Land Corporation was like going into the hyena's den, she must have been threatened, feared them. But then why did she go? For the same reason journalists get killed all the time – because they keep digging for the truth.

THE CORONER HAD LIED about the fresh water in Sylvia's lungs, but now what difference did it make? He wasn't going to sing, not with his brother in the clutches of Lanai Land Corporation. They were just doing to him what they did to everyone on Lanai who opposed the wind turbines and Cable: intimidate them, fire them, evict them, chase them off-island. Scorched earth capitalism: works nearly every time.

What it *did* prove, however, was that Kim was still trying to help me, she didn't disbelieve my story.

Or did she? How could I be sure she'd really had this conversation with the coroner? It could be just another story to make me trust her so she could track me down. But she'd had a chance to locate me by her phone, said she hadn't.

But had she?

So I went to see Joe Krill.

HE WAS A TERRIER like Kim said, about five-eight, knotty knuckles and hard little hands, narrow cheeks, stringy eyebrows and bushy graying hair with lots of dandruff on his pink pinstripe shirt. His skinny fingers picked at his tie as he sat in the driver's seat of his new silver Jag in the darkened parking garage and tried not to tremble.

He had no reason to be scared but didn't know it: I wasn't going to fire Charity's little gun I held on him. "So who," I said, "tells you change your story?"

"Just a voice on my cell. Caller ID said *Private*."

"What'd they say?"

"Not to tell my brother. If I told him he'd get fired just the same, lose his house. Lanai Land Corporation owns everything, could chase him off the island. Ruin him for life."

I tried to imagine this guy fucking Kim. "What else they say?"

"I had to reverse my finding that it was fresh water in her lungs."

"How'd you know it was fresh?"

"When her body came in it was early morning. I'd just got to work and they called me right down. To the morgue, I mean…" Krill shook his head. "I felt so bad for her. Such a pretty young woman, excellent physical shape, slender with strong core muscles, probably a surfer given her lean legs and arms…" He wet his lips with the tip of his tongue and I wondered what he'd truly felt, looking down on Sylvia's body.

"So she had to be a good swimmer," he went on, "and I wondered if maybe she didn't die from drowning. Though you could tap her chest and hear the water in her lungs…So I said let's pump her out and right away I noticed it didn't smell right –"

"Yeah?" I waited.

"Chlorine. First thing I smelled was chlorine." He nodded in recollection. "Like from a swimming pool."

"So you *knew* she was murdered."

He stared at me bleakly. "My brother's worked hard all his life…They said they'd kill my kid."

I sat back, stunned. He looked down at my gun. "You wouldn't shoot me –"

"Of course not."

"Then let's put it away."

I shoved the gun in my pocket. "How we going to solve this?"

Again the mild persevering glance, as if he'd seen everything evil that humanity could produce and didn't expect much else. "If we bring these people down," I added, "there'll be no danger anymore. Otherwise your brother'll never be safe. Or your kid."

"He's twelve. Has Down Syndrome." He looked at me. "You love them just as much, you know, as a regular kid. Maybe more."

"I need your help," I said, "to bring these people down."

"Lanai Land Corporation? They'll kill you. And no one'll ever find your body."

"They've been trying to kill me for weeks. It isn't working."

"For weeks?" He smiled. "Then your time's running out."

"Sylvia was murdered. You don't care?"

"People get murdered all the time in this country. You know how many get solved? Barely sixty percent."

I glanced at his wedding ring. "Your wife isn't going to like it, you sleeping with other women."

"My wife's been dead seven years, Mr. Hawkins."

"Okay," I sighed, defeated. "When I reveal all this, it'll bring you down."

Again the almost-kindly smile. "You're not *going* to reveal all this. Because you're going to be dead." He nodded at the door handle. "Now get out of my car."

Roadblock

"THEY BIT!" Mitchell on the phone, laid-back like this news was nothing big.

"Tell me."

"When you comin in?" *In* meaning his place.

"*Tell* me!"

"Simon got our email at 15:47 and called Gerry Cruwell at Lanai Land Corporation at 17:11. At 18:29 they called Hen Lu. That was just after noon in Hong Kong…"

I waited, finally had to say it. "And?"

"They don't seem to have that same brotherly closeness we had in SF…"

"Get to the point, Mitchell –"

"They're too smart to ever say anything useful. But they gave us something noncommittal. What we got was, *Please advise as to what this refers. And to your terms.*"

"Fuckers want to know how much we know –"

"And what it'll cost them."

"So what do we say?"

"I already did. Told them ten million –"

"Ten million *what*?" I put in, not understanding.

"The more we ask for, the more they'll think we know. The more they'll fear us."

"You told them it was me?"

"Who else?"

"And where I am?"

"We *can* tell them. Whenever you want."

"The moment they agree to pay they're up shit creek –"

"Used to be a beautiful little stream ran out into the Bay. Then they diverted an outlet from the Pearl Harbor sewers into it. And people started calling it Shit Creek…"

"Stay on target, Mitchell."

". . . but that was in the old days. Now we're far more sanitary, dump it on the coral reefs instead…"

"*Please*, Mitchell."

He paused. "They're just playing, trying to track us."

Back to Jim Corbett again. "The hunted hunts the hunter."

"Or the hunter hunts the hunted hunting him."

"Can you track *them*?"

"They replied from an untraceable location. Just like us."

"But that they answered, it proves they responded to the email."

"It proves nothing. We could have created the untraceable location ourselves."

"So I have to be the prey, and wait."

"And see how they want to deliver the ten million."

I was so tired of it all I almost wanted to give up. "Fuck it, let's find me a hole and send them after me."

"Not yet," Mitchell says, and rang off.

"NO GPS," Charity assured me, snapping her gum. "It's an old phone."

She'd pulled off the Diamond Head Highway by an overlook. Nothing there seemed out of normal, a few families with food hampers, two pickups talking story, a couple arguing in a blue Audi convertible; they'd all been there when we arrived. "The cops can still triangulate us," I said. "In seconds."

"You know what, Pono?" She slid a comforting palm down my forearm. "At some point you just got to trust her."

"Kim?"

"Your very own." She punched in Kim's number, still snapping her gum. "Hi Kim? This's Charity – that friend of Pono's? Yes," she smiled at me, "he *is* a total bastard. I don't know how you stood him, long as you did…"

I felt like a lamb between two wolves. "Just *tell* her," I begged silently.

"He's not with me right now, but wanted me to pass on what he's learned – yeah well me too, honey, but we don't need to go there…Anyway he wants you to know that Sylvia went to a Lanai Land Corporation benefit the night she died. And he asks can you look into that?" Charity popped her gum, listening to Kim. "And also Sylvia might have taken a taxi, her car was being fixed, and can you run down any taxi trips, you know, like from or to her place –"

I made a choking hand motion: *End it.*

"Yeah goodbye to you too, sweetheart," Charity added, "and all the worst. Speak up honey, don't be bashful…Okay sure I'll tell him…But you got to admit, he's a great lay –"

She dropped the phone in her bag. "She'll do it. Said they had no fucking idea Sylvia'd gone there. That since it was an accident they didn't look into her recent background or activities." She ran her hand soothingly up my wrist. "In a day or two, honey, you could be out of this."

That really spooked me. Not the idea of being out of danger but of imagining it could happen. Afghanistan teaches many things but the most important is this: *You're never in more danger than when you think you're safe.*

AFGHANISTAN OF COURSE made me think of Mitchell. He answered on the second ring like always. "Can you get into Lanai Land Corporation's email history?" I said.

"When you want?"

I explained him about her going to the benefit the night she died. "Any calls from a week before, to and from the Foundation to Lanai Land Corporation, any emails to Sylvia?"

"I may not get them all…"

Then the thought hits me: "Sylvia's laptop and notes disappeared –"

"You already explained me that," he says, making fun of me, "at least three times."

"But could you find her email history, like on a server somewhere?"

"If you took a board out in the waves could you ride it?"

"One more thing – can you get the calls on this number?" I gave him Joe Krill's cell, "for the five days after six a.m. April 27?"

Traffic was slowing ahead. The road was down to one lane each way, cars slowly getting through. "Maybe an accident," Charity said.

There were no side roads ahead, just a steep ragged cleft up the cliff and the ocean on the other, the blue flashing lights of cop cars in front of us but no fire trucks or ambulances. "Turn around!" I yelled, but the road was too clogged and we couldn't reverse in our own lane, cars blocking us ahead and behind.

"There's a shave ice stand about a half mile beyond this roadblock," I said. "Be there in twenty minutes." I got out and pretending to open my fly walked casually into the brush then sprinted up the cleft in the rocks, clambered to the top and ran along its jutting lava spurs till I could look down on the roadblock, the flashing lights and busy policemen small as Lego figures, a black unmarked Mustang like the one I'd been in with Kim.

"They weren't looking for you," Charity said after she'd pulled into the shave ice stand. "Said it was for stolen cars."

"Yeah," I said, trying not to breathe hard. "Sure."

TEN MINUTES LATER Kim calls. "What do you see in her," she snapped, "you don't see in me?"

I glanced at Charity intently driving and watching for cops, biting an edge of her lower lip in concentration, coils of auburn hair dangling down her temples. "There's nothing," I said low to Kim, "I don't see in you."

"Then how come you *see* her at all?"

I faced out my side window. "She's helping me. Just like you."

"I don't think so. She works for WindPower. She's a friend of Manny's, and more and more I'm thinking Manny was no friend of Sylvia's."

"What are you saying?"

"I checked the Lanai Land Corporation benefit? Sylvia never showed. The Lanai Land Corporation guy, Cruwell?"

"Gerry Cruwell –"

"Had his secretary call Sylvia at four-thirty that afternoon to confirm and she said she was coming. But they say she never showed."

"They say –"

"But, get this, she did take a taxi, at nine-ten p.m."

"Where to?"

"Hippolito Urbano's."

The Escher Stairs

NOTHING WAS TRUE anymore. My head spun. "*Why?*" I said to Kim. "Why would she go see Hippolito? How'd she even *know* him?"

"We haven't talked story with him. Not the right time yet."

I covered my other ear with my hand, trying to hear the phone over the traffic noise. "Lou Moreno."

"What about him?"

"Maybe that's how she knew Hippolito. Maybe Lou knew him."

"Maybe the whole weed shipment fiasco was set up by Hippolito?"

I motioned for Charity to stop the car. "But why?"

"Maybe Hippolito had him killed?"

I thought of Hippolito's patient kindness, how he'd protected me, his rule to never kill or hurt even your enemies. "He says you did it."

She half-laughed. "Yeah, right."

"He's been on my side, all through this."

"Yeah. Right."

I got out of the car, walked a few feet down the sidewalk, Charity watching me through her dirty windshield. "Kim?"

"Yeah?"

"Am I ever going to get out of this?"

"Maybe." She thought a while. "If they don't kill you first." She was silent; I thought she'd rung off. "I want to see you," she said.

That scared me. "What for?"

"I want to hold you, see you're okay. I want to talk you into coming in."

That scared me even more. "They'll drop all charges?"

"They drop the B&E on Sylvia's, but not on WindPower. And they want you for Lou Moreno."

"Did you do it?"

"You fuckhead, I never killed anybody."

"This sucks."

"I know. I'm working on it."

"How?"

"Let's see what Hippolito says."

"When you see him?"

"Tomorrow early."

"You trying to locate me?"

"We can't. You keep coming up empty. You're not there at all."

I remembered what Rico Morales said, that the Lanai Land Corporation guys who tried to kill me didn't kill Sylvia. And since Rico had no reason to lie, given that he planned to kill me anyway, I sort of believed him.

I explained Kim a little of this. "So if Lanai Land Corporation didn't kill her, who did?"

"That's what we're gonna discuss with Hippolito."

"But the conversations between my three perps..." I started to say then realized I'd never told her about Severina's recording of Simon, Gerry Cruwell and Hen Lu discussing how to "resolve" me, and that they hadn't done it "right" with Sylvia.

To tell Kim all this was to let her in on everything I'd learned from Hippolito, from Severina. Not to speak of what I was learning from Mitchell's coverage of the perps' emails and cell phones. That didn't seem like a good idea. Not yet.

"So let me know," I says, "what you learn from Hippolito." I didn't mention that I intended to see him first.

That was when Mitchell called back to give me the last number Sylvia called before her phone disappeared.

You already know: Hippolito.

Now I had him.

FIRST I WROTE a summary of everything I'd found out, the sordid links between WindPower, the Governor, High Stakes, Lanai Land Corporation and IEEC, the compromising conversations and emails, everything I could remember. And mailed hard copies to Kim, Mitchell, Marcus and Rebecca Wild on Hawaii, my buddy Tom Shapiro on Lanai, Tank on Molokai, and one to my old adversary Leon Oversdorf who was now trying so hard to find me. And I ended by saying I was on my way to see Hippolito, and if I disappeared he would be the reason.

"You used all my stamps," Charity said.

IT SEEMS I was always going back to Hippolito's because he'd done something that imperiled me but then he always convinced me he hadn't, that he'd been on my side. But this time was different: if Sylvia'd been there the night she died, he probably knew why she died. Or killed her. In which case he wouldn't mind killing me.

He'd first threatened to kill me if I didn't lead him to the ones who'd framed him with the boatload of weed. When I'd pulled out my knife at the Outrigger Club he'd pointed his gun at me but didn't fire.

He'd kept me at bay with lots of nice talk and a possibly faked recording from Severina, had tailed me but said it was for my own good, then said he'd protect me because I'd saved his nephew from getting gang-banged in the slammer, let me use his safe house. Just to keep tabs on me?

Was he waiting for the price on me to rise before he sold me to Lanai Land Corporation?

As usual the question was how to get past his security. Finally I did what I always did, called him up but got somebody else, maybe Victor, the guy who made martinis, or Virgilio Mendes, the one who'd tailed me. When Hippolito comes on I says, "Why'd Sylvia Gordon come your place, the night she died?"

I heard him scratch his chin in confusion. "Who the fuck this is? This you, Pono?"

"Who else?"

"What the fuck you asking me questions?"

"*Why?* That's all I want to know, Hippolito –"

"Why the fuck *what*?"

"Why she come there?"

"Where you at? Come in."

"Yeah so you can kill me too? *Why*, Hippolito?"

"Christ stop using that stupid word. It's too complicated."

"I'll come in. I've told lots of people I'm here, so you go down if I do."

"I'm not going down. I've told you that. So you won't either." There was the sound of him breathing into the phone as he pulled bolts and opened the door. He stepped out into the light. "So where the fuck are you Pono?" he calls.

AS USUAL we sit in a corner of the living room on the long white leather couch overlooking the sea. "So you really did suspicion me?" he says, chewing pistachios and putting the shells on the glass table. "Want a martini?" he says, not giving me time to answer, shakes his head as at some great mystery.

With the side of his palm he scraped the pistachio shells into an ashtray. "You got some balls to come here accusing me."

"The cops think *I* killed Sylvia."

He snorted. "That's a joke."

I watched him. "So why'd she come here?"

"Lou Moreno was in love with her." He stared toward the ocean, hands clasped, pensive and formal as an old don, a retired conquistador. "What a crazy kid. A great kid. I loved that kid, Pono," he turned toward me, "like he was my own."

"You *knew* him?"

"He was a kid I took care of, growing up. His Ma and Pa died when he was four or five, he spent a few years in foster homes, they beat him, didn't feed him right, then the last one moved away one day and didn't take him. He was fifteen then, when I heard about it. So I sorta adopted him. He grew up just fine, graduated University, was making good money as a diver…He'd only known Sylvia a couple weeks, he said. Was crazy about her."

I shook my head. "I never knew this –"

"The night she died he called me, asks can I send a guy to drive her to and from a meeting, she was going to some Lanai Land Corporation thing. But when I call her she tells me no, she's got a taxi coming in five minutes. So I says do me a favor come here first, pick up my car and driver, and she gets a little pissed at my intruding into her life. I'd only met her once, such a lovely girl. No, she says again, she's got some interview after the Lanai Land Corporation thing, somebody wanting to talk behind the scenes, an off-record guy. I says all the more reason to pick up my driver. She says that's silly, good bye. Last I ever heard from her."

"She never showed?"

"No. I didn't expect her to, after she told me no."

"Taxi driver says he dropped her here."

"If he did she never rung the bell. One time a little later I hear noises out front, so I go look and it's some couple arguing in a parked car on the far side of the turnaround. Go fight somewheres else I was going to yell at them, but it's sad when people are unhappy with each other, so I left them alone."

He popped a pistachio into his narrow mouth, looked at me a while. "Next day Lou calls, tells me she's dead. Even then, we thought she'd drowned on a midnight swim."

"Who was the off-record guy?"

"I'd like to know. But if she didn't make it to the benefit she didn't make it afterwards to meet with him."

"Maybe. Why didn't you report this?"

"To the cops?" He smiled at my naïveté, at a question too stupid to answer.

"We can track it down. The taxi."

"*We?*" His brows raised. "You and that cop cunt?"

"Since then you've done nothing."

"What do you mean *nothing*? We're helping you with it and working other angles you don't even know about."

"Sylvia felt threatened, wanted Lou to go with her."

"She didn't sound like that, when we talked. Anyway he couldn't. Some night dive he had to do."

"So who killed him?"

Hippolito smiled patiently. "They say you did."

"They?"

"Cops. The media. All that crowd."

That made me smile too. "So you know it's not true."

"Yeah," he smiled back. "I know it's not true."

"That's why you've helped me?"

"That and like I said, my nephew Inside." He squinted at me. "And because you help people, teach those foster kids, take care of wounded vets–"

"You know all that?"

"You think I didn't check you out, after Kapu asks me to meet you?"

"So who killed Sylvia? Who killed Lou?"

"For a while I actually thought your cop cunt –"

"Stop saying that."

"– was who did Lou but it wasn't." He sat back, looked across at me. "Only answer I've come up with is I don't know."

It was like Escher stairs, where each step leads logically to the next but never leads you anywhere, and when you look at the whole thing it's impossibly introverted, could never happen.

Hippolito walked back through the house with me to the door looking out on the turnaround. "I shouldn't have come here," I said.

"I don't give a shit they have you all points," he said. "I had no way of knowing. I don't read the paper any more. Don't give a damn about the news." He soft-punched my shoulder. "You're doing good. Use the safe place, you want."

"I will."

He looked over my shoulder at the street. "That car –"

"It's Manny's. He lent it to a friend who lent it to me. It's safe."

"The night I wanted Sylvia to come here, like I said, when I heard voices arguing and looked out, it was that car."

Badger Hole

T HAT'S WHEN Mitchell calls saying our perps offered five million for my locate. "So," he says, "I told them get lost."

I said goodbye to Hippolito and got in Manny's car. "Wait a minute," I says to Mitchell, "I thought we *wanted* them to deal."

"Yeah but for ten million."

I drove a few blocks and stopped. "Never happen."

"They have millions to throw around. They've bought the Governor and most of the Legislature and lots of mainland Senators and Congressmen, and the last thing standing between them and five billion dollars is this bungled operation to get rid of Sylvia. C'mon, Pono –"

"But *everybody's* against the damn project –"

"Just the people. But the politicians make the decisions. And they don't give a damn what the people want." He snorted. "Though they pretend to."

"So we tell the perps where I am, they come for me, I get them. Then we have proof."

"We'll find a badger hole that works for both of us." Meaning him in his wheelchair with two AKs and various other accoutrements.

"No, we need you in front of your computer. Inside their brain."

He thought about that a moment. "This really sucks."

He meant being crippled and not able to cover my back, go into the fight with me. "I know," was all I could say.

"We have to think terrain. What approaches they'll have…"

"Anybody I take –" I'd started to say *kill* but thought of Hippolito – "we need the path back to who they are. Who hired them."

"We have their emails and every number they talk to."

"Yeah but maybe do they know that? It's starting to worry me."

You could feel Mitchell shrug, over the phone. "Sooner or later we'll know."

A BADGER HOLE'S hard to find and easy to defend, where you can see but not be seen, control all your approaches yet have a choice of covert exits. As mentioned earlier, a badger's about the fiercest animal on earth, and that's the attitude you take.

Hippolito's safe house was one option, but if I still wasn't sure of Hippolito, why place myself in his hands? And who else might also know about it?

Another option was the mountain rain forests on Molokai, Maui or the Big Island. Trouble there was dogs: on the ground you're easy to track down.

Or an apartment, long as you had at least two hidden exits. Or a warehouse, or a somewhere on the docks. But anywhere you moved outside, a chopper could find you. And anywhere you went on foot the dogs would get you.

Staying safe also depends on how many people are after you. If it was just Rico's two buddies that was one thing – somebody who can't hunt you openly, has to be covert. But if it was the cops, they can do whatever they want, openly or covertly. And send hundreds of people after you if they want.

Being of a cautious and suspicious nature I long ago had sussed out a good place half way to Punaluu off Kamehameha Highway. There aren't many lava caves on Oahu, and no one even knows about this one. About two hundred feet mauka the highway on a volcanic rubbled slope is the stone foundation of an old farmhouse and fifty feet behind it a milking shed from back in the days when Hawaii had its own dairies. Inside the rear of the shed a small louvered door opens on a hole in the hillside about the size of a normal person's chest. It inclines sharply down into total darkness, a narrow long lava tube deep into the earth. It's nice and cool, and back in the day they maybe stored milk cans in there.

At first it's so narrow you have to inch along with your arms in front of you. After about two hundred feet you reach a circular room with a domed ceiling and a caved-in floor. With a rope and pitons I'd climbed the ceiling to a blowhole in its center and squeezed upit till it vented in a narrow slit opening further up the hillside. From this slit you had a good view of the hillside, the highway, the lower valleys and the ocean beyond. What you couldn't see was what was behind and above.

On my way back down the blowhole I'd pitoned a rope to the side, slid down and left it hanging. Any time I wanted I could climb it and pull it up behind me and no one would know I was there.

From the room with the domed ceiling a single corridor curves down to the left, about six feet high and eight wide, its smooth rippled walls colored iron-red and brown, with flow lines at varying heights from previous eruptions of lava. After about a quarter mile it ends in a slick steep cliff you can slip off and fall a hundred feet. This is where I'd put in a climbing ladder a few months before, to explore below.

So though my killers outnumbered me I had a safe exit and knew this place by heart. And they wouldn't even know what it was, or how to deal with it.

And because I knew it I could operate in total darkness, while they needed light.

I HADN'T GONE FAR when the phone buzzed again. "I been workin on Joe Krill," Kim says.

I pull in beside a warehouse, a tacky smell. "Like I said he's a lucky guy."

"He's gonna announce there was a mistake and two samples got mixed up. Sylvia's lung contents and one from somebody else. He's figured out how to do that, in the records. So you're the lucky guy."

I looked out at the damp dark street smelling of vegetable ordure, down at my dirty shorts and sweat-stained chest. "How's that?"

"Because how can they blame you if it was a swimming pool?"

"Just as easy."

"But it gets us one step closer."

"To what?"

"To finding who did it. That's the only way to prove you didn't."

"Why'd he change his mind?"

"He told his brother. It's an old Hawaii family. With a sense of honor. His brother was furious with him."

"So the brother loses his job."

"Not if Lanai Land Corporation goes down first." She cleared her throat. "Remember the taxi driver? We brought him in. Vietnamese guy, no English. The kind with a long thumbnail? Through a translator he says when he dropped Sylvia in front of Hippolito's a car was waiting. A small black car. We showed him lots of pictures but he couldn't pick one out."

"Show him a black Subaru."

"Why's that?"

"Manny's car. And Charity sometimes drives it."

"I told you that girl was trouble."

"And she knew Sylvia."

"*What*? How?"

"They met at WindPower when Sylvia interviewed Simon, had lunch a couple times, went out for drinks. Sylvia may have been fishing for info on WindPower. Oh, and Charity introduced Sylvia to Manny."

"So if we start at the beginning, Manny glommed on to Sylvia when she began working on Big Wind."

"And Manny lived in the same apartment complex as Charity, she borrows his car sometimes. The black Subaru."

"Oh fuck, shoot them all. They're all guilty."

"What do you make of this?"

"It's time for me to go see Manny."

"You should bring him in."

"For what?"

"Existing."

She snickered. "We do that for everyone who has it coming there'd be nobody left."

I told her goodbye because Mitchell was calling. "They agree," he said.

"To the five million?"

"Ten. I said we're going to trade you to the cops and they don't seem to want that."

Ludicrous that anyone would pay ten million just to kill me. *Hell*, I thought, *I'd do it myself for less.* "We'll route the funds via a Paki bank," Mitchell was saying, "one of the ones the Agency uses. Then to a construction account at Mehltidi Bank in Kuwait then an investment account in the Caymans. Once the money hits Mehltidi we give them your coordinates. The funds stay in Mehltidi escrow till they locate your coordinates and identify you."

"I'm supposed to let them *see* me?" I said in a *have you lost your mind* tone.

"No, stupid, leave some evidence of your recent presence, we'll have to think about it – something with your prints on it maybe –"

"I'm not worth ten million."

"Not you, but what you know."

"You too."

"They don't know about me. Not yet."

"These accounts, you set them up?"

"Amazing what you can do with modern technology. The banks think we're a small Dutch company that makes turbine bearings and is doing work in Pakistan."

NOT DARING to go back to Charity's I parked at the Waikiki Yacht Club. The gate to the slips was locked and well-lit with cameras on it, so I put my stuff in a plastic bag, walked beyond the lot and swam out to a slip with a lovely fat motorboat, no one aboard. I unzipped the canvas, crawled in and slept for five hours on the double bed in the master cabin, in the morning made coffee and toasted frozen croissants, borrowed a yachting outfit and a small backpack from the closet, a pen and yellow notepad from the desk, cleaned up, zipped her shut and strolled toward the parking lot in the clear plumeria-fragrant light.

Across car rooftops glinting with early sun I made out a tan Taurus with four guys in it parked near the Subaru. Then a gray Taurus beyond, same thing. As I slowly turned and backed away, all eight guys got out, one with a Belgian Shepherd on a leash. They spread across the parking lot, two coming my way.

Pretending to have a phone at my ear I walked toward the harbor then along a dock till they were behind me. When I glanced back they were going boat to boat. If I'd left five minutes later they'd of had me. That pissed me off. At myself.

Now I had no vehicle. And couldn't return to Charity's. How the cops found the car I couldn't figure. Unless Charity told them.

Though hadn't I just told Kim?

In my yachting duds I walked an hour in the sweaty sun to Clyde Fineman's. "You're a famous guy," he says.

"It's getting worked out. I'm not guilty of anything."

"You never are." A quick grin. "So, what you want? You didn't visit to be nice."

I glanced toward his garage. "You drive that Sportster much?"

"All the time." He realized, stopped. "You want to use it?"

"Or anything. I'm temporarily out of wheels."

"Take it."

I'm not fond of Harleys and don't like the noise they make but they work just fine once you figure what all the switches and dash lights do and how to turn off the stereo, and long as you forget there's a quarter ton of steel flying down the road under your crotch.

I parked it in a eucalyptus grove a half mile past the Badger Hole, took a ten-inch crescent wrench from the Harley's tool kit and hiked up to the old milking shed. It looked disused as ever. The spider web across the door hadn't been broken. I turned the wood latch on its rusty nail, opened the door and stepped inside. Ten stalls on each side, pitted concrete floors and withered wooden dividers with their whitewash nearly gone, a hay bin at one end littered with rat droppings and alfalfa dust.

I called Mitchell, told him to give the perps my coordinates, then sat at the bottling table by the door and on the notepad wrote, *To the Honolulu Post from Pono Hawkins*, dated today, followed by a few paragraphs proclaiming my innocence and who had really killed Sylvia.

I stopped mid-sentence with a quick slash of the pen, dropped the pen on the ground and let the chair topple back. I stuck the crescent wrench in my back pocket, opened the louvered door and slid down the lava tube to the room with the domed ceiling, climbed the rope up the blowhole and pulled it up behind me and stretched out on the warm stone to watch through the slit for guests.

The noon sun gleamed down on the blue ocean and the rugged green hills and ebony cliffs of Molokai and Lanai. For an instant I remembered the old stories of warriors who dared attack Molokai dying in their canoes before they reached the shore, and wondered if maybe it was true.

My phone vibrated in my pocket. "You seen today's *Post?*" Mitchell says.

"*How* am I going to –" I started.

He cut me off. "The Coroner recanted. Says two samples got mixed, there was fresh water in Sylvia's lungs."

I couldn't tell him I already knew. "That doesn't change anything."

"Yes it does! Here's why: The latest email from Simon to Gerry Cruwell, with a cc to Hen Lu, quote: *Noted your latest screwup in today's Post. Will conference you and HL re this at 3 pm today. Be ready to explain and provide recovery strategy. You, and we, must be entirely blameless in this matter*, unquote."

"We can prove they make the call," I said, "but we won't know what they say."

"What matters is they're getting scared. And when you're scared you make mistakes."

I looked back out the slit: no change. It made me think of the tiny gap in their helmets medieval knights could see through as they fought to death with swords and sledge hammers, and of the *hijab* Muslim women have to wear, their slit of sunlight. I didn't like being contained like this, but told myself I had a safe exit.

Simon Says

SEVENTY-TWO MINUTES later my guests arrived.

A maroon Land Cruiser with a surfboard rack pulled off the road below the dairy farm. Four guys got out, went to the back of the Land Cruiser and took out black shoulder bags. They could have been Korean, all slender and muscular. All wore dark aloha shirts, dark sweatpants and black running shoes. Two were scanning the hillside with binoculars; a third climbed the slope toward the milking shed holding a GPS in front of him.

I killed my phone and slid further back in my hole. The driver drove the Land Cruiser back down the row of eucalyptus to the highway and turned toward Oahu. The four guys pulled handguns from their bags. Two stayed outside while the other two went into the milking shed and came out a minute later, one holding my note. They were talking fast but I couldn't make out the words. One was speaking on a phone in a high singsong. He sounded angry.

They fanned out and began to search the slopes around and above me. Lying by the slit I heard one's feet rustle past, a crunch of dry grass and the slick whisper of his clothes. I feared for a moment he'd seen the slit but he kept climbing, steadily and effortlessly.

After a while all four gathered round the milking shed for more aggrieved phone talk. Three went inside and searched again, must have opened the louvered door for there was much loud talking and the fourth went in too. Finally one came out and sat on an old upside down milking can in the sun, and soon I could hear voices in the lava tube coming toward the domed room beneath my blowhole.

Mentally I counted them again: one had driven off in the Land Cruiser, one was on guard outside, so three should be in the tube. After a couple of minutes dim lights began to play across the sweaty cold rock of my blowhole, then they were in the domed room below, whispering to each other.

If they had flashlights that meant they needed one hand to carry them, and with the slippery footing and frequent handholds maybe they'd holstered their guns. But when I took a quick glance down the blowhole one passed beneath with an LED headlamp that he then flashed up the blowhole and nearly caught me.

They stopped whispering and I could hear their footfalls in the curving lava corridor. After three minutes I slid down the rope, tied it against a lava pillar out of sight to one side, and followed my three guests down the corridor toward the subterranean cliff.

Coming around the curve in darkness I could see their headlamps darting over the roof and walls ahead. They were moving fast and silently; I tried not to look at their lights and kill my vision.

As I got closer I saw they'd stopped at the cliff by the rope ladder. *Go, you bastards*, I urged them. *Go!*

They did as they were told. Two went over the side down the rope ladder, their voices echoing up from the cavern below. I waited till they reached bottom then crept up in the dark and whacked the third guy hard on the temple with the crescent wrench, grabbed him before he slid off the edge and took his headlamp, gun and shoulder bag. With the wrench I unbolted the top of the ladder from the two pins I'd set into the rock and let it slide over the edge. It made a great slap when it hit bottom and the two guys below started yelling. I cuffed my friend hands to feet backwards with his own flexcuffs, turned off the headlamp and headed back up the corridor watching for a light ahead.

In the domed room I climbed up the blowhole to my slit, pulled up the rope and checked outside. The fourth Korean was pacing in front of the milking shed, gun on his hip. The Land Cruiser was still absent.

If I came out of the lava tube into the milking shed the remaining Korean would probably shoot me. An alternative would be to break open the rocks of my slit and work my way downhill in hopes of dealing with him.

At this instant he turned resolutely into the milking shed and I could soon hear him laboriously clambering down the lava tube toward the domed room. Now I either had to wait for him to go past the room and down the long corridor, or break out of my slit. Either way once I was out I could lock the louvered door, pile something against it and shut him in with his friends.

I glanced through the slit at the bright hills, black rocks, snaky road and blue-white sea, kicked the rocks free of the slit and stood up in the warm afternoon sun, stretched and took a deep breath.

"No move," said a voice behind me.

This was the end. I would die. I raised my arms slowly. His steps came closer. "Where are they?"

"They?"

"My guys." He whacked me across the back of the skull with his gun, a stupid move for two reasons: one, it hurt – and that pissed me off – and two, it turned the muzzle away from my head giving me time to grab the gun and smash his wrist with the crescent wrench. He doubled up over his broken wrist. "Who's paying you?" I screamed at him.

He snorted with disgust at the question. My skull howled with pain; I hungered to shoot him and he knew it. I pointed at the milking shed. "Get down there."

I took his phone and made him crawl into the lava tube. "Keep crawling all the way in the dark till you get to a round room. Stay there. If you come back I'll shoot you."

When he was a good ways down the tube I locked the louvered door, flipped over the bottling table and dragged it against it. One by one I carried lava boulders from the pasture outside and piled them on the inverted table until there was no way anyone could open that door.

I drove Clyde's Harley a few miles, pulled in behind a Burger King and told Mitchell what happened. "Now we have them," he said. "We sent them an email, they responded by wiring money to locate you, then sent people to kill you. That locks it up."

"Like you said, when you're scared you make mistakes."

"You were scared, down there."

"We're always scared, guys like us."

"But you didn't make mistakes."

"Yeah I did. I thought the fifth guy had gone but he drove around to come down from above. Stupid."

"Yeah, that *was* stupid," Mitchell said thoughtfully. "Amazing how tiny things make the difference, life and death, a few seconds…" and we were both thinking not only of my surviving the fifth Korean but also that if in Afghanistan Mitchell had been a few feet further from where the RPG hit, a truck would have blocked it and he wouldn't be in a wheelchair now. But there was no point of saying *it's not fair* or anything like that, because *not fair* makes no difference in this world.

NEXT I CALLED KIM and explained her about the Koreans and where they were. "Can you send some guys down there, bring them in, hold them a while?"

"On what charge? Trespassing? I don't see how –"

"These may be the guys who killed Sylvia."

She thought a moment. "They do any damage?"

"Damage? To the *cave*?"

"It coulda been used by the ancient Hawaiians…Pillaging our cultural sites, ain't that a federal offense?"

I couldn't explain her about Mitchell without risking his job, and didn't want anyone to know we had cracked the perps' emails, or what Simon had emailed to Cruwell and Hen Lu. So I repeated the basics: these were the perps who killed Sylvia, and probably Lou, and tried to kill me.

"On this evidence, not all that indictable." Her voice softened. "Pono, let *us* take over now –"

"I got one more thing to do."

"I don't like hearing that –"

"You got a stun gun, something like that?"

"A Taser? We all got em."

"Lend me one?" I had two guys to bring down yet keep alive to tell their stories. Unlike a stun gun a Taser can hit from fifteen feet and its fifty thousand volts will knock you down for several minutes, freezing your muscles. Hurts like Hell, too. It's legal in forty-five states but not Hawaii, not that that concerned me right now.

"I can't, Honey." Whenever she says *Honey* I know she's lying.

"Make a deal?"

"I don't do deals."

"You give me a Taser and twenty-four hours and I'll come in."

She thought about this, the odds of my surviving with a Taser as opposed to without, the promise of my coming in. "I don't do deals like that," she says.

"What other kinda deals you do?"

"How far are you from our place?" she says. By *our place* she means where we used to meet up sometimes, just to say hi.

So ten minutes later I park the Harley behind Queen Emma's Summer Palace and meet her in our favorite alley. "I shouldn't do this," she says as I hold her, not wanting to let go.

She was loving and beautiful but scared and not wanting to show it. "If you come in now," she said, clasping my face in her hands, "we can pick up whoever you want, question them –"

"That won't do it."

She looked up at me near tears, and I realized she didn't think I'd make it. "I'm hours away from finishing this," I whispered. "Help me." It sounded plaintive but was true. I was burned out, beyond exhaustion, couldn't figure what else to do next.

From her handbag she pulls a heavy weapon like a handgun, in a nylon holster. "It's an M-26," she says. "The latest one. Don't hit anybody more than once. It's a drop, nobody knows about it. So when you're done get rid of it. I don't want to see it again."

My whole body ached to be with her, just to feel her touch. "See you," I called, ran out the front so she'd think I was on foot then circled back for the Harley.

Soon as she drove off I called Charity. "Simon there?"

"Where else?"

When are you leaving tonight?"

"Same as ever. But oh," she said, "I have a date –"

"Doesn't matter, you and I can catch up later."

"It's only Manny, he got two tickets for the Jimmy Buffet concert."

"Before you leave the office, can you let me in? If Simon'll be there-"

"He'll be here. Something big has hit the fan and he's here all the time now. Him and Damon both."

"Damon there now?"

"He's picking up the Hong Kong guy at the airport. They're all flying to Lanai tomorrow."

"So we meet at your office door, seventeen-seven?"

"Seventeen-seven?"

"Five-oh-seven." I hopped on Clyde's Harley and headed downtown into a fine rain that glistened on the oily road and hissed under the tires. A double rainbow rose over Honolulu and for a few moments it even seemed a lovely town.

I BARELY HAD TIME to drop off the Korean's phone with Mitchell. "Can you send another email?" I says.

"To who?"

"Our perps. That I've moved and here's the new locate."

"They won't bite twice."

"They might."

"Where at?"

"A container down in the Matson docks."

"It's all concertina wire down there. You'll never get in."

"Yeah I will. And so will they. It's their last chance to get me."

"Who's they?"

"Two guys I met on Molokai. Friends of the guys who tried to drown me. Maybe even one of them."

"Who they with?" Mitchell sighed, like *this is too much.*

"If we assume the Koreans worked for Hen Lu, these guys must work either for WindPower or Lanai Land Corporation. Or both." I caught a breath. "Oh, and I've got a phone for you. From the guy that drove the Land Cruiser."

"The one who came down the hill behind you." Mitchell turned the phone over in his big hand. "Be interesting, see what numbers he called."

"Gotta run," I said, and headed downtown, as with every time I left Mitchell, feeling I owed him more.

AS CHARITY came out the WindPower office door she let me in, gave me a quick smile and a whiff of lovely perfume. "Still there," she whispered, eyes flashing to the side. I shut the door silently, did a quick check of the other corridors then went silently along the executive corridor toward Simon's office.

Two offices, one after the other on the right, then a little room on the left with a coffee machine, table and whining refrigerator. Noise of someone humming. A bigger office on the right, leather swivel chair and expansive desk. Damon's. Nobody there.

One door straight ahead.

Simon was bent over his screen examining something, his back to me. His skull was pale and freckled with a few long hairs straggling up. He wore a blue-stripe shirt. He was humming *My eyes have seen the glory of the coming of the Lord*. The screen showed a Google Earth shot of a hilly, rocky landscape and a road below.

It was my GPS locate, where the five Koreans had just tried to kill me.

I buried my fingers in his spindly neck hard enough to numb him, got him on the carpet and cuffed both wrists behind him to the opposite ankles so he looked like a Cornish game hen ready for the oven. "You make a fuckin noise I'll kill you," I informed him, and from the wide look in his eyes he seemed to believe me.

"Who killed Sylvia?" I asked. "Who sent those goddamn Koreans after me?"

His eyes got wider. "I did *nothing*, don't know what you mean –"

I thought of how tough he'd sounded on Severina's recording, talking to his buddies about killing me. I sank my fingers into his biceps till his eyes bulged. "You explain me everything, you live. Otherwise," I nodded at the balcony, "I toss you over."

Even in the poor light you could see him blanch, making me remember what Charity had said, *Crazy that he took the office with the balcony – he never goes out there 'cause he's afraid of heights.* So I picked him up by a cuffed arm and lugged him out there.

"Please," he said. "Let's go inside, let's talk."

I bent him over the rail, tiny streets and cars and flashing lights. "This is where you're headed," I says, "if you *don't* talk." I took another look at the street far below. Flashing lights. On the car roofs. Cops. Right downstairs.

I shoved him half over the rail. "*Who* killed her?"

He began to vomit, little crying gasps. "I don't know please…"

I dropped him on the balcony and raced from the office and fast and silent down the back stairs, listening for steps coming up. Some of them would be in the elevator but the real danger was the stairs.

Halfway down, twentieth floor maybe, you could hear them coming. Rubber soles slapping the concrete stairs, panting voices, rattle of uniforms. I ducked into the corridor till the feet thudded by, then ran all the way down to the eighth floor, had to dive inside again, stood there panting in the bright corridor as a man and woman embracing pushed suddenly apart and stared at me.

"Sorry," I says running through the cubicles to a far corridor down the opposite staircase, the last story full of cigarette butts and the song of birds and I come out into the blinding sunset watching everywhere for cops, wiping away sweat and trying not to gasp too hard, trying to look like any other passerby on Alakea Street.

The building's security cameras were what caught me, I decided later as I stopped to buy a little portable radio, plastic bag and roll of duct tape, unable to think of a safe place or how to get there, afraid any other shopper could be the one to turn me in.

And now I'd never get near Cruwell or the other perps. Now they'd all be waiting for me.

Containment Strategy

I HID the Harley in a stinky alley behind the Pacific fish plant figuring nobody would go near the place, sprinted across Nimitz Freeway between the fast-moving headlights and down to the waterside, shoved everything in the plastic bag and swam out to the far end of the Matson pier where a storm drain from the pier exits underwater.

It has a rusty cage over the outflow to keep people out but there are holes big enough to squeeze through if you can hold your breath that long. Then if the drain isn't full you can get your head above water and swim then crawl the hundred feet up to the inflow grate on the pier where there's another battered rusty screen you can squirm through.

A wide alley runs down the middle of the pier with rows of containers stacked on either side. Some stacks were butted tight; others had space between them, sometimes enough to squeeze into. In such a narrow space between two stacks I set up the little radio, tuned it low to a sports talk station so you could barely hear the rumble of male voices, checked the GPS, hunted around till I found three bottle caps, then sat on the concrete edge of the pier with my feet over the side and called Mitchell to give him my new coordinates. "These guys won't bite again," I said, "after what happened today."

"Here's what I told them," he said. "*Will provide new coordinates. Please advise what problem you had this afternoon. You may have a foreign virus in your system.*" I thought that might motivate them —"

"You *sent* that? What about Charity! What if they think it's her!"

"They'd never think that – we know too much."

"So does she!"

"Don't make sense, why would she…Where *is* she?"

"On a date. With Manny."

Mitchell huffed, and I knew he was thinking *what I would've done with a woman like that.* "Manny don't know what to do with women," I said.

"Maybe *he* killed her?"

"Never. He was crazy about her. She was killed by WindPower, Lanai Land Corporation, and High Stakes. We have the evidence – their emails, the phone numbers called, Severina's recording –"

"But if it's illegally obtained it can't be used."

"And we've got the Koreans."

"Which reminds me there's a new email from Simon to Hen Lu and Cruwell: *She wants us there at nine so we meet 7:30 HNL private terminal. Damon will fly us to Molokai…*"

"Who's *she*?"

"Old lady Steale?"

"She's on Lanai. Why would they all go to Molokai?"

"They're working on a containment strategy?"

"If we can prove they're calling Gerry Cruwell, or he's calling them, and we've already proved they came to kill me –"

"That's what the email history will say."

I sighed, beyond exhaustion. "Sometimes winning is so hard by the time you get there you don't care."

"We aren't there yet."

"When you're scared you make mistakes," I said again, more to myself than him. "And when you're tired, too."

What I was really thinking about was what if Sylvia's killers thought Charity was the "foreign virus" in their system? And that she was out somewhere with Manny.

A BLACK NEEDLE BOAT slipped quietly out of the night and tied up at the pier. Two guys got out and climbed the cyclone fence, cut the concertina wire and hopped down on the inside. One was tall, burly and light-haired, the other shorter and slender and moved like a cat. Both had night goggles, short-barreled shotguns and probably handguns and other crap.

I felt very lonely, the kind of scared that goes up your spine and makes your arms and legs weak, afraid I'd made the wrong choice, thinking how many more things turn out bad than we like to remember, and feared this was something that was going to turn out bad.

They moved silently down the center aisle between the containers, one patrolling each side row to the end then back to the center. I followed them, staying out of sight when they moved down the center and advancing when they checked the side rows. After they'd done this several times, meeting up in the center then going down the next aisle, one on each side, the tall one signaled to the other and pointed toward the distant voices on my little radio. They leaned together conferring a few moments then the tall one turned right, toward the voices, as the other moved left between the rows in a flanking maneuver.

I followed the guy to the left one row behind him, waited till he reached the far end, tossed a bottle cap onto the concrete and as he swung toward it out of sight of his partner I Tasered him good and he went down with a *whump*. I grabbed his weapons, taped his wrists behind him to his ankles, taped his mouth and locked him in an empty container.

The Taser had made the usual little *clack* and I feared the other guy had heard, then caught a glimpse of him moving between the rows ahead of me, closing in on the radio. Row by row I moved up behind him and when he stopped to listen for his buddy I zapped him good, took his guns and taped him like the other guy.

This was the big guy that long ago someone, I couldn't remember who, said was a Russian and had a piece missing from his ear. I flashed my headlamp on his ugly pain-contorted face – yeah, the right earlobe was short by a good inch.

He was starting to quiver as he came out of it, a violent muscle-rigid shake. When he stopped hyperventilating, I said in a friendly fashion, "My buddies are chatting with your friend. If they keep Tasering him I'm afraid he'll die, so maybe you can help us…"

He said nothing. "You just got one way out of here," I went on, explained him I needed to know who he worked for, but as usual he didn't know, so I Tasered him again and he remembered more, till we got to the final question: "How'd you guys kill Sylvia?"

Silence, then, "That is shit."

"Explain me."

He explained me all right. Turns out far as I could tell they worked for some guy who worked maybe for somebody on Lanai or maybe in Honolulu but they had nothing to do with killing anybody. He'd never killed anybody, all his life. Strangely he had an Arab accent, not Russian.

I remembered a little of the Koran in Arabic, from Afghanistan and then my first time Inside when I wanted to understand the mindset of a man who would burn his own daughter alive. "Where you from," I asks in bad Arabic.

Again he jumps. We dance around the question a bit more but when I offer to electronically stimulate his memory he says, "Cairo."

"Who killed my dog and cat? And nailed their heads on my wall?"

"I am sorry to hear of this," he said. "This is not my style."

"So who did it?"

He tried to shrug. "No one I know could do such a thing."

"Who hired you?" I repeat.

"I do not know, honest. This one guy he calls me, voice on the phone. Maybe he work for somebody on Lanai, maybe here in Honolulu."

"How do you contact him?"

"I never do. Only he calls. The money's always a drop somewhere, cash."

"What'd he want you to do?"

"One hundred thousand, he promised to me."

"For what?"

He tried to shrug, like the answer was obvious. "Kill you."

"Then what?"

"Take you out deep, give you to the sharks. I am sorry about this."

I locked him in another container, threw all their weapons down the drain, took the cigar boat to shore, picked up the Harley and raced to Charity's place.

She wouldn't have Manny's black Subaru because the cops had no doubt impounded it after they'd looked for me at the Yacht Club. But her tan Honda wasn't in the parking lot either. Nor did she answer the door, and when I climbed the roof and dropped down on the lanai, her apartment was empty.

The Voice

I WAS GOING NUTS trying to find Charity. She wasn't home and not answering her phone and all I knew was she'd been out with Manny the night before while I was dealing with my two pursuers down on the docks. This worried me because Sylvia had died after being with Manny, and if there was a link then Charity could be next in line.

So I headed for Manny's. On the way I called and woke Mitchell to explain him that my two pursuers were contained and I was going to call Kim to have someone bring them in. "What's with Charity?" he says, sleepy-voiced.

"Can't find her."

"You call her?"

"Goes to voice mail."

My second call got Kim asleep with her husband. She was pissed off and rough-voiced and I heard her get out of bed and turn on the light somewhere and say, "Oh shit," and sat down and said, "*What*, Pono?"

I explained her *what*, that I had these two guys in Matson containers, seventh and twelfth rows from the end of Aisle Eleven and if the Koreans didn't kill Sylvia then these guys did.

"Christ, couldn't you wait till morning?"

"You might get the whole story from these guys." I explained her more about the three perps, the Governor and IEEC.

"So *what*, you have these emails," she snapped, "and call logs and some recording made by an escort service, and we're supposed to convict somebody for Sylvia's death based on that? When we're not so sure she was killed?"

"The fresh water in her lungs –"

"But you don't have enough to nail anybody. Except yourself. And even if you can prove you didn't kill Sylvia, you're still suspected of killing Lou."

"What motive would I have had?"

"You went to see him, lady doing her laundry saw you leave, then he was dead."

"He was already dead."

"That's when you shoulda called us."

"Leon would've arrested me."

"He still will."

"When do you go on duty?"

"Noon."

"Let's go see Manny."

"Whatever for?"

"Charity was out with him last night and now she's disappeared."

"Good. Maybe she stays disappeared."

"*Kim –*"

"What time's it?"

"Almost five." I gave her Manny's auntie's address. "Can you be there by six?"

She yawned. "Fuck you, Pono. You've ruined another day."

WHEN I PULLED UP in front of Manny's auntie's I tried Charity again. She answered on the seventh ring. "Where the Hell you been?" I almost screamed at her.

"Pono!" she says, "calm down!"

"I been calling all night for you! I was worried about you!"

"I can take care of myself. In case you haven't noticed."

"Where've you been, dammit!"

"What, are you jealous?"

"You were out with Manny –"

"He wanted me to go home with him and I wouldn't."

"His auntie's place?"

"Then he wanted to go to my place and I still said no. I didn't want to sleep with him. He grabbed me and tried to pin me down so I clawed him good."

"You didn't go home – I been trying for hours, went by your place –"

"I got so spooked I went to my friend Linda's place, slept on the couch…"

"Why didn't you answer your damn phone?" I was still yelling at her, tried to calm down.

"It died. I had to recharge it, plugged it in the kitchen by the toaster. I couldn't hear it."

I wanted to strangle her. "God I'm happy you're okay…"

"He spooked me, Manny did. Like I said, I think he killed Sylvia."

"You may be right. I'm going to see him now. Anything I should ask him?"

"Yeah. Ask him why he's such an asshole."

"When WindPower goes down, you're going to be out of a job. Got any money?"

She got cautious. "A little."

"I do too. Let's go somewhere –"

"New Zealand?"

"I can enter surfing competitions, make enough to stay alive –"

"Sounds like Heaven."

Kim came up behind me. "Who you talkin to?"

"Gotta go," I told Charity. "Friend of Manny's" I said to Kim, "who doesn't like him anymore," and banged the big brass loop on Manny's auntie's mahogany door.

"That bitch is trouble and you know it," Kim said. "Why you keep calling her?"

Manny opened the door, ashen-faced and sleepy.

"We got good news for you," Kim said.

He stared at her, not focusing. I realized he wore contacts, hadn't put them in. Four long red scratches ran down the left side of his face.

"Can't you come back later?" He tried to look at his watch but it wasn't on his wrist.

"We know how much you cared about Sylvia," Kim said. "And wanted you to know we may have found her killers."

He scratched the top of his head. "Good."

"There's a few things you can help us with, about Lou. So we can tie that up too." She smiled encouragingly. "Sorry to come so early, but it's important to do it now. Can we come in, sit down?"

"Sure," he hesitated, trying to consider options. "Whatever."

We sat in the living room, Manny on the loveseat with his robe wrapped tight.

"So Manny," she says, "when'd you last see Lou?"

"Like I told *you*," he pointed at me, "it was a few days after Sylvia died."

"What'd you talk about?"

"Sylvia a little. But it got really too painful…" He tugged at his robe. "About his work, a little."

"Diving?"

"Yeah," Manny almost grinned. "If that's what you call it."

"How'd you end up friends with the guy who stole your girlfriend?"

"Well you see he didn't *really*. It was more sister-brother, what they had."

"So who called who first?"

This startled him. "Oh, you mean *that*? Well, he called me."

"What'd he say?"

"Said he had some stuff of hers, did her family want it. I told him Sylvia had no family except some cousins in Iowa, I'd send it to them. He asked can he bring it over, so he did."

"Did he seemed worried, concerned, about anything?"

Manny shrugged. "Just Sylvia."

"So why," she backed off, "would anyone kill him?"

Manny smiled devilishly. "Lou ran drugs."

"What kinda drugs?"

"Big Island weed to Oahu. By boat."

"That didn't make him worry about anybody? Anything?"

"He said he was safe because he'd revealed the whole operation in an email that would go out if anything happened to him."

"He told you all this, from when he barely knew you?"

"People feel confident with me. Safe."

"So who killed him?"

"Whoever he bought from, sold to or competed with." He cocked his head. "Can you go now?"

"Did that email get sent out, telling everyone?"

"You'd be the one to know."

Kim got up. "You sent Sylvia's stuff that Lou gave you to her cousins in Iowa?"

"Not yet."

"Can we see it?"

"You know what, I threw it away." Manny spread his hands in explanation. "Hurt too much to keep."

I got up too. "How'd you get those scratches down your face?"

"Oh that." He fingered them gently. "Darn kiawe trees. All those thorns."

"Charity give them to you?"

"Charity? I haven't seen the bitch."

"Explain me again, how you met Sylvia?"

He swung on me. "I did not."

Kim sat down. "Did not what?"

"We know the truth," I said. "Just want to hear your version of it."

"I could call my lawyer –"

"For Chrissake Manny," she leaned toward him, hand on his knee, "no one's accusing you of anything. But with your help we can nail these guys not just for Sylvia but for Lou's death too. But we need to move fast –"

I swear he gulped. The shining path to salvation had opened before him. "Totally accidental how I met her. I'd done a little surveillance, private dick stuff, sometimes got calls, can you do this, do that, find me info on such and so, you know the drill..."

He sat back, fingers laced over crossed knees. "So I get this call, guy saying his niece got some threats from an old boyfriend...he wanted someone watching over her. Without her knowledge of course, because she'd be furious. And I was to report to him every morning on what she did the day before."

"You followed her day and night?" Kim said.

"Just from after work till she went to sleep."

"How'd this guy find you?" I said.

"My website. Amazing, all the calls I get."

"So how'd you report to him?"

"I called a number. Never was anyone there, I just read out my report and hung up. After Lou died the number didn't work anymore."

"You have it? The number?"

"Five three seven nineteen forty-two. But like I said, it doesn't work anymore."

"How much he pay you?"

Manny glanced at me superciliously. "Two grand a week."

"Wow," Kim put in, "she musta been in some danger."

"Though I never saw anyone stalking her." He grinned, "'cept me of course."

"How'd he pay you?" I said.

"A hundred twenties in an envelope, he'd call and say where it was."

"How many weeks you do this?"

"Till she died. Five, maybe? Yeah, I got paid for five weeks. After that nothing…No point in surveillance on a dead person, is there?"

"But she was going out with you?"

"I took her out a few times, just a beer, you know. She never knew."

"Never knew what?"

"That I was reporting to him."

I watched him. "What was she like to sleep with?"

He glanced away. "I know I told you I did, but I didn't. She wouldn't let me." He checked out a dolphin mosaic on the wall then added, "So when I realized she was…It made the difference."

Kim waited. "She was *what*?"

"Doing sex with him."

"Lou?"

"Yeah." Manny sat upright. "Now I never *thought* she was sleeping with Lou Moreno – why would she? What could she see in *him*? Foster kid, scrapes out his living selling drugs? I thought Sylvia was into manhood. Sylvia was into males."

"Like you."

"Could have been me, coulda been some other heavy-duty guy. She got me."

"Lucky girl," Kim says.

"So that made a difference?" I says.

"In how I thought about her, you know. She wasn't right anymore."

"What did that mean?" Kim asked encouragingly.

He put his hands flat on the table. They were big and strong-fingered. "It meant I had to find someone else. That Sylvia was a false hope, a what do you have in the deserts, one of those –"

"Mirages?"

"Yeah, that's it."

"Weren't you angry at her for screwing Lou? Didn't she *need* to be punished?"

He smiled that huge gold tooth. "Yeah but God punishes. *We* don't have to."

"Did she get punished?"

Again the wide smile. "Ended up dead, didn't she?"

"The night she died," I said, "what were you and she fighting about?"

He looked at me sharply. "We *never* fought."

"The night she took a taxi to Hippolito Urbano's, but you got there first?"

"I don't know *anyone* named that. *I* didn't go there."

"C'mon, Manny. You and she were arguing in your car, the black Subaru."

He sat silent a moment. "This is nuts. I'm calling my lawyer."

"You know what that does, Manny?" Kim said. "That makes you a suspect. Anyone who calls a lawyer has something to hide. So what you hiding?"

He looked at her primly. "I have nothing to hide."

"So who killed her?"

"Yeah," he nodded. "That's the sixty-four thousand dollar question… you know *those* game show questions were rigged, don't you? Like what *you're* throwing at me."

"Whoever killed her, Manny," Kim said, "didn't she have it coming?"

"Oh she did," he sat back. "She *sure* had it coming."

I looked at his big strong hands. "So who you think the guy is, who called you – paid you all that money?"

He flashed that phantom smile. "Why don't you ask Charity?"

Kim leaned suddenly at him. "What did you and Sylvia argue about, sitting in the car that last night?"

He sighed, looked out at the magical view but didn't seem to see it. "I'm guiltless in all this."

"We know that, Manny," Kim said, "just explain us how it happened."

"It was after I'd watched her the night before, you know. Doing sex with him."

"Because the Voice told you to –"

"So when the taxi dropped her off, you know, I was waiting." He got a faraway look in his eyes, and I wondered how many times he'd fantasized it, the last scene with Sylvia.

"How'd you kill her, Manny?" Kim said softly. "I know she deserved it, but to get the credit you have to say how."

He looked surprised, smiled the gold tooth. All that was unscrupulous and evil, all that hurt other beings gratuitously, seemed to beam from him like a beacon. It was in his greasy sweaty brow and hairy crossed knees. "She had it coming," he repeated, more to reassure himself than us.

With a beatific smile he glanced out at the azure pool beyond the lanai. "That's the water," he said proudly, "they found in her lungs." He nodded again, and for a moment I misunderstood it as regret, but no, it was awareness of his place in fate, his role in human destiny. Due to him Sylvia would never "do" sex again with another man, her very genes excised from our race before they could create another life.

"How'd you get her to come with you," I said, trying to control the urge to kill him, "when you were parked outside Hippolito's?"

He looked at me. "You're not the only person with a gun."

"She was a tough girl," Kim said. "How'd you hold her down?"

He looked at her quizzically as if the answer was obvious. "I pushed her in, jumped on top of her and did it." He smiled. "She fought a lot."

"Why'd you take her to the beach?"

"Oh to cover up the traces. Even though she needed to be punished, killing her was still illegal, you know."

"But you followed your own star, didn't you, Manny?" Kim said.

He nodded with a martyr's pride and I wondered two things: why should we have to feed and house this man for the rest of his life? And could he get released before he died? But I was reassured to remember that once they get Inside, killers of young women and children don't often live long. Even Inside has its morals, often more than outside.

"We want you to come downtown, Manny," Kim said. "And explain this more." While she called for backup and read Manny his rights I went out on the lanai and called Mitchell to track down any calls between Manny, Lou and Sylvia the week before she was killed, and also between Manny and Lou after she died.

Just then my nemesis arrived – good old Leon Oversdorf. I almost jumped off the lanai and headed for the hills. "Morning, Pono," Leon says. "You're overdue for a piss test."

I felt my whole world collapse, imagined never surfing again. "You going to bring me in?"

Leon gave me that lugubrious smile like he was being fed to the lions but was being Christian about it. "I could have done that days ago, when you were at the yacht basin in that ridiculous boat of yours."

This got me mad. "She's a fine boat."

"I wanted to give you plenty rope to hang yourself. Instead you hung Manny."

Mitchell called back. "Manny called Lou seven times the week after Sylvia died."

"Lou didn't call him?"

"Never. Manny called Sylvia the last time at 20:41 the night she died."

"That's when he went to Hippolito's to intercept her." I went inside to tell Kim that Manny had lied about Lou calling him. And that he'd talked to Sylvia before driving to Hippolito's.

Then I went out on the lanai again. The world was alive with sunrise, the mynahs cheering the new day, the green hills and blue ocean sparkling, a lovely taste of sea and plumeria in the breeze, yet I felt nothing. My weeks of confusion and danger were over, but I felt empty, unfulfilled. "So WindPower, IEEC, Lanai Land Corporation, High Stakes, the Governor – none of them had anything to do with killing her," I said to Kim.

"Doesn't seem so."

When my phone buzzed I almost didn't answer, then saw it was Charity. "Oh my God," she said, her voice husky. "They're all dead!"

Tectonic Shift

F EELING SAFE AT LAST, I couldn't imagine what she meant. "What
are you saying?"

"Simon and Damon, Mr. Lu and Mr. Cruwell too –"

"Slow down, slow down – they did what?"

"Damon was flying them all to Molokai…a meeting at High Stakes…
It was real foggy, they should've turned back."

I remembered Mitchell mentioning an email about them flying there.
"They died?"

"He hit some tower…It's going to be all over the news, I got to go, the
other lines are ringing –"

"Leave the phones. Leave the office. Go home."

"Why?"

I glanced around for Kim. She was talking to Leon and another cop who
was taking notes. "I'm coming to your place," I told Charity. "Fast as I can."

Manny was standing there in a blue sweatsuit and tennis shoes, getting
cuffed. "I'll tell you who killed her."

"You said you did, Manny," Leon said.

"But maybe who *really* killed her was the Voice? The guy who paid me?"

"Why's that?" Kim said, acting disinterested.

"Wasn't he trying to *get* me to kill her? Telling me all this sex she was
doing with Lou? Getting me so mad I took his ten thousand dollars? Didn't
he kill her? And Lou too?"

"What ten thousand dollars?" Leon said, quiet-like.

"What he offered. Make it look like she drowned, he said."

"Which guy?" Kim said.

"At night, I'd be sleeping, he'd call and say, 'Do you know what Sylvia's doing right now? She's fucking...'"

"Was she?"

"He told me go to Lou's house, listen to them. I listened, outside the window. I could see them. She was moaning, you know, like they do."

"They?"

"Women. When they cheat on you."

"Manny," I reminded him, "you told me you never went to Lou's place, didn't know where it was."

"Yeah well just that one time."

"And the time you killed him –"

"He gave me ten thousand for that too." Manny nodded, thinking it through.

"The same guy," I said, "the one who called you?"

"Yeah. The one who wanted me to follow her. The Voice."

IT ONLY TOOK THREE DAYS to track down the throwaway phone that had called Manny. It had been bought at the airport the day before it was first used to call him. A tourist shop at the airport sold three phones that day out of four hundred forty-nine transactions. Two of them had been bought by members of an elderly tour group from Shanghai. The third had been bought for cash, but the salesgirl recognized Damon's photo.

By that time Manny was saying it wasn't his fault Sylvia died because the man kept calling him. And then after the man talked Manny into killing Sylvia he called again about Lou, that Lou was telling everyone that Manny'd done it, and was Manny going to put up with that? Didn't he want vengeance?

So WindPower got Manny to kill Sylvia, then to kill Lou Moreno a week later. They had to kill Lou because he was chasing down clues just like I was. Which is why Rico Morales told me he and his two buddies had nothing to do with Sylvia's death. They were hired solely to kill me, because I was trying to find out who killed her.

Kim learned it was the DEA that had dumped the weed in the ocean, low-grade Big Island stuff not even worth bringing to Honolulu. They were trying to deflect attention from another shipper because they wanted to make friends with him to catch a bigger fish elsewhere. At least that's what they told her. At this point she doesn't believe anything anymore. Which is one of the reasons I love her.

"So what's Hippolito got to do with this?" I says.

"Nothing," she scoffed. "But they been wanting that boy for years."

"What for?"

"He help people who get in trouble. DEA doesn't like that."

"So how'd Lou Toledo get caught up in it?"

"Your perps – WindPower, IEEC and all them – somebody called DEA on him."

"Lou wasn't running weed –"

"Of course not. That doesn't keep him from being a suspect, though, does it? When somebody calls him in. And don't forget, he was a friend of Hippolito's."

Next day I returned to the Waikiki Yacht Club to return the clothes I'd taken from that boat and left fifty bucks on the counter for the food I'd eaten. No doubt they'll never figure it out so maybe it'll seem a little gift from heaven. And I was more than glad to polish and fuel Clyde's Harley and get it back to him, Charity giving him a big kiss of thanks at the same time.

I called the Molokai Paddle Club and explained them what happened to their canoe and sent a check for nine hundred to buy another just like it. The Hulk was easy to find – the Korean tied it up near Sand Island but Leon's guys had located it and hitched it back at its usual slip.

Meanwhile Leon's holding the Koreans on Murder One – he says some guy showed up in the ocean off Kalaupapa with a bullet hole in him, and the Koreans apparently had landed about three hours earlier and were hunting someone. And he's holding Rico's two friends for the same reason, though they claim they were hunting boar.

And it only took a few days for Godfrey Slink (good old *God's Peace* himself) to run an editorial calling for a federal investigation of Big Wind, the Cable, and the perps, including the Governor, Lanai Land Corporation and Miranda Steale herself. But given that the ringleaders are all dead, there isn't much chance to prove who else was involved. Though it looks like Big Wind and its multi-billion-dollar useless Cable will be shot down, even by Hawaii's easily purchased politicians.

And though I never could track down the guys in the false Courtesy Electric van, the ones who ransacked my house, the best Kim could figure was they were friends of somebody in the Governor's safety detail, but she could never prove it.

And of course the Governor's still pushing the Cable, but he's coming up for re-election with the worst approval rating in the country, so maybe he and his Napoleonic schemes will go away before they hit our taxes and electric bills.

High Stakes Ranch is giving up on putting casinos on Molokai. And IEEC, long rated the nation's worst utility, has fallen to junk bond status and may soon be split into three companies in the vague hope that will make things better.

Old lady Steale, that vicious termagant, has gone bankrupt too, unable to come up with the millions she borrowed using Lanai as collateral. For the very rich, though, being bankrupt is a relative term: she still gets to keep two of her private jets but only nine of her fourteen homes.

A rumor surfaced that Old Lady Steale had once been a *he* – but when he realized that women have a longer life expectancy than men he'd had a sex change to gain some extra years – but you know how rumors are.

The PUC (Protect the Utilities Commission) is still protecting IEEC, the Corporate Advocate is still shilling for the corporations, and Hawaii's still the place to be if you've got lots of money and want to ruin other peoples' lives.

Turns out that the tower Damon's plane hit on the approach to Molokai airport was for the new wind speed monitor WindPower's subcontractor had built. Nearly a million in cash was scattered around the crash site but nobody knows what it was meant for – Ecology Profits' "community benefits" maybe? Ironically, the last transmitted message from the tower before it was hit said *No wind*.

Reminds me of the old saying: when enemies attacked Molokai they died in their canoes before they ever reached the shore.

BACK IN MY OLD NEIGHBORHOOD everything looked the same, as if I'd been away a weekend. My house smelled empty and closed-up but with the windows open it soon filled with warm sea air. There was still Longboard in the fridge, five surfboards in the living room and leftover dog and cat food on the shelf. And in the driveway down the street the black fat-wheeled Ford 150 was back.

I pulled the spike from the wall where Mojo and Puma had been hung and took it down the street to the big guy's house. A black-spotted pit bull came dashing at me and I knelt down to say hello and talked story with him a minute. He was young and full of piss and vinegar and just needed some reassurance.

When the guy comes to the door, ugly as ever, I take the spike out of my pocket and hand it to him saying I brought you this back, and when his eyes showed fear and comprehension I punched him in the adam's apple and the crotch and generally went to work on him till he was about the sorriest man on earth.

"You're quitting your job tomorrow," I explained him, "giving all your money to the Humane Society, and moving to the mainland within a week and never coming back to Hawaii." I dumped the bills out of his wallet, nine hundred twenty bucks no less. "Planning to buy something, were we?" I asks but he's unable to speak. I took all the ID and credit cards too, then did a quick check of the bedroom finding a Glock 19 in the drawer beside the disheveled smelly bed and a Colt .38 in a shoe box on the closet shelf. Plus ammo, cleaning rods, the usual.

"My buddies loved my animals and really want to kill you," I explained him further. "So even if I'm not around you will do what I've said." He nodded, too zoned out with pain to care about anything else. Nor would he for a long time.

I searched his sticky kitchen cabinets annoying many cockroaches till I found a jug of Wal-Mart high fructose corn pancake syrup, emptied it in the gas tank of his big black boytoy and put a nice rock on the pedal to speed up the process.

After about five minutes it began to hiss and moan and shake and fart then *glug-glug-glugged* to a wretched halt as the sugar in the corn syrup exploded in the cylinders and cooked the metal solid. I grabbed my inert and moaning friend by the neck and explained him that if he didn't give me the pin numbers to his three credit cards he was going to feel a lot worse than he did now, so he was quite accommodating. I found a leash, snapped it on the pit bull's collar and took him down to the Humane Society on Waialae Avenue, stopping on the way to max out the three credit cards, and gave the Humane Society the nine hundred twenty dollars cash plus the seventeen hundred eighty from the cards.

"A dog like him, he'll go fast," the pretty freckled girl at the counter said.

"Don't give him to anyone does dog fights –"

"No, for a family," she said. "They're great with kids."

After I got her phone number so I could take her surfing next Tuesday I hopped in the Karmann Ghia and took the guns, ID and credit cards to the Waimanalo Gulch landfill and tossed them into a truck of sewage sludge waiting to unload. Seemed like the best place on earth to put them, given that outer space was not an option.

JUST LIKE THE TECTONIC SHIFT that created these beautiful islands, I thought as I drove home, we need a tectonic shift in governance, so we can actually control what happens to us. As Thomas Jefferson said, most bad government results from too much government, and when corporations tell politicians what to do it's always the people who pay.

After going through all this I've become more aware how the slimy symbiosis between politicians and corporations overrides the public will and our common good. I was lucky in my battle with Big Wind to have a friend inside the enemy camp, plus a genius SF buddy to decode my enemies' communications, and a tough cop to back me up. To say nothing of Hippolito, a true uncle in the Hawaiian sense.

But there are lots of Big Winds happening all over our country destroying beautiful places from Maine to California and everywhere in between, and many other ugly taxpayer-gouging scams like them, totally unneeded but very enriching for big companies and their fully-owned politicians. Maybe the folks fighting these other Big Winds are lucky enough to have as much help as I had – let's hope.

And when I thought about it, the second Iraq War that little Bush started because he – a draft dodger like Cheney – wanted to look tough. And how that War killed so many of my friends and beggared our economy. Like Big Wind and the Cable, something evil that enriches the politicians, bankers and huge companies. And I realized we've come to a time when our government has become the enemy of the people.

On a personal level, Sylvia kept haunting my dreams, and it took a while to realize how she'd healed me. Afghanistan and Iraq had left gaping wounds inside me, places of horror and pain. I had come to believe in nothing, trying not to care because caring did no good and only made the hurt worse. But by the process of hunting her killers I'd come to believe again in protecting the good, the fair, the honest and loving. In not letting evil win.

But we'll never have Sylvia back, this brilliant, warm, good-hearted and beautiful young woman. She's gone, down the drain of all the men who have murdered women.

And like so many journalists she was killed because she was trying to find the truth. She could have had a marvelous life, done a lot of good. She might have married Lou Moreno – he was a straight-up guy, tough, smart and kind, and they would have been happy together for maybe fifty years – who knows? Who knows all the kids and grandkids they might have had, and on and on down through the ages.

And Lou died simply because he loved Sylvia. Their deaths are metaphors for what's happening to Hawaii. How we've been given a pearl and are crushing it into concrete. How criminals like the Governor and many of the legislators are selling off and destroying what they're sworn to protect.

The idea of writing surfing articles again and going to competitions and being in the frothing sea and golden sun now seems the most gorgeous of possible worlds. Along with tutoring my foster kids, being out there every morning at six when the ocean's rippling its shoulders after a restless night, and each ride takes you to a place you've never been before.

And getting back in touch with Angie. The thought of having her and Charity and Kim was almost overwhelming. And all the other women the gods of surfing bring you.

Soon as I'm up to it I'm going to the puppy penitentiary for another surfing dog. Don't have to worry about cats, though, one's sure to show up. Though she'll probably never learn to surf.

Mitchell has invested our Caymans ten million in money market funds so it can be withdrawn as we decide how best to spend it. My ancestor Father Hawkins did enormous good with few resources, trying to soften the blow of invasion, protecting the Hawaiian people, giving them the schools and knowledge to defend themselves. Couldn't Mitchell and I do the same?

There's lots of foster kids and wounded vets out there, and other people who could use some help. That's true aloha – loving and caring for others.

How much do we love Hawaii?

Mitchell and I, we can do a lot of good with ten million.

THE END

The first two chapters of

Assassins

Mike Bond's next novel.

One man's story of the wars behind the wars in Afghanistan and Iraq
– due soon from Mandevilla Press

From its terrifying beginning in the night skies over Afghanistan to its stunning end in the explosive streets of Baghdad, *Assassins* reveals the covert and often self-destructive history of America's two most recent wars. Based on the author's extensive experience in the Middle East and his knowledge of both Islamic terrorism and covert operations, *Assassins* is not only a thriller and multiple love stories, but also a meditation on war and religion and their impacts on nations and individuals.

Assassins conveys the terror of battle from inside a Soviet tank and in deadly firefights in snowy mountains, of assassinations in city streets and desert valleys, and of an operative alone in a foreign and dangerous country. It also reveals how politics and apathy in Washington allowed Al Qaeda a safe haven in the U.S., why the Bush Administration gave Osama Bin Laden free passage out of Afghanistan in November, 2001, and how Islamic terrorism and nonexistent Weapons of Mass Destruction were used as pretexts for the disastrous and costly invasion of Iraq.

Death Mountains

H E FELL THROUGH SPACE, grabbing for the ripcord but it wasn't there. Icy night howled past, clouds and black peaks racing up. Spinning out of control he yanked the ripcord but it was his rifle sling. He snatched for the spare chute; it was gone. *I packed it*, he told himself. *I had to.*

Falling out of the dream he felt great joy it wasn't real, that he was safe in his bunk. Then waking more he realized he was in a thundering tunnel, huge engines shaking the floor, the aluminum bench beneath him vibrating. The plane, he remembered.

"Jack!" The Jump Master in a silvery space suit shook him. "Going up to drop height! Twenty minutes to the Afghan border." The Jump Master bent over the three others and gave them a thumbs up: *The mission is on.*

He took a deep breath. The engine roar loudened as the two Pratt & Whitneys on each wing clawed up through thinning air. He bent his arm, awkward in the insulated jump suit, to check his altimeter. *8,600 feet.*

"You're falling at a hundred twenty miles an hour," Colonel Ackerman had reminded them last week in Sin City, "at sixty below zero. Guys die if they wait one extra instant to deploy their chute. Always remember, *Maintain Altitude Awareness.*"

Tonight anything could happen over the Hindu Kush. MiGs, high winds, tangled chutes, enemy waiting on the ground. Hindu Kush meant *Death Mountains.* He thought of his father's last chopper into Ia Drang twenty years before, the green hills below the Huey's open door, the rankness of jungle, guns and fear. Do you *know* when you're about to die?

Glancing round the rumbling fuselage he was stunned at how lovely and significant everything was: a strip of canvas dangling from a bench, the rough fabric of his jump boot, a rifle's battered stock, the yellow bulb dancing on the ceiling, the avgas-tainted air. Next to him Owen McPhee stood up, awkward and bearlike in his Extended Cold Weather suit, smiled at Jack and shrugged: *Never thought we'd do it.*

"They might still abort," Jack yelled over the engine noise.

McPhee grinned: *Stop worrying.*

Jack turned to Loxley and Gustafson. "Time to get ready, girls."

Bent over his rucksack, Sean Loxley gave him the finger. Beyond him Neil Gustafson glanced up, his broad face serious. "I been afraid," he called, "that we'd get scrubbed."

Jack tugged his kit bag from under the bench to final-check its contents: padded wool Afghani jacket, long wool shirt, trousers, two goatskin bags of grenades and AK cartridges, a blackened tin pot of rice and dried goat meat, two Pakistani plastic soda bottles of water, a woven willow backpack, a Soviet Special Forces *Spetsnaz* watch. He slid on his parachute, nestled the canopy releases into his shoulders, secured all the straps and turned to help Loxley. "If these chutes don't open," Loxley yelled, "we'll never have to do this again."

At first Jack hadn't liked Loxley, his own New England conservatism put off by Loxley's cheery California surfer cool, Loxley's wide gregarious grin and the bad jokes about Home Office and military politics. Loxley talked too much, Jack had thought. A lightweight. But Loxley had always backed it up, always come through, always put his buddies first. And he made them laugh; even tough-faced sarcastic McPhee with his small hard mouth, tight on the balls of his feet as a welterweight, couldn't keep from grinning. "You dumb hippie," he'd growl, trying not to laugh.

The Jump Master raised both arms sideways, bent his elbows and touched his fingertips to his helmet. Jack nodded and slid his padded leather helmet over his head, tucked the goggles up on its brim, settled the Makarov pistol on his thigh. Now the JM raised his right hand, thumb to his cheek, and swung the hand over his nose. Jack took a last breath from the plane's oxygen supply and slipped on his radio unit and mask, gave the JM a thumb up to say his own oxygen was working.

22,500 feet.

"To avoid Soviet and Paki radar," Colonel Ackerman had told them, "it has to be a Blind Drop."

"No marching bands?" Loxley had snickered. "No girls waving panties?"

"We've calculated your Release Point based on your DZ," Ackerman said. "And where we think the wind'll be."

"In the Hindu Kush," Loxley added, "I can't imagine wind would be a problem."

"There'll be no external resupply. No exfil. We've devised an Evasion and Escape but you may want to change that on the ground."

"You're making it sound like we're not really welcome."

Ackerman glared at him. "Remember up there, *Maintain Altitude Awareness.*"

"That's right, girls. Know when you're high ..."

"If this mission existed, which it does not, its purpose would be to build an Afghani guerrilla movement against the Soviets, not tied to the Pakis but on your own. By themselves the Afghanis can't beat the Soviets. But with our help – *your* help – we might just reverse the Soviet conquest of Asia *and* get the bastards back for Vietnam. But we don't intend to start World War Three or fuck up our relations with ISI. So once you drop out of that plane we can't help you."

Slender and rugged with a black moustache and graying curly hair, Levi Ackerman had lost his right forearm in the same Ia Drang battle that had killed Jack's father. Ever since then he'd watched over Jack, got him into West Point, then after that fell apart and Jack had finished at University of Maine, Ackerman got him into the military ops division of Home Office – "I want you near me, kid." Would Ackerman now send him to die?

In the thundering airless fuselage the JM swung up his left hand and tapped the wrist with two fingers of his right, opened and closed his palms twice: the Twenty-Minute warning.

34,000 feet.

"When I was a kid," Loxley said, "my Grandma use to make Afghans–"

"Your Grandma," McPhee yelled, "was a chimpanzee –"

Jack plugged in his backpack oxygen and checked his AIROX on/ off valve.

"Whatever you do, guys," Ackerman had added, "don't get split from Jack. He's your squad leader, knows the lingo, the country. Lose Jack and you die."

The Red Light over the rear ramp flicked on. *Courage isn't the absence of fear,* their weapons trainer, Captain Perkins, used to say in Sin City, *but action despite it.*

They could still abort. The JM would give the abort signal if an Unsafe Condition existed either in the aircraft, outside it, or on the DZ. As if the whole damn mission weren't insanely unsafe.

Haloed in the Red Light the JM gave the Ten-Minute warning. Eight times his hands closed and opened: *Wind speed 80 knots.*

Way too fast. They'd have to abort. But the JM swung his arm outward, the command to check their automatic ripcord releases. Jack slid his combat pack harness up under his parachute, its seventy-pounds added to the chute's forty-five making him stagger backward. He checked that the sling of his AKMS rifle was fully extended and taped at the end, that the tapes on the muzzle, front sight, magazine, and ejector port were tight and not unfurled except where he'd folded over the ends for a quick release.

"*Strela?*" Jack called. McPhee lifted up a long heavy tube wrapped in sheepskin and lashed it vertically on one side of Jack's combat pack. Jack helped Loxley and McPhee lash two more *Strela* tubes to their packs. Jack secured his rifle muzzle-down over his left shoulder, the curved magazine to the rear so it nestled against the side of the chute and wouldn't tangle in the lines.

With a fat gloved thumb he pushed the altimeter light. *39,750 feet.* The JM gave the Two-Minute command. Jack tightened his straps, checked everyone's oxygen pressure gauge, patted their shoulders. *Be safe,* he told each silently.

His breath was wet and hot inside the mask; his beard itched. His goggles fogged, the Red Light danced. Buzzing filled his ears. The plane shivered, the ramp cracked open, began to drop. Air sucked past. Beyond was black. A styrofoam cup scuttled down the fuselage and blasted out the hole. The JM gave the salute command: *Move to the Rear.*

Jack switched on his bailout oxygen and disconnected from the plane's oxygen console. This was what happened when you got executed, you numbly stood up and let them put a bullet through you.

The JM gave the thumbs up *Stand By* command and Jack gave it back. He thought of his father in the chopper, his father's Golden Rule: "Do what you say, and say what you do." *Keep your word, and speak the truth.* So when you die you've lived the way you should.

The Green Light flashed on. The JM swung his arm toward the hole and Owen McPhee dropped into the darkness. A second later Neil Gustafson. Then Sean Loxley.

Jack halted on the ramp. *You're going to die. That's all.* The JM swung down his arm. Jack arched his back and dove into the night.

Tao of War

H E SLAMMED INTO the plane's wake, spinning wildly, stars flashing past. He flung out his arms into the Stable Free Fall Position but the offbalanced *Strela* on his pack made him spin faster. He was icing up, had to *Maintain Altitude Awareness*, tumbling too fast to see his altimeter. Cold bit through his gloves into his fingers and into his elbows and knees where the jumpsuit was tight.

You drop a thousand feet in five seconds. How long had he fallen? He hunched to balance the pack but that made him spin worse. He shoved the chute left to offset the *Strela* and combat pack; the tumbling slowed, the huge white-black Hindu Kush rushing up. Grabbing his left wrist he pushed the altimeter button. 29,000: he'd dropped ten thousand already. In a few seconds, at 25,000, he could deploy the chute.

Safe now. Thicker air hissed past, the black ridges and white cliffs of the Death Mountains rising fast. To the east, behind him now, Chitral Valley and Pakistan. To the west the snowy peaks, barren slopes and desert valleys of Afghanistan.

27,500. He couldn't see the red chemlites on the others' suits. But no one had broken silence. *So they're fine too. We made it.* He felt a warm happiness, the fear receding.

26,500. He reached for the main ripcord handle.

25,250. He pulled the ripcord; the pilot chute yanked out the main bag and he lurched into a wide downpulling arc. Tugging the steering toggles he swung in a circle but still couldn't see chemlites, only frozen Bandakur climbing toward him, the snow-thick valleys eight thousand feet below, dim lights to the east that could be the village of Sang Lech. He lined up to fly northwest across Bandakur so he'd hit the DZ on the mountain's western flank. The stars above the black dome of his chute were thick as milk. The great peaks rose past him, entombed in ice. He sucked in oxygen, felt peace.

A huge force smashed into him collapsing his chute; he somersaulted tangled in another chute, somebody spinning on its lines. "Cutaway!" he screamed. They looped round again, caught in the lines. Jack wrenched an arm free but that spun him the other way, the tangled chutes swung him down and the other man up then the stars were below him so for an instant he thought he was falling into space. He yanked the chute releases and dropped away from the tangled chutes, accelerating in free fall till with a great *whoof* the reserve chute jerked him up and the tangled chutes whistled past, the man wrapped in them. "Cutaway!" Jack screamed into his radio. "This is Tracker. *Cutaway!*"

"This is Domino," McPhee said. "What's your situation?"

"Tracker this is Silver," Loxley said. "I can't see you. Over."

"Come in, Whiskey!" Jack yelled at Gustafson. "If you're caught, cut away the main chute and deploy reserve. *Maintain Altitude Awareness.* Cut *away!*"

His hands had frozen. "Whiskey!" he screamed, "what's your situation?"

He switched off his oxygen. Bony ridges climbed past. Below was a tiny chemlite. "Whiskey," McPhee radioed Gustafson. "Do you read me?"

Rocky ridges coming up fast. If Gustafson hadn't deployed his reserve he'd have hit by now. A fierce wind was blowing snow off the peaks; they had to land into it. Short of the DZ, way short. Maybe in the boulders. *Bend your knees. Roll with the fall.* He snapped off his chemlite.

"Whiskey," McPhee radioed. "Do you read me?"

Bend your knees. Loosen shoulders. Adjust rifle so it doesn't smash ribs on impact. The ground raced up. He dropped the combat pack and *Strela*. The mountain slammed into him; he tumbled backward his head whacking boulders. He leaped up and scrambled downhill unbuckling the chute harness and stamping on the chute, dragged it together and knelt on it.

A steep stony slope, wind screaming, shaly rock clattering down. He snatched off his helmet and clutched his head, blood hot between his fingers, the pain unbearable. He untaped his rifle, checked the safety. "Tracker here," he whispered, gripping his skull to hold in the agony. He feared his skull was broken, the way the blood poured out. "Touchdown. Over."

"Silver here," Loxley answered. "TD. Over."

"Domino here," McPhee said raggedly. "TD. Over."

"Whiskey!" Jack called. Silence, hissing of wind in the radio. "Stow your chutes in your packs and link up," he told them. "Look for my chemlite. Over."

"Domino here," McPhee said. "Come to me. Over."

"I want us uphill." Jack gritted his teeth. "Get up here."

"Hurt," McPhee grunted. "Not going anywhere."

The blood running out Jack's nose had frozen in his moustache. Clutching his skull he steadily descended the slope, each step jolting new agony into his head. When he reached McPhee, Loxley was already there. "Goddamn rocks," McPhee groaned. "Goddamn leg."

Clamping a light in his teeth Loxley eased off McPhee's boot. "Tibia and fibula both broken."

Behind the wind Jack heard a faint rumble through swirling snow. *How could a helicopter be up here at night?* "Wrap it," he snapped. "Chopper!"

"Can't see us in this," Loxley yelled into the wind. "What happened?"

"Gus hit me from above," Jack yelled back, making the pain worse. "About eighteen. We tangled. I cut away at the top."

"He streamed," McPhee said, as if stating the worst might prevent it. He gripped his radio. "Whiskey! Do you read me?"

"Stop sending!" Jack said. "We'll get the Russians on us." He stuffed all their jump gear under a boulder and jammed it with snow. Now except for their *Spetsnaz* watches, Russian field glasses, AKs, pistols, and *Strelas*, everything they had was Afghani. "Leave the channel open. In fifteen minutes try again."

"Gus is our medic," Loxley yelled. "Owen's got a broken leg. If we abort, try for Pakistan –"

"Abortion's for girls," McPhee snarled. "We find Gus."

Jack thought of Gus falling tangled in his chutes, icy rock racing up. "If his reserve didn't open his body's way behind us and there's nothing we can do. If it opened he's somewhere on this ridge."

The radio buzzed, stuttered. "That's him!" McPhee said. "Whiskey!" he coaxed. "Come in Whiskey . . ."

The radio was silent. *One man gone, another injured.* Jack's head pounded like a jackhammer. He'd failed, the mission screwed before it even started. He broke away the chunks of frozen blood clogging his nose and mouth, slung McPhee's rifle over his own, and pulled McPhee up.

"You asshole," McPhee hissed, "you're bleeding."

"Bit my tongue when I landed," Jack spit a dark streak on the snow. "No big deal."

Loxley shouldered McPhee's combat pack, stumbling under the weight, stood and looped the *Strela* tube over his other shoulder. "Where to, Boss?"

"We find a place to stow Owen," Jack said. "Then we find Gus. Before the Russians do."

WITH McPHEE HOBBLING between them they climbed Bandakur's south ridge through howling snow that froze their beards and drove icicles through their coats. Every fifteen minutes they tried the radio but there was no sound from Gus.

It was worse than Jack could have imagined; they might not live, let alone complete the mission. Pakistan seemed the only choice. *If* they could get McPhee back across the Kush without being caught by the Soviets or Pakis. He saw Ackerman's taut angry face. *You didn't do what we trained you for.*

"It's not to put you in shape that we drive you so hard," Ackerman had told them in Sin City, speaking of the five a.m. runs with full packs, the crawling on hands and toes under machine gun fire, the rappelling down cliffs and buildings. "You men were already hard as steel when you came here."

"Not McPhee," Loxley snickered, "he's never been hard at all."

Ackerman ignored him. "It's so you *know* you can do them. Once you've done them, even in training, you'll *know* in Afghanistan you can endure almost anything . . ."

"And you're going to learn everything you can about ordnance," Captain Perkins added. "From Makarovs to SA-7s, about setting ambushes and nailing a guy in the head at eight hundred yards. How to set Claymores and dig pit traps, how to get the jugular when you cut a throat, how to recognize Soviet infantry units and tell a T-72 tank from the later T-72S, and the RPG-7 from the RPG-16 . . .

"And *no*, RPG does *not* stand for 'rocket-propelled grenade'. It's Russian for rocket anti-tank grenade launcher – *Reactiviniyi Protivotankovyi Granatomet*, and I want you girls to know how to spell that."

"We've been agitating these damn Afghanis for years," Ackerman said, "fed them fanatic Islamic stuff till we finally got a fundamentalist government going in Kabul and the Soviets *had* to come in, for their whole soft Moslem underbelly – Tajikistan, Uzbekistan, and Kazakhstan, *and all that oil* – was at risk . . . Now," he'd added, "We're going to do to them in Afghanistan what they did to us in Vietnam. We're going to bleed them dry."

Now the peaks blocking the stars and the sheer icy canyons filled Jack with a vast, desolate despair. A perfect place to bleed and die.

"The Special Forces man is the essence," Ackerman said, "of the Art of War. He's not *where* he appears to be, nor *what* he appears to be. He strikes where and when the enemy's not ready. He inflicts great harm with few resources because *he* is the Tao of War."

"The SF man," said Perkins, "makes losing part of the enemy's fate."

Jack smiled, shook his head. "That is *such* bullshit."

"Some day, if you're good enough," Levi Ackerman had answered, "it won't be."

Now within two months they had to report to Ackerman in Rawalpindi. Even if Gus was dead, they might still be able to reach Jack's old village, Edeni, where people would care for McPhee. Then Jack could find his former enemy Wahid al Din, now a famous warlord fighting the Soviets. They could still start a third front uniting the Afghani opposition . . .

He took a breath, bit back the agony in his head, spit a clot of blood snatched by the wind. "Edeni," he yelled. "Even if we can't find Gus we're going to Edeni."